LUCIFER'S
GOLD

Also By Robert W. Barker

The Devil's Chosen, A Search for Understanding
(Decision processes of the Holocaust)

Nuclear Rogue
(First of the Peter and Maria Thrillers)

LUCIFER'S
GOLD

Robert W. Barker

LUCIFER'S GOLD

Cover art by Justin Barker-Detwiler

iUniverse books may be ordered through booksellers or by contacting:

*iUniverse
1663 Liberty Drive
Bloomington, IN 47403
www.iuniverse.com
1-800-Authors (1-800-288-4677)*

ISBN: 978-1-5320-7437-0 (sc)
ISBN: 978-1-5320-7438-7 (e)

Print information available on the last page.

iUniverse rev. date: 05/07/2019

Dedication

This book is dedicated to my wife,
and to all my family,
who have kindly tolerated my eccentricities and obsessions.
You are my world.

Preface

Not too many years ago, a small gold exploration company in Canada announced a major new gold discovery in Indonesia. Drill results were astonishing. Within a year the deposit was estimated to contain more than 70,000,000 ounces of gold, and the company's Vice-President of Exploration estimated the ultimate potential to be 200,000,000 ounces.

Originally a penny stock, the company's stock price, adjusted for splits, reached a peak of $286.50 Canadian, and the company had a capitalization of over $6 billion Canadian. During the fantastic story of this discovery, some few observers were unconvinced, but most investors simply reveled in the fantastic story and their amazingly good fortune. To this point, this is history.

In *Lucifer's Gold*, Peter Binder, an international exploration geologist and former SEAL, and Maria Davidoff, his partner, are recovering from an Arctic confrontation with nuclear terrorists (*Nuclear Rogue*). In that confrontation they created many powerful enemies. As Peter becomes involved in the Indonesian gold discovery, he and Maria find themselves in the center of a dark and violent conspiracy. Their enemies multiply. The confrontations become deadly. This is the story of *Lucifer's Gold*, and it is fiction.

Chapter 1

Peter Binder jerked upright in bed. His heart pounded, and he realized he was panting. His skin was slippery with sweat. He shut his eyes and forced himself to hold his breath. He exhaled slowly.

He pushed against the violent images from his dream. The images shattered and collapsed, but he couldn't push away the old, familiar fear.

"Damn."

At least I'm not screaming. He looked at Maria Davidoff. Her breathing was quiet.

He was sure she was pretending to be asleep.

Peter swung his feet out of the bed and stood up in the darkness, naked, shaking slightly. He steadied himself with a hand on the wall above the low, cluttered table next to the bed. His heart was still racing.

After a moment he took two steps and stood at the glass door to the small balcony on the fifteenth floor. Only the faintest hint of pink colored the eastern horizon. Peter looked at the twin to Maria's apartment building across the large courtyard. He saw only a few lights. He absently scanned the view of downtown Toronto and past downtown to Lake Ontario. He continued to breathe deliberately, but it took less of his attention.

Peter heard movement behind him.

"You okay, babe?" Maria asked.

"Not really."

"Dreams?"

"Yeah."

He heard her get out of bed, and the whisper of her feet against the light gray carpet. She put her arms around him and hugged him to herself. He could feel her breasts against his back. She slid her hands down his wet chest, across his tight stomach.

1

"You feel like you've just run a marathon," she said.

"Yeah."

"Peter, what we did up north? It's finished. It's over."

"I'm not so sure."

She hugged him a little tighter. "Come on back to bed."

Peter didn't reply.

"Come on," she said again.

"Give me a couple of minutes."

Maria kissed him on his neck and he felt her back away. He heard her feet on the carpet again and then the slight noise of the bed springs and the covers. He continued to stare out over the city.

What am I waiting for?

The day was slowly slipping into early morning twilight of what promised to be a beautiful, mid-summer day. His ringing phone startled him, and he took a half step to pick it up from the low table beside the bed.

In the same instant, with a sharp, explosive sound, the bullet punched a hole in the glass door just above his head. A few shards of glass bounced off his neck.

Without any conscious thought, he jumped to the side, sheltering behind the wall next to the glass sliding door.

"What the hell?"

"Get down on the floor! Now!" Peter shouted.

Maria tumbled out of the bed.

His heart was racing again, but Peter's breathing was almost normal. He picked up the still ringing phone and looked at the number. "Unidentified." Peter swiped the phone to answer.

"Who the hell are you?"

A flat male voice, "Just stay out of sight." The caller disconnected.

"Christ almighty," Peter said and threw the phone onto the bed.

He looked at the glass door. The small, round hole was surrounded by neat radial fractures. He glanced across the room and saw the new, dark hole in the white wall. It had just missed the black frame of a Japanese print. Peter turned back and pulled the cord to close the heavy blackout drapes.

"What the hell is going on?" Maria asked.

"Hell, I don't know." Peter stepped quickly to the closet and pulled out his backpack. "Looks like somebody wants to kill me."

"Jesus! In Toronto?"

"Yeah. In Toronto."

Peter rummaged through an outside pocket on the backpack, tossed out his exploration and geology supplies, and found his binoculars. He turned to Maria and said, "Stay here. I want to take a look."

"I'll call the police."

"No," Peter said. "Let me look first."

He stepped quickly into the hallway that connected the two bedrooms and bathroom to the kitchen and the living/dining area of the apartment. Crouching down behind the cupboards, he reached up and turned on all four burners of the electric stove. Then he turned on the oven and opened the oven door. When waves of heat were rising from the stove, he stood up, with the stove between him and the kitchen windows. With the increased morning light, it would be difficult for the shooter to see through the glass into the dark apartment with a normal sniper scope, and the heat from the stove would help confuse an infrared scope, if the shooter were using one.

Peter took a deep breath and slowly scanned the apartment building across the courtyard, at least the part he could see through the kitchen windows. The building was one of four identical buildings built by one developer around the park-like space.

Almost immediately Peter saw the man, sitting perfectly still, at a table behind an open glass door. He was straight across the courtyard. Same floor as Maria's apartment. Peter had the sense that he was looking directly down the barrel of the man's rifle.

He had short, dark hair. Black shirt. He looked up from the telescopic sight and slowly set his rifle down. Peter could see his large black moustache.

As Peter watched, the man's head exploded, followed by the loud report of a gunshot. Reflexively, Peter crouched behind the cabinets again and swore.

"What's going on?" Maria asked.

"I don't know," Peter replied. As he stood up, he glanced quickly at Maria. She was standing at the end of the hallway in her white, terrycloth bathrobe. Peter turned back and trained the binoculars on the same doorway in the building across the courtyard. Nobody in sight. "I think we've got a bloody war out there."

"Peter! Just tell me what you saw."

Peter put the binoculars down and took a deep breath. Whatever was happening, it was over now. His heart still raced. He breathed slowly and deeply several times. He reached over, turned off the burners and the oven, and gently closed the oven door.

"I think somebody just killed the guy who took a shot at me," Peter said. He was not nearly as calm as he sounded. "This might be a good time to call the police."

"I thought when we were in Toronto we didn't have to worry."

"You were wrong," Peter said softly. "We were both wrong."

They looked at each other for a moment, and Maria asked, "You want Captain Durban and his Mounties?"

"No. After last summer I don't trust him. Just call the Toronto police."

"You're crazy."

As she called the police, Peter picked up the binoculars again and looked at the now empty door. He could still see the rifle lying on the table. He heard Maria briefly tell the dispatcher that someone had shot through her apartment window.

Another person came into view in the door to the balcony across the courtyard. This one wore a black balaclava and a plain, black jacket.

A man or a woman?

With a brief look in Peter's direction they stepped out onto the balcony. They wore black, baggy pants and black boots. They looked to their right and raised one hand with a thumbs-up salute. With one more, quick look in Peter's direction, they stepped back, shut the glass door to the balcony, and closed the drapes.

Peter stood motionless, still naked, in the kitchen. Most of the sweat from his nightmare had dried, but Peter shivered. The rush of adrenalin was ebbing, leaving behind a familiar and vague discomfort as his heart rate slowly returned to normal. He stared at the empty balcony across the courtyard.

Okay, Peter thought, *and just who the hell are you?*

Chapter 2

Peter lowered the binoculars and continued to stare across the courtyard. He listened to the sounds of the city as Maria completed her call. Nothing. No sirens. Nothing.

Gun shots are an unusual sound in Toronto, he thought, *but still...* All he heard was the background sound of traffic, which was always present, even with the windows closed.

Maria put her hand on his shoulder. "We ought to get dressed."

"Yeah. You're right. They'll be quick." He put the binoculars back onto the counter.

They returned to the bedroom and threw on the first clothes they found. Peter reached into the bottom of his pack and pulled out a .44 revolver and a box of shells.

"Are you crazy? I did call the police."

Peter stepped over to the table beside the bed, found his keys and unlocked the trigger lock on the pistol. He opened the cylinder, loaded the pistol, and flipped it closed again.

"I don't trust anyone," Peter said, "particularly when somebody just took a shot at me. Even if they are blown away a few minutes later."

After a quick look at Maria, Peter turned and headed toward the living room. "Let's get ready for our visitors." He sat on the light blue Donghia sofa, facing the entrance to the apartment, with the apartment's hallway, kitchen and dining area to his left. He tucked the pistol between the cushion and the arm of the sofa, just as Maria answered her phone.

"Yes. We're expecting them. You can send them up." She disconnected and put her phone in her pocket. "Two Toronto cops," she said. "Frederick checked their ID at the door."

"Make them show their badges before you let them in."

Maria shook her head. When the police knocked on the door, Peter watched as Maria checked their badges through the peephole and opened the door. Peter guessed that the older policeman was in his late twenties or early thirties, and the other probably no more than twenty-two. The older one introduced himself. "I'm Sergeant Dickerson, and this is Constable Winters." Peter got up and shook their hands as Maria shut and locked the door behind them.

"So, you think someone shot into the apartment?" Dickerson asked. "Can you show me where this happened?"

"Sure. Follow me," Maria said. The two policemen followed her down the hallway to the bedroom, Maria explaining what had happened along the way.

Peter settled back on the sofa. He always loved this room. Simple. Calm and peaceful. Mostly white. Maria had two, spare, pen and ink life studies on the wall to the side of the entry. The coffee table was a simple glass top on a metal and crackled glass base. A blown glass vase with ribbons of clear and dark blue glass sat on the table. The painting behind him and above the sofa reminded him of a Winslow Homer painting, Sailing Off Gloucester, with the light lines of a sailboat against a pale gray sky.

Peter snapped out of his daydream. He heard noises in the hall. It sounded as though someone was scraping at the door. He pulled the .44 out of the sofa and stood up. He took four steps and stood behind a large chair under one of the life studies to the side of the door. The door would open toward him and initially hide him from any intruder. He felt the first surge of adrenaline. He muttered a curse.

Peter stuffed his revolver into his belt and took out his phone. He quickly sent a text to Maria. "We've got company at the door," he wrote. Maria's phone beeped in the bedroom, and he heard her read the text to the police. He wasn't sure what the sounds at the door signified, but they continued.

Constable Winters showed up in the living room at the end of the hallway, looked at Peter and asked, "What's going on?"

Peter saw the door open, and Winters jerked his head around to focus on the opening door. "What the hell?" Winters said. With a look of shock on his face he shouted, "Drop the gun, now!" He reached for his pistol.

Before Winters could pull his pistol out of the holster, Peter heard four sharp pops. Winters staggered backward and crumpled to the floor. His gun never left his holster.

The shots were remarkably quiet, not much more than the popping of a champagne cork. All Peter could see of the attacker was the silencer on the end of the pistol. The door hid everything else. Peter flattened himself against the wall and waited.

He heard a voice in the hall. "You fucking idiot. You just killed a cop."

The man behind the door said, "Big fucking deal." They continued with a second exchange in Russian.

Peter watched as a tall man entered the living room. He focused on the hallway leading to the bedroom.

Peter heard Dickerson yell, "What's going on out there?"

Peter watched the man raise his pistol.

"Drop it," Peter said. The command came out a lot louder than he had intended.

The man jerked around, swinging his pistol toward Peter.

Peter's instinct and training took over. He shot the man, once, between his left eye and his temple. The report of the .44 was like a thunder clap inside the apartment, and the massive exit wound was accompanied by a spray of blood and brain matter before the man fell to the carpeted floor with a thud.

Peter heard two shouts at the same time. Dickerson, swearing, ran toward the living room. A second man ran into the apartment in a crouch, firing toward Dickerson and the bedroom.

Dickerson returned fire, hitting the man once in the chest, and Peter fired twice, hitting the man once in the neck and once halfway down his left torso.

Peter watched the man twist and jerk in the combined fire and fall to the side. He hit his head on the dining table as he went down and exhaled loudly when he hit the carpet. He didn't move once he hit the floor.

Peter heard someone running in the outside hallway. He shouted at Dickerson, "There's someone else. I'm going out."

Peter stepped over the first body and looked around the door jamb. He saw someone exit into the fire escape at the far end of the hall that connected the four apartments on the floor. Peter stepped out into the hallway and toward the disappearing man. He stopped. Chasing the man was useless.

Inside the apartment, Dickerson called for backup. Officer down. Multiple shootings.

People in the three other apartments on the floor opened their doors, curious, looking out. "Get inside and lock your damn doors!" Peter shouted.

The neighbors took one look at him, with his pistol at his side, and they slammed and bolted their doors.

"Dickerson?"

"Yeah?"

"I'm coming back in." Peter was breathing deeply and slowly. His heart was still pounding. He knew his body would continue in high gear for at least another ten or fifteen minutes.

Just as well, he thought.

When he stepped into the living room, Peter shut the door. Dickerson was on his knees beside Winters. Maria stood behind him. Dickerson's radio crackled with all the conversations of the police rushing toward them. Peter could already hear some of the sirens.

"He's dead," Dickerson said.

"I'm sorry," Peter said.

Dickerson got to his feet and took two steps toward Peter. He looked emotionless, almost paralyzed. Peter had seen the look before when he was with the SEALS. Sometimes, in a firefight that was going really badly, when everyone was falling around them, some of the fighters could go crazy. Sometimes it was a good thing.

This is not a good thing, Peter thought.

Dickerson raised his Glock 22 handgun and aimed it at Peter. The conversations on his radio were steady. Radio discipline was holding, but only barely.

Peter didn't move a muscle. He held his pistol in his right hand at his side, pointed toward the floor. He waited.

"Give me your gun," Dickerson said over the noise of his radio.

"You sure you want to do this? One of them escaped."

"All part of the plan, I'm sure. Give me your gun! Now!"

They heard the sound of multiple gunshots coming from somewhere outside the apartment building. Dickerson diverted his attention, and his aim wavered away from Peter.

Maria took two steps toward Dickerson's back and brought her right leg across his ankles with all the strength she had. Dickerson fired a wild shot that hit the ceiling in the far corner of the room. He lost his grip on his pistol as he fell.

Peter stepped forward and grabbed Dickerson's pistol off the floor, and then he stepped back again. Dickerson grimaced as he got to his feet and put weight on the ankle Maria had kicked. For five seconds, he and Peter stared at each other in silence. The radio chatter filled the room.

Dickerson reached for his radio.

Peter raised his pistol. "Don't even think about it."

Dickerson slowly moved his hand away from the radio. "You're crazy," he said.

"Maria keeps telling me that," Peter said. "Put your hands above your head and lean into the wall. Maria will relieve you of your radio."

"What are you going to do? Shoot me?"

"I hope not."

Dickerson hesitated, but he turned toward the wall, raised his hands, and leaned into the wall.

Maria removed his radio from his belt and backed away.

"Okay," Peter said. "Now move toward the sofa. Once you're there I'll put both of these pistols on the floor."

"Just listen to my radio. Half the Toronto police force will be here in a couple of minutes. There's a dead policeman on the floor. You've just attacked me, you're holding me hostage, and they're sending the Emergency Task Force. You don't want to screw with them."

For two or three more seconds, Peter and Dickerson continued to stare at each other, listening to the radio chatter and the growing sound of sirens.

"Move," Peter said.

Dickerson, still watching Peter, took a few limping steps into the living room and positioned himself beside the far end of the glass coffee table.

"Maria," Peter said, "go into the kitchen. Call Commander Branch. He'll want to know we're in the middle of this."

"He's not on duty today," Dickerson said.

"I'll call his cell phone," Maria said.

Peter listened to Maria on the phone with Bill Branch. Peter began to smile. He placed his .44 and Dickerson's Glock on the floor, but he didn't move to join Dickerson. Not yet.

Dickerson's radio continued to crackle with rapid fire orders. Then there was a change. They listened to Commander William Branch's distinctive voice on the radio. Dickerson tilted his head to one side. Peter watched a look of disbelief appear on Dickerson's face as Branch issued his orders.

"Back off and secure the area. Take no further action until I get there. Make sure no one enters or leaves the building."

"This is Superintendent Bredich, Commander. This is an active shooter situation. We have a policeman down. We have to go in."

"I know all about the situation, Superintendent. Secure the area. Secure the floor. Do not enter the apartment. Is that clear?"

"Yes, Sir."

"Don't do anything stupid. Back off and wait for me."

"Yes, Sir."

The radio continued its noisy reports, but now it was more methodical. An ambulance for a gunman down, in the alley behind the apartment building. Orders positioning the police in and around the building. Evacuation of Maria's neighbors.

Peter knew that the moment of danger with Dickerson had already passed.

Dickerson looked at Peter and then Maria. "You have friends in high places," he said.

"Friends? Maybe," Peter said.

Dickerson stared at Peter. Then he shrugged and sat on the sofa. "It's gonna be a while."

Peter turned to Maria, "Stay in the kitchen, but put your hands on the counter, where they can see them when they come in." Then he moved and sat on the near side of the sofa, about three feet from Dickerson. The two of them put their hands on their knees and stared at the entrance.

"Who the hell are you two?" Dickerson asked.

Peter continued to stare at the door. "You don't want to know."

Dickerson said. "I guess it's a good thing I didn't shoot you."

Peter didn't respond.

Except for the ongoing radio communications, they waited in silence for the fifteen minutes it took Commander Branch to arrive on the scene. Two minutes after the radio announced his arrival, they heard footsteps in the hall outside the apartment.

"This is Commander William Branch. Peter Binder, you in there?"

"Yes, Bill. I'm here."

"You okay?"

"Yes."

"Who else is in there with you? Maria Davidoff?"

"Maria's here, and Sergeant Dickerson of the Toronto Police, and three bodies."

"Sergeant, is there any reason I shouldn't come in?"

"No sir, and I think the door's unlocked."

"All of you, please stand facing away from the door, legs apart and hands on your heads. Two men will enter, pat you down, and secure the apartment."

Peter opened his mouth to respond, but he quickly closed it again. He didn't like being blind and helpless. He wanted to see what was coming through the door, but he didn't have any choice. He stood, turned away, and put his hands on his head. After he looked at Maria and Dickerson he said loudly, "Ready."

Peter heard the door open. One person came into the room, and moved to the side behind him. Peter heard the soft sound of the second man coming toward him. The second man said, "I'll pat down all of you to check for weapons. Please do not move until I say so."

He started with Peter. He was very thorough. After he finished with Dickerson, he moved into the kitchen to Maria. Peter turned his head slightly and got a good look at the man. He was dressed all in black with body armor, black pants with large, bulging pockets, and a black helmet with a dark visor that covered most of his face. As he moved while searching Maria for weapons, Peter could see large white letters spelling out "TORONTO POLICE" across his chest and back.

When the man finished with Maria, he checked the three bodies for any signs of life. "Anyone else in the apartment?" he asked.

"Not that I know of," Peter said.

"Dickerson?"

"I don't think so."

"Okay. Stay where you are and don't move."

He began a complete search of the apartment, including closets and the cupboards in the kitchen. He carried an MP5A3 submachine gun, standard issue to the Emergency Task Force officers in Toronto. Peter assumed that the man behind him was similarly armed and equipped. As the one man searched the kitchen, he asked Maria to move once. When he was finished, he stayed in the apartment hallway. He said, "All secure, commander."

A voice from the entrance said, "Okay. Everyone relax, put your hands down and turn around."

Peter turned to see Commander Branch standing in the doorway. Bill looked around the bloody scene and muttered, "Christ." Turning to Peter he said, "Everyone clear out except for myself, Peter Binder and Maria Davidoff. Sergeant, you'll be debriefed at headquarters. Everyone else back off down the hall to the fire stairs."

The man who had completed the search asked, "Leave the weapons?"

"Yes. Forensics will take care of them. Just leave, close the door behind you, and give me ten minutes."

"Yes, Sir."

When the door clicked shut, Bill took a deep breath and looked first at Peter and then at Maria. "Peter, what the hell is going on here?"

"I don't know."

"Maria?"

Maria raised her hands. "We pissed off a lot of nasty Russians up north last summer."

Bill frowned. "Obviously. And rumor has it that one of them, some guy named Rostov, is still out there. Somewhere."

Bill Branch contemplated the three bodies on the floor. "I have direct orders from the Prime Minister regarding your safety. He will not be pleased." He gestured at the bodies of the two attackers. "You know these guys?"

"I don't think so," Peter said.

Maria shook her head.

Bill kneeled down and took a closer look at Constable Winters. "God, I hate this. He didn't work for me, but he must be brand new. He probably has a young wife and a kid."

"I'm sorry, sir," Maria said.

"Doesn't look like he had a chance. Never got his gun out of his holster." Bill straightened up. "You two seem to collect dead bodies." He looked at Peter and said, "Maria, give me a quick summary of what happened. Just the high points. We can do a detailed interview at headquarters. You said over the phone that the initial call was for someone taking a shot at the apartment, right?"

Maria provided a brief description of the sniper shot and the arrival of the police. Peter covered the two men breaking into the apartment and the death of the policeman.

"You saw the sniper, Peter?"

"Right after the shot," Peter said. "I went into the kitchen and searched the apartment building across the courtyard. I saw someone with a rifle. I didn't see him, or her, take the shot."

"Can you show me the location?"

"Sure. It's the fifteenth floor, same floor as we're on. Second balcony from the right."

Bill walked into the kitchen, careful to not disturb anything. He saw the binoculars. "These yours?" he asked Maria.

"Peter's."

"You mind, Peter?"

"Have at them."

Bill picked up the binoculars and looked out the window. He gazed at the balcony Peter had indicated. "Not much to see," he said.

"No," Peter responded, "but I'll bet there's another body and plenty of blood behind that curtain."

Commander Branch stepped away from the window, replaced the binoculars, and said, "Let's go down to headquarters and let the forensics people have their fun here. They'll have plenty to do." He sighed. "And you'll both have a long day giving your statements."

"How long before we're allowed back in the apartment?" Maria asked.

"I don't know. Tomorrow night maybe?"

"It'd be nice to take a few things."

"Sorry. Can't do it. We'll set you up with a place to stay tonight."

As they left the apartment, Bill said, "I'll have to bring in Dick Durban and his counter-intelligence team."

"I was afraid of that," Peter said.

"I'm not surprised," Bill responded.

Chapter 3

By the time the Toronto police, and the Royal Canadian Mounted Police from Durban's office, had completed their separate interviews of Peter and Maria, and debriefed Sergeant Dickerson, it was after four in the afternoon. Peter was tired of the process and tired of the stark, windowless and claustrophobic interview room. Except for brief breaks, he had been in the room for over six hours.

Peter kept repeating to himself, *I'm just a geologist. I'm a consultant. I help companies find and develop gold mines. That's what I do for a living. Yes, I have a license for the pistol. I work alone in the Arctic. Two armed men broke into the apartment. It was a home invasion. Maybe if I repeat it enough I'll actually believe it myself.*

Peter looked at one of the two video cameras in the room. He thought he understood why lions constantly pace back and forth in their cages. He stood and began a series of stretching exercises, and then sat on the floor in a *hakina mudra* position. He closed his eyes, focused on his breathing, and felt his heart beating, slow and strong. He was drifting away into his endless white sea, when he heard the knock.

Peter didn't look up. "Come in."

"Peter?"

Peter opened his eyes and saw Bill Branch at the door. "Yes?"

"You look like you've survived today's interviews."

Peter stood up. "Boring," he said. "I'm tired of this room, too."

"Well, you'll be glad to know we're finished."

"So, Maria and I can leave?"

"Let's join Maria. I'll bring you both up to date. Then you can leave."

They walked down the hall and took the elevator to the eleventh floor. Peter followed Bill into a large conference room and saw Maria standing at the windows that looked out over College Street. "Hey," he said.

"Peter!"

Peter walked around to the table. "You okay?" he asked.

"It's been a long day, but I'm okay. You?"

"Well, they didn't beat me up, like they do in the movies."

Maria smiled. "Glad to hear that."

Bill Branch closed the door with a soft click. "Before we sit down," he said, pointing to a table at the end of the room, "if you'd like coffee, tea, or a soft drink before we start, help yourselves."

Peter got two Cokes with ice and sat down next to Maria, facing away from the windows. An oak table with sixteen brown, leather chairs took up most of the room. Pictures of all twenty-three police chiefs since the Toronto force was founded in 1834 hung on the walls on either side of the entrance.

Bill sat across from them with his coffee. They sat silently for almost a minute. Finally, Maria asked, "So what's our status, Bill? Are we free to go or what?"

Bill took a deep breath. "We searched the apartment where you said you saw the sniper, Peter. We can't find a body."

"That's not possible. Nobody walks away from a head shot like that."

"Oh, there's enough blood and bits of brain in that apartment that I don't have any doubt someone was shot, and unless they don't need a brain they're dead. But there's no body, and no gun either."

"Somebody removed the body?" Maria asked.

"Looks like it. Somebody doesn't want the body identified."

"Any idea who that might be?" Maria asked.

"Not really, but everybody we can identify in this incident seems to have some connection to Russia."

"How long was it before someone actually checked on the shooter's apartment?" Peter asked.

Bill shrugged. "Two hours after I arrived. Maybe a little more."

"Somebody moved fast," Maria said.

"Yes."

"That's pretty strange," Peter said.

"So far, nobody official, or unofficial, is taking credit for the kill or removing the body," Bill said. "The two dead guys in the apartment were recent visitors from Russia. The one we shot in the alley immigrated from Russia fifteen years ago."

"Did he survive?" Peter asked.

"He's back in the operating room at Toronto General. With a little luck we should be able to question him in a few days. He's a Canadian citizen and has nothing negative on his record. Interpol is working on the other two. Russia doesn't always cooperate, but for some reason they seem to want to help on this one."

The three of them sat in silence for a full minute, and Bill finally spoke again. "Look, I know a little about what went down last year up in northern Nunavik, but not a lot. Can you fill me in? It would help a lot."

Peter looked down at the table. "No."

"No?"

Peter looked up at Bill. "No. We can't tell you. We're not allowed to tell you anything."

"Maria?"

Maria just shook her head.

"Well, this is great," Bill said. "I've got three bodies and nobody will tell me the start of the story."

"You should talk to Dick Durban."

"I have. He and the RCMP won't tell me anything. All highly classified."

"Then you had to know we couldn't tell you anything," Peter said.

"I had to try."

"No, you didn't."

"Look, if the Prime Minister ordered you to protect us, talk to him," Maria said. "Tell him you can't do your job unless somebody tells you what happened in Nunavik last year."

"You never answered Maria's question," Peter said. "Have you charged us with something, or are we really free to go? Can we go back to the apartment?"

"No charges. Self-defense in a home invasion. With a little encouragement from Durban's bunch, Sergeant Dickerson and the department will decline to pursue charges of assault and battery of a police officer." Bill hinted at a smile.

"I guess I should thank you for your restraint," Peter said.

Bill ignored Peter's comment and continued. "I also know you have a permit for your pistol, strange as that is in Canada." Bill focused on Peter. "So, yes, you're both free to go, but not back to the apartment."

"Why not?" Maria asked.

"It's still an active crime scene. We'll be done early tomorrow morning. The building manager will have someone there tomorrow to clean and do repairs. I arranged for a room for you on an upper floor of the Royal York."

Bill reached into his shirt pocket, pulled out a phone, and handed it to Peter. "Here's your phone. I have a couple of jackets for each of you and a small suitcase in my office. We picked up some basics for you from the apartment, tooth brushes, and so forth."

"If you don't mind," Peter responded, "I have a friend up in Cabbagetown with a B&B. I'd rather stay there tonight if he has space."

"You sure?"

"I'm sure."

"I could put on some security."

"Thanks, but I want to disappear tonight," Peter said. "If you want, you can put some extra security on the apartment."

Bill Branch did not respond immediately. If he felt insulted, he didn't show it. Peter didn't really care.

Finally Bill said, "Your pistol and the box of ammunition is in your suitcase."

"Well," Maria said, "then we should pick up the suitcase and get ourselves out of here."

"Before you go," Bill said, "there are a couple of things I'd like to say. First, I don't know what's going on here. Unless the surviving shooter talks, or unless the PM tells me more, there's a limit to what I can do." Bill paused. "Second, you're obviously in danger here in Toronto. If I were you, I'd go to ground for a while."

"Really? And for how long?" Peter asked.

"A few weeks. A month. Let's see what happens. Call me or email me in a couple of weeks."

Peter and Maria exited the police station and stopped on the sidewalk about half a block away. People were passing in both directions. No one paid any attention to the two of them standing there. "I've got to find out if we have a place to sleep tonight," Peter said. "A little public, but it'll have to do."

Peter called his friend in Cabbagetown. "Devin! This is Peter Binder. I was wondering if you had space available tonight in your B&B…. Super. I'll be up there in about half an hour…. It's a long story. I'll see you in a bit."

"We've got a bed for the night?" Maria asked.

"Yep. The Cabbagetown Homestead. I think that's what he calls his B&B." Peter turned his phone off and waited for it to shut down. Then he opened the back and pulled out the battery. "You do the same, Maria. I don't think it's healthy for us to be connected right now."

Maria shook her head as she shut down her phone. "I think you're getting carried away again, but after today I won't fight it." She pulled the battery out of her phone and dropped both back into her small, black leather purse.

"Okay. Let's find our bed for the night," Peter said.

"You really want no one to know where we are tonight?" Maria asked.

"That's the idea."

"Where's our bed?" Maria asked.

He leaned over and whispered in her ear, "Just south of Wellesley on the west side of Parliament."

"Let's start with a cab."

Peter hesitated for a moment. "Okay. Lead the way."

Maria stepped out into the street and flagged down a cab. They got out at Bloor and Bathurst. Maria spent a few minutes looking at the shop windows. Then she turned quickly, retraced her steps and entered the subway. They rode thirteen stops east and exited to the street. Crossing quickly to the other subway entrance, they walked down the stairs and entered the next westbound train. Just as the doors were closing, they stepped back onto the platform and took the next train instead. They got off at Saint George, walked up to Cumberland Street, pausing at a number of shops, got in a second cab, and exited on Amelia Street, just east of Parliament. They crossed over Parliament, walked to the north and stepped into a doorway just south of Wellesley.

"That was interesting," Peter said.

"Didn't see any followers. If they're out there, they're good."

"I didn't see anything suspicious either, but I'm impressed."

Maria smiled. "I read all of John le Carré's spy novels. Besides, don't you know that all Russians are spies?"

Peter nodded. "Right." He gestured to the stairs. "Let's go upstairs to Devin's apartment and get our keys. Maybe he can call in a dinner reservation for us at Opus One."

Maria followed Peter up the somewhat ragged stairs. "Not all that inviting," she said.

Peter laughed. "It's a bachelor apartment, first floor, with a back door. It's clean, convenient, quiet, and best of all practically invisible."

After they dropped the suitcase in the apartment, and after they used the bathroom, Peter and Maria exited from the back door. The small patio had a tall privacy fence. A locked security gate opened onto Darling Lane. They turned left, walked down to Prospect Street, and after a few blocks to the west back up to Wellesley to catch a cab. Opus One, in the western part of the upscale Yorkville district, was a quiet oasis on Wednesday night. They took a corner table in the back of the restaurant and sat on the same side of the table, looking out across the restaurant to the front door.

Peter picked up the wine list, a rather thick book. "I think we need a good wine." He looked through the thirteen pages of Bordeaux reds, found the one he wanted, looked up, and signaled the waiter.

"How can I help you?"

"We'd like to have a bottle of the 2005 Chateau Leoville Las Cases, please."

"Certainly, sir. That's a recent addition to our wine list. It's quite drinkable, but it is in the early stages of its life."

"I've had the 2003, and I thought it was excellent."

"I'll bring it right away." The waiter took the wine book from Peter and turned to leave.

"If you don't mind," Maria said to the waiter, "I'd like to look at the wine list myself. I know you have one of the best cellars in Canada, and there might be something I would particularly like for a second bottle."

"Certainly, madam," he said, and handed the wine list to her. "Please take your time." He bowed slightly and left.

"I haven't been here for at least a year," Maria said as she opened the book. "I notice you're not cautious about prices tonight."

Peter reached over and put his hand on Maria's. She looked up from the wine list. "Maria, both of us need to slow down and relax."

"What do you mean?"

"Look, someone took a shot at me today. It should have killed me. You were probably his next target. I shot two men who would have happily killed me, you, and the two policemen. One of them murdered a cop right in front of me. You attacked a cop who was thinking about shooting me. We were both grilled for half the day by the Toronto Police."

Peter gestured toward the front of the restaurant. "Frankly I'm still nervous as hell, but this should be a safe place. Let's just sit back and enjoy a fine wine and a great meal."

Maria looked at him and slowly closed the wine list. She put her left hand on top of his and said softly, "Okay. Let's do that." She took a deep breath.

Peter thought he saw a note of sadness in her face. Maria never fell apart. She didn't scream. She never hesitated to act in a moment of danger. Usually she didn't weep, except quietly, later, and even that was rare. It wasn't her style to be overly dramatic, but Peter knew she was not untouched by the violence of the day.

They turned their attention to the waiter when he returned with the bottle and a decanter.

The wine was sturdy and rich. They shared an appetizer of Fogo Island snow crab. Peter ordered rack of lamb, and Maria the wild halibut. They talked about the state of the world, and Toronto politics, which was much calmer than it had been. They passed on dessert and ordered coffee instead.

As she sipped her coffee, Maria looked pensively at Peter and said, "So, babe, what do we do now?"

Peter smiled. "I'd say we head back to our apartment for the night and hop into bed."

Maria smiled in return. "You're so dependable sometimes, Peter. Actually, I was thinking about tomorrow and maybe the next month or so. Bill Branch did suggest that we get out of town."

"Yes, and I think he's right," Peter said. "I do have one appointment tomorrow morning at eleven, Ontario Helicopters out in Waterloo. It's my flight check in the MD 500, and hopefully my first solo. I don't want to miss that."

Maria smiled. "I'd forgotten all about that. I should go with you."

He laughed. "No, you shouldn't. You don't want to ride with me on my first solo flight."

"It can't be any more frightening than sharing an apartment with you."

"I suppose there's some truth to that, but, really, you should not go with me."

"What about after tomorrow?" Maria asked. "I don't know about you, but I don't feel safe in Toronto. I guess I don't really want to leave either."

"I did think we could retreat to my cabin on the lake," Peter said.

"Isn't that a little obvious?"

"Oh, I don't know. We can be entirely off the digital grid up there. No cell coverage, and I've got a pretty good security system. But we still have the option of a secure connection when we want it. Satellite telephone. Satellite internet. We can check in with Bill occasionally, and otherwise we can rest... and heal."

"Okay. So that takes care of a month or so, but what about a year? What about our future? I don't want to live like this, on guard all the time."

"Maybe after Nunavik we don't have a choice."

Maria shook her head. "That can't be true."

Peter took Maria's hand. "We're safe tonight. Let's pay the bill and go back to Devin's B&B."

With a slightly crooked smile she said, "And what do you think we should do when we get there?"

"Oh, we can find something interesting to do. Maybe there's a good show on television?"

Maria laughed.

The cab dropped them at the corner of Rose and Prospect. Peter didn't want to be visible on any of the main streets. They held hands as they took the short walk over to Darling Lane and up to the apartment. Peter unlocked the back door and held it for Maria.

Once inside they removed their coats and turned to look at each other. Then they embraced. Her embrace held a sense of urgency. "I'm sorry," she said.

Peter held her back and looked at her. He was surprised to see the tears on her cheeks. "I'm sorry," she said again.

"It's okay," Peter said.

Maria shook her head. "No, it's not. I'm Russian. This is all about Russians."

"Maria."

"No. I'm Russian. You know almost nothing about my life."

Peter took a half step back. She was right. He thought about how easily she had watched for followers and hidden their movements. She had been so confident that no one had followed them. "I love you Maria, and you love me. That's real, isn't it?"

"Yes. That's real."

"That's enough for me tonight."

Maria reached up and caressed Peter's cheek. "Oh, my beautiful man, I do not deserve you."

"Then neither of us deserves the other, and I don't want to believe that."

Peter held her again. He felt her slowly raise her arms and embrace him. They stood in silence before Maria said, "Let's not watch television."

Peter almost burst out laughing. "What do you want to do?"

Maria pulled back slightly. "I want to get ready for bed, and when we're in bed I want you to hold me. I want to feel safe and warm in your arms."

"I'm not sure I can make you feel safe."

"You can. You have before." She reached up again and caressed his cheek. "Now, you go first."

When Peter came out of the bathroom, Maria was lying on the bed in her nightgown. She smiled at Peter and got up. While Maria was in the bathroom brushing her teeth, Peter took his pistol out of his suitcase, loaded it, and put it in the drawer of the small table next to the bed. He made sure that both doors were locked, and he wedged two chairs under the door knobs. *Won't stop anyone, but it might give me a little time.*

He turned off all but one light, threw half the pillows onto the floor, and climbed into the bed. He didn't wait long before Maria climbed in the other side. She looked at Peter in silence before she closed the space between them.

Peter felt her sense of urgency as she held him.

"I do love you, Peter," she said. "That is real, but I'm afraid."

"We're okay."

"You don't know these people. I've lived with them. They are brutal, and they never give up."

"You're not in Russia anymore."

"Part of me is still Russian."

"We'll be fine."

"We weren't fine this morning."

"We're fine tonight."

"And even here, you barricade the doors."

"Just to make you feel safe."

"Peter.., What are we going to do?"

"We're going to love each other. We're going to live a long and happy life."

Maria said something in Russian that Peter didn't understand. She held his face in her hands and kissed him. Hard. She started to rub her body against his. When she pushed him onto his back, it was obvious to Peter that she wanted to take the lead tonight. He stepped back mentally and let her take him where she wanted to go.

Their loving was fierce and a little noisy, and when it was over, Peter lay on his back and held Maria on his chest. He took a deep, shuddering breath.

Maria looked up at his face. "You okay?"

"I need you, Maria. More than you know."

"No. I know."

"I'm afraid I'm going to lose you."

"Don't be afraid. I'm not going anywhere. I can't."

They slipped apart and rolled onto their sides, facing each other. "Keep holding me, Peter. I want to fall asleep together."

When Peter was sure she was asleep, he gently pulled his arms away. She moaned slightly and rolled onto her right side, facing away from him. He gently pulled the covers up, turned off the light, and lay back in the bed.

He wondered about this woman sleeping beside him. He knew the risks. *No, I just think I know the risks.*

"Someday, Maria Davidoff," he whispered, "you will tell me."

Chapter 4

Peter woke once in the night with a dream. He didn't move. He forced his breathing into a regular rhythm, and after a few minutes he could feel his heartrate gradually return to normal. It was always the same dream. The same bodies and the same blood. Always the same man, in the shadows. Peter could never quite make out the details of the man's face.

For a while Peter sat on the edge of the bed. His left arm ached, and he rubbed the rough scars. They were a lasting gift from Nunavik. Though he lay back in bed, he did not sleep well. He got up a little after six.

He pulled the chairs away from the doors before he showered and shaved. He shook his head at the image in the mirror. His curly, auburn hair was a little longer than he liked.

While Maria showered, Peter dressed in clean jeans and a clean shirt he found in the suitcase. He retrieved his pistol, unloaded it, and put it and the ammunition into the suitcase. He laid out clean clothes for Maria. He considered using his telephone but decided against it. He went upstairs to pay Devin.

When Devin answered the door, he was in his bathrobe. "I thought I ought to settle up," Peter said. "I hope I'm not too early."

Devin laughed. "Nope. You know me. I'm up early but slow to move. Come on in."

Peter knew that Devin inhabited a different world at night. He chose not to ask questions. As Devin ran the credit card, Peter asked, "You mind if I use your phone?"

"You want my personal phone or my business phone?"

Peter smiled. "I think the personal phone, thanks."

Devin handed Peter a phone from the table, and Peter punched in the number for Bill Branch. It rang three times.

"Yes?"

"Bill, this is Peter. Can you talk for a minute?"

"Sure."

"We're going over to the apartment. Anything new I should know?"

"No. We're out of there. Nothing new on the shooters."

"You think it's okay for a couple of days?"

"I think so. Yesterday was a major setback for the bad guys. At a minimum, it'll take a while to regroup."

"I agree."

"We have some assets around the building."

"Thanks."

"It's all Toronto assets. Dick Durban doesn't want anything to do with it."

"Interesting."

"What the hell did you do to him?"

"Not entirely sure. Sorry about yesterday."

"That's okay. It's your game."

"Yeah."

Peter hung up. Devin had a rather quizzical look on his face.

"What?" Peter said.

Devin put his hands up. "Nothing. You know me. Don't ask and don't tell."

"Good idea," Peter said and handed back the phone. Devin handed him his credit card and collected a signature.

By eight Peter Binder and Maria Davidoff were out the door with the suitcase and quickly found a cab at Parliament and Wellesley. It was a bright, summer day, with the promise of real heat.

As the cab pulled up to the apartment building, Peter noticed the police patrol car halfway down the block. "You see the cop car?"

"Reassuring," Maria said.

Frederick, the doorman, asked how they were, but he didn't pry. He never did. "Things are a little busy up there."

"Who's there?" Maria asked.

"The carpet cleaners are already in the apartment. Painters should be in later."

They chatted with the cleaners when they got to the apartment. The cleaners were making good progress. One of them said, "By the time we clean the whole carpet, you'll never notice a thing."

Maria looked up from her computer when Peter came into the kitchen in his black leather pants, jacket, and boots, with a pair of running shoes inside a rolled-up pair of blue jeans.

He poured himself a cup of coffee. "You'll be okay today?"

Maria thought about it. "I'll be okay. I've got a lot of work to do for some of the boards I'm on. Pitcairn Gold wants me to negotiate a joint venture."

"That police car is probably just one of several."

"Nothing's going to happen today. It's too soon." She looked up. "Anyway, I'll keep the door locked. I'll work on getting the keyless deadbolt installed."

"The pistol's in the suitcase."

"Thanks, I guess. What about you?"

Peter shrugged. "Gotta live my life."

"I guess so."

"We just need to be a little careful."

"Or a lot careful," Maria said.

"Yeah. Maybe a lot careful."

Twenty minutes before ten, Peter waited for the garage door to open. He was already hot. His helmet was matte black with a dark smoke face shield. The BMW K1600 GTL, also black with chrome and silver trim, idled with its confident but soft-throated sound. With the 160 horsepower, six-cylinder engine, the 800-pound motorcycle was capable of performing to a level that could be a little frightening even for Peter. He pulled up to the sidewalk, looked, and turned into the street. He saw in his mirror that the police car did a U turn and followed him.

Peter headed to the Gardiner Expressway, which was not clogged with traffic for a change. *A good time of day for the ride to Waterloo.* Peter hit a few slow spots on the 427, and again around Missauga on the 401, but generally the traffic was light.

Past Missauga, he moved into the far-left lane and sped up to the flow of traffic. Peter didn't see the police car anymore, and the speed cooled him in his leathers. A large, white SUV began to crowd him from behind.

The road was clear in front of him, but Peter moved to the right, behind a semi, to let the SUV pass. The SUV pulled in behind him.

Peter couldn't see much detail in his rearview mirrors. He took no action for a moment.

The SUV pulled closer.

Too close.

"Screw this," Peter said.

He checked the left lane. Open.

Peter shifted down and shot to the left just as the semi hit the brakes for a driver who had cut him off. Peter shifted quickly through the gears and sped up to 120 miles per hour.

Peter took a quick glance at his mirrors. No sign of the white SUV. Peter closed on the traffic in front of him, braked hard, and pulled into the lane to his right.

He became the motorcyclist that every automobile driver hates. He wove from one lane to another to put as many cars and trucks as possible between him and the SUV.

Peter pulled off at exit 278 and checked his rearview mirrors. No white SUV. He relaxed. When he pulled up at Ontario Helicopters, he parked near the front door.

He closed his eyes. "Shit," he said. He inhaled deeply. He wanted to be calm for his test flight.

Peter took off his helmet, took the key, and grabbed his jeans and running shoes. He changed in the men's room and still had about ten minutes to spare.

He went to the front desk with his flight helmet. "Brewster ready for me?"

"He's with another student. He should be on schedule."

Brewster Bannister, chief pilot for Ontario Helicopters, did all the final flight checks. He could be gruff and crusty, but Peter liked him. He was battle scarred, literally. They had a lot in common. Peter sat down to wait.

He thought about the incident on the 401. The intentions of the SUV driver seemed pretty clear, but maybe it was just another idiot on the road.

He never got a good look at the driver or the license plate. It was a large Jeep, presumably a Grand Cherokee. Newer model. *I could be overreacting. I don't think so.*

"Nuts," Peter muttered.

"Mr. Binder. You ready?"

Peter looked up at Brewster. "You bet. Let's go."

"How was traffic this morning?"

"Pretty calm," Peter replied.

Peter talked with the tower and took off to the north. He flew up to an area of open fields near the little town of Alma. They practiced maneuvers over the empty fields for half an hour before heading back.

When he landed, Brewster said, "Keep it running, Peter." Brewster unplugged his helmet from the cabin communications system and opened his door. "Just take it up to Alma and back. That'll be enough for today." Brewster had a rare smile on his face. Peter saluted.

Peter loved flying the little MD 500. It was his motorcycle in the sky. The winds were calm, and the sky was blue with small puffy clouds. For the moment he didn't think about anything except flying, and in a little more than twenty minutes he was on the ground again, shutting down. He took a deep breath. He had a long way to go before he could add a helicopter license to his fixed wing license.

After a quick lunch at the restaurant across the street, Peter changed back into his leathers and got on his bike.

Traffic should be light at this hour.

"Just keep cool," he muttered. He started the bike and headed down the road.

Once he hit the 401 he sped up and headed into the far-left lane. The traffic was moving fast, up around eighty miles per hour. He watched the traffic around him as the cars and trucks shifted from one lane to another to gain an imagined advantage.

Nothing alarming.

By the time Peter rolled into his parking space at the apartment building, he was having some very bad thoughts.

I've been lucky, so far, but these attacks have been too easy.

Maria had told him she needed to make a lot of phone calls today. Peter assumed they had seriously diminished the capabilities of the Russian attackers. Peter and Maria had both turned on their cell phones in the morning.

They knew exactly where I was, Peter thought.

"Idiot," he muttered.

Maria's parking space was empty.

Chapter 5

Peter unlocked the door to the apartment and stepped inside. "Maria?"

No answer. Maria hadn't told him she was going out.

I am getting paranoid, he thought, *but I'm not sure it's a bad thing.*

In the bedroom, Peter stripped off his leathers, showered, and dressed in his jeans and tee shirt. He sat down with his computer at the dining room table. He disconnected from the internet, inserted a small memory card, and opened an encrypted word file.

He paged down through his notes on the Nunavik incident from last year and quickly added what happened on the 401. He saved the additions and closed down the computer. He knew every word of the file, but he struggled to understand all the implications.

He did, however, understand Rostov. Zakhar Rostov was easy. He was very rich. He had been the most powerful of the Russian oligarchs. Even in hiding he had supporters. He had dreamed of creating hell on Earth, and Peter had denied his dream.

"And Maria, too," Peter said softly.

Everyone fails you, Rostov. Someday you will come for us... yourself.

Peter took the computer back to the bedroom. He returned the memory card to the small, hidden pocket in his backpack. He thought again about the white SUV on the 401.

That was too close. There's too many of them, and from too many directions.

He grabbed a cold beer and sat on the sofa in the living room. He switched on the television. He noted the bullet hole above the television had been patched but not yet painted.

Ten minutes later, he was into his second beer and watching the start of the CBC news when he heard the key in the door.

For the briefest of moments, after Maria stepped into the apartment, she stopped and looked at Peter.

Are you surprised to see me? He couldn't tell.

Maria took a quick breath. "How did it go today?" she asked.

As she carried two grocery bags into the kitchen, Peter said, "No problems."

"And you soloed?"

"I did."

"And you survived, which is a good thing." She put some of the groceries into the refrigerator. "I still wish I could have been there with you."

"Well, I'm glad you weren't. I was sweating enough as it was."

"I still say it couldn't be any more frightening than just living with you."

"Sorry about that."

"Anyway, I knew you'd have a good day, so I bought a nice red wine to celebrate." She held it up with a small smile.

"That sounds like a great idea."

She came over and sat down beside him. "Now, before you pick up the rest of the groceries from the car, tell me more about your solo."

"Well, the flight test was a bore, and the solo was only twenty minutes. Nothing exciting."

She stared at him for a moment before she said, "Well congratulations for having such a boring day."

"And you? How was your day?"

She looked away. "I was on the phone most of the time. Nothing exciting. Stupid property owners."

Later that evening, Peter prepared two small tenderloin filets for dinner and topped them with Maria's hot, Cajun lobster sauce. They added plain green beans, and rice with diced onions and carrots, topped with Parmesan cheese. The wine they had with dinner was Australian, a solid and respectable Penfolds Shiraz. Maria was mostly silent as they ate.

After dinner, they finished the wine watching the evening news. At one point the news anchor reported, "A major accident this morning tied up the westbound 401 for several hours. A white SUV struck a large truck, rolled, and severely injured the driver and one passenger. Police say the two were Russian tourists. They would not comment on the cause of the accident."

Maria turned to Peter. "Lucky you missed that."

"I must have been right in front of it." Peter put his arm around Maria's shoulders. "If you ask me, with one exception, there are too many Russians around here."

After a moment, Maria said quietly, "Even this Canadian Russian might agree with you."

"You dealing with yesterday okay?"

Maria shrugged and frowned. "I don't know. I try my best to control it, but I'm still a little jumpy, and I'm depressed and angry about it. I feel hunted. It hasn't been this bad for a long time, maybe not since I left Russia. I want to hide." She turned to Peter. Without a hint of excitement, she asked, "So when are we going to the lake?"

"Let's leave early tomorrow. I know we agreed we could turn on our phones this morning, but I think we should turn them off again and remove the batteries. I don't want anyone to find us too easily."

Later, when Maria was in the shower, Peter sat at the edge of the bed and composed a short email. He frowned and hesitated before he sent it. He returned his computer to his backpack. When Maria came out of the bathroom, she turned off the light, and without a word joined him in bed.

She rolled over to Peter, and he put his arms around her and held her. Neither of them said a word, and Peter thought he knew why.

We're both afraid, he thought. *We're afraid of each other.*

He did not understand why, but for some reason the fear also drew them together. They held each other tighter, and he kissed her.

Maria responded with a sigh and dug her fingers into his back.

Peter woke at three. There was no dream, just a sense of emptiness. He lay awake for a long time listening to Maria's measured breathing.

Why do I feel so alone? he asked himself. He knew the answer. *Too many secrets.*

He woke again at six, and he got out of bed and showered.

Maria was awake when he returned to the bedroom to dress. "You're eager today," she said.

"We should get going before the morning rush."

Later, when Peter heard Maria come out of the bathroom, he said, "I'm taking the groceries down to the car. I've got six bottles of wine. That enough?"

"Make it a case, mostly red."

"Okay," Peter said. By the time he had loaded the groceries, wine and his backpack into Maria's Mustang, she was ready to go. He added her suitcase. It was half past seven, still before the height of the rush.

As Maria pulled out of the garage, Peter said, "Let's make sure no one's following us."

"You think that's necessary?"

"Probably not, but let's do it anyway."

Maria exited the garage and drove around the block. Then she did it twice more, expanding the exercise by two blocks each time. "You see anything?" she asked.

"Not a thing. You?"

"Nothing." He had watched her as much as he had watched behind them. She was totally focused. If she was jumpy or nervous, she hid it well.

It's second nature for you, he thought.

He wasn't as sure as he sounded with regard to possible followers. There were two cars that seemed to follow them for a while before they broke off. He thought the first one might be behind them again.

"You do realize that I don't know the way," Maria said.

"Just head west on the Gardiner. I'll guide you from there."

A little after nine, they pulled into the small but popular Palmer Café. It was long past the peak of the breakfast business. Only a few of the local regulars remained, and Peter liked that. Anyone else, Peter and Maria included, stood out like tourists.

A blue pickup that had followed them for some time also pulled into the restaurant. The two young men from the pickup sat four tables away. One was busy texting. They looked to be in their late teens or early twenties.

Too young to worry about, Peter thought, *but I'll watch them anyway*. He turned his attention to the menu.

The waitress came to the table. June had worked at the café since opening day. "How are you, Peter," she said. "Haven't seen you for a while."

"I'm good. How about you?"

June shrugged. "Except for sore feet, I'm great. What can I get you?"

Peter and Maria both ordered scrambled eggs, toast, potatoes, and coffee. Their order seemed to appear almost before they finished giving it.

Peter said, "Nobody's come in after us but those two guys from the pickup. You notice anyone else following us on the road?"

Maria shook her head. "Just the pickup. It's been behind us for a long time, but there was no reason to pass. I was quite a bit over the speed limit."

"Let's see what happens when we leave."

As they headed out of Palmer, the blue pickup pulled in behind them again. The empty road developed longer and sharper curves as it wound around small lakes and streams.

Peter said, "You know, police patrols up here are pretty rare. I'd like to put a little distance between us and that damn pickup truck."

"Really?"

"Yes."

Maria smiled. "Okay. Hang on." Maria increased speed and began to drive much more aggressively. Peter could never quite escape the feeling that when she drove her Shelby Mustang on roads like this one, that the car became an extension of her. Somehow it seemed to be excited that it could run.

Three and a half hours after leaving Toronto, Peter directed Maria to a two-car garage he rented behind the small general store in Pierceville. "You don't want to drive your Mustang down the road to the cabin," Peter said. "I'll open up and you can park next to my pickup."

As Maria got out of the car, Peter closed the garage door. "What's next?" she asked.

Peter looked out at the road through a glass window in the top of the side door. Maria stood beside him. "Let's see if the blue pickup shows up," he said. "Shouldn't be long."

A few minutes later, Maria said, "That looks like them."

The truck sped by. *They're in a hurry*, Peter thought.

Peter said, "Let's see if they come back. The general store has a couple of tables where we can have coffee and a bite to eat."

They entered the store from the back and sat at a small table by the front window. They helped themselves to coffee.

At noon, after an hour of watching, they bought a sandwich and something more to drink. They continued to watch. No truck. After two hours Peter said, "I think they went fishing."

Just as he spoke, the blue pickup showed up again, heading toward Toronto at a rather sedate pace. "Maybe they're going home," Peter said.

"You want to wait a little longer? Just to be sure?"

"We'll never be sure," he said. "Maybe they weren't following us in the first place, or maybe they were and realize they lost us. Anyway, it looks like they're leaving."

I don't think they were going fishing, unless they were fishing for us.

Peter got up from the table. "If we're going to last two weeks, we need more groceries and a few supplies, like toilet paper. This place isn't elegant, but it has the basics."

After they picked up a few more things at the general store, they headed down the road in Peter's pickup. "Now," he said with a smile, "we travel a little more slowly."

Two miles west of Pierceville they turned into the woods on a narrow, dirt track, barely wide enough for the truck. It was full of muddy potholes and an occasional rocky outcropping. "It's mostly paper company land," Peter said. "My only neighbor is a small fishing lodge five or six miles away at the other end of the lake. They'll be busy, but they don't come up to my end of the lake much."

After a wide spot in the road, Peter stopped at a heavy steel gate. In large letters a sign read, "PRIVATE PROPERTY, NO TRESPASSING."

"It discourages tourists and honest people," he said.

And hopefully it at least slows down the bad guys when they come calling.

After he locked the gate behind them, Peter said, "I have a couple of video cameras at the gate, and a magnetic sensor. Haven't used them for a while. Let's hope they still work."

Maria said, "I feel like we're headed to a redoubt."

"Not a very secure one," Peter said with a small smile.

After they passed a second gate, Maria said, "Of course somebody could come in by air."

"Lots of noise, and nobody flies into this lake. Unlike a lot of the fishing lodges, there's a road to this one." Peter pulled into a small clearing on the north shore of the lake and stopped.

"Here we are," he said. "My cabin, the garage, and my little Zen garden."

Maria pointed at a rock and gravel jetty that connected to a small wooden dock. "You have a boat?"

"There's a big freighter canoe in the garage, and a little outboard motor for it. There's a kayak, too."

Peter opened the door to the oversized, one-car garage behind the cabin and drove the truck inside. He and Maria grabbed some of the groceries and walked to the entrance to the cabin.

He stopped at the door and put down the bags he was carrying. "Before we go in, give me a minute to look around." He stepped up on a deck on the south side of the cabin. He wasn't sure what he was looking for, but his security systems were designed for privacy, not protection from killers. *Just look.*

Finding nothing out of order, Peter returned to Maria, unlocked two deadbolts on the door and swung it open.

Peter raised the steel shutters over the bank of four large windows that looked over the deck to the lake. Light flooded into the cabin. Everything was as he had left it. "That's better," he said.

He switched on the electrical system, heard the refrigerator come to life, and shut the door. "Now we're all connected to my local, solar energy system," he said with a small smile of satisfaction.

Maria put the grocery bags on the counter, looked out the window to the lake, and said, "This is nice."

"You want the full tour?"

"Sure."

"Well, I know this is pretty remote and may seem primitive, but we have indoor plumbing and hot and cold running water. The system is small, though. Use it gently. I have a washing machine in the back."

"This is most of the cabin," Peter said. He gestured around the large open room. "Kitchen. My hand-hewn dining table. Too many chairs. My desk over there, with my books and files, and what you might call the living room with the sofa and chairs." Brightly colored geological maps and Peter's photographs of wildlife and exploration camps covered most of the walls.

Peter pointed to the wood stove against the wall opposite the door. "That's our main heating system until it gets really cold."

"We've got satellite telephone and internet, and," he pointed to a flat screen above the desk, "satellite television. It all works great, until there's a bad storm."

"There's a loft upstairs with a desk and a futon for an extra bed." They stepped into a short hallway and Peter pointed out the bathroom. "It's small, but it works."

He opened a door on the other side of the hallway. "This is the bedroom. A queen-sized bed, two closets and two bureaus. One for each of us." Peter opened the shutter over the large window.

"This is amazing," Maria said.

"It's not Toronto."

"I love it, though it does look like it was built and furnished by a geologist."

"That's a fair observation," Peter said, laughing.

"But I really do like it."

"I'm glad. I think it's our home for a while." Peter grew silent as he looked out the window at the trees.

Now all I can do is wait, Peter thought. *Somebody will find us.* He took a deep breath. *Let them come.*

He turned around and said, "I guess we should get the rest of the stuff out of the truck and put it away."

Once Maria put the groceries and supplies away, she went outside to the deck.

As Peter finished with the last of the chores to open the cabin, he looked at her. *She doesn't seem worried or scared. She should be. I am.*

Peter joined Maria on the deck. He sat next to her in the double Adirondack-style chair. It and two smaller chairs surrounded an iron brazier.

"You like the view?" he asked.

"All I can hear are the birds, and the little waves hitting the rocks."

"When there's a storm, the wind can really howl, but at times like this I feel like the quiet swallows me alive."

Maria reached over and held his hand. "I think I can almost feel safe here."

They both sat silently, looking along the lake to the trees and hills in the distance.

Peter said, "Feeling almost safe is probably the best we can do for a while."

Chapter 6

A week later, in the evening, Peter and Maria sat together on the deck. It was a cool evening, and a fire blazed in the brazier. She asked, "What did you do up here when you were alone?"

"Mostly I thought of you."

Maria poked him in the ribs. "I'm serious. It's pretty lonely."

"Well, my field work was mostly in the summer. I had to write my reports somewhere. It's amazing how much work you can get done in a day of quiet solitude."

"Seems pretty extreme to me."

Peter didn't answer for almost a minute. "After I got out of the SEALs, I was in bad shape. I hated crowds and noise. My nightmares were much worse then. There's a lot I haven't told you. Some I probably never will. I barely managed to survive my time at the University."

Peter turned his head and looked directly at Maria. "All the security around this cabin is because of my demons. Right now, it seems like a good idea."

"Well, having you beside me keeps me from being petrified most of the time."

"I think we're a mutual aid society."

They watched the fire. "It's a beautiful evening, but the mosquitos are getting to me," Maria said. "Shall we head inside?"

"Sounds good to me."

They went into the bedroom, which was still warm, even with a window open. They pulled back the covers and lay on the sheet. They held each other quietly for a long time. They gradually shed their clothes. Peter pulled Maria close and whispered, "Do you think we could make this last all night?"

"Oh, I think that's up to you," Maria said.

In the early morning calm, there was barely a ripple on the lake. Maria was out in the kayak. Peter could see her, stroking smoothly, near the center of the lake heading south.

He watched as a twin-engine Otter floatplane banked over the lake and turned back toward the cabin. It flew low and close to Maria. For a moment Peter thought it would land on the lake, but it climbed again and continued flying, only two or three hundred feet above the ground when it passed the cabin.

You were quick, and you've found us. Where do we go now?

Peter answered his own question, aloud, "Nowhere."

After more than two weeks, Peter's contact had finally responded to the email he had sent after the incident on the 401.

Peter frowned as he read.

The two men in the SUV died from their injuries. Interpol says they were low level associates of the Russian mob. Police found two assault rifles in the SUV. Both men were on a "no entry" list for Canada, but they entered on false Ukrainian passports. No clear connection to Zakhar Rostov. The email ended with the comment, *You are not helping by being invisible.*

Easy for him to say, Peter thought, *and that floatplane tells me we're not invisible. You want Rostov and so do I. I'm just not sure I'll survive the hunt.*

Peter picked up the satellite telephone and punched in the number for Bill Branch's cell phone.

"Bill Branch."

"This is Peter Binder."

"How are you doing?"

"Well, it's more than two weeks," Peter said, "and I'd like to make a quick visit to Toronto. What do you think? Have things calmed down?"

"No action on this end. The guy we caught in the alley apparently committed suicide. He jumped, or was pushed, out the hospital window. He never answered any questions."

"Nice."

"You're pretty good at leaving no survivors, Peter."

"You accusing me of throwing this guy out the window?"

"No, but there are a lot of bodies around."

"I can't help that."

"By the way, did you hear about the crash on the 401, just before you left town? Killed a couple of Russian tourists?"

"Yeah, I saw the news before we left," Peter said. "I thought the guys in the SUV survived."

"Died in the hospital. A witness said a black motorcycle left the scene at high speed. Was that you?"

Peter was silent.

"You still there, Peter?"

"Yeah."

"Look, I'm not accusing you of anything. The trucker said he braked hard to avoid a car that cut him off, and the SUV hit him as it was changing lanes to go around him. He said the motorcycle was gone before the SUV hit him. If that was you, what was going on?"

Peter hesitated. "I don't know. A white SUV tried to shove me under a truck. I jumped into the far-left lane and got the hell out of there. I really don't know what happened after that."

"What were you doing up there anyway?"

"I was headed to Waterloo for a flying lesson."

Peter heard Bill exhale loudly. He could almost see him shaking his head.

"Listen," Peter said, "I called because I want to come into Toronto. What do you think?"

"Hell, I don't know. They seem to have a lot of resources."

"Seen anything since the incident on the 401?"

"No."

"You think it's safe to come to the apartment?"

"I don't know," Bill said, "but I wouldn't recommend it, not yet. I'd stay at a hotel, and if you need to go to the apartment for some reason, do it during the day and don't be obvious about it."

"You're probably right."

"You know I'm right."

"Okay, but if you haven't had any action, I think both of us will come to town tomorrow morning. At least I'm sure I will."

"I'll put a little extra security around the apartment building. How long do you plan to stay?"

"Let's see what, if anything, happens," Peter said.

"Does Dick Durban know what you're doing?"

"No."

"Then who does?"

"The Prime Minister, I think."

"Christ. Does Maria still work for Durban?"

"I don't think so," Peter answered.

"Shit. Who the hell do you really work for anyway?"

Peter was silent.

"Just be careful, man, and keep in touch when you can. Okay?"

"I'll do that," Peter said.

Peter dialed another number.

"Bob Williams here."

"Bob, it's Peter Binder. You going to the IndoGold presentation tomorrow?"

"Yeah. I can't help myself."

"Look, I know what you think about their Endang gold deposit. If I buy you lunch after the show, would you let me pick your brain a bit?"

"Sure. You're the only one these days who has any interest in my views on that subject."

"I'll try to get there a half hour early. Hang around the entrance to the meeting room. We can sit together."

"No problem. See you there."

After dinner Peter and Maria sat quietly at the table finishing a bottle of wine.

"Have you heard anything from Bill Branch?" Maria asked.

"I talked with him for a few minutes this morning."

"Jesus. When were you going to tell me? Tomorrow?"

"Sorry."

"Well, what did he say?"

"Not much," Peter said.

"He must have said something."

"I told him that I wanted to come to Toronto."

"And?"

"I think he's afraid."

She frowned. "I'm not surprised."

"He doesn't want us to stay in the apartment. If we want to go there, we should take a taxi into the basement garage. Don't talk to Frederick. Leave the drapes closed, and don't turn on any lights or show ourselves at the windows."

"That's a pain. Where are we supposed to stay?"

"We can stay at the Bond Place Hotel," he said.

"That funky place?"

"It's not bad. Besides, funky is good. Nobody would expect us to stay there."

Maria shook her head. "Okay. So, I want to go buy some wine. Why do you want to go to Toronto?"

"You remember IndoGold and their Endang deposit from your time with World Nickel?"

"Sure. It's supposed to be the biggest gold deposit ever. The company's worth billions."

"I bought 200,000 shares really early, at eleven cents," Peter said. "They're worth about twenty million now, and I'm getting… Let's just say I'm very uncomfortable."

"How come?"

"It doesn't make sense. I want to go to their presentation tomorrow and talk to a friend of mine after. He's always been really down on that company, and I want to know why."

"You think we might stay in Toronto?"

"I doubt it. Let's see what happens, if anything."

"Well, I sure don't want to hang around here alone," Maria said. "That plane this morning makes me nervous as hell. Too close. They were staring right at me."

"I thought they were going to land."

"That's the thing. They came down really low, looked at me, and flew away."

"Probably scouting for moose, ahead of the hunt."

"Do I look like a moose?"

The next morning, they left early and got to the Bond Place hotel a little after ten. Maria parked in the garage across the street, and as they had agreed she took a cab to the apartment building.

Peter took the subway down Yonge Street to Union Station and crossed the street to the Royal York hotel. IndoGold was hot news on the stock exchange. They needed the main ballroom of the old hotel for their presentation.

Bob Williams was easy to spot. A bit taller than six feet, he was dressed in a red and black plaid shirt, tan twill field pants, and light tan boots. With thick, unruly gray hair, he looked like he had just stepped out of the woods with a pocket full of gold nuggets. He was a major anomaly among the investment bankers and brokers in their dark pinstripes.

Peter shook Bob's hand. "Good to see you, Bob. It's been a while."

"We should go in," Bob said. "It'll be a full house."

Bob was right. The room was full. Everyone in Toronto wanted a piece of the Endang action. The presentation started on schedule when the chairman of IndoGold, Robert Talon, walked to the podium.

"I'll bet he's had at least two glasses of gin already this morning," Bob said.

Robert Talon was no more than the ring master for the circus, and after brief comments he introduced the president. Wayne Richards presented a wildly positive report on their huge and potentially fantastically profitable Endang gold deposit in Indonesia.

The numbers are crazier than ever, Peter thought.

One hundred million ounces of gold made it the largest single gold deposit in the history of the world. And the economic estimates made it the most profitable mine ever.

The old saying kept running through Peter's mind, over and over. *If it sounds too good to be true, you can bet it's not true.*"

Wayne Richards introduced Dr. Teunis Dulaigh, the chief geologist, to talk about potential to expand the already giant gold deposit. Teunis was huge, morbidly obese.

Peter turned to Bob Williams, "Is he really a field geologist?"

"Ask me over lunch."

After the presentations, Peter and Bob headed down to a restaurant along the lakefront. They sat by a window with a view of the water, and each ordered a beer and a light lunch.

"Okay," Peter said, "is Teunis Dulaigh really a field geologist?"

"Did you know we worked together?"

"No."

"Well we did." Bob leaned back. "We worked for an American company in Indonesia. He was the laziest damn geologist I ever knew, and that was before he got so fat."

"He has an amazing reputation," Peter said. "I invested in IndoGold because of his reports on Indonesia geology and gold potential."

"All those early reports, the ones that built his reputation, he stole them from the company files." Bob took a swallow of beer. "I know. I did the field work, and I wrote the reports."

"You're kidding."

"No, I'm not. Of course, the company doesn't care. They left Indonesia and don't plan to go back. I think he wrote the more recent reports, half drunk, in a pub. I've been to some of those places, and his geology is absolute bullshit. Endang is bullshit too."

"Every stock broker and investment banker in the world loves the bloody thing," Peter said.

"You really want to know what I know? This is for you only?"

"I don't work for the stock exchange, and I'm not a reporter."

"Well, I have to be careful. They've threatened to sue me."

"You have been a little vocal and rather public with your opinions."

"Look, Peter, the brokers and bankers are happy because they're making heaps of money off the IndoGold story. They don't want to mess it up with the truth. I've been to Endang as a geologist, before IndoGold picked it up. There's no gold in the streams. No gold in the soils. No gold in the rocks. I've seen a hell of a lot of gold mines, and I can tell you Endang is not a gold mine. There's no gold there. Period. It's a total fraud."

Peter sat back in his chair. "A fraud that size would be really hard to maintain. Too many people involved."

"It's possible Dulaigh is the only one who knows exactly what's going on," Bob said, "but I'll bet that sleaze ball Wayne Richards is in it up to his eyeballs. Talon's just the happy, drunk promoter. He doesn't have a clue."

"Do you really understand what you're saying?"

"Yeah. I know exactly what I'm saying."

"You think it's just a giant stock fraud?"

Bob took his time answering. "I don't know what it is, but I do know what it isn't. I think it started off small, maybe a simple stock fraud, pump and dump, but then something happened. Somebody wanted it huge. Something really bad is happening over there, but I don't know what it is." Bob shrugged and said, "I'm just a geologist. All I know is that Endang is no gold mine."

"I have a lot of respect for you, Bob, but this is really hard to believe."

"Believe it."

As Peter walked back toward Union Station, he decided to continue past the station and walked up to the brokerage at the TD Centre. The IndoGold presentation had been well received. The stock was up five dollars to $110 per share with a huge trading volume. He sold his entire holding in IndoGold at market.

Chapter 7

Peter took a cab from the TD Centre to the apartment building and into the garage. As Peter entered the apartment, Maria looked up from a book.

"You get all the wine you wanted?" Peter asked.

"I did, and I also got some good cheese. I have a feeling we're heading back to the cabin, and that funky little store in Pierceville has its limits." Maria stood up. "There's something I want to show you in the bedroom."

Peter followed Maria and they stood in front of her bureau.

"We've had a lot of workmen in the apartment making repairs, but I don't understand this." She opened the drawer that contained her underwear and socks. "You see anything odd?"

"Not really. Just your usual neatness."

She picked up a brown sock. "I almost never wear brown socks. For that reason, they're always on the bottom of the stack. They're on the top. I didn't put them on top."

I don't like this, Peter thought.

"You're sure about that?" Peter asked.

"Yes. I did not rearrange my socks." She shut the drawer. "Let me show you something else." She opened a drawer where Peter kept his gym shorts and shirts. "See anything odd here?"

This is getting really strange.

"The drawer's reversed."

"That's what I thought. And there's one more thing in my office." They went across the hall to the second bedroom, where Maria kept a desk and several file cabinets. "Both cabinets were locked, but when I searched for a file today I found this." She opened a drawer and pulled up a file. "This file is backwards. I don't do that."

"It's not just a simple mistake?"

"Look, I've spent a big part of my life as a glorified file clerk. I do not make that kind of mistake."

Peter took a deep breath. "Someone searched the apartment."

Maria nodded.

"They either didn't do a very good job or they wanted us to notice. I don't know which is worse. I suspect if we took the time we'd find a few other things that aren't quite right."

"What do we do now?" Maria asked.

"They wanted to find something. Probably wanted to know where we were. If we've been careful enough they shouldn't know we're here right now."

But I bet they know we're here, Peter thought.

"I think we need to get back to the hotel," Peter said. "We'll take the wine down to the garage. You can stay there, and I'll come back for you with a cab. I can't believe they have more than one person watching the apartment building."

A few minutes later Peter exited the back entrance of the apartment building into a narrow alley. A light, summer rain was beginning to fall. He stopped at the door, and looked, and listened. Then he started down the deserted alley. Ten minutes later he returned to the basement garage in a taxi.

A little after three in the afternoon Peter paid the taxi at the parking garage on Bond Street, across from the Bond Place hotel. The normal traffic of the city surged past on Dundas, but Bond was quiet. In the daylight, on the sidewalk, Peter felt dangerously exposed, but he still took a moment to watch the traffic and the hotel.

If they're good, I won't see anything. He didn't.

"If anyone got curious about the taxis in and out of the apartment parking garage, we've got real problems," Peter said. He looked at Maria and shrugged. "Let's get off the street. The wine should survive one night in the garage."

They dropped the two cases of wine into the trunk of Maria's Mustang, but Peter took one bottle with him. They took their suitcases, the cheese, and Peter's backpack, and quickly walked across the street to the hotel.

Their room was ready, a business suite, the best room available. They got their keys and headed up the elevator to the room.

"It's the best they've got," Peter said, as they entered the room.

"Better than I expected," Maria responded.

Peter hunted in a pocket of his backpack and produced a Swiss army knife. "Not much of a knife," he said, "but it does have a corkscrew."

As he opened the bottle of wine and found two glasses, he said, "I sold all my shares in IndoGold this afternoon."

"Really?"

"I have a little cash in my brokerage account."

Maria laughed. "That's an understatement. You won't like your tax bill."

"I don't think I'll complain."

They took their wine and sat on the white sofa. Peter leaned back and said, "I don't know about you, but, aside from selling my shares, I'm beginning to think it was a bad idea to come into town."

"Probably right. We could head back to the lake right now."

"No," Peter said. "We haven't been to a decent restaurant in weeks. I'm going to call La Fenice and reserve a table for tonight. The theater district is crowded. Under the circumstances, crowds are good."

"So, you're planning the last supper?"

Peter laughed. "I hope not, but it is Italian."

Early the next morning, when he loaded the Mustang, Peter pulled his pistol out of his backpack and dropped it into his jacket pocket. They pulled out of the garage at six-thirty.

"Any special requests this morning?" Maria asked.

Peter looked behind them. He saw a white SUV pull out of its parking space. "Yes," he said. "Let's see if that white SUV wants to follow us."

Maria completed two expanding loops around the hotel. The SUV stayed behind them. When they stopped by the garage, it came around the corner two blocks away, and settled into an open parking space.

It's like they don't care if we know they're following, Peter thought.

"What do we do now?" Maria asked.

"Just drive up to our breakfast in Palmer. We'll see what happens."

It was easy to keep track of the SUV in the light traffic in the city. Not so easy on the main highways. When they got closer to Palmer, Peter would catch a glimpse of it on the longer straight stretches. "They're not too sophisticated," he said.

As they pulled up to the café, he said, "Park on the street, where they can see the car." Maria took the last parking space in front of the café.

The café was nearly full and noisy, with only a few tables available. Peter and Maria sat down at a table by the window.

Just as they sat, the SUV pulled in and parked behind the café. Shortly after, two heavy-set men came in, both looking like they hadn't had a chance to shave. They had the solid, somewhat battered look of professional boxers who have lost too many fights. The only remaining table was in the back of the restaurant next to the entrance to the ladies' room.

June arrived at their table, set down two coffee cups, and filled them without asking.

"How are your feet?" Peter asked.

"Same as always. You want your usual?"

"Sure. You Maria?"

Maria smiled. "Sure. I'll have his usual, too."

They sipped at their coffee. Peter said softly, "Go to the ladies' and see what you think."

Peter looked out the window. When Maria returned, she said one word, "Russian."

Lots of empty road ahead of us, Peter thought. *Maybe a little too empty.*

They ate in silence. About half-way through his breakfast, Peter pushed his chair back. "I'll be right back."

He walked across the restaurant, down a short hallway to the right of the kitchen, and past the men's room. He looked back. Except for two tables near the door, no one in the restaurant could see him. At the end of the hallway he opened the fire exit to the parking area behind the cafe. He put a small pebble in the door jamb to prevent the door from locking behind him.

The white SUV was right in front of him. He saw no one in the parking lot. He examined the SUV more closely. Black tinted windows. Jeep Grand Cherokee. On the side it said, "Track Hawk".

"That's interesting," Peter said. He took a knife out of his pocket and walked around the car. He bent over at each tire.

Peter removed the pebble from the door jamb and carefully shut the door. He stopped by the cash register. He was struck again by the noise level of the small café. As he handed June the cash for the bill and a generous tip, he leaned closer, "You know those two by the ladies' room, the guys who came in right after us?"

"Never seen them before. What about them?"

"Can you delay them a bit?"

She raised her eyebrows. "How long?"

"Oh, just a couple of minutes. That'll be enough."

She smiled. "For you, no problem."

Peter sat down again at the table with Maria. As he worked on his breakfast, he said, "We're all paid up. When I'm done, let's go, and let's be quick about our exit. Okay?"

"I'm ready when you are."

A few minutes later they both got up and walked toward the door. Peter saw that the two Russians had already stood up, trying to pay. Peter and Maria got in the Mustang.

"Let's get the hell out of here," Peter said

"Won't they just keep following us?"

Peter reached into his pocket and dropped the ends of four valve stems into one of the cup holders between them. "Not with four flat tires."

"Man, they'll be royally pissed."

"Probably, but it gives us a couple of hours head start. If they know where we're going, at least we can be ready for them."

"I could always outrun a big SUV like that."

Peter shook his head. "I'm not so sure. That's a Grand Cherokee Track Hawk. One engine option has over seven hundred horses under the hood and can probably do zero to sixty faster than your Mustang. It's a tank, but it might be a very fast tank." Peter looked back. "I think those boys are serious."

Maria made good time to Pierceville. They followed the same routine as before, parked the Mustang in the garage, transferred the groceries, wine, and baggage to the pickup, and added a few items from the store. They quickly passed through the two gates on the road to the cabin.

As they pulled the truck into the garage, Peter said, "We should have a while before they show up, but this could be a long day." He looked out the garage door toward the lake. It was a clear, hot, July day. The wind was blowing hard, and the lake had little white caps.

Peter grabbed some of the groceries and headed toward the cabin. Maria followed with her arms full. He unlocked the door, stepped inside, and turned on the lights. "Maybe you can put this stuff away, and I'll empty the truck."

"Uh… I hate to say it, but barricading ourselves inside this cabin doesn't seem like such a great idea to me."

"Let's get everything out of the truck and put away," Peter said. "Then I'll show you what we can do."

"Okay."

On the third and last trip, Peter locked the garage door and closed the cabin door behind him.

"Okay. What now?" Maria asked.

Peter sat down at his desk and turned on his computer. "First I want to be able to monitor the gates." He checked the video feed. "Looks like we're good so far."

"Now let's button up this place. If you make sure all the shutters are locked shut, I'll bar the door."

When they were done, Peter said, "Okay. That's as secure as it gets."

"But won't they just smash the door?"

"Well, it looks like wood, but it's a steel door in a steel frame. It'll take quite a pounding. There are a few other things that make this building a little tougher than it looks, but all it does is buy us time."

"Time for what?" Maria asked. "If we're inside we've got no place to go."

"Just follow me." Peter went into the bedroom and opened the door to the second closet, where he kept his clothes and boots.

"Don't tell me you have a secret passage."

"You're ruining the surprise." Peter took out the two pairs of boots, a 12-gauge pump shotgun, and his .460 Weatherby rifle. He reached around to the right on the inside of the closet. There was a click followed by a hum as the floor sank about four inches and slid out of sight to the left.

"Really? You've got an escape tunnel?"

"Really." Peter got down on his knees, reached under the edge of the flooring and switched on the lights. They lit the top of a ladder.

As Peter got up he said, "There's an opening in the garage and another about fifty feet into the woods on the other side of the Zen garden."

"You really were paranoid when you built this."

"Yeah." Peter frowned. "I guess I'm glad I was."

They stood in silence for a moment.

"We need to get moving. If those guys know where we are, they're already mad as hell."

They put two light weight, camouflage jackets and two olive drab hats on the bed. Peter added his pistol to the pile. He loaded both the shotgun and the rifle.

"Time for a little makeup," he said. He pulled three sticks of face paint out of his bureau.

"You first," he said to Maria.

He quickly painted Maria's face a mix of greens and brown. Then he turned to the mirror and did the same for himself. He looked at the results. "Not perfect, but it's better than nothing."

"Now we wait, I guess," he said. "There hasn't been an alarm from the magnetic sensor at the gate, but let's look at the video."

Peter looked at his computer. No one at the gate. He started to turn away, but at that moment the alarm sounded for the magnetic sensor. Peter turned back to the computer.

"Well, look at that," he said. Maria looked over his shoulder. A white SUV pulled up to the gate.

"I think our friends have arrived," he said. "Let's see what they do next."

Two men exited the vehicle and examined the gate. Then they opened the back of the SUV. When they came back into view, they both carried a rifle. One of them also carried a slightly bulkier item.

"Shit," Peter said. "You see the thing that guy on the right is carrying?"

"Yeah."

"I'll bet that's some sort of anti-tank weapon. Might be an AT4."

"That's like an RPG?"

"Yeah. It'll blow a hole in the side of this cabin big enough to walk through."

One man appeared to lock the car, and the two began to walk down the road to the cabin. They were quickly out of sight.

Peter stood up, closed the computer and locked it in the filing cabinet next to the desk. "We've got about fifteen minutes. Let's get going."

They put on their jackets and hats. Peter grabbed his rifle and dropped the pistol and extra ammunition into his jacket pocket. "You first," he said, and handed the shotgun to Maria.

Maria climbed down the ladder and Peter followed. He pulled the closet door shut, and once he was below the floor level he pushed a button to slide the floor back into place. He switched off the power to the hydraulic motor and joined Maria at the bottom of the twenty-foot ladder.

"Follow me," he said, and he started down the narrow, seven-foot tall tunnel to the right. Small lights lit the way.

"Watch your step," he said. "The floor's wet and slippery."

After a hundred feet, they came to the end of the tunnel.

Peter looked up the ladder. "I'll go up and open the hatch. Hopefully a tree hasn't fallen on top of it."

"You didn't need to say that."

Peter opened the hatch without any difficulty and called down, "Come on up."

After she climbed out, Peter closed the hatch and said, "There's a large log near the edge of the trees." He looked at his watch. "We have about five minutes. Follow me."

They made their way through the thick mass of young fir trees and lay down by the large log, Peter at the right end of the log and Maria just to his left.

The wind blew through the trees, creating a constant background noise.

Peter chambered a round in the rifle.

"Pump a shell into the shotgun," he said. "When I tell you, yell in Russian and English for them to drop their guns and put their hands up."

They didn't have to wait long before two men entered the clearing. One of them went up to the door to the cabin. The other held back.

When the door didn't open, he stepped back and shouted in English, "Peter Binder! We know you're in there. Come out. We need to talk."

These guys are not very bright, Peter thought.

The man who had stopped at the edge of the clearing was carrying an AT4. The two rifles looked like newer versions of the Kalashnikov.

The man who had yelled in English looked around the clearing.

He's getting nervous, Peter thought.

The man spoke to his partner with the AT4.

"Russian," Maria whispered. "He's going to look around the cabin."

Peter watched the one man disappear onto the deck. He thought he heard breaking glass. The other man looked around nervously. Peter kept absolutely still.

The man came around the other end of the cabin, and the two conversed some more. Then the one with the AT4 came further into the clearing, put his rifle down, and prepared the AT4 for firing.

"Now," Peter said.

Maria shouted at them, first in Russian. She didn't need to do it in English. She ducked back down behind the log.

Both men turned to the sound. The one with the rifle fired in their direction. Peter heard two or three rounds hit the heavy log with a thud.

Peter braced. Unconsciously he lowered his aim to compensate for the shortrange shot. He aimed for the man's heart, just to the side of the center of his chest.

Peter fired one shot and absorbed the heavy recoil of the rifle.

He didn't watch the man fall. He chambered another round and turned the rifle on the second man, who still held the AT4. The man was desperately searching for the source of the gunfire.

Maria yelled at him, again in Russian, to put it down.

The man appeared to focus on the sound of Maria's voice. He made no move to put down the AT4. He aimed it.

Peter fired the same shot, this time slightly under the man's raised, left forearm.

As the man fell backward, he fired the AT4. The rocket-propelled round arced high over Peter and Maria. It exploded in the woods behind them.

The exchange had taken less than thirty seconds. Peter exhaled. He hadn't really heard the sound of the gunfire. Now the sound of the wind and the waves seemed quite loud.

He stood up, slowly. He laid the rifle against the log and stared in the direction of the cabin and the two bodies lying on the gravel.

"You idiots," he said. The comment was nearly lost on the wind.

Maria stood up cautiously.

"Damn it," Peter said. "They didn't have to die."

"You didn't have much choice."

"Yeah. They're still idiots." He picked up the rifle, chambered another round, and handed it to Maria. "Stay here. This kicks like hell if you have to use it." He pulled the pistol out of his pocket. "I'll check on them. Cover me if I need it."

Peter looked at Maria. There was a moment of doubt, but he pushed it away.

"Watch yourself," she said.

He stepped around the log and into the edge of the clearing. He looked up the road. Nothing. He moved over to the first man, the one who fired the rifle. He kneeled down and checked for a pulse. Nothing. He stepped over to the second man. No pulse.

Peter had no eagerness to examine them more closely. He stood up, shook his head, and walked back to Maria.

"Stay here," he said. "I'm going back into the cabin. I'll check the video cameras. If everything looks safe, I'll take the bars off the door. Keep out of sight until I get back."

Peter disappeared back to the entrance to the tunnel. When he got to the cabin, he checked the videos for both gates. The white SUV was still at the first gate, blocking the road. Nothing else.

He took the bars off the door, went back to the desk, picked up the satellite telephone and punched in the number for Bill Branch.

"Bill Branch."

"It's Peter Binder."

"What's up?"

"I'll call you back in a few minutes with the details, but I've got two more dead Russians."

Chapter 8

Peter returned through the tunnel to the entrance in the forest. He carefully closed the opening and concealed it with gravel and leaf litter. He looked around and listened. All he heard was the wind and the waves. He took out his pistol, walked through the small fir trees again, and stood beside Maria. He dropped the pistol back into his jacket pocket.

"So?" she asked.

Peter shook his head. "Looks like these two were here on their own."

"That's a relief."

"Yeah."

They stood in silence.

"Everything was self-defense," Maria said. "These guys were trying to kill us, for God's sake."

"I know, but I don't understand it. Somebody's sending stupid amateurs after us. They were way too careless following us, but they knew about the cabin."

"We both know where that information is coming from," Maria said.

"Perhaps. What really scares me is that these guys preferred to die than surrender."

"They thought they had us out-gunned. Maybe they thought we were bluffing."

Peter kept staring at the two bodies. *This conversation doesn't make any sense.*

Maria said, "Let's go inside."

"Yeah. I guess we're done out here," Peter said. He bent over and picked up the rifle from where it lay against the log. "You bring the shotgun."

As Maria passed the bodies, she said, "Strange how violent death can look so peaceful."

Peter said nothing.

Once they were back inside the cabin, Peter picked up the satellite phone. "I called Bill Branch when I was in here, but I have to call him back. I'll put it on the speaker." He entered the number for Bill.

"Branch here."

"Bill, it's Peter Binder and Maria Davidoff."

"You're both okay, right?"

"Yes," Peter said.

"Good. I've got the Ontario Provincial Police on their way, and an ambulance. Can they get past your security gates?"

Peter hesitated and then said, "Bill, how do you know about my security gates, and the location of my cabin? You didn't get any of that from me."

"Dick Durban told me. Can they get by your gates?"

"The first one is blocked by their SUV. I haven't searched the bodies for the car keys. There's no rush for an ambulance."

"We have to pick up the bodies," Bill said. "I'm flying up with Dick Durban and a crime scene investigator. We should be there in about an hour."

"Durban?"

"This may be my business in Toronto, but this is his territory. Like it or not, he's involved."

"Just so you know," Maria said, "I don't like it."

"Look, I have to maintain certain protocols, and Dick Durban will be with me. Right now I have to get to the airport. Don't move the bodies, but find the keys so the OPP officers can move the SUV. Unlock the gate and be there when they show up. See you in a bit."

Peter pushed back from the desk. "We should wash our faces before we greet the police. They'll be nervous enough without seeing us all painted up."

The wind calmed down while Peter waited for the OPP officers when they arrived. He gave them the keys to the SUV, and they moved it out of the way. When they got to the cabin, they used crime tape to surround the area around the two bodies, the deck, and the large log where Peter shot the two men.

Peter and Maria sat at the dining room table waiting for the helicopter. He kept the shutter closed over the broken window, but they still had a good view of the lake.

"You want a drink?" Peter asked.

"I think that's a good idea."

Peter got up from the table and went to the cupboard. "Ardbeg?"

"Anything strong will do."

Peter poured two ample glasses of the smoky scotch whiskey. When he sat down they touched their glasses together.

"I'm getting tired of this," Peter said.

"Me too."

"If Rostov's behind this, he seems to have an inexhaustible supply of amateur assassins, and they know way too much about us."

"I told you he'll never give up. He'll keep trying to kill us until one of us kills him."

"I don't want to spend all my life looking over my shoulder," Peter said, "but I'm beginning to think that's our normal."

"Our history catches up with us."

They both heard the helicopter, just before it came into view. It landed in the Zen garden. Peter stood up and removed the empty glasses. "Let's not tell them about the tunnels," he said. "They'll probably find them, but I'd like to keep a few secrets, if I can."

As soon as the helicopter landed, Dick Durban exited one side, and Bill Branch exited from the other with a third man. Peter always thought Dick looked like a caricature of General Montgomery, misplaced from the Second World War. Thin, with a small moustache, Peter thought he also shared Montgomery's abrasive character.

Peter stood at the door and watched the three men speak briefly with the two OPP officers. Then they came into the cabin, and Peter shut the door behind them.

They shook hands all around. Bill Branch introduced John Maitlan, the investigator, a short, thin man, with buzzed, very light blond hair. He had a smooth face with bright blue eyes. Peter tried to estimate his age. He couldn't.

Dick said, "Seems like you keep attracting nasty people."

"Not exactly our objective," Peter said. "These guys knew exactly where we were, and they came ready to blow this place to pieces."

"You may not understand," Dick said, "but you've been investigated by everybody, the Russians, the RCMP, the CIA, probably a bunch of countries in Europe. A lot of people know a lot about you, Peter, and you, too, Maria. Besides, Maria, you did work for me."

"I don't work for you anymore."

Durban laughed.

Peter thought Durban's laugh was, at the very least, inappropriate.

After an awkward silence, Bill Branch said, "Let's sit at the table? You can tell us what happened today."

"Fine," Peter said.

Bill Branch placed a small recorder on the table. Peter told the story, with Maria occasionally adding details. He started with Maria's discovery that someone had searched the apartment, and he finished with the details of the shootings at the cabin. Neither of them said a word about the tunnels.

Dick Durban looked at Peter. "Have you wondered who took out the sniper at the apartment?"

"I assumed it was one of your people."

"Nope. Not us."

"Then who was it?" Peter asked.

"Thought you might have an idea. Very professional. We think it has to be the CIA or the SVR out of Russia. You know anything about that?"

"No, I don't. Besides, they were damn slow. I shouldn't have survived."

"But you're still alive," Dick said, "both of you, and that's rather amazing. Isn't it?"

Prick, Peter thought, but he remained silent.

"What about you, Maria?" Dick asked. "You know anything about who might have shot the sniper?"

"And why should I know anything about that?"

"As I remember, you do have a few Russian connections."

"Are you planning to arrest me as a Russian spy? That would be a little awkward for you, wouldn't it?"

Dick smiled. "I think I might survive it."

"Then do it," Maria said. She put her hands together and stretched her arms out toward Dick Durban. "Just handcuff me right now."

Just a little bit of venom there, Peter thought. *On both sides.*

After an uncomfortable silence, John Maitlin spoke up. "I'll need both of you to help me with the details outside."

"Perhaps you could start with the bodies right now," Dick said.

John smiled slightly. "I'll do that." He picked up his bag and went out the door.

After John left, Bill said, "We're not arresting anyone here. It's obvious that one or both of you are still targets. Do you have any thoughts?"

"They're all Russian, one way or another," Peter said. "At least these last two spoke Russian. I assume it's all related to Zakhar Rostov. He seems to have a lot of people, though most of them aren't too bright."

"The Russians want to kill us," Maria said. "Rostov's in hiding, but he still has money and power. He'll give up when he's dead."

An hour later, after Peter and Maria had gone over the scene with Maitlin, Bill Branch and Dick Durban appeared to be satisfied that the investigation was in good hands. They prepared to fly back to Toronto. John Maitlin said he'd need the rest of the day and part of the next. He'd hitch a ride back to Toronto with the OPP officers. When Durban was in the helicopter, Bill Branch turned to Peter.

"Call me tomorrow morning. Use the VoIP phone I gave you, and call the number I gave you. We need to talk. Alone, if possible."

"Maria usually goes for an early paddle on the lake. Is eight okay?"

"That's fine." Bill Branch shook Peter's hand and got on the helicopter.

By five, John Maitlin had finished up for the day. The ambulance had collected the two bodies. John asked them to disturb nothing, but he cleared them to use the deck. "I'll be back early tomorrow," he said, and left with the OPP officers.

After they had finished dinner, Peter and Maria sat on the deck watching the stars. There was no moon, and the stars seemed very close in the thick darkness. The logs that fed the fire in the brazier crackled and spit. There was enough smoke to keep the mosquitos at bay.

"There's a lot going on between you and Dick Durban," Peter said.

"I don't trust him."

"Someone's selling us to the Russians. You think he's behind that?"

Maria stared at the stars.

"I can understand that he might be happy if some crazy Russian managed to kill me," Peter said, "but I really resent it."

She turned to him and the light from the fire lit her face with a soft, orange glow. She seemed ready to say something, but then she turned away and stared at the stars again.

"You have to tell me what's going on between you and Durban," he said. "Do you still work for him?"

Maria was silent for a long time. Then she turned to Peter. "You know almost nothing about me. Are you sure you want to ask questions? You may not like the answers."

"Like them or not, I have to know." Peter got up and added two logs to the fire. He didn't press. He had waited to ask the question, and he could wait a little longer for her answer.

Maria stared into the fire. "When I was a teenager, the SVR recruited me to be a foreign agent." She looked at Peter. "I was young and naïve. My English was very good, and I had a sort of vulnerable beauty." She paused. "They trained me to seduce American businessmen."

Peter shut his eyes. *They trained you well.* His lips curled into a hint of a smile.

"I got through training, and I worked for a little over a year, mostly in Moscow. Compromising stupid Americans. I hated it. I quit, and I talked my way into Canada."

"They let you quit?"

"Uh… They weren't exactly happy, but I was pretty small stuff. I didn't hang around. I didn't want to test how upset they were."

And Durban? Peter waited. *She'll get to it.*

"Do you remember the story I told you, about the night my ex-husband tried to kill me? How when he ran at me, I flipped him off the balcony?"

"You said your old boss bought you the best lawyers in Toronto, and that's why you worked for him for so long."

"That's part of the story. The other part, the worse part, is that the Canadian government threatened to deport me back to Russia because of the murder charge. I wouldn't have survived."

"But you said the lawyers got you off on self-defense."

"It was all Dick Durban. He fixed it. For a price. The price was I had to work for him."

Peter remained silent.

"It was mostly small stuff. Keep an eye on Serg, my boss. Attend meetings of Russian societies and clubs. It was easy. I had escaped Russia. I had walked away from the SVR. They understood."

Peter focused on the stars. "They didn't suspect you were still with the SVR?"

"I can be pretty convincing."

"I know."

Maria took her time. "Are you sure you really want to know? The whole story?"

"Yes."

She took a deep breath and exhaled. "It was my last assignment."

Peter waited.

"He asked me to kill you. I was supposed to make it look like an accident."

Peter wasn't completely surprised, but to hear her say it left him almost breathless. He leaned his head against the back of the chair. "But you didn't do it."

"I finally realized I was innocent. He didn't have a hold over me anymore. The Prime Minister supported me. I told Durban to go to hell. I walked away."

"How'd he take it?"

"Not very well. He still hates me for it."

"And he hates me for killing his lover," Peter said quietly.

"Yes."

"He's sold us to the wolves."

"Yes," she said.

"I don't know how we prove it."

She turned to him, "I carry a lot of baggage. I ran away from my training with the SVR in Russia. I ran away from Durban and the RCMP. I'm always running away from my past, but it always catches up with me. I'm sorry."

Peter took both her hands in his. "Don't be sorry. We can't always tell all our secrets, but once we can we're free."

"How can you trust me?"

"You could have killed me any number of times, but instead you've saved my life four times, I think. Besides, I love you. How can I not trust you?" He felt her body tense as he spoke.

"We'll be okay. We have to be," he said. He held her, and slowly he felt her relax.

"Yes," she said. "We have no choice." She kissed him.

Peter shut his eyes. *She told me. When do I tell her my secrets? Not for a long time.*

Chapter 9

Watson MacDonough sat alone, with his eyes closed, in a featureless cube of a room in the basement of the White House. It was, perhaps, the most secure room in all of Washington. He looked to be asleep.

He opened his eyes as the recording finished. He removed the headphones and moved the cursor on the computer.

What am I doing? What am I listening to? He blinked his eyes. *God, it's black. I'm listening to the beating heart of darkness.*

He was also feeling something he hadn't felt so strongly since he was a young field agent in eastern Europe, over thirty-five years ago.

I felt it in Moscow, too, but mostly for my people, not for me.

He was "spy of spies" in Moscow, when he ran the CIA office there for fifteen years before he was forced into retirement. Watson MacDonough did not welcome the return of fear.

Now I'm the president's boy, he thought, *and the CIA is afraid.*

Overweight and out of shape, his clothes a mass of wrinkles, he felt the full measure of his years, but his brain was as acrobatic as ever. He rubbed his forehead. He could sense the shifting pieces of the puzzle, but the picture remained fuzzy.

Watson stroked his bushy, gray moustache and decided to listen one more time. This time he didn't bother to plug in the earphones.

Harold James was first. He spoke of the "IG" project. Watson thought about the Director of the CIA. The Director was the privileged product of an upper-class New England family, and his schools were the best money could buy. Watson would never be part of Harold's world. Watson hated Harold's pedantry, his heritage, his blatant arrogance.

You pompous twit.

"We don't have anything solid," Harold said, "but we're getting close."

"It's a lot of gold," Gerhardt Weber said. "In the right hands it could raise a lot of hell. It could put our man right where we want him."

Watson thought the former Vice President's heavy German accent sounded completely out of place. *He even sounds like a Nazi.*

Brayden Davenport, assistant to the Secretary of State, was next. Watson couldn't stand him. He thought Brayden was even more pompous and elitist than Harold. "It's worth a try, Harold," Brayden said. "We provide a little help and let it happen, but it won't work. Too complicated. Too many people involved."

"You always underestimate the stupidity of the masses and our leaders," Gerhardt said. "It doesn't have to be perfect."

"Give it a try," Brayden said. "It can't be traced to us. Even if it fails, it won't do any harm. The gold will not evaporate."

Watson knew that there was a fourth man in the room, Derek Bunting, the head of Military Intelligence, but he never spoke in these meetings.

You understand better than the others, Watson thought

When the recording was finished, Watson sat back in his chair. "Bastards, all of you," he said softly.

"I think I have another job for you, Peter Binder," he said. "Something right up your alley."

Watson laughed.

Maria headed out with the kayak a little before eight in the morning. John Maitlin and the two OPP officers showed up shortly after to complete their work on the crime scene.

Peter waited until Maria was well down the lake. He opened the filing cabinet and pulled out the VoIP phone. With its encryption active, it would work with only one other phone in the world. He punched in the number printed on the phone and waited.

"Bill Branch."

"It's Peter Binder. You know anything about the two bodies?"

"Their papers say they're German. Been in the country for nearly three months. So far that's all we have."

"That's interesting. We were sure they were Russian."

"Why'd you think that?"

"Well… Maria walked by them when we were having breakfast and said they were Russian. Then she said they were speaking Russian at the cabin. I would have known if they were speaking German. The wind was pretty noisy, though. When she shouted at them in Russian to drop their weapons and put their hands up, they reacted instantly. That's when the first one started shooting at us."

"You don't know that they understood Maria, just that they reacted. Right?"

"True."

"You're not sure they were speaking Russian, are you?" Bill asked.

"True again, but I don't like where this is headed."

"Even if they were speaking Russian, we don't know for sure they're from Russia."

"You have a point," Peter said. For a moment they were both silent.

"You do understand she worked for Dick Durban?" Branch asked.

"Yes, but she doesn't work for him now."

"And she had agent training in Russia with the SVR before she left?"

"So I've been told."

"Who told you?"

Peter paused before he answered. "Maria, and now you."

"Okay. I want to be sure you understand."

Both men were silent for perhaps half a minute.

"Bill, you asked me to call. Is this what you wanted to talk about?"

"Yes… in part." Peter waited for him to continue. "We both have secrets we can't share with the other. I don't know your precise connections, but I suggest you call on some of them. You should leave Canada, with or without Maria."

"What are you saying? Is the government throwing me out?"

"No. The government is saying… Actually, I'm saying it. I'm worried about your safety in Canada. Someone is feeding information to your enemies. You need better security coverage."

"I don't like this at all," Peter said.

"Neither do I."

After a long silence, "I'll see what I can do."

"If you have connections with the CIA, you should use them," Bill said. "And by the way, though you may not like this question, do you really trust Maria?"

"Absolutely."

"I think I understand, but let me give you a piece of advice. The world you are living in is a world of gray. There is no white and no black. You understand?"

"Yes. I've known that for a long time."

"Be careful," Bill said.

"I'm always careful, even with the ones I love."

"Keep in touch when you can."

"I will."

Peter disconnected the phone and put it away. He leaned back in his chair and closed his eyes.

He felt like he and Maria were being abandoned.

I can't really blame him, but that doesn't mean I have to like it.

He signed in to his computer and drafted an email. He gave an update on the call with Bill Branch, sent it, and stayed signed in to see if there would be a quick response.

There was. Two words. *Call me.*

Peter took a deep breath and closed down the computer. He picked up the satellite telephone and dialed a Washington, DC number. After the phone rang three times, a robotic voice requested identification. Peter carefully enunciated five words. Then he heard several clicks.

"Watson MacDonough."

"Peter Binder. You asked me to call."

"Sounds like they're kicking you out."

"I'm not sure I blame them."

"You're a hot commodity right now."

"Well, Watson, you know more than most why that is."

"So far we've got nothing but small fish."

"A few too many of them, if you ask me."

"It may be time to give you a break," Watson said. "Give you and old Zakhar a vacation."

"Really?"

"Yes. I've got another job you might find interesting."

"I'm not sure I like that."

"This is a geological job," Watson said, "and it takes you into the South Pacific, which should be remote enough to give your cat and mouse game with Rostov a rest."

Peter didn't respond immediately. Finally, he said, "So what do you want me to do?"

"Come down to Washington," Watson said. "We'll talk about it."

"You do realize that, unless Maria bails, she and I work together?"

"Yes."

"She can't know that you and I have been working together all along."

Watson laughed. "You sure she doesn't know already?"

"No, I'm not sure."

"It's your life, but she carries some significant risk."

"I don't think so."

"Love is blind."

After Peter did not respond, Watson said, "I can send a plane to pick up you, or both of you, tomorrow."

"I'll talk with Maria and email you."

"This is part of your contract, Peter. No excuses."

Peter hung up and sat at the desk for a long time.

What am I doing?

He heard a small, insistent voice in his head telling him, over and over, *You cannot escape.*

Maria returned to the dock, and Peter watched from inside the cabin as she pulled the kayak out of the water.

"I'm a fool, but I love you, and I will trust you," he said.

He watched Maria walk toward the cabin and talk briefly with the police. She opened the door and came in.

"I'm getting better, and stronger," she said. "The cops are packing up to leave."

"That's what they told me a few minutes ago." Peter poured two cups of coffee. He held one out. "The coffee's fresh, hot, and we need to talk."

Maria took the cup. "Coffee's good. I'm not so sure about the 'talk' part."

They sat down at the table. "I had a couple of phone calls this morning. The first one was with Bill Branch. He's telling me to leave the country."

"What?"

"He says he can't guarantee my safety, our safety."

"What the hell are you going to do?"

"Well… That brings up the second phone call. You remember Watson MacDonough? You met him once. He was with the CIA."

"Yeah. I remember. At the hospital. An older guy. I thought he retired."

"I think he did, but now he's some sort of special advisor to President Pelton. He offered me a job."

"What kind of a job?"

"He wouldn't say. Some sort of a geological job, somewhere in the Pacific. I told him we worked as a team, unless you decide otherwise. He's sending a plane for us tomorrow. He wants to talk about the job in Washington."

Maria seemed to consider the proposition. "There are way too many bullets flying around for me to hang out alone here or in Toronto."

"Whatever he offers, it won't be a vacation."

And no safer than here or Toronto, Peter thought.

"That's okay," she said. "I'm ready for a change. When do we leave for Washington?"

"I suggested four, tomorrow afternoon. It takes a while to close up here and get to Toronto." Peter paused. "Nothing from Watson comes without serious personal risk."

"I know."

"I should tell Bill Branch we're coming into town. He won't be happy, but we won't be there very long."

"You think we can go to the apartment? I don't have clothes for Washington."

Peter thought about it. "Being at the apartment has nearly killed us a couple of times. I'm probably a little crazy to think it's okay to go there now. I'll see what Bill thinks. If he says we can go to the apartment, we'll go."

After dinner they went to bed early. Surrounded by the forest, and miles from the nearest light, the cabin held a darkness that was almost tactile in its density. Peter normally slept naked, but Maria usually wore a nightgown. This night, when she rolled over against his back, he felt her nakedness against him. The effect was instantaneous.

He felt Maria's breath and then her kiss against his neck. "I want you," she said.

Peter rolled over and put his arms around her.

Their sex was quiet, soft, peaceful. It held none of the usual urgency. Peter held on. He did his best to make it last a long time.

He slept soundly. He dreamed of being a geologist on a tropical island, with palm fronds rustling in the light trade winds. He and Maria swam naked in the warm and intensely blue waters. They lay together, under the sun, on a large, white towel on an endless white sand beach. They made love at the edge of the sea.

The next morning Peter and Maria followed the usual routine to get from the cabin to the apartment in Toronto. The only change this time was that, when they exited the road from the cabin, a police car met them. It followed them all the way into Toronto.

When Maria turned into the garage, Peter noted the police car across the street, and the police officer standing at the front entrance to the apartment building. He was a little surprised to see another policeman at the end of the hall when he and Maria exited the elevator on the fifteenth floor.

They left the drapes closed and spent ten minutes checking the apartment. Everything looked normal.

They're probably just getting better.

"Well, I'm not afraid of being in the apartment today," he said.

They had plenty of time, and the taxi they called arrived at Skycharter nearly twenty minutes early. Their plane was ready, and they were onboard the small executive jet and taxiing toward the runway by five minutes before four.

Once airborne, the copilot showed them an assortment of sandwiches, soft drinks, beer and wine. "Should be clear sailing, until we get close to Washington. We'll catch up with a storm just west of the city."

After they brought their drink selections back to their seats, Peter looked out the window. The rain-washed air provided a crystal-clear view as they flew over upstate New York.

"I think that's Cayuga Lake," he said. "When I was a kid, I used to help my grandfather on his dairy farm up here. I think my father thought it would keep me out of trouble."

"Did it?"

"Pretty much. Long hours, but the local farm girls thought this kid from New York City was exotic. Actually, my grandparents tolerated teenage hormones better than my parents."

"You've never told me much about your family."

Peter turned away from the window. "My grandfather had a fascinating life. He was the son of a Ukrainian rabbi. Emigrated before the First World War. He converted, bought the farm he worked on, and married his neighbor's daughter. The great American success story."

Maria smiled. "You're almost part Russian."

"I suppose you could say that."

Peter remembered how his grandfather, in his old age, had tried to contact his extended family in the Ukraine. There was no one. The Germans had annihilated his entire family.

Fifty minutes into the flight, the copilot came back to the cabin. "We'll catch up with the storm in a few minutes. We'll land at Joint Base Andrews in Maryland. The Secret Service will meet you there and take you to Blair House."

When the copilot returned to the cockpit, Peter said, "We're getting the VIP treatment. Blair House is usually reserved for visiting dignitaries. Maybe Watson's trying to impress us."

Or he's worried about our safety, even in Washington, which is not a good thought.

He turned to Maria. "On a totally different subject, let's be careful of what we say on this trip, no matter where we are."

"You think people are listening?"

"I guarantee it."

"Don't you trust anyone?" Maria asked.

"In the world we're entering, we shouldn't even trust ourselves."

"You're right." She looked away. "I don't think you can ever fully understand my intense hatred of that reality."

When they arrived at Blair House, they had a light dinner, two glasses of wine, and watched several of the news shows in their room.

"Christ! The news is so depressing. What in God's name are you doing in this country?" Maria asked.

"We're just trying to experience true democracy and mob rule by the ignorant."

"Oh, you are nasty," Maria said laughing.

"Yes, and cynical and depressed about all things political."

"Well," Maria said, "having accomplished very little of substance today, I'm really tired."

"It's been a long day of doing nothing," Peter said.

Blair House was silent now they had turned off the television. All they could hear was the occasional murmur of a passing car. While Maria readied herself for bed, Peter opened his computer and checked his emails. He clicked on one from Watson. *I'll see you tomorrow morning at 7:30 for breakfast at Blair House.*

Peter disconnected from the internet and retrieved the small memory card from his briefcase. He opened the encrypted file on Nunavik, but he closed it again. He created another encrypted file labeled *INDO*.

We're starting something new.

He wrote his thoughts on this new work proposal. *I don't know it's Endang*, Peter thought, but Bob Williams' comment kept running through his mind, *Something really bad is happening there, but I don't know what it is.*

Maria came out of the bathroom as Peter shut down his computer. "It's all yours," she said.

"Watson MacDonough says he'll join us for breakfast tomorrow morning. Half past seven."

A few minutes later, when Peter came out of the bathroom, Maria was already asleep. He undressed and turned out the lights. He looked out the window at the bit of the White House that was visible from their room.

"So, Watson, what are you putting on the table?" he asked in a whisper.

Peter turned away from the window and got into bed. *Whatever it is, we don't have much choice. Unfortunately, you, my dear Watson, know that.*

Chapter 10

When Peter and Maria came down for breakfast, Watson MacDonough was already sitting at a table. Peter glanced at his watch, almost exactly half past seven.

Watson was a presentation of wrinkles. His brown suit, white shirt, and even his face all looked like they could use a good ironing. In an odd contrast, his tie was sharp edged and smooth.

Watson gestured to the two chairs across from him. "Have a seat. They always have a good breakfast here. You're my excuse for enjoying it."

"Happy to help," Maria said as they sat down.

Nice edge to that, Peter thought.

A young woman appeared, introduced herself as Marcy, and offered coffee. "There is no menu. We can prepare most anything you want for breakfast. Just let me know what you'd like."

After Marcy left with their orders, Watson sat back with his coffee and said, "You two have been leading a rather interesting life recently."

"A little too interesting," Maria said.

"We like normal," Peter said.

"You may as well forget it. You're not ordinary people."

"There's only one reason we can't live ordinary lives," Maria said, "and that's Rostov. How can he send so many people to kill us and nobody can find him?"

"It's not as easy as you might think."

Peter watched.

"You're using us as bait," she said. "You don't give a damn if the bait lives or dies."

Watson took a deep breath. "This is part of the world you both live in. I'm sorry, but that's the truth. There are limits to what we can do."

Maria shook her head. "I know these people. Find Rostov and kill him, or he will kill us."

"I have never been guilty of not caring about the lives of anyone who works for me," Watson stated.

"But we don't work for you," Maria said. "At least not yet."

"I have a great interest in what is happening to you, for many reasons, some of which I cannot discuss. I do care about your survival. That's why I brought you down to Washington. It's why you have Secret Service protection while you're here. It's why you're staying in Blair House. It's why I'm offering you a job on a remote island, where Rostov can't possibly find you."

Maria stared at Watson. "There is no island that remote."

"You may be right," Watson said with a nod, "but remoteness can protect you for a while. Besides, Rostov is getting careless. He's making mistakes. This will give us time, while you're out of sight, to follow up on those mistakes."

Marcy appeared with breakfast. She refilled coffee cups, left the pot on the table, and asked, "Will there be anything else?"

"I think we'll be fine, Marcy," Watson said. "Perhaps you could see that we're not disturbed?"

"I'll see to it," she said and left the room.

The three of them were silent as they began to eat, but Peter put down his fork, "I don't mind taking a break from Rostov and his buddies, even for a short time. However, no job for you ever comes without major risks."

"You're such a cynic," Watson said without looking up.

"Realist."

"Well, this is a simple job," Watson said, looking up at Peter. "You look at a new gold discovery. The company says there's a lot of gold there. You tell us if all that gold is really there. That's your specialty, isn't it? Exploration, ore reserves, mine development?"

Peter ate a part of his omelet. "You want me to look at Endang?"

Watson laughed. "I'm really that transparent?"

"Actually, there aren't many other possibilities. Why's the US government so interested in Endang?"

Watson took his time answering. "Think about it. We're talking a hundred million ounces of low cost gold, ten million ounces of new gold produced each year for at least ten years. That can have a hell of a negative impact on the price of gold, something of interest to the Treasury."

"The Treasury may not have much to worry about. A good friend of mine says there's no gold there at all."

Watson smiled. "And I think I know your friend's name. But answer this question. If it's a fraud, what kind of a fraud?"

"Stock fraud? Mining the investors?" Peter shrugged. "Who knows. It's happened before, and it'll happen again."

Watson sat back in his chair and closed his eyes. "You're right, of course, but let's just suppose it's something more. Suppose there's a hundred million ounces of bloody, dirty gold hiding out there somewhere. Suppose Endang, a mine with no gold, is just a way to launder that gold, remine it, make it clean and legitimate."

Peter shook his head. "Not possible. Historical gold production is pretty well accounted for. I don't think it's possible to hide a hundred million ounces without the secret leaking out. And to grind it up, send it through a mill, and pour new gold bars? Too complicated. Too many people. The secret would never hold."

Watson opened his eyes. "Right again, except for one thing. We do think there's a hundred million ounces of dirty, hidden gold. We're beginning to think we know where it is."

"I'm not sure I believe this." Peter returned to his breakfast and finished off the sausage.

"That's a lot of gold," Maria said. "Where'd it come from?"

"At peak gold price, a few years ago, it was close to two hundred billion dollars. Right now it's worth a bit less than one hundred thirty billion. I'm not going to talk about the source or location."

Watson sat forward in his chair. "But if it does exist, even by the standards of the richest men in the world, it's a lot of money. In the wrong hands it could destabilize nations, buy elections, buy nuclear weapons, fund civil wars, and who knows what else."

"For that amount of money," Maria said softly, "I know some men who would happily kill thousands, maybe millions of people."

And I'm sure I don't want to know any of them, Peter thought.

"The job I want you to do," Watson said, "both of you, is to go to Endang and figure out what the hell is going on. Period. It's a simple geological exercise. Nothing more."

"You should hire my friend, Bob Williams. He already knows more than I do about Endang. He's cheaper, too."

"He doesn't have your reputation, Peter, or some of your other capabilities."

"What do you mean 'other capabilities'?" Maria asked.

"Oh dear," Watson said. "You're being rather tough on an old man today."

"All I want is simple answers. No bullshit."

"Ah, no bullshit. Not easy, Maria. This is a geological exercise. I don't expect any problems. However, if Endang is a gigantic fraud, designed to secretly launder a hundred million ounces of filthy gold?" He let the question hang between them.

"It'll attract the usual bad actors," Peter said.

Peter turned to look at Maria. Her attention was focused on Watson.

"You want us to go to Endang," she said, "because we know how to kill people."

"No. I want you to go to Endang, because Peter can do the geological work, and you both know how to stay alive. I don't want to send someone who's a good geologist but is also helpless and naïve."

"Right. Because we're good killers."

Peter smiled. He almost laughed out loud. *Maria's in fighting trim.* He gestured with his hands. "Admit it. She's right. You want us on the job because you know we can handle crazy shit and survive."

"Yes, but it's not because I think you're such good killers. This should be a piece of cake. It's remote enough that you should be able to get in, do your work, and get out, before anyone has the opportunity to really react."

"What about the fact that IndoGold has never allowed anyone to do a proper evaluation, or even to take any samples?" Peter asked.

"An interesting question. First of all, you won't officially be working for me, the CIA, or the US government. You'll work for a major investor in IndoGold, a man named Saul Bernstein. You'll be his consulting geologist. He insists on full access to all records and freedom to collect samples from outcrops and drill core. With his stock position in the company, they really can't refuse."

"There are still a few problems," Peter said. "It's public knowledge that they ground up most of the drill samples for their gold analyses. To prove the gold is there, or not, will not be easy."

"That's one of the reasons we're hiring you. It won't be easy, but we think you'll find a way."

Peter picked up the coffee pot and poured fresh coffee for himself and Maria. He offered it to Watson, but he declined. "What do you have planned for us for the rest of today?"

"If you agree to do the job, we need to discuss what equipment and support you need, and we need to arrange for Saul Bernstein to meet you tonight. I'll also have to move you to a hotel and arrange for proper security."

"Okay. Before we agree to anything, Maria and I need to talk. I'm not going to talk in Blaire House. Please arrange with the Secret Service for us to take a little walk in about half an hour, and tell them to keep their bloody distance."

"I think you're being a little paranoid," Watson said.

"Yes. And you think I shouldn't be?"

With a hint of a smile, Watson looked at his watch. "I'll plan to come back here at eleven. That enough time for you?"

"I don't think either of us is prepared to make a commitment until we talk with Mr. Bernstein," Maria said.

Watson stood up. "That's good enough for me. I'll make arrangements with the Secret Service. They should be ready for your walkabout in a few minutes. See you in a few hours."

Peter and Maria sat on a low bench in front of the Washington Monument. It was already hot and humid. Their two Secret Service agents stood fifty feet away, one on each side. The area surged with large groups of visitors and the ebb and flow of their shouts and conversations.

"This is as good as anywhere," Peter said. "Just speak softly and cover your mouth with you hand."

"You really believe people are listening to us?"

Peter shrugged. "I don't know. It would be difficult with all the noise here, but they could watch our lips, or use a parabolic listening device."

"Okay. What do you think about Watson's offer?" Maria asked.

Peter didn't answer immediately. "I want to get away from Rostov's people for a while, and I think this should do the trick. However, I do think it's a lot more dangerous than Watson is letting on. We'd be out there on our own. He and the US government want to keep their distance."

"I agree. If things get nasty, they'll deny we exist."

"And it will get nasty. If I'm allowed to collect the samples I need, and if Endang has no gold, they will worry that I'll discover the fraud. There's too much money involved. Whatever the reason for the fraud, they'll want us to disappear. Permanently."

"And you still want to take the job?" Maria asked.

"I think it's safer than sitting around, waiting for Rostov's army to arrive."

"Perhaps."

Chapter 11

Watson MacDonough looked at his watch. *Plenty of time before I meet with them.* He pushed the memory card into the side of his laptop, moved the mouse and clicked on the icon to open the recording. The first voice was Harold James, as usual.

"I have to report a rather serious development. Watson MacDonough is nosing around. Apparently he's looking at Endang for the Treasury."

"That's inconvenient," Braden Davenport said.

"Get rid of him, Harold," Gerhardt Weber said.

"Not so easy. He works for the President now, not me."

"For Christ's sake, you control the whole CIA," Weber said. "Conjure up an accident and eliminate him."

"I have to wait for the right opportunity," James said. "Most of the time he's surrounded by Secret Service."

"Just find a way."

"We're working on it, Gerhardt," Harold James continued, "but it won't be right away, and it won't be easy. He may look like a sleepy moron, but that's all an act. He's a bright and experienced agent. One of the best. Anyway, he's the least of our concerns."

"What's supposed to be our greatest concern?" Davenport asked.

"He plans to hire an expert ore deposit geologist, Peter Binder, to look at Endang. You should remember his name. If he gets full access, and if he survives, and if he produces a report…"

Watson heard a grunt. He assumed it was from Weber, who then said, "That's at least one big 'if'. Endang's pretty remote. Easy. No Binder. No report."

"There's plenty of opportunity, and incentive enough for IndoGold," James said.

"Still way too many people involved," Davenport said, "and some of them aren't too bright."

"Ja. Ja. You're always complaining," Weber said.

"And I'm usually right," Davenport responded.

"You're a wimp, too, just like everybody else at State," Weber said. "However unlikely, this might work, and there's no risk to us. See if you can get rid of that damn geologist, Harold. Then deal with MacDonough."

Watson heard Harold James laugh and say, "You don't ask for much, do you?"

"Considering your position, no."

"In case you haven't noticed, Binder isn't easy to kill," James said.

Watson switched off the recording. He'd heard enough. "Well, Peter, it's up to you, isn't it?" He shook his head and frowned.

Dead or alive, I think I'll have what I need, but I'd like some insurance.

Watson packed up his computer and prepared to walk to Blair House to meet Peter and Maria.

Sorry Peter, and sorry Maria. You're both on your own, and so am I.

At eleven, Peter and Maria found Watson at the same table where they had breakfast earlier.

Watson rose as they entered. "Did you have a good walk?"

"Yes," Maria said as she sat down. "Our escorts were quite discreet."

"And did you make a decision?"

Peter nodded. "The first decision is easy. We'll meet with Saul Bernstein tonight. We'll make a decision regarding Endang after that meeting."

Watson paused before responding. "But your inclination is to take the assignment?"

"Peter wants to do the job, and I'll go with him if he agrees to do it," Maria said.

"And I have a small list of requirements and special equipment for you," Peter said. He pulled a folded sheet of paper out of his pocket and gave it to Watson.

Watson read the list and looked up. "Most of this you should discuss with Saul Bernstein tonight. He has very good contacts with the Mossad. He should be able to handle these matters." He paused. "I don't think I can be in Jakarta."

"That's not negotiable. We'll be on site for no more than five or six days, and in country maybe two more days. While we're in Indonesia, I want someone in Jakarta whom I know and trust, and who has the clout to bring in the cavalry if we need it."

"You should make arrangements for backup with Bernstein."

"Look, Watson, just because Bernstein's our cover, that doesn't mean you can wash your hands and walk away. Ultimately, we work for you. While we're at the Endang camp, while we're in Indonesia, you have to be in Jakarta, ready to support us if we need it."

"That will be very difficult."

"Tough," Peter said. "You're either in Jakarta and accept some responsibility for our well-being, or we go home and forget the whole thing."

Watson shook his head. "You'd be crazy to go home right now."

"We'd be crazier to let ourselves be hung out to dry on the island of Sulawesi."

Silence hung between them for several minutes. Watson closed his eyes and said, "Okay. Meet with Bernstein tonight. If you still feel you need me in Jakarta, I'll agree to be there."

"Thank you." Peter watched Watson open his eyes and look directly at him. *I wonder what you know that you aren't telling me.*

"You want lunch?" Watson asked.

"Sounds like a good idea," Maria said.

"Good. After we're finished, I want you to meet Alden Sage at the White House. He's a special advisor to the President, and he's your last resort contact if you take this on. He should meet both of you."

"If we do this job, I need some additional field equipment, a couple of metal boxes I can lock, and we both need some different clothes. It's all in Maria's apartment or her storage locker. Either we go get it, or someone gets it for us."

"Give me a detailed list this afternoon," Watson said. "If you agree to do the job, I'll have someone get it for you. I don't want you in Toronto, and particularly not in that apartment."

Watson got up from the table and pressed a call button for the staff. "After lunch, take a few minutes to pack. I'll move you to the Four Seasons in Georgetown. You'll have a suite on the top floor." He paused. "In case you're wondering, we have excellent security in place already."

After lunch, Peter, Maria and Watson went with the Secret Service to the West Wing of the White House. Watson led the way to Sage's office and stopped at the open door. "Alden, I have Peter Binder and Maria Davidoff with me. You said you'd like to meet them."

The three of them stepped into the room, and a small, thin man rose from his desk. "Welcome to the White House. I'm Alden Sage, special advisor to the president." He shook hands first with Maria, then Peter.

A surprisingly strong handshake from such a small man, Peter thought.

"Let's go across the hall to the Roosevelt Room. We can talk there. We won't be long."

Once they were seated at a table, Alden Sage said, "I'm very glad to meet you both. Watson has informed me of some of your more recent activities." He smiled.

"I don't wish to be rude," Peter said, "but Watson indicated that you are our 'contact of last resort.' I'm curious. What exactly does that mean?"

"It's very simple, Mr. Binder. Assuming you and Ms. Davidoff agree to visit and evaluate the gold potential of Endang, if you get into serious trouble, and neither Watson nor Saul Bernstein can help you, you call me."

"Why are you involved at all?"

"Well, now you're asking why President Pelton has an interest in this matter, and I can't answer that." He focused on Peter. "You have one question to answer for us. Is Endang real?"

Alden Sage reached into his pocket and handed a business card to Peter. He pointed to a hand-written number on the back. "That number is my cell phone. Actually, I do have one more question for you and Ms. Davidoff. Have you decided?"

"We will do this together, and I think I'll let Maria answer your question."

"I suspect we'll agree to do the job," she said, "but our final decision will wait until after we meet with Mr. Bernstein."

Sage turned to Watson. "You'll let me know?"

"Of course."

"Good. Then I'll leave you in Watson's very capable hands."

As they walked down the hallway, Maria asked, "Is there a ladies' room around here somewhere?"

"Of course," Sage said. "Just down the hall on the right."

They watched in silence as Maria disappeared into the ladies' room.

"I put an envelope in your briefcase," Watson said to Peter. "For you only."

Peter remained silent.

Alden Sage continued to look down the hallway. "Seems to me the drama's a little thick."

"Don't worry," Peter said. "I'll do it, alone if I have to. Just let the drama play out."

"Small price, I guess," Sage responded.

As the Secret Service delivered Peter and Maria to the Four Seasons Hotel in Georgetown, the agent handed them each a card. "Please call that number if you want to leave the hotel. You can consider the interior of the hotel secure."

When they checked in at the desk the clerk gave Peter a note. *Mr. Saul Bernstein requests that you join him for dinner, in the main dining room, at 7:30 this evening.* He showed the note to Maria. "Our dinner is arranged."

Peter looked around the lobby. *Lots of men in suits standing around and wearing one ear piece*, he thought. He couldn't tell who was Secret Service and who was hotel security. When they got off the elevator to go to their room, there was one more at the other end of the hall.

"Since they said the hotel is secure, I think I'll go to the gym," Maria said as they entered their room. "I need some exercise."

Peter sat at the small desk and pulled out his computer. "I'll join you in half an hour or so. I want to check on the world."

When Maria left the room, Peter pulled Watson's envelope out of his briefcase. It contained two passports under the names of David and Nancy Madeaux. They looked to be well used, and both had a long series of stamps and visas. His entries, he noticed, were quite accurate. There were also driver's licenses for both of them, and two credit cards for each. *Do we really need these?* He inserted all of them under the lining in the bottom of his briefcase.

The next items were two round-trip, business-class tickets for Washington to Jakarta on United Airlines. One was for him, under his real name, the other for Maria. They had an additional flight, two days after arrival in Jakarta, to Manado on Sulawesi. *Thank God for that extra day in Jakarta,* Peter thought.

Departure for Indonesia was in three days. *We'll see.* Departure from Jakarta was eight days after arrival. *Four full days on site. Parts of two others. Should be enough.*

Peter dropped the two tickets into his briefcase. Twenty-four hours to Jakarta, with a stop in Tokyo. He hated crossing the Pacific. He locked his computer in his briefcase, changed into his exercise clothes, and joined Maria in the gym.

Just before half past seven, Peter and Maria entered the dining room. At the mention of Saul Bernstein's name, they were led to a small, private dining room.

Saul rose from his seat and extended his hand to greet them. "Mr. Binder and Ms. Davidoff. A pleasure to meet you."

They shook hands and Peter said, "Please use our first names."

"Yes, and call me Saul." He gestured at two chairs. "Please sit down." An open bottle of red wine sat in the middle of the table.

Saul was a short man, well dressed, dark complexion. He projected an air of confidence. He was not young. Peter guessed his age at eighty years old, perhaps older, but he was certainly not frail. On the contrary, Peter felt a sense of strength and intensity. He thought Saul's dark eyes might be able to see the inner workings of his mind. Peter watched him and said nothing.

"I understand you want to evaluate me before you accept this assignment," Saul said to them.

"Well," Maria said, "neither one of us wants to work for someone we've never met."

"I do have a few questions," Peter said, "and a list of equipment and requirements." He handed a folded piece of paper to Saul, a copy of the one he had given Watson.

Saul looked at the piece of paper and back at Peter. "This should not be a problem. Any contacts you may need are already in place on Sulawesi."

"I'm also concerned about the ability to take samples."

"Let me explain a few things. I come into the picture as a major investor in IndoGold. The chairman, Robert Talon, has promised full cooperation for my geologist when he visits the property. That's you, if you accept the job."

"You do know that they destroyed most of the core with their crazy assay process," Peter said. "That makes proper sampling very difficult."

"Yes, but you can take small samples of the representative core they have kept from the ore zones. Not ideal, but better than nothing." Saul picked up the wine. "Would you like me to pour the wine?"

"Yes," Maria said, "and perhaps we should look at the menus and order."

After they made their decisions and placed their orders, Peter picked up the wine glass and sampled a very good and well-aged wine. He sat back. "I'm sure you are something more than an investor. What more can you tell us about yourself? Why are you so interested in Endang in the first place?"

Saul drank some of his wine. "Did you Google me?"

"Yes," Peter said. "I didn't find much."

Saul smiled. "Good. That's the way I like it. You're correct. I am more than an investor. I've worked on and off for the Mossad for many years. I also have a good relationship with Watson MacDonough."

Saul poured more wine. "I also lead a group that is trying to trace the gold the Nazis looted from the treasuries of eastern Europe, and the gold they secured by selling everything they stole from the Jews."

"I thought the Swiss banks had sorted that out by now," Maria said.

"What they have paid is a pittance. We know the approximate value of what was looted from the Jews. We know what was stolen from the national treasuries. Even accepting some normal loss, some ten to fifteen percent is simply missing. We cannot account for it."

"You have any idea where it is?" Peter asked.

"Perhaps." Saul shrugged. "But that is only an obsession of mine. More to the point, I am heavily invested in Endang, and I have heard some unpleasant rumors that I would like to see resolved."

Peter drank. He asked softly, "On a totally different subject, where were you born?"

"I was born in Germany, in 1937."

"And your family? How did they fare in the war?"

Saul sighed. "My father sent me as a baby to live with my uncle Mordicai in Brooklyn. I was his insurance policy, I suppose, for his family, maybe for his genes." Saul shrugged. "Everyone in my German family disappeared, like six million others."

"I'm sorry," Maria said.

"Yes. I'm sorry too." Saul paused. "I'd like to turn our attention back to Endang, if you don't mind."

The waiter arrived with the first course, a paté for Peter and Cesar salad for Saul and Maria. They ate in silence for ten minutes.

"It's really quite simple," Saul said as he put his fork down. "I invested early and quite heavily. I own about fifteen percent of the company. I want to know the truth."

"The truth can sometimes be both excruciatingly elusive and very unpleasant to hear."

"True enough, Peter." Saul pulled an envelope out of his briefcase and handed it to Peter. "I've prepared a contract, and I've signed it. $4,000 per day for the two of you, all expenses, business class travel, hotels arranged. You're to prepare a confidential report on the resource at Endang, though it might be leaked to the Toronto Stock Exchange."

"In that case, my name will not appear anywhere on the report," Peter said.

"They'll probably know anyway."

"I will deny it."

The waiter arrived with his helper to remove the first course. They delivered the main course of a small beef tenderloin for Saul, salmon for Peter, and coq au vin for Maria, and promptly disappeared.

"If you agree to the contract, I'll provide you with emergency contacts. All the equipment you've asked for will show up locked inside a leather bag in your baggage, Peter, when you arrive at Endang. The combination lock will be set for the last four digits of your Social Security number."

Peter looked at Maria. "We'll make a decision on the contract tonight. How do you want us to give you our decision?"

"Let's meet here for breakfast tomorrow at half past seven. On another note, perhaps you could give me your passports tonight."

"Why?" Maria asked.

"I want the Mossad to prepare backup passports for you, and I need to make sure they're accurate."

"Watson should be able to handle that," Peter said.

"Probably has already, but I'd like to give you an alternative."

Peter pulled out his passport. He hesitated, but he handed it to Saul.

"Well, I have to get mine out of the safe in the room," Maria said, "and I'd like to finish my meal first."

Later, after dessert and coffee, Maria left to get her passport.

Saul watched her go. "You sure you should trust her?"

"Yes."

"She has a complicated history."

"I know."

"She's killed before."

"She could have killed me many times, Saul. She didn't."

"Maybe none of those times were the right time."

Peter was silent.

"You will do the job. Right?"

"Don't worry. We'll get the job done." Peter paused. "You know that I have demanded that Watson be in Jakarta while we're in Indonesia?"

"Yes. He told me. I'm not sure he can help much. The CIA has only a few assets in Indonesia."

"I know, but I want him there. Where will you be?"

"I'll be in Tokyo, Peter. I can do little myself on site. I'll give you some excellent native contacts, on the ground in Manado and in Jakarta. They can get you out, under a different name if necessary. That's why I want your passports."

Saul glanced at the door to the private room. "You understand that in Indonesia, if you're sleeping together, you must present yourselves as husband and wife? Even if you are not?"

"I'm quite familiar with the Islamic sensitivities on that subject," Peter replied.

They were silent until Maria returned to the table and handed her passport to Saul. They parted a few minutes later, and Peter and Maria went to their room.

"Are you going to sign the contract?" Maria asked.

"We have to read it. You in particular. You know more about contracts than I do."

"But you want to do it?"

"Yeah. I feel a little obligated."

"Obligated?"

"For a couple of reasons."

Maria looked at Peter for a moment. "I have to ask you something. You don't have to answer."

"Okay."

"Do they all tell you not to trust me?"

Peter looked at her with a hint of a crooked smile. "Yes."

"So why do you trust me?"

"Because I love you."

Chapter 12

Watson knocked on the door frame at the entrance to Alden Sage's office. "You got a minute?"

Alden looked up. "Always. They met with Saul?"

Watson stepped into the office and closed the door. "Yeah. They'll go over the contract tonight. Peter will sign. He doesn't have much choice."

"And Maria? She'll sign too?" Alden asked.

"Yes. They're in love, for Christ's sake."

"That happens to be the nuttiest thing I can imagine."

"I don't know. I think it's just love."

"Maybe. What do you need?"

"Listen," Watson said, "I want the Secret Service to do something for me."

"Yeah?"

"Peter and Maria have a day before they head for Indonesia. I want to play tourist with them. I want to see how my buddies react, and how Peter and Maria react. I need the Secret Service to keep close cover, but they have to make it invisible."

"That's a big ask. A bigger risk," Alden said.

"I know the risks. There's one additional thing. We need to keep the lid on this a little longer. If somebody makes a move, a serious move, I want them dead. It's too early for press interviews and the courts."

"Jesus! I knew I shouldn't know you."

Watson shrugged. "You volunteered."

"I'll arrange it. Just give me the details. I have to tell the President. He has to sign off on this stuff."

Watson pulled a sheet of paper out of his pocket. "Here are the details, and my plans for the day." Watson smiled. "The Secret Service should be ready tomorrow morning. No later than ten."

Peter and Maria sat at the small table in their suite, reading two copies of the two-and-a-half-page contract from Saul Bernstein. Maria took her time, carefully dissecting the legal language. Peter finished first. He stared out the window.

When she looked up, he said, "I hate reading these things. It looks okay to me, as far as it goes. There's no extraction language if things get nasty."

"There never is."

"True. It's always a question of faith, but we do have a choice of saviors."

Maria shook her head. "They won't answer any of our prayers. We'll be on our own."

"I'll sign it," Peter said. He looked at her. "You don't have to go with me."

"I really wish you'd stop saying that. It's annoying."

Peter said nothing.

Maria reached across the table and rested her hand on Peter's hand. "Look, you say you trust me because you love me. I trust you. I want to be with you. Besides, right now we're both safer together."

"Sometimes, Maria, I'm just sorry that you have to live my life."

"You think my life has been much different?"

"I suppose not."

Maria sat back in her chair. "Do you know the Bible? The book of Ruth?"

"I've read it."

"There's a passage. 'Ask me not to leave you, or not to follow you; for wherever you go I will go also.'"

Peter smiled. "Where the hell did my favorite Russian learn that?"

"I have a broad education," she said. "Let's sign this damn thing and go have a drink."

The bar was busy with a noisy crowd of business men and women, lobbyists, and all varieties of governmental acolytes. The hotel was a little too up market for most tourists. Peter and Maria sat at a corner table, each nursing a whiskey. *I want my back against the wall*, he thought. *Too many damn people.*

He watched her. Her eyes moved systematically across each person in the bar. *She's as on edge as I am.*

"Sometimes I do wonder about us," Maria said. "Look at these people. Most of them lead quiet and peaceful lives."

"I think we chose our lives."

"We didn't know what we were choosing."

"I think I did."

"I didn't," she said.

"Are you sure all these people are living quiet lives? No spies? No threats? No killers?"

"Oh, there are spies, and threats, and maybe killers," she said, "but not many. We're safe, for the moment."

"I hope you're right."

Peter listened to the conversations around him. Occasionally a few words stood out from the background, but nothing made any sense.

"When are you going to tell me all your secrets?" Maria asked.

The question startled him. "You want an honest answer?" he asked.

"Yes."

"Well… The honest answer is never. There are some things… I don't want to tell you some things. Some hurt too much. Some are too dangerous. Some are top secret. Isn't it the same with you?"

"That's not what I want."

"Do either of us have a choice?" he asked.

"Not really."

"Watson asked me if I trusted you. I said I did. Do you know what he said next?"

"No."

"He said, 'Love is blind.'" Peter paused. "And that's okay."

Maria shook her head. "I'm not sure that works for me."

They sat in silence for several minutes until Peter said, "Would you like another drink, or shall we call it a night and go up to our room?"

"Let's pay up and go."

When they closed the door to their suite behind them, they embraced.

Maria pulled back a bit and started to unbutton his shirt. "I'm feeling very Russian tonight," she said. "I'm a Russian SVR agent, and I intend to possess you."

"You sure you can?" Peter asked.

"Yes," Maria said as she finished with his shirt, "I'm well trained. I know you will be a good boy for your Russian spy."

"For you," he said, smiling, "I will always be a good boy."

Several hours later, after midnight, they kissed one last time and rolled apart. He tried to think of something to say to her. *My Russian spy. My lover. Sometimes it's better to keep your mouth shut.* He reached out for her. She wrapped her fingers around his hand. A few minutes later they were both asleep.

In the morning, Peter quietly got out of bed, put on his exercise shorts, and sat at his computer. He prepared a list of items for Watson to retrieve from the apartment in Toronto.

"What time is it?" Maria asked from the bed.

"About six thirty. Is there anything special you need from the apartment? I'm sending a list to Watson."

"Just clothes, but let me do it," she said as she got out of bed. "I don't trust your translation."

An hour later, showered and dressed, they made their way down to the lobby.

Saul was already sitting at a table when they got to the restaurant. "Good morning to you both. I trust you had a good night."

"Yes, we did," Peter said as he and Maria sat down. He handed an envelope to Saul. "That's your copy."

"Good." Saul took out the papers and glanced at the signature page. "I understand you have tickets from Watson?"

"Yes," Peter said. "We leave the day after tomorrow."

Saul pulled a business card out of his pocket and handed it to Peter. "Do not call me when you're in Indonesia unless it's absolutely necessary. The same with email. If you need assistance, call the number on the back. They should be able to provide any help you need, even if Watson cannot."

"How will we recognize them?" Maria asked.

Saul smiled. "There is a simple recognition code. The first person says, 'I seek the golden star of David.' The second replies, 'It will be found on an island nation.'"

"That's amusing," Peter said.

"Should be good enough."

"Sure. Assuming the code isn't stolen, or given away."

"It is my experience that the Mossad and their agents do not leak secret information."

"Nobody's perfect." Peter stood up. "I'm hungry. Let's see if we can get a waiter to take our orders."

A few hours later, Peter and Maria sat in the hotel lobby. "I don't know what he's up to," Peter said.

"Maybe he just wants to show us around Washington," she said.

"Nothing's that simple. There's some reason for our outing with him."

"Well, if there's a reason, we won't know what it is unless he decides to tell us."

"I just feel a little helpless, and I don't like that." Peter stood up as a man in a suit and dark glasses entered the lobby, looked around, and headed in their direction. "I think our escort has arrived."

"Mr. Binder? Ms. Davidoff?"

"That's us," Maria said.

"Mr. MacDonough is waiting for you outside. Please follow me."

Outside the man opened the rear door to the White House SUV. Watson sat in the front. "So, what's the plan for today?" Peter asked.

"Well, you've got a little time before you leave. I thought you might like to see some of Washington, like the African American History and Culture Museum. I know you have an interest in the Holocaust, Peter, so I thought we'd a visit the Holocaust Memorial Museum. Maybe the main Smithsonian or the National Air and Space Museum. I can get you past all the lines."

"Aren't you a little busy to be playing tour guide?"

Watson smiled. "You two are a big part of my being busy. I have a special interest in your welfare."

"I thought we were to stay out of sight," Maria said.

"Sometimes the safest place is the public square," Watson said, "surrounded by thousands of other people."

Peter looked around when they entered the National Air and Space Museum. He could see the museum security, but no sign of the Secret Service. *Is he trolling? If he is, for what?*

"I come here a lot," Watson said. "I always find a surprise. It's like my grandmother's attic, on a national scale."

Watson gave an animated, knowledgeable tour. Peter watched the crowd. Gradually, he began to notice that part of the crowd always followed them.

I see you.

After their lunch stop, he saw some of the same men, with different shirts, first at the Holocaust museum and later at the African American museum. Their final stop was a visit to the Jefferson Memorial. It was nearly deserted.

Outside the memorial, Peter and Maria followed Watson as he walked around the grounds. There was no one visible around them, no security, no tourists. Peter had a growing sense of discomfort, and he felt the adrenaline building in his system.

This is crazy. We may as well have targets painted on us.

He stopped. "Watson!"

Watson looked back.

"We're going to the car." Peter didn't wait for an answer. He simply grabbed Maria's hand and turned around.

"What are you doing?" she asked.

"We're going back to the car."

"Okay, but don't pull my arm off."

They nearly ran back to the SUV. They were sitting in the back seat when Watson, breathing hard, caught up with them.

"What the hell is the matter with you?" Watson asked.

Peter glared at Watson. "Play your game by yourself."

"What do you mean?"

"You've had us on display most of the day," Peter said. "You've had people shadowing us. I hope they're your people. But I don't see them here. I don't know what you're up to, but I think we're the bait, and I've had enough."

"I'm just trying to give you a bit of a tour."

"Right. You want to play these kinds of games? Fine. We all know it's part of the business, Watson. Just include us in the planning, or find somebody else to play with. Now, take us back to the hotel."

Watson and Peter glared at each other. Watson was still breathing hard. "Go back to the hotel," Watson said to the driver.

No one talked on the way. Peter was too angry to trust his own judgement. When they pulled up to the front of the hotel, Watson said to the driver, "Wait here. I may be a while."

Peter and Maria exited the SUV and walked briskly into the hotel. Watson caught up with them at the elevator.

"We need to talk," Watson said, still breathing hard.

"Okay," Peter said. "Where?"

"Go up to your room. I'll get a bottle of scotch from the bar and join you."

"Fine."

When they got to their room, Maria closed the door and asked, "Don't you think you're overreacting? There was a lot of security around today."

"They didn't want to be seen."

"A couple of Hawaiian shirts doesn't do much to hide the look of professional security."

"Do you know who they belong to?" Peter asked.

"No."

"That's my point. We were told nothing, and there was no one around the Jefferson Memorial." Peter sat on the sofa. "Watson was testing someone. When nothing happened at the museums, he really exposed us at the Memorial."

"Maybe he was just testing us?"

"Maybe, but I think it's more than that."

When Watson arrived, he took three glasses from the bar, poured three ample glasses of scotch, and sat down. "I'm sorry my tour upset you."

"Before you start, I want to say something, Watson. Maria and I signed a contract with Bernstein, but we really work for you. You know why I want you in Jakarta? Because I thought I could trust you. This job can get ugly in a hurry, and we need somebody in Indonesia to cover our backs. You were setting us up today. So, why should we trust you, or work for you?"

Watson took a good drink of the scotch and sat back in his chair. He closed his eyes. "There are some aspects of my work that I cannot discuss with you. You don't have the clearance. Yet. Even if you did, there still are some things that I shouldn't tell you."

"I don't think that excuses today," Peter said.

"Probably right." Watson opened his eyes. "Look, I'm in the middle of an investigation of some really bad actors. They know what I'm doing. I set up today, with a lot of plain-clothes security at the museums, to see if they'd react."

"I didn't see much security outside the memorial," Maria said.

"More than you think."

"What did you find out?" Peter asked.

"Nothing. They're being careful, but that does not lessen the danger."

"Maybe they're smart enough to recognize your setup," Peter said. "We did."

"Maybe."

In the silence, Watson refreshed their glasses.

Peter picked up his glass and took a good swallow of the whiskey. "Look," he said, "you can't pull another stunt like this, without at least involving us in your planning. We need to know enough to be prepared. We don't need any surprises from our side."

Watson stared out the window and did not answer for a good half a minute. "Alright. You've got my word on that, but you won't always know all the details." Watson raised his eyebrows. "Does that work?"

Peter shrugged and looked at Maria. She nodded.

"We understand the need for secrets," Peter said, "but get us our clearance. It would be nice to be able to understand the whole picture."

"I'll do the best I can, but you both have complex histories. Clearance can take a while." Watson drained his glass. "Does that sort us out for now?"

Peter and Maria looked at each other. "I think so," Peter said.

Watson stood up. "I guess I'll leave, then. I'll see you in Indonesia. Remember, when you're in Indonesia you're a married couple." He turned, and shut the door.

Maria stared at the door. "So, if this was all a test," she said, "who was Watson testing? The bad guys or us?"

"Good question. Both, I think."

The next day, Peter and Maria arrived well rested at the airport. "We get lie-flat seats on the first leg to Tokyo," Peter said, "which is good, considering the flight time is over fourteen hours."

Peter was never sure there was anything good to say about a fourteen-hour flight. He didn't particularly like flying into the unknown, either, though once past airport security he didn't worry too much about the crowds in the airports.

A little over twenty-five hours after departing Washington, they arrived at the Sheraton Bandara International Hotel, just outside of the Jakarta airport, with Peter's backpack, a duffel bag, and a briefcase with Peter's computer. One additional piece of baggage was an empty steel chest, three feet long, two feet wide, and eight inches deep. Peter adjusted his watch to local time, just after one in the morning.

At check-in the clerk handed Peter a note from Watson. *See you for lunch at noon at your hotel.*

"I'm not sure whether I should be awake or asleep," Peter said as they entered their room.

"It's dark outside," Maria said. "I'm going to bed."

Peter made sure to lock the door and latch the security chain in place. He checked the locks on the sliding doors to the balcony. Then he followed Maria to bed.

Chapter 13

Peter and Maria were both slow in rising in the morning, but a little after eight the morning sun awakened both of them.

Peter groaned. "I feel like I've been hit by a truck."

"I'm not hurting, but my body doesn't quite know what to think," Maria said with a laugh.

"I should get up," he said.

"Why? We have nothing to do until we meet Watson."

"I suppose."

"You know, I was thinking last night. You haven't told me who you work for, but that's okay. I already know. You work for the CIA, or Watson, or someone else. Who cares? What I realized is…. We're the same."

"We're the same?"

"Yes. We both are, or have been, paid warriors. And I think, when we can, we should take some time for ourselves. Walk in the gardens. Make love in the middle of the day. We don't know how much time we have."

Peter rolled over to face her in the bed. "You're really upset."

"No. I'm not upset. I think I'm just recognizing us… for the first time."

Peter smiled. "I know I smell like an old goat, and my breath is probably just as bad, but I would like to kiss you."

Maria shook her head. "I don't think so, but you can shower and brush your teeth. And I could, too. Maybe we could even do it together."

"It's a deal," Peter said. "Then maybe we could find a garden to walk in."

Peter stood on the balcony. It was almost time to meet Watson for lunch. The immediate view was a lake, with a limited amount of vegetation and walkways under the balcony and beside the water. He scanned the area methodically with his binoculars.

Nothing unusual, but this is not my home turf. He felt uneasy. *It's just a lack of control,* he decided. As Peter lowered the binoculars and retreated into the room he heard a knock on the door.

"Can you get that," Maria called. "I'm in the bathroom."

"Who is it," he called.

"I have a flower arrangement for the room."

Peter stepped over to the door and looked through the peephole. He saw a short, slender man. *He looks Balinese*, he thought, *with a hotel uniform. Nothing to be afraid of.*

"We didn't request any flowers."

"Oh no, sir. This is our gift, a welcoming bouquet."

This makes no sense, Peter thought.

"Just a minute," he said, and stepped over to the pile of luggage. He opened his backpack and pulled out a four-pound, one hand sledge he normally used for sampling rock outcrops.

Back at the door, Peter took a second look. *Same small man. Looks innocent enough, but...* Peter reached across the door, opened it a crack, and stepped back. The safety chain clanked as the man in the hallway opened the door against it.

With a thud, and a snap of the security chain, the room door flew open and banged against the wall. A man over twice the size of the one Peter had seen in the peephole stumbled, off balance, into the room. A maroon balaclava covered his face, but he wasn't hiding the small revolver he held in his right hand.

Sure as hell no friend of ours, Peter decided.

Before the man could regain his balance, Peter swung the hammer. He aimed at the man's hidden face, and the flat of the hammer head smashed vertically across the nose and mouth. Peter grimaced at the wet cracking sound of breaking teeth, bone and cartilage.

Peter took one more step back into the room. The attacker stood motionless for several seconds. Then he grabbed his face with his hands, and he made a sound that was something between a scream and a moan. He fell to the floor.

"You fucking bastard," Peter muttered. He kicked the pistol away from the now unconscious attacker.

"What the hell?" Maria shouted.

"Call hotel security," Peter said. "Tell them somebody with a pistol broke down our door."

Peter looked at the man on the floor. He wasn't moving. He made a gurgling sound as he breathed through the blood in his mouth. *No threat.*

"Watch this guy if he comes to."

Peter ran into the hallway. He stopped, looked down the hall, and saw the back of a hotel uniform before the door to the fire stairs closed. "You son of a bitch," he said, and he ran toward the fire stairs.

He pulled open the door. It slammed against the wall. He heard feet pounding on the stairs below him, just before another fire door opened and slammed shut.

"Useless," Peter muttered. He stepped back into the hall and let the fire door shut behind him. A bouquet of flowers sat on a table near the elevator, somewhat off center with a little water spilled onto the table. He shook his head. "I'd never be able to prove it." He ran back down the hall.

Before he got to the room, he heard Maria shout, "Don't move." Then he heard a thud and a loud grunt.

As he turned to enter the room, Peter saw Maria standing over the masked man. He was curled up, his hands between his legs, groaning.

"He was trying to get the gun," Maria said. "I kicked him in the nuts."

Peter was breathing hard. "You called security?"

"Yeah. I told them somebody just tried to kill us."

Peter kicked the man savagely in the head. He stopped groaning. Peter bent down, put the hammer on the floor, stripped off the man's belt, and rolled him on his stomach. He pulled the attacker's hands together and tied them with his own belt.

"Give me a hand to roll him onto his back," Peter said.

Peter tied his shoe laces together. "That should keep him," he said and stood up.

Peter heard someone running down the hallway, and he looked out to see two hotel security guards. "Right here, guys!" he shouted.

Peter stepped aside to let the two guards enter the room. When they saw the man on the floor, they had a hurried conversation in Bahasa. Then the older of the two turned to Peter. "What happened?"

"This man broke down the door. He had a pistol in his hand," Peter said. "I hit him in the head with the hammer."

"We will call the police," the senior guard said. He spoke briefly to his associate, who made a call on his cell phone.

The guard reached down and pulled the balaclava off the man's broken and bloody face.

"I'm sorry. I think you need to call an ambulance," Peter said.

This time the older of the two guards made the call. When he was done he said, "Please sit down in your room. The national police will want to question you."

Peter and Maria stepped back into the room and sat at the small table. They were partially hidden by one of the bathroom walls.

Peter looked to see that the guards could not see him. He quickly tapped out a text message to Watson. *Get here NOW. Attacked in room. Police arrive soon. Awkward. P & M.*

"Contacted Watson," Peter whispered.

Two members of the national police, the POLRI, arrived just ahead of Watson.

"What the hell is going on here?" Watson asked loudly when he arrived.

The scene quickly descended into a noisy confusion of shouted conversations, demands for identification, telephone calls, more police arriving, crime scene photographers, and an ambulance crew. Through the entire noisy scene, Peter and Maria sat quietly, waiting.

Eventually, Watson managed to convince the police that he should be allowed to talk to Peter and Maria, and he worked his way into the room.

He looks a little like a standing Buddha in a blue batik shirt, Peter thought.

"You guys are high maintenance," he said. "I've got Alden Sage working on this. We'll have someone from the embassy over here shortly. They've got a lawyer coming, and when he gets here the police will interview you. Now, tell me exactly what happened."

When Peter and Maria finished, Watson shook his head. "Okay. When the lawyer and the embassy people get here, I'll introduce you. Then I'll disappear. I'll keep in touch with what's going on, but I'll reschedule our lunch meeting for supper."

"I don't think this police interview will be like the one we had in Toronto," Peter said.

"That's a reasonable expectation," Watson said. "Don't worry too much. It's pretty obvious what happened here, and the White House carries a lot of weight, even in Jakarta. We'll get this sorted out in short order."

When they walked into the hotel restaurant a little after six in the evening, Peter spotted Watson immediately. "You look very comfortable," Peter said as they approached the table.

"Have a seat," Watson said. "I hate the humidity of Jakarta, but I love ditching the suit. The police have let you loose?"

"Things seem to have cooled off a bit," Maria said. "We have a new room. They've told us we can continue on our trip."

"You must have pulled out all the stops," Peter said. "I figured, at a minimum, we'd have to spend a day in the police station." Peter shook his head. "I was hoping to avoid an Indonesian jail. We had to show them our tickets, and we have to check in with the police when we get to Manado."

"Well, the POLRI are notoriously corrupt and inept to start with," Watson said. "That can be good, or horrifyingly bad, depending on how you handle it. At the moment we have a good relationship with Indonesia, and that is definitely to your benefit."

"It's a hell of a start for the two of us," Peter said.

Watson nodded.

"Do you have any idea of what's going on? Who's behind this?" Maria asked.

"Not really. I don't think it has anything to do with Rostov, if that's what you're wondering. The POLRI think someone noticed all your luggage and decided to rob you." Watson raised his hands and shrugged. "Who knows? The guy appears to be Japanese, but he has no identification. The police say they don't know anything about him. His fingerprints are going to Interpol. A current picture of his face doesn't help much."

"I feel a little bad about that," Peter said.

"Don't."

"This is crazy," Maria said. "This wasn't somebody trying to rob us. This was someone trying to kill us. If they wanted to rob us, they'd wait until they knew we weren't there. This guy did the opposite. He made sure we were there before he broke the door down."

Watson nodded. "In this case, we should let the police believe what they want to believe. Anyway, let's not talk about it here." He picked up the menu. "Let's get something to eat. We can talk in your room after dinner."

Peter shook his head. "I'm with Maria. This is crazy, but I'm also hungry. It's been about twenty hours since I last ate." He looked at the menu. "I'm no expert on Indonesian food, but I've rarely been disappointed by their rice dishes, like nasi goreng, and the spicy grilled chicken and fish is always good."

"If we were in eastern Europe or Russia, I could help you," Watson said. "Here it's pretty much pot luck for me."

They didn't waste too much time on conversation as they ate, and in deference to Muslim preferences, they didn't drink any variety of alcohol, though it was available. The food was spicy and good, and the service by the Balinese staff was excellent and quick. In less than an hour Peter and Maria were seated with Watson at the small table in their room.

"Do you have any idea of who's behind what happened in our hotel room today?" Maria asked.

"No," Watson said, "but perhaps you now understand why I wanted the two of you here, rather than some naïve geologist."

"I still say you want us here because we know how to maim and kill people really well," Maria said. "But if this isn't Rostov – and I'm not so sure I believe it isn't – who the hell is it? And why?"

"IndoGold knows we're coming... right?" Peter asked.

"Yes, they know you're coming," Watson said.

"This is somehow related to IndoGold," Peter said. "I don't know how, but I'm sure of it. If we were smart, Maria and I would head back to Canada right now, on the next available flight out of here."

"You're saying we're not smart?" Maria asked. "We're staying?"

Watson looked at Peter with raised eyebrows. "I hope that's what you're saying."

Peter looked at each of them with a very small smile. "I think there's some whiskey in the minibar, and in spite of this country having over two hundred million Muslims, I'm going to have a drink." He stood up. "Either of you want to join me?"

Chapter 14

At ten that evening, Watson MacDonough sat at a small desk in a secure room at the Jakarta embassy. He punched in a number for the US embassy in Geneva, Switzerland.

"Terry Whincup."

"Terry! It's Watson MacDonough. How are things in Geneva?"

"Jesus, Watson. I thought you were dead, but now I hear you're working for the President?"

"Don't worry. This old cat has a few lives left. I need a favor."

"Why am I not surprised?"

"I've been reading some of your reports, Terry. You say the Mossad has been spending a lot of time in Zürich. They bought a building?"

"Yeah. They're tearing it apart. They say it's just an investment. Their front man is a guy by the name of Saul Bernstein. You know him?"

"I've met him. What do you think they're up to?"

"I have no idea, Watson. The building's right next to the Swiss International Bank. Maybe they plan to rob it. How the hell should I know?"

"What's the bank like?"

"It's old. Family owned. Been around forever. One of those old fortress-style buildings, all stone, bars, and battlements."

"A boutique bank?"

"Yeah. Pretty much. It's small, but it's very solid financially."

After a brief pause, Watson asked, "Do they offer to provide secure storage of critical papers for their clients, that sort of thing?"

"Probably. A lot of the old banks provide that kind of service."

It's a risk, Watson thought. *I could be exposing too much.* He shook his head. *I don't have the luxury of time.*

"I want to know what's in the vaults that are next to the Mossad building. I want to get someone into the bank to have a look."

"Jesus! You're crazy, Watson. You realize just how tough that would be? It really is a fortress."

"See if Irish will do it. If anybody can do it, he can."

"I can't do that! He's too expensive. I can't hide it. Anyway, it's impossible."

"Impossible is exactly what Irish does on a regular basis, Terry, and you know it."

"You know I can't help you."

"Just give me his contact information."

"I can't do that."

"You know who I work for." Watson waited for Terry to answer.

"Jesus, Watson. You know Irish?"

"Yes."

The silence lasted for a long time. Watson waited.

"Call this," Terry said and recited a number. "Let it ring three times and hang up. Call a second time and let it ring two times and hang up. Wait. He'll call you."

"Thanks, Terry."

"Yeah. Don't ask for any more favors. Okay?"

"I won't."

"This conversation never happened. Whatever you're doing, don't get me involved." Terry hung up without another word.

Watson shook his head as he hung up. "Man, Harold must have them shitting in their pants over me."

The next afternoon, just before four, the Garuda flight came to a stop at the terminal in Manado. "I never enjoy these Indonesian flights," Peter said. "They're much improved now they're using 737's, but when they used turboprops they tended to crash on a fairly regular basis."

"Thanks for not telling me that until the flight was over."

Peter pointed to the MD500 helicopter parked off to the side of the terminal. "I bet that's our next ride," he said. "I'd prefer they don't know I can fly the thing."

"Why?"

"Secrets can be good."

"True."

Peter quickly spotted Teunis Dulaigh beside the baggage claim area. "That's a surprise. I didn't expect the chief geologist to meet us at the airport. He puts a bit of a dent in the helicopter's payload."

Maria laughed. "You're terrible."

"You're right. I am."

Peter and Maria walked across the baggage claim area, and Peter extended his hand to Teunis. "How are you, Dr. Dulaigh? I'm Peter Binder, and this is my wife, my assistant, Maria Davidoff."

Teunis smiled as he shook hands. "A husband and wife geological team is a first for me. No problems on the trip?"

First test, Peter thought.

"Actually, one small problem in Jakarta," he said. "A man with a pistol broke down the door to our room while we were there. A bit nasty, but nothing was stolen."

Teunis frowned, and said, "Sorry to hear that. Jakarta has a few problems sometimes. I'm glad you escaped unharmed."

Can't tell, Peter thought.

"We weren't hurt," Maria said, "but we do need to check in with the police before we go to the camp."

"Really? Why?"

"We, ah, did a little damage to the attacker," Peter said. "He'll need some serious facial surgery. I think they just want to keep track of us until we leave the country."

And I have a suspicion that you know all about it.

Teunis looked at his watch. "We've got plenty of time. Collect your bags. We'll leave them with Rahmat and the helicopter and take a cab to the police in town. It shouldn't take long, but police in Indonesia are an unpredictable bunch."

Once they arrived at the police station there was a lot of talking, mostly warnings about reporting again before they leave Manado, and that they should restrict their travel to IndoGold's exploration camp.

"What is that smell?" Maria asked, as the cab took them back to the airport. "It smells like an open sewer."

"You're insulting Indonesian cuisine, my dear," Teunis said. "That's the enticing aroma of ripe durian, the most fantastic fruit in the world."

"Good grief. How do you get past the smell to actually eat it?"

"It's an acquired taste, but you should try it at least once."

It was a tight squeeze with all three of them in the back seat of the helicopter. It took a bit of maneuvering for Teunis to buckle his seatbelt.

As they took off, Teunis said, "Visibility's terrible today. You won't see much of central Sulawesi. The farmers set fires to clear the land, and they get out of control. This year it's really bad. It's about a hundred miles to the camp, a forty-five-minute flight."

"This is a nice machine for this type of work," Peter said.

"It's what we can get. We have to use the Indonesian military, so we don't have much choice."

"The pilot's military?" Peter asked.

"Oh, yes."

I can barely see the ground at all, Peter thought. *It's almost instrument flying.*

"He just flies with the GPS?"

Teunis shrugged. "I assume so."

Rahmat landed at a log helipad at the IndoGold camp. The camp was a collection of log buildings, made from the local timber, with the typical, Indonesian curved roof lines and large verandas at the entrances. "I love Indonesian camps that have no road access," Peter said. "They're like a real village, not like the flimsy tent camps in Canada."

"It's what everybody does in this part of the world," Teunis said. "They'll take your baggage to your cabin. We don't usually have any married couples in camp, but you have a nice cabin to yourselves."

"I'm sure we'll be fine," Maria said.

"Well, follow me to the cook house, and we'll talk about your plans."

In the cook house, the largest building in the camp, they sat at a table and benches roughly hewn from local timber. Plastic table clothes covered the tables, and bowls of tropical fruits were set out on each table. Several large fans stirred the air and caused some of the Bahasa posters on the walls to rattle.

"What are the posters about," Peter asked.

"Oh, mostly employee rights," Teunis replied. "Same the world over."

One of the kitchen helpers, dressed in white, arrived with a fresh pot of coffee and filled a cup for each of them.

"I will ask you to be discreet while you are here," Teunis said. "No public displays of affection. It can create some serious problems with the Muslim staff."

"I think we can control ourselves," Maria said with a smile.

"Good." Teunis turned to Peter. "Now, I understand you're working for Saul Bernstein?"

"That's right."

"Well, he's a very important investor for us. Whatever he wants, he gets. Robert Talon says you should have full access." Teunis raised his hands. "So you have full access. Where do you want to start?"

After tasting the strong, dark coffee, Peter stirred in some sugar. "I've read most of the reports you've filed with the exchange, but I wouldn't mind revisiting the latest ones."

"Not a problem," Teunis said. "I've already put them in your cabin. I'll need them back, but if you want I can copy sections for you."

"Tomorrow morning maybe we could start with a surface tour with the maps of the geology and surface sampling," Peter said. "I'll probably spend a day or so collecting samples from the surface. Later I'll want to look at the representative samples you have from the drilling in the heart of the orebody."

"I'll have a geologist show you around tomorrow, after breakfast. Do you want samples of the drill core?"

"If that's possible."

"One of our local workers can use the diamond saw to cut disks from the small pieces of core we saved. Most of the core was ground up for the bulk assay procedure. The samples will be small, probably no more than a half inch thick. How many do you think you'll want?"

"Fifty to one hundred should be fine," Peter said

"That shouldn't be a problem."

Interesting, Peter thought. *No objections. That's a surprise.*

"It's almost dinner time," Teunis said. "We may as well stay and have dinner. I'll take you to your cabin after we're finished. You can look at the reports tonight, or just relax."

The evening meal was simple, but ample, as is the case in most remote exploration camps. Peter and Maria lingered with Teunis over dessert, long after most of the other workers had left for their rooms.

"I'm curious," Peter said. "Have you had any conflicts between Muslim workers and some of your expatriate, Christian workers?"

"Not anymore," Teunis answered. "I think I'm the only non-Muslim in the camp, except for the two of you. We did have some problems early on."

"What sort of problems?" Maria asked.

"We had two expat geos from Canada, a man and a woman, and they started sleeping together. The more hard-core Muslims in camp demanded that I fire them for adultery."

"That must have been interesting," Peter said.

"It was. Under strict Sharia law, you need four witnesses of the actual physical act of intercourse. They had them. Peeping Toms, you might say."

Peter shook his head.

"I had to fire the two expats. Haven't had any non-Muslim geologists since. Much more peaceful."

Teunis took them to their cabin. It was spacious, a bit separated from the other cabins in the camp, with ample sitting area and two twin-size beds. It was obviously meant to be shared by two workers. There were shelves and hangers for clothing, and two small desks and chairs for reading and work. With no air conditioning, the room was hot and humid.

Sitting at one desk, Peter flipped through the stack of reports. "This is all public information," he said, "either from their website or from the stock exchange. I don't need to spend much time on these."

"Good. We can relax for the rest of the night," Maria said. "Maybe we could take a walk around the camp."

"This is a bad time for that. The anopheles mosquito is most active at dusk and dawn, most of the night actually. A walk right now is a good way to end up with malaria."

"I guess we relax by going to bed, then," Maria said with a smile.

"Not a bad idea. We'll have a long day tomorrow, I suspect."

"And a sweaty one."

"Indeed," Peter said.

As they prepared for bed, they emptied most of the clothing out of the duffel bag. Peter lifted out a locked leather bag.

"What's that?" Maria asked.

"Just the special equipment I asked Saul to provide."

Maria didn't ask any more questions. Peter unlocked the bag and looked inside. *Looks in order*, he thought. Two pistols, a satellite telephone. He left them in the bag.

Peter pulled out a plastic bag. It held two passports, some credit cards, and what looked like driver's licenses. He left the bag unopened. The passports, at a quick glance through the plastic, looked well worn.

He riffled through a small pile of hundred-dollar bills, he estimated about $10,000, and a much larger wad of local Rupiah notes. The latter mostly the 50,000 and 100,000 denominations. He examined an unsigned credit card with the name of Charles Manson. A small piece of paper was taped to the card with a passcode and the note *$20,000*.

Peter looked up at Maria. "I think we're reasonably prepared," he said, smiled and dropped everything back into the leather bag and locked it. He dropped the bag into the stainless-steel chest and relocked the four combination locks and the two circular key locks on the chest.

"You think that's secure enough?" Maria asked with a smile.

"Probably not, but I should know if someone breaks into it."

They undressed and began the night in one bed.

"I actually like this," Maria whispered. "Slippery sex."

"It's fine by me," Peter whispered, and he pulled her down and kissed her.

Later, alone in his bed, lying naked and uncovered, except for the mosquito net, Peter struggled to fall asleep in the heat and humidity.

Why is Teunis so relaxed about sampling? Peter wondered. *He must be sure I'll find high grade gold. Or he knows I'll never write a report. I can deal with the first conclusion*, he thought. *What about the second?*

Peter listened to Maria's quiet and measured breathing. He got out of bed and unlocked the metal chest. He opened the leather bag again and removed the larger of the two pistols, the .357 Magnum with the three-inch barrel.

More reliable. Better stopping power, he thought.

He loaded the revolver and wrapped it and its holster in a canvas sample bag. He gently laid the bag back in the chest.

As he slipped back into bed, he considered the chance of discovery. *There's a greater risk than that.*

In the morning, Teunis assigned Gusti, an Indonesian geologist, to show them around the surface. Peter listened to the young man discuss the geology of the Endang gold deposit. *It sounds good*, Peter thought. *He's got all the right words, but it doesn't make any sense.*

They ended up at a long, low outcrop of soft, weathered rock, along one of the drill trails. It wasn't really a road, just a scar in the jungle where they winched a drill rig from one site to another. "This is the longest surface exposure with high gold values," Gusti said.

"I noticed a few others on the map with higher gold numbers," Peter said.

"Yes, but none of them are very long or well exposed."

"We'll probably get to some of those tomorrow," Peter said, "but we'll spend most of the afternoon here, mapping and taking samples."

"That should get us sweaty and dirty enough," Maria said.

After lunch, Gusti left them at the outcrop and walked back to his work at the camp.

Peter watched him go. "I can't believe they're letting me collect my own samples with no supervision."

"Seems like they're not worried about us."

"Yeah. And that worries me. The more I see, the more I believe Bob Williams."

"Maybe he's wrong," she said.

"Well, from what I've seen so far, this sure doesn't look like any gold mine I've ever seen. I think it's a joke."

"Why are you so sure?"

"Look, this is supposed to be the biggest gold deposit in the world. Huge amounts of hot water and steam should have moved through these rocks, altering them beyond recognition and leaving millions of quartz and sulfide veins." Peter shrugged. "There's none of that. Where the rocks aren't weathered, they're fresh and unaltered."

Peter looked at the low exposures of weathered rock on the side of the hill. "This outcrop is a perfect place to start."

Peter dropped his backpack on the side of the trail and began to pull out his sampling gear. "We'll sample one hundred feet of this outcrop, in five-foot intervals, two samples per interval."

"One sample isn't enough?" Maria asked.

"Nope. We're concerned about salting, adding gold to the outcrop. There's lots of ways to do it. One of the best is to load a shotgun with tiny grains of gold and blast away. That one's hard to detect, but the gold's only skin deep."

"So… We chip off one sample. Then we do the same thing again, but only taking rock from below the surface. Is that it?" Maria asked.

Peter smiled. "Ah, my fine assistant, you get an A-plus. Your reward is… You're in charge of the bags, sample tags, and numbers."

"Thank you so much," Maria replied with a smirk.

By the end of the afternoon, they had forty small samples and a detailed map of the outcrop with the sample locations.

As Peter closed his backpack, he said, "That's a good start. The samples are a little small, but they're good enough. Now we lock them up so nobody can add any gold to them, and get them to an approved lab in Canada for the gold analyses. If the surface is high grade, and below surface is barren, we know this is a hoax."

"It's that easy?"

"Yes, it's that easy. We'll take more samples, including tiny samples of the core, but these twenty samples should tell us what's going on here."

"Do you suppose Teunis really understands what you're doing?" she asked.

"Yes. Unless he's a total idiot."

"That's a little scary."

"Yes, it is," he said.

They began to hike back to the camp. About a third of the way along the trail, Gusti met them.

"Did you have a productive day?" Gusti asked Maria.

Peter smiled. *I think he's flirting with her.*

"You'll have to ask Peter," she said.

"A good first day," Peter said.

"Would you like me to lock your samples in the core shack, so they'll be safe?"

"No. I think they'll be fine in our cabin," Peter said.

Back at their cabin, Peter unlocked the steel chest. He dropped the samples and his field notes into the chest and locked it.

Later, when they arrived in the cook house for dinner, Teunis gestured for them to sit with him.

"Everything go well?" Teunis asked.

"It's a good start," Peter replied, as he served himself. "We sampled along the road by drill hole twenty-five."

"You should get some good gold values from those samples," Teunis said, "but there are some other outcrops with higher grades."

"Gusti showed us some of them, and they're marked on the map. We'll get to them tomorrow," Peter said.

"When do you want to look at the core?" Teunis asked.

"The day after tomorrow and probably the next day after that," Peter said. "That gives us the morning before we fly out to Manado to sort out any last-minute issues."

"If we have time, I'd like to show you another gold system on the way out."

"Really?"

"Yeah. We control the concession," Teunis said. "I think it's bigger than Endang. You want to see it?"

Peter nodded. "Sure. Let's plan on it."

"If you want, I can lock up your samples in the core shed. They might be safer there."

"Thanks," Peter said, "but I think they're fine in the cabin. I have them locked up. It's not perfect, but I'll know if someone screws around with them. You know how it is. Protocol for my work says I'm supposed to maintain custody of the samples."

"I understand. Just thought I'd offer." Teunis ate some of the highly spiced rice and then said, "Those small samples you're planning on collecting from what's left of the drill core won't be very representative. With the coarse gold we have in the high-grade portions of the deposit, gold values in such small samples will be extremely erratic."

"That's not really a problem," Peter said. "I just need to confirm the presence of gold and the presence of some high grades. They don't have to match your assay values precisely."

"That's good," Teunis said. "I know you'll find gold in those samples. Probably some crazy numbers." Teunis filled his coffee cup. "I'll make sure someone lays out the drill samples tomorrow. They'll be ready for you."

I bet they will be, Peter thought.

Chapter 15

Watson listened as the secure telephone at the embassy ring. He answered on the third ring, "Watson MacDonough."

"You called me." The man's voice had a soft, clear, tenor ring.

Watson knew the man's actual name, but he respected him enough to always use his chosen code name, *Irish*. Watson had heard him recite poetry and sing in an Irish pub once. He would never forget the man's voice. "I have a job for you," Watson said.

"You freelance these days?"

"No. I work for POTUS."

"This a secure line?" Irish asked.

"Yes."

A pause. "What's the job?"

"The Swiss International Bank in Zürich."

Silence.

"You know it?" Watson asked.

"Yes, I know it. Better than most. I've been there before for another client. Not easy, but it can be done. What are you looking for?"

"Someone bought a building next door. They're tearing it apart. I want to know what's in the bank vaults along the common foundation."

"You're kidding."

"I'm deadly serious," Watson said.

Silence.

"You can do it?"

"Yes. There's a large vault there. It may be the owner's vault. I've never been in it. I think that's what you want." Irish paused. "You can afford me?"

"What's your price these days?"

"Half a million. US dollars. In my account in Zürich. Half up front. Half when I'm done."

"I can afford you."

"Can you give me a hint of what I'm looking for?" Irish asked.

"A hell of a pile of gold bars."

"You want a report only? No samples?"

"Take nothing. Leave nothing. I need to know what's in that vault. If it's gold bars, I want to know how many, what they weigh, and if they're international standard bars. That's all. Nothing else. Don't get greedy."

"I follow directives precisely. You know that, Mr. MacDonough."

"Yes, I know that."

Irish paused. "The storage vaults are easy. The cash vault is another story, but that's not your concern. I know how I can get into the bank and into the vaults. I do not need any preparation time."

"How long before I get a verbal report?"

"I will leave for Zürich as soon as I receive confirmation of the advance deposit. I should have an answer for you in three to four days following receipt."

"That's sooner than I expected," Watson said.

"I try to give good service," Irish said and terminated the call without another word.

Watson hung up. "Now who the hell did he work for when he got in there before?"

It could be anybody, even a businessman who just wanted some records to disappear.

Peter and Maria completed the surface examinations and sampling the next day. Peter examined the less weathered outcrops for alteration and veining. He found little of either. They spent two days examining and sampling the representative drill samples.

When they were alone in the core shack, at the end of the fourth day, Peter examined several samples.

"These samples are from a very high-grade section of the deposit," he said to Maria. "They're volcanic rocks, almost fresh. With the kind of gold content they're reporting, these rocks should be full of veins and altered beyond identification."

He picked up one sample. "Look at this with my hand lens. You see the metal along the cut surface?"

"Yes."

"I think someone deliberately rubbed their wedding ring along the surface," he said. "That's another old trick to add gold to rock samples."

"Isn't that a little obvious?"

"I'd say so," Peter said, "which is a little scary."

By the end of the fourth day of sampling, they had sixty-four samples from rock outcrops on the surface, all reported to contain high gold values. They had 106 small samples sawed off of the representative pieces of core from some of the highest-grade portions of the drill holes.

Peter made sure they were alone. "Well, that's it," he said. "Now all we need are the analyses."

"We sure haven't had any problems of access," Maria said. "Saul seems to have done his job in that regard."

"That scares the hell out of me."

"You still think this is a fraud?"

"I don't know what this place is," he said, "but it sure as hell doesn't look like a gold mine. If it's really a fraud, things could get nasty really quickly."

"We're in the middle of nowhere, and we're still in one piece," Maria said.

"Too many witnesses here." He looked down at the last of the samples. "The only way out of here is by helicopter." Peter shrugged.

"The pilot's military. He can't be in on any fraud, can he?"

"I suspect the military are paid crap, so an opportunity to make a pile of money would be a huge temptation." Peter paused. "Let's put these last samples away in the chest, and head to dinner."

As they approached their cabin, Peter made sure they were alone. When they walked in, he bolted the door behind them. "It's time to show you something," he said.

He unlocked the metal chest and proceeded to put the last samples into the chest. Before he put his pistol away, he pulled it out of the bag and showed it to Maria.

"You've been carrying that every day?"

"Yes."

"You could have told me."

Peter ignored her comment. "I have something for you." He unlocked the leather bag and took out a small Glock 19 handgun. He snapped in a clip, chambered a round, and flipped on the safety.

"You're kidding. Right?"

"No. Teunis wants to show me another gold system on the way out. It doesn't make sense. I'm getting really nervous about the flight out to Manado."

Maria shook her head.

"You familiar with the Glock 19?" he asked.

"No, but it looks pretty simple. Show me the safety."

He showed her and handed her the pistol. "It's cocked and loaded. Just flip off the safety and fire. You've got one bullet in the chamber and fourteen more in the clip."

"Should be enough."

"Don't forget. It's a 9mm cartridge. Not a lot of stopping power."

"An old Russian once told me, 'If you have to shoot somebody, five or six well placed bullets beats a single shot every time.' I always try to follow his advice."

This time Peter shook his head. "Sometimes I forget some of your history."

"You shouldn't."

"Theoretically we'll be stopping tomorrow to do some geology," he said. "We'll wear our field vests. We can carry our pistols in one of the baggy pockets."

"Jesus! And if they find out?"

Peter shrugged. "Worst case? If they discover them, we're both dead. Worst case? If we're not prepared, we're both dead."

"You're always so damn optimistic."

Peter held out his hand. "I'll lock both of them up with the samples. Then it's time for dinner."

They walked past Teunis' cabin on a stone walkway designed to reduce the mud problems. It was the second largest cabin in the camp, after the cook house, and the front of the cabin served as the main office.

Peter followed Maria, and as he passed below the office window he heard Teunis speaking. He stopped to listen. Maria kept walking. She looked back, and Peter put his finger to his lips.

It sounded like Teunis was on the camp's satellite telephone.

"From where you're sitting," Teunis said, "in a nice air-conditioned office, I know it seems easy. It's not so easy here." Teunis coughed as he listened.

"I'll see what I can do," he said. After a pause he continued. "Yeah, yeah. I know. I'll call late tomorrow."

"What did he say?" another man in the office asked.

Sounds like Rahmat, the helicopter pilot.

"What do you think?" Teunis responded.

"Shit."

"Just follow my lead," Teunis said.

Peter walked silently away from the office cabin and caught up with Maria. He shook his head. They walked in silence to the cook house.

They were half-way through dinner, when Teunis and the Pilot came in and sat down across from them.

"So, are you ready to go tomorrow morning?" Teunis asked.

"Yeah, we're done," Peter said. "We'll pack up tonight. We can leave any time tomorrow morning."

"What flight are you on?"

"We're on the 4:15 PM Garuda flight," Maria said.

"We'd like to get to the airport plenty early," Peter said.

Teunis looked at the pilot. "We don't need the helicopter for anything here in the morning, do we?"

"No," Rahmat answered.

Teunis turned back to Peter. "I need to get some supplies in Manado anyway. Let's leave early, right after breakfast. We'll have plenty of time to look at that other system. We'll get you to the airport in plenty of time for your flight."

"Sounds good to me," Peter said. "Saul Bernstein will be happy to know you have another super deposit up your sleeve."

"Well, early days. We'll see," Teunis said with a smile.

Peter and Maria finished their meal. Peter asked Teunis some geological questions about the Endang deposit. As usual, Teunis had quick answers for every question.

Their answers always sound good, but they almost sound memorized, Peter thought.

"You planning on taking your samples as checked baggage?" Teunis asked.

"Yeah," Peter replied. "It's a pain, but I really have to do it."

"Make sure it's no more than seventy pounds. That's Garuda's limit for baggage. If you're in first class you can get a total of about eighty-eight pounds of checked baggage each, but the maximum for any item is still seventy pounds. We can ship the chest for you, if you want."

"We might have to move a few samples to the backpack, but I think we'll manage," Peter said.

Teunis shrugged, "Your decision."

A few minutes later Peter and Maria departed for their cabin.

"Let's go sit by the river, up by the helipad," Peter said.

"Okay."

They sat next to each other on the rocks. The noise of the river obliterated all the other sounds of the camp, except for a few bird calls from the surrounding jungle.

"Just a little planning," Peter said. "Be ready for anything. Hopefully I'm nuts, but you focus on the pilot. I'll keep my eye on Teunis. He's big enough that a 9mm bullet might not make much of an impression."

"You're really worried?"

"Probably just being paranoid, as usual."

They sat silently for several more minutes.

"Well, we'd better get packing," Maria said.

Peter shook his head. "In more ways than one."

"Sick," she said.

Peter smiled and got up. "We shouldn't be sitting out here this time of day anyway."

Maria stood up. "You don't suppose, after we pack, of course, we might be able to try some of that slippery sex again?"

"I suppose," Peter said, smiling, "but only if you insist."

Back in the cabin, Maria bolted the door. They faced each other, and Maria said, "Maybe before packing." She began to undress Peter. It was easy. Neither of them wore much in the heat and humidity.

Standing naked, they embraced and kissed for a long time. Then Peter lay down on the floor, on his back, and pulled her down to him.

"You'll get splinters in your beautiful ass," she whispered.

He grinned. "No problem, as long as you pull them out."

Maria laughed.

Chapter 16

Watson sat in the bare and secure communications room at the embassy when the telephone rang. He looked up from his computer and answered the phone.

"Yes."

"Rahm Blake. This Watson?"

"Yes. You have anything?"

"Yeah. We ran his prints through Interpol. Had a hit in Japan."

"Not a huge surprise."

"He's an enforcer, for an ultranationalist Yakuza named Akihiko Uehara."

"I've heard of him," Watson said.

"He's a real piece of work, that one. Mostly money laundering and really nasty, heavy armament sales."

"So, what about the enforcer?" Watson asked.

"Small trash. The Japanese told Indonesia to put him away for as long as they can. They don't want him back."

"What the hell was he doing here?"

"Don't know, but I'll guarantee it was no simple robbery, no crime of opportunity. Your people should be dead."

"Thanks for the help, Rahm."

"No problem, Watson. Anytime."

"You mean that?"

"Actually, I do. I didn't like the way the CIA threw you out a couple of years ago, like a piece of rubbish."

"Thanks."

After he disconnected, Watson shook his head.

What the hell is the Japanese connection? One thing, it's sure as hell not accidental.

Watson looked back down at the encrypted email he had been reading. He'd called in a whole hat full of favors to get this report from an old MI6 connection. He didn't want to go to the CIA files and give Harold James any more clues than he already had. The email was a dump of the MI6 information on the Swiss International Bank and its activities during the Second World War.

MI6 knows more than the CIA anyway, Watson thought. He went back to the summary.

1. *The Swiss International Bank handled approximately ten percent of the hard currency and gold transactions for Germany during the war.*

2. *The man who handled these transactions for Germany was an SS Officer, Friedrich Glock. He disappeared near the end of the war, apparently in the final defense of Berlin.*

3. *During the war, the bank owned its own precious metal refinery, which produced a surprising amount of refined gold in stamped, 400-ounce, .9999 gold bars.*

4. *The bank exchanged and sold large amounts of precious and semi-precious stones, stock certificates, bonds, and works of art. The bank converted the proceeds into gold bars.*

5. *The bank's refinery also melted gold bars stolen from the treasuries of eastern Europe, and poured new 400-ounce, .9999 gold bars with the bank's refinery stamp.*

6. *The services for Germany resulted in an extreme level of prosperity for this small, family-owned bank.*

7. *The bank denies that it holds any of the Holocaust gold or any other gold left over from these dealings with the Germans. No significant amount of gold shows up on the bank's books as an asset.*

Watson frowned. Denials of inconvenient truths are always easy. *How much gold is in that owner's vault? Irish says it's a big vault. How good was the skim, and who was the skimmer?*

Watson sat back in his chair. *It has to be someone who could cook the books. Hitler's books.*

Watson saved the report on a small memory card and destroyed the original communication.

I'll know how much gold is in there soon enough. There has to be a contract. Who has a copy? The bank. And Herr Glock, but he died in Berlin.

Watson closed his eyes. He sat motionless for a good three minutes. When he opened his eyes, he nodded. "Another job for the Secret Service," he said. The words seemed to disappear into the dead air of the soundproof room. "Later."

He sat forward, consulted his list of contacts, and picked up the secure telephone. He punched in a number for an office in the Kremlin. He waited for Ivan Dinisovich, of the SVR, to answer.

Ivan was a thin and almost haggard man of sharp angles. Strangely, they had moved from being bloody and deadly enemies to cautious friendship.

Who would understand this transformation? Most would call it treason.

Early in the morning, Peter and Maria finished packing up their baggage and the metal chest. Peter lifted the chest. *About seventy pounds, maybe seventy-five,* he thought. "We'll have some issues on weight, but with a little adjustment we should get by," he said.

"Let's get some breakfast."

"We should put on our field vests now," Peter said. "We don't want to draw attention to them later."

"Good idea."

As they walked to the cook house, they both saw Teunis and Rahmat, the pilot, conversing next to the helicopter.

The hunt is on, Peter thought, *and we're the trophy.*

Peter and Maria were half way through their breakfast, when Teunis and Rahmat appeared.

"You all ready to go?" Teunis asked.

"All packed."

"You're heading back to Jakarta today and stay the night there?"

"Yeah."

"You said you're taking the 4:15 Garuda flight?"

"You got it."

"That's good. We'll have plenty of time at that other property." Teunis looked at his watch. "Let's try to take off around eight-thirty. That good?"

"If you don't mind, I'll have a bit more coffee," Peter said.

"That should be fine. See you at the helicopter."

Peter poured himself another cup of coffee and watched them go. "I must be wrong."

"Maybe you are," Maria said.

They sat in silence as Peter drank his coffee. When he put his cup down, he asked, "You ready?"

"Ready as I'll ever be."

"Let's go then."

Back at their cabin, they each dropped their pistol in the pocket on the right side of their canvas field vests. The pockets were large, and the vest pockets were baggy. The pistols were not obvious.

Peter put on his backpack and carried the duffel bag. They both grabbed a handle of the metal chest.

"Not too heavy," Maria said.

"Probably a little over seventy pounds, though."

At the helicopter, the pilot tied down the metal chest in a cargo basket on the side of the helicopter. Peter and Maria sat in the back, with the backpack and the duffel bag between them. They all put on their headphones. The pilot checked the intercom, made sure everyone was belted in, and took off.

Almost immediately the smoky haze from the jungle fires cut visibility. The pilot flew just above the forest canopy. Occasionally Peter saw small clearings and openings along the streams and rivers. The buildings and small gardens disappeared as they climbed higher into the mountains.

Twenty minutes into the flight, Teunis said, "We're almost at our stop."

Peter felt a surge of adrenalin.

Teunis spoke up again. "You won't believe it. It's a fantastic outcrop, high grade gold, and I think it's richer and larger than Endang. I haven't even told the head office about this one."

"Why are you showing it to me?"

"I just want to see the look on your face. Besides, it'll give you something exciting to report back to Saul Bernstein."

His happy conversation is not reassuring. Peter put his hand in his vest pocket. In the noise of the helicopter he cocked the revolver and put his finger next to the trigger.

They landed smoothly on a small, sandy beach at the edge of a fast-flowing river. "Let's wait to get out until Rahmat shuts down completely," Teunis said. "I prefer to avoid getting sandblasted."

"Sounds good," Peter said.

When Rahmat stopped the rotors completely, they all got out. Teunis carried a small bag and walked across the sand with the pilot toward the edge of the jungle.

Peter and Maria followed, about ten feet behind them.

Peter's senses were on overload. He could hear, smell, and feel the jungle, the sand, and the river. He was already inside Teunis' head. He knew what would happen next.

At the edge of the jungle, Teunis and Rahmat stopped and turned to face Peter and Maria.

Peter felt a familiar sensation of time slowing down.

Teunis reached into his bag and retrieved a small revolver. He pointed it directly at Peter.

Rahmat pulled a small semi-automatic out of his pocket and aimed that at Maria.

Peter didn't move. *There's time.*

At a distance of less than ten feet, he saw that all the exposed cylinders in Teunis' revolver were loaded, but Teunis was not quite ready.

There's still a chance, Peter thought.

Teunis' hand shook slightly, but not enough at this close range to make any difference.

"You ought to put those things away before you hurt someone," Peter said.

Teunis laughed. "You know, Peter, I'm not a total idiot." He and Rahmat took two steps back. "You both know too much. We can't let you wander around writing reports on Endang."

Peter wasn't sure whether the expression on Teunis' face was a grin or a grimace.

Peter stood perfectly still. He looked at Teunis for about five seconds. The time was gone. He decided on surprise. He didn't take the pistol out of his pocket.

Peter pulled the trigger. His aim was not great. He hit Teunis in the left, lower abdomen.

Teunis staggered backward. He fired and missed, before he dropped the pistol in the sand.

The unexpected report of Peter's .357 Magnum momentarily stunned Rahmat, but he quickly recovered, turned, and aimed at Peter.

Before Rahmat could fire, Maria pulled the Glock out of her pocket and fired six shots in rapid succession.

If someone had pinned a target over the pilot's heart, all six of Maria's shots would have hit the target.

Rahmat stepped back two steps, with a startled look on his face, before he fell face first into the sand.

Teunis was still alive, but there was no possibility he'd survive the massive damage of the gunshot to his gut. He was still on his knees, clutching his lower belly. He looked up at Peter "You son of a bitch." Then he looked down and reached for his pistol.

Peter and Maria both fired at the same time. Both shots hit Teunis in the middle of his forehead. The back of his head exploded, and he fell into the sand.

Peter took several deep breaths and turned to look at Maria. For a full minute neither of them said a word.

Peter exhaled loudly. "Surprise, surprise," he said.

Chapter 17

"Watson MacDonough! It is good to hear your voice," Ivan said in Russian. He had the scratchy voice and cough of a life-long smoker. "Are you reborn?"

"Well, I haven't gotten any younger," Watson replied in Russian.

"And working for the President I hear. Is that a promotion?"

"Not sure about that." Watson paused. "Look, Ivan, I need a favor."

Ivan laughed. "I am completely astonished! I thought you had called to enquire about the health of my sick aunt."

"I hope she's doing better," Watson said. Ivan always liked the slow and more complicated approach. *He won't like me rushing.* "And you? We haven't talked since you were released from the hospital."

"I'm much better. You know I am not a vindictive man, but I felt much better after I witnessed the death of the unsuccessful assassin. It was slow and delightfully painful."

Watson cringed. "Back to the favor." He chose his words carefully. "I'm looking for something that might have fallen into Soviet hands in Berlin, at the end of the Second World War."

"Much of that is open to researchers now," Ivan said. "What ancient Nazi secret interests are you looking for now?"

Watson hesitated. *What am I handing to him?*

"There was a man named Friedrich Glock, an SS officer. Part of Hitler's inner circle. He managed the transfer of gold to the Swiss banks to pay for the German war effort. I think he visited a specific bank, the Swiss International Bank, sometime in either 1939 or 1940."

Ivan remained silent.

Watson hesitated again. *I'm crazy.* "There should be a contract between the bank and Glock, or the SS." Watson shifted his weight in the suddenly uncomfortable chair. "Perhaps a copy fell into Russian hands? Maybe it's in your files… somewhere?"

Watson waited. He pictured Ivan at his desk, an antique once used by Lenin.

"So… you are looking for the mythical hoard of Nazi gold?" Ivan Dinisovich finally asked. "The Holocaust gold? I thought that was the Mossad's turf. I don't think I can help you."

Watson felt sudden anger. "Look, Ivan, this is a little more than the Jews trying to recover their family trinkets. There may be enough money here to finance some really bad shit. It could come down in Russia just as easily as somewhere else."

Ivan remained stubbornly silent.

Watson was still angry. "Ivan, I pulled your ass out of the fire. I saved Moscow. You owe me."

A full minute of silence passed. "Yes, I owe you a favor," Ivan said, "but our presidents are not on the best of terms at the moment." He paused. "I'll see what I can do. You may have to come here to get a copy."

Why the hell does he want me to do that?

"I can come to Moscow."

"Watson, you have to understand. We don't get involved with anything to do with the Jews. Not the atrocities of the Second World War. Not modern Israel."

"Yes, I know."

"I can sympathize. My family suffered under Stalin. I came close to the Gulag myself. But this policy, I do not have the strength or power to go against it."

Watson leaned back in his chair and smiled. "I understand."

"How soon do you need this?"

"As soon as possible."

"If we are lucky, I can get back to you in two or three days. Will you still be in Jakarta?"

Watson shook his head. "I don't know. Do you?"

Ivan laughed. "Perhaps."

They said good-bye.

Watson closed his eyes. *It might work. Who knows?* Then he dialed another number.

"Alden Sage."

"Watson MacDonough. I need the Secret Service to do a well-hidden stakeout for me."

"Where?"

"The Swiss International Bank in Zürich, Switzerland."

"Shit. How long?"

"Starting right now and until I tell you to stop."

"You are a pain in the ass, Watson. What are you looking for?"

The echoes of the gunfire had faded, but Peter could still feel his heart pounding. He could feel the usual sense of depression closing over him, and he pushed it away.

No time for that.

"What the hell do we do now?" Maria asked.

"Not entirely sure," Peter answered. "Still have to work out the details. Right now, I have to take a minute to calm down."

He walked over to a rock at the edge of the sandy clearing and sat down. Maria joined him. They sat silently for several minutes.

Maria held out her hand. It was shaking. "I'm no good at this anymore."

"Oh, I don't know. That was pretty good shooting."

"Yeah. But look at me now. I can barely function."

"You're not alone."

They looked out at the two bodies, the helicopter, and the rushing river cutting through the dense green of the jungle. "They chose a beautiful spot," he said. "No witnesses."

"That's good," she said.

"We've got one dead geologist, and one dead military pilot."

"That's not so good."

"We still have a helicopter," he said, "and I know how to fly it."

"But we can't just land the thing at the Manado airport and walk onto our flight."

"Yeah. We have a few problems, but I think we can deal with them."

Maria shook her head. "I'm glad you're confident."

"I didn't say I'm confident. We've got a satellite telephone. I think it's time to call Watson. Maybe there's a nice aircraft carrier just off shore with a helicopter that can race in and pick us up."

Maria looked at him as if he were completely crazy.

"Yeah. Rather unlikely, and maybe not the best alternative. Anyway, first things first. Let's figure out where the hell we are." He pulled out his Garmin GPS unit and a large-scale map of Sulawesi from one of the big pockets in his vest.

"The map isn't very detailed." It took a few minutes, but when the GPS unit provided his location, he plotted it on the map. "We're about fifty miles from Manado. With me flying, thirty to forty minutes in this haze."

"Do we want to go to Manado?"

"Not really, but if Watson can't help us it's the only way out." Peter paused. "Somehow we have to get rid of the helicopter."

He pointed to a spot on the map, about ten miles east and a bit south of Manado. "Some nuts out of California bought a bunch of land here, maybe fifteen years ago. They built a stupa and set up a Buddhist prayer retreat. I visited it a couple of years ago. It's a pretty big dome. If it's still standing it should be easy to spot."

Peter marked the approximate location of the stupa and calculated a set of coordinates. "They abandoned it six or eight years ago, and the road's in terrible shape. There was a clearing at the end of the road, next to a ravine. A good place for us to land…. I hope."

Maria looked at the map. "How the hell do we get from there to the airport? And what do we do with the two bodies?"

"We'll have to depend on Saul's contact to get to the airport." Peter looked at the two bodies in front of them. "As for Teunis and Rahmat, they have to disappear, permanently."

"What about the helicopter? How does that disappear?"

"I've got a couple of ideas."

Peter looked at his watch. "I'll get the satellite phone out of my backpack. Time to start yelling for help."

When he returned with the telephone, Peter looked up the number for Watson's cell phone and called him.

"MacDonough."

"This is Peter. Can you get to a secure telephone?"

"Yes."

"What's the number?"

Watson gave him the number. "I can pick up right now."

"Okay." Peter disconnected and called back immediately.

"MacDonough."

"This is Peter again. We've got a problem. IndoGold's geologist and the Indonesian, military pilot, landed the helicopter on the way out to show us another gold property."

"And?"

"They tried to kill us." Peter paused. "They're both dead."

"You're both okay?"

"We're fine, but we have to get out of here, out of Manado, and out of Indonesia. I think these two bodies have to disappear. I'd like to make the helicopter disappear. And two people named Peter and Maria would like to disappear, at least for the time being. Other than that, everything's just great."

"Where the hell are you?" Watson asked.

"We're in the middle of the jungle in the middle of the northern arm of Sulawesi. What I want to know… Can you call in the US air cavalry from some convenient carrier group to come and get us?"

"I doubt it, but I can check. I'll have to call someone on another line."

Who does he call to answer that question? Peter wondered.

"He's checking, Maria. He's not optimistic."

They waited in silence.

"Peter?"

"Yes. I'm still here."

"We've got nothing," Watson said.

"So, no convenient helicopter on a ship offshore of this tropical paradise?"

"No such luck. Maybe in three or four days, but we don't really want to get you out of Indonesia that way. If we're caught doing it, we could be in serious trouble. So, can you tell me exactly where you are?"

Peter covered the mouthpiece of the phone. Turning to Maria he said, "He thinks they might have something in three or four days. I vote for not hanging around."

"Sounds reasonable," she said.

Peter turned back to the telephone. "Look, Watson, I don't think we can wait for three or four days. Stay at this number for a while, maybe an hour or two. There may be another way. We might be able to get to Jakarta tonight or tomorrow, traveling under different names."

"How do you get out of the jungle?"

"We should be able to handle that," Peter said.

"You plan to use the passports I gave you?"

"No."

"Shit. Be careful. Being caught with a bad false passport is not pleasant."

"Just stay put, Watson. If this works, you'll just have to get us a hotel room, in a different Jakarta hotel than last time, and get us out of Jakarta tonight if possible."

Peter ended the call before Watson had a chance to object. He studied the topographic map, where he had plotted the location of the stupa. *It's the best I can do.* He called the number for Saul's contact in Jakarta.

When a man's voice answered, Peter said, "I seek the golden star of David."

"It will be found on an island nation," the man responded. "What do you need?"

Peter outlined the situation.

"I have someone in Manado with a vehicle. Can you get to an isolated spot, close to a seldom-used road?"

"I'm not really familiar with the Manado area, but there was a group from California that built a stupa about fifteen kilometers east and a bit south of the city. It was abandoned when I saw it, about two years ago. You know it?"

"Yes."

"The road was in terrible shape when I was on it last, but it goes another kilometer past the stupa to a clearing beside a ravine. If I can, I'll land in that clearing. If not, somewhere closer to the stupa."

"Someone will meet you there," the man said.

"Have them bring two five-gallon cans of gasoline."

"It will be done."

"How will I know your man?" Peter asked.

"It's a woman. Use the same recognition code."

"I'll try to be there in maybe an hour and a half."

"Anything else you need?"

"That's it for now."

"Good."

The man disconnected.

Peter took a deep breath. "Well, nothing quite like trusting someone you've never met." He looked at Maria. "Let's drag the bodies to the river."

The pilot was easy. Teunis was not.

"We have to drag them into the river." Peter removed his boots and pants. "No sense traveling in wet clothes." Maria did the same.

"This will work?" Maria asked.

"It should. This whole scene needs to disappear, bodies, weapons, helicopter. The river's convenient for the first two."

Peter searched the two bodies for wallets and identification. The pilot had his name on his uniform. Peter cut it off. He put the wallets into one of the pockets of his field vest. "Let's start with Teunis," he said.

They grabbed Teunis' body by the legs and pulled him into the river. Once the current caught the body, they let it go. It turned several times before it floated out of sight and over a waterfall. Rahmat did not float, but the current carried him away along the bottom of the river.

"The river and the jungle beasties should take care of the bodies," Peter said. He turned and walked to the shore. They dried off with a couple of shirts from the duffel bag.

"Keep your little pistol for now," Peter said. "I'll wipe down mine and toss it and the other two into the river. I'll clean up the blood-soaked sand, but after that we'd better get going."

Fifteen minutes later, Peter looked around. *I think that's everything.* He joined Maria back at the helicopter. He pulled a pair of gloves out of his backpack. "I don't want my fingerprints on the controls for this puppy."

The pilot's helmet was much too small, and Peter exchanged it for one of the headsets they had used in the back seat.

In the helicopter, Peter plugged into the intercom system and said, "Put the headphones on that Teunis was using. If this next bit works, we might be home free."

He latched his flight harness. "You said you wanted to fly with me on my first solo flight. You're on my second."

"Just fly the damn thing."

"Yes ma'am."

Peter turned his full attention to the helicopter. He breathed a sigh of relief when it actually started, and a second when the engine and rotor blades reached operational speed. He smiled at Maria. "We'll be fine," he said over the intercom.

"Oh, I'm feeling better already. We killed two guys. We threw their bodies into the river. We're stealing a military helicopter. Sneaking out of the country on a bogus passport should be a piece of cake."

Peter smiled.

Plenty of fuel. He turned off the emergency beacon. He didn't want that to go off under any circumstances. He turned off the radar transponder and the radio.

"Now we should be radio silent and radar invisible," he said.

Peter felt sweat running down his back. The coordinates he'd marked on the map agreed with what he saw on the GPS in the helicopter. He punched in his estimated coordinates for the stupa, and he took a deep breath.

He rested his hands lightly on the cyclic and the collective, and his feet on the pedals. He made slight movements with the pedals, which controlled the tail rotor, and the cyclic, that controlled the angle of attack of the main blades and direction of movement of the helicopter.

"Everything feels good," he said.

He looked around. Plenty of room. He pulled up on the collective, increasing the bite of the main blades into the hot and humid jungle air, and, with a few adjustments to the pedals and the cyclic, they were airborne. He pulled up a bit more on the collective, increasing the angle of the main blades, and they rose out of the valley. "Don't expect a lot of conversation from me."

Maria remained silent, staring straight ahead.

Once out of the valley, the thick haze closed in. *The haze hides us, which is nice, but I can't see a damn thing. Thank God for GPS.* He used the compass to aim for his destination.

"I'll be a little wobbly," he said. "Hard to see the horizon."

Maria looked at him, but she said nothing.

Peter flew slowly and tentatively, but after a bit he began to relax. The GPS showed the distance to the stupa slowly growing smaller.

He glanced at Maria. She was sitting completely rigid, staring straight ahead.

"Try to relax," he said. "I'm pretty sure we'll make it."

"Stop talking."

Peter laughed.

Chapter 18

The smoky haze grew thicker as they flew about fifty feet above the tallest trees and approached the coordinates for the stupa.

"We're getting close," Peter said. "Watch for that damn stupa. It was a pretty large dome. Who knows what shape it's in now."

He slowed down.

"Is that it ahead?" he asked.

"Looks like it," Maria answered.

Peter banked to the right and dropped down even closer to the tops of the trees. "That's it. Looks like the dome's falling apart. I'll turn south and follow the little track. Should take us to the clearing by the ravine."

Maria leaned forward. "I don't see anyone coming up the track."

"I'm not sure what we do next if she doesn't show."

Peter followed the crude and partially overgrown dirt road until he came to a grassy clearing next to a small, rocky ravine. The road appeared to end at the clearing, but Peter flew a bit farther south to make sure.

"I think they used the ravine as a garbage dump," Peter said.

"Not a very Buddhist action if you ask me."

Peter approached a landing on the very edge of the ravine. He set down with the front of the skids hanging precariously out over the edge of the small, rocky cliff. He felt the sweat drip off his chin.

"What the hell are you doing?" Maria asked.

"Hold that thought," Peter replied. He gradually lowered the collective. The helicopter hesitated before it started to pitch forward. Peter quickly pulled up on the collective. With a delicate movement of the cyclic, he backed up about a foot.

This time the helicopter seemed to settle solidly at the edge of the cliff.

Peter waited to make sure.

"Okay," he said. "I'm going to keep the power on. You get out. Get our baggage out of the back. See if you can drag the sample chest out of the cargo basket. I don't want to shut down until we've got everything off this thing."

"What are you going to do?" Maria asked as she opened her door.

"Don't worry. I'm not planning to go over the edge with the helicopter."

Maria stepped out.

Peter focused on the stability of the helicopter.

"Got everything," Maria shouted a few minutes later.

"Good. Now get away from this machine."

Peter lowered the collective completely. The helicopter settled firmly on the ground. He began to shut it down.

Sooner the better, he thought. *Helicopters always draw crowds. All I want to see is one woman.*

When he stopped the rotors and the helicopter was finally quiet, the pain in his shoulders registered for the first time.

God I'm tense.

He took a moment to consciously try to relax.

Peter stepped out of the helicopter. It was strange to suddenly hear the noises of the jungle. The only sound from the helicopter was the normal snapping and popping as the engine and exhaust system cooled. He took a few deep breaths and stretched.

"Nobody yet," Maria said.

Peter looked at his watch. "We're about fifteen minutes early. I'll put off the panic mode for a while."

He looked around the clearing. "Let's pull the baggage and the sample chest a little farther away from the helicopter and throw these vests into the duffel bag." Peter put the contents of the vest in his backpack, and Maria put her small pistol in a day pack that doubled as a purse.

There wasn't much to say as they waited.

Now I am getting anxious, Peter thought after twenty minutes had passed.

"I think I hear something," Maria said.

"Yeah. Me too."

The sound grew louder, until a small, black pickup truck bounced into the clearing. Peter could just see the top of the driver's head.

It looks like a child, he thought.

The truck stopped quite close to the helicopter, and a slim, dark-skinned woman stepped out, a clove cigarette clamped firmly in her mouth. She smiled tentatively at Peter and Maria.

Peter stepped up to her and said, "I seek the golden star of David."

"It will be found on an island nation," she replied, her smile broader now. "You can call me Atin."

Atin appeared somewhat amused by the situation. "The gasoline cans are in the back."

So far, so good, Peter thought. "Thanks, Atin. I'll need them in a few minutes. First, we need to tip the helicopter over the cliff. We may need the truck to give it a push."

"That's how you make it disappear?" Maria sounded unconvinced.

"First step. This is as good a place as any to start the disappearing process."

The three of them gathered at the back of the helicopter. "All we need to do is rock this thing up and down," Peter said. "Hopefully I've set it close enough to the edge that if we get the tail up high enough it'll slide over the edge."

Atin looked at him as if he were crazy, but she said nothing.

After a few tries, they coordinated their efforts and the helicopter started to swing up and down. On the fifth oscillation, it hung in the air, as if it were questioning its own future. Slowly, it continued to tilt forward. In a tumbling, crunching slide, it crashed down to the bottom of the ravine.

That's a lot less noise than I expected, Peter thought.

"Now to finish the job." Peter turned to Atin. "Do you have a book of matches I can have?" She nodded and gave them to him.

Peter grabbed the two cans of gasoline. "Stay back from the edge of the ravine. Don't even look over." He looked at the truck. "You might move the truck back a bit."

He stepped over the edge of the ravine, sliding down the loose rocks on the steep slope. Peter was pleased to see the lack of vegetation on the side of the ravine.

Should work.

The helicopter lay on its side. Some fuel had already leaked out. *It doesn't look much like a crash*, he thought. *Maybe this'll help it along.*

As he slid to a stop by the helicopter, he opened a damaged front door. He took the wallets for Teunis and the pilot out of his pockets and emptied the identification and credit cards into the passenger compartment of the helicopter. He soaked the seats in the front part of the cabin with gasoline and made sure the identification and credit cards were in a little pool of gasoline.

He stood back for a moment. *Good thing it's cooled off. Less chance of a premature explosion.*

The rear door was more badly damaged, but he still managed to force it open. He dropped in the empty wallets and soaked them and the seats. He poured some gasoline on the tail and fuselage and underneath the helicopter.

He collected both cans and walked about twenty-five feet away, leaving a trail of gasoline behind him. He stepped back ten more feet, lit a match, then lit the whole book of matches and threw it at the trail of gasoline-soaked soil and rocks.

Peter scrambled away from the helicopter along the rocky bottom of the ravine as the gasoline ignited with a small "whump" of an explosion. Peter felt the force and heat on his back. He stopped and turned around.

"Impressive."

Peter climbed up and out of the ravine and made his way back to the truck. He turned as he heard another explosion when the aviation fuel ignited.

"Jesus," Maria said. "I was a little worried about you."

"Safe and sound," Peter said and threw the empty gasoline cans into the back of the truck.

The fire was smokier now with the addition of jet fuel. He saw that Maria and Atin had loaded the samples and their baggage.

"Let's get out of here. The haze should hide the fire, but I don't want to hang around."

"You're going to the airport?" Atin asked.

"Yes," Peter said, "but stop down the road before we get to any settled areas. I need to make a telephone call, and I don't want anybody listening."

They bounced down the poor excuse for a road, banging against each other in the cab of the small pickup. Peter looked back as they passed the half-collapsed stupa. Already the haze hid the smoke from the fire.

"Won't the searchers find the helicopter pretty quickly?" Maria asked.

"Burned like that, it won't be easy to spot from the air, and the government has no idea of where it is. This is well off the flight path from the camp to the airport. I'm counting on local junk pickers chopping it up and selling it." He turned to the driver. "I think it'll disappear, don't you?"

"Absolutely."

After another quarter mile of bouncing, Atin stopped and said, "This is a good place for you to make your call."

"Okay. Come with me, Maria." Peter stepped out of the truck and walked about one hundred feet back along the rough track.

"You calling Watson again?"

"Yeah, but first you need this." He handed her a travel-worn passport along with the credit cards and driver's license. "You are now Mary Manson, courtesy of Saul. It has all the right stamps, and the home address is 185 Ferris Road in Toronto, where you grew up. Should be easy."

Maria looked at the passport. "You never told me you had this."

"Didn't think we needed it. It's from when he borrowed our passports that night in Washington. We have a choice, but right now I think it's best to use Saul's passports, and his false identity, rather than Watson's.... I'm not entirely sure why I say that. Maybe because Saul seems to be more thorough."

"Well, I agree we don't want to be Peter and Maria right now."

"Yes." Peter punched a number into the satellite telephone. "Now a quick call to Watson." He pulled his own Mossad passport out of his pocket. *Christ, what a choice for a name.*

"Hello. What's going on?"

He sounds really impatient, Peter thought.

"The party expects to arrive on the 4:15 flight from Manado. It stops at Makassar and gets in at 6:35. The names are Charles and Mary Manson. Have one of your people meet the party at the airport. Get them on a flight to Singapore tonight, if you can."

"Done. I will meet them."

Peter started to respond, but he realized Watson had already disconnected. "That was quick."

"Is your name on your passport really Charles Manson?"

"Dumb, right? Just call me Charlie."

Peter stopped at the back of the truck and opened the metal chest. "We need to change identities. Give me your Maria passport and all your Maria identification. Replace it with the Manson stuff."

Peter made the shift of identities in his wallet. He took all the Peter and Maria identification and credit cards, put them in a plastic bag, and placed them in the center of one of the weathered rock samples. "Best I can do," he said with a shrug. "At least the x-ray won't see them."

"Now, let's sign the credit cards." Peter laughed. "I feel like a new man."

"Let's head to the airport," Peter said as they got back into the truck. Turning to Maria he said, "You still have that little pistol, right?"

"It's in my day pack."

"Give it to our driver. She can probably use it."

Atin smiled as she pocketed the small pistol and the extra clip of ammunition. "You could take it with you," she said. "The x-ray machine and magnetometer never work at the Manado airport."

"No thanks. I want to be in Singapore tonight, not in an Indonesian jail. All we have to do is find some room on the flight." He looked at Maria. "It shouldn't be all that hard."

"I do know of two people who won't show up for the flight," Maria said.

"Yeah. I just hope the police aren't waiting at the airport for that missing couple to check in with them."

Maria nodded. "Me, too."

Chapter 19

Atin pulled into the parking area at the airport. "I won't go into the terminal with you. Too many people know me." She maneuvered close to the terminal but behind two rows of parked cars.

"This will work," Peter said.

"Please be quick," Atin said.

Peter and Maria got out of the truck and pulled the baggage and the chest out of the back. Peter hit the back of the truck and waved. Atin was gone before they could even pick up the luggage.

"I wonder what makes her so nervous about the airport," Maria said.

"Probably the same reason I'm nervous. Too many police."

With their baggage in hand, they went to the Garuda desk and handed their Manson passports to the lady behind the counter.

"Any space on the 4:15 flight to Jakarta?" Peter asked.

"I'm sorry sir," the agent said. "The only space available is in First Class. I have two adjacent, First Class seats. Would you like them?"

"Yes, please."

"And how much baggage do you have?"

"These three bags. The metal chest is heavy."

By moving some samples from the chest to the backpack, they lowered the weight of the chest to under the maximum of 70 pounds. Peter threw the locks inside and secured it with carabiners, as the agent requested. All the adjustments took a while, but eventually Charles and Mary Manson, and their baggage, were checked in for the 4:15 flight.

"That was a little annoying," Peter said as they sat at a table in the coffee shop. "If someone's watching for a geologist and his wife, I might as well have held up a big sign saying 'Here we are!'"

"The police don't seem to have any interest," Maria said.

"Low level guys." Peter watched a man he had noticed earlier. "See that guy standing against the wall? The one with the little white bandage on his left hand?"

"Blue shirt and black pants, just like almost every Indonesian man in the terminal, except that he seems to be attached to us?"

Peter smiled. "Yeah. That's the one. The only reason I've been able to keep track of him is the little bandage on his hand. He was at the check-in. Right behind us. He could have moved when we took so long, but he didn't."

"He's watching us, but he's trying not to make it too obvious," she said.

Peter looked at his watch. "We've got almost two hours. You want to test him?"

"What do you have in mind?"

"Walk around a bit. See if he follows us."

"He might not, if he's good. He knows we have to go through security soon."

"Let's see," Peter said.

They finished their coffee and began a slow walk around the terminal. They stopped at the few small shops. Bandage, as they called the man, did not move, except to turn so he could follow their movements.

"Let's step outside," Maria said.

No more than ten seconds after stepping out of the terminal, Peter looked down the walkway. "Well look at that, Bandage moved."

"That's pretty obvious," Maria said.

"Let's go back to the coffee shop."

Thirty minutes later, when they headed through security, Bandage was close behind. On the plane, he sat two rows in front of them, across the aisle.

As the plane descended through the thick haze to land at Makassar, Peter showed Maria a photograph of Borobudur from the airline magazine. "This is the biggest Buddhist temple complex in the world. Ninth century and in amazing shape. Too bad we can't visit it."

"When will we be able to relax?" she asked.

"Not right away."

"I feel like nobody's telling us anything. We have no idea of what to expect around the next corner."

"I agree."

"Is there anyone you trust?" Maria asked.

"Not really."

"What do we do?"

"We stay on high alert. We get through this, and then we hide," he said.

"Hide? For how long?"

"I have no idea."

Peter grimaced at the exceptionally hard landing at Makassar. They didn't get off the plane, but he got up to use the bathroom. Bandage was sending a text message, and he didn't look up.

When they took off for the second leg to Jakarta, Maria turned to Peter. "So tell me, what's our immediate plan?"

"Probably shouldn't talk about it in the plane. We'll see what Watson has to say, and Saul. We don't have to hurry back to Canada."

"I don't think Canada wants us back right away," she said.

"I was thinking we might stay a few days in Tokyo and take a trip down to Kyoto. I think you'd like Kyoto. You haven't been there, have you?"

"Never spent any time in Japan."

"Kyoto is a special place," Peter said softly. "I love the temple grounds, simple, beautiful. Then there's the Philosopher's Path. It's wonderful."

Though the Garuda flights tended to be erratic, their arrival at Jakarta was delayed by only a few minutes. Peter and Maria made their way through the normal noise and confusion of the Jakarta airport. Watson stood against the wall opposite the exit from the concourse.

Peter was reminded again of Watson's economy of motion. *He expects the world to come to him.* Peter plowed his way through the crowd with Maria close behind him.

Watson shook their hands. "You two look pretty good, considering our last conversation."

"I don't think we're entirely alone," Peter said.

Watson raised his eyebrows. "Let's head to the baggage claim area. Was the plane full?"

"Pretty much," Maria said. "Fortunately, they did have two first class seats."

"Do you have a hotel for us?" Peter asked.

"I booked you into a room at the FM7 Resort Hotel. It's right at the airport. I couldn't get you on a flight tonight. Your flight leaves tomorrow at 7:55 AM. It's the best I could do."

"I was afraid of that," Peter said.

"Just for your information, I've checked. Charles and Mary are not on any watch list."

"Hopefully it'll stay that way," Maria said.

As they waited for their luggage, Peter looked around at the crowd. Bandage was looking at them, but he quickly looked away.

"Watson," Peter said, "you see that Indonesian guy, dark blue shirt, black pants? He's standing against the opposite wall. He's not moving. Not with anyone. He has a small white bandage on his left hand. We've been calling him Bandage."

Watson took a moment to scan the crowd. "Yes. I see him. What about him?"

"He's been shadowing us, watching us, starting at the Manado airport. He was on the plane with us, and I think he's still watching us."

Watson looked at Bandage. "I think you have an overly active imagination."

"Don't do that," Peter said.

"Okay, but I'm just telling you what I think."

"You're outnumbered two to one," Maria said.

Once their bags arrived, Watson called the embassy driver. He stopped at the curb a few minutes later. Peter and Maria loaded their bags, and the driver headed to the hotel.

They checked in, showered, changed clothes, and joined Watson at a corner table in the bar off the lobby.

"This is too public for the conversation I really want to have," Watson said, "but I can deal with a few simple issues." He handed them each an envelope.

"I have reservations for you, Business Class, Singapore Air, tomorrow at 7:55 AM. There's also a hotel reservation at the Crowne Plaza at the

Changi airport in Singapore. Two nights if you need them. You're on your own to get back to Canada, or wherever you want to end up."

"Sounds like you're sick of us," Maria said.

"You're supposed to be working for Saul, not me. I'm bailing you out in Indonesia, but it's up to Saul after this."

"Seems to me we signed on with you," Maria said.

"And you agreed to work for Saul."

"Not without your backup," Peter said.

"I'm there, but I'm behind Saul, not in front of him."

"I told Peter that when it got tough you'd abandon us."

Watson looked at Maria. "If you call this abandonment, you're living in a strange world."

"Look, Watson," Peter said, "we had to make choices, if we were going to survive. And we aren't out of the shit yet. Don't get all pissed off at us just because we didn't do everything your way. Your offer wasn't particularly attractive."

Watson was silent for a moment. "Okay. I take your point, but Saul is still your primary contact, particularly after some of the choices you've made. I can help. I can help you right now, but I can't be standing beside you all the time."

All three of them nursed their drinks in silence for a while.

"We were thinking of stopping in Tokyo for a couple of days," Peter said. "I'd like spend a day in Kyoto with Mary."

Watson shook his head. "I wouldn't, if I were you."

"I suspect we're safer in Japan than we are in Canada," Peter said.

"Hell, they don't even want us in Canada," Maria said.

"Still, lots of unknowns in Japan," Watson said. "The guy you met up with in your room before you went to Endang was Japanese."

Peter frowned. "That's interesting. What's the connection?"

"Don't really know. Interpol says he's some sort of hit man for a Japanese yakuza, a mobster named Akihiko Uehara. I have no idea of why he was here, but it suggests you have some real risks in Japan. If you're going to stay in Tokyo, tell Saul. He's already there."

The conversation stalled as all three of them watched Bandage come into the bar and sit at a nearby table.

Peter scratched his chin. "Let's go up to our room. We can talk there."

"Probably a good idea," Watson said.

"I don't know about you two, but I'm going to need dinner pretty soon," Maria said. "I've had nothing to eat since breakfast."

Watson stood up. "Let's have a quick talk in your room. Then we can come down to the restaurant."

The lobby was nearly empty. Bandage stayed in the bar.

When they got to the room they sat at a small, round table by the window. The room was decorated with completely inoffensive photographs of temples and gardens, hung on the uniformly beige walls.

"I think hotels like this buy their decorations by the container load," Peter said.

"Perhaps you can tell me what happened today," Watson said.

"It's a pretty simple story." Peter gave a quick summary of the day. By the time he finished, Watson was leaning back in his chair with his eyes closed.

"I didn't know you could fly a helicopter," Watson said.

"Maybe you need to do more thorough background checks on the people you hire."

Watson opened his eyes. "You may be right.... They will do a thorough search for the helicopter. After all, it's military. And the bodies, too."

"It's a big jungle out there," Peter said. "The critters will take care of the bodies. They'll never be found."

"But the helicopter's another matter. The jungle animals can't eat that," Watson said.

"It's off the normal flight path by a few miles," Peter said. "Well past the airport and probably nowhere anyone would be looking. Besides, there won't be much left of it, and what there is will be very hard to spot from the air."

"You must have left a pretty good burned spot."

"That isn't unique, and it won't last long. We were lucky. There was nobody around, but I'll bet junk pickers will pick what's left to pieces, and the government will never find anything."

Watson was silent for a moment. "You seem to have thought of everything."

"I'm sure we haven't," Maria said, "and Bandage is a reminder. But for the moment a helicopter, a pilot, and three passengers have disappeared without a trace. It'd be nice if it could stay that way for at least a couple of days."

"It probably will," Watson said, "and so far, you haven't attracted any attention. I assume you're using passports supplied by Saul?"

"Yes," Peter answered.

"Why did you use them rather than the ones I provided?"

"I don't know. It just seemed like a good idea at the time."

"Could you let me see them? I'd like to check their quality." Watson smiled slightly. "It's a free service."

Peter and Maria handed the Manson passports to Watson, who leafed through them, looking closely at some of the stamps, before he handed them back.

"The Mossad does good work," he said. "You shouldn't have any problem with them, so long as they got you into the critical computer databases as well. You're definitely in the Indonesia database."

"What about Singapore or Tokyo?" Maria asked.

"And what about Canada and the United States?" Peter asked.

"I'd advise you to use either your actual passports or the ones I gave you when you're leaving Singapore," Watson said. "They're both in the US database with a note to expedite passage."

"What the hell does that mean?" Peter asked.

"It means that when they put your passport into the computer a message tells the customs agent to let you through with no questions."

"Isn't there a problem with not having any entry stamp for Singapore?" Maria asked.

"If you give them to me, I can provide that. You'll be fine after Singapore, as long as you keep using the same passport."

"The Peter and Maria passports are inside one of the samples in the chest, but I'll get the Madeaux passports from my briefcase."

"Another identity I didn't know about," Maria said. "How many more do you have?"

"That's it," Peter said with a small smile. He handed them to Watson. "Now let's go down and get something to eat."

"About those samples," Watson said. "I want to get them to the embassy and ship them under diplomatic seal. I'd like to get them tonight if possible."

"They're pretty well locked up in that chest," Peter said.

"What I'm worried about is someone taking the whole chest."

"Well, go downstairs and get a table then. I'll get the Peter and Maria passports out of the samples and join you in a few minutes."

Peter watched as Watson and Maria left the room. He listened to the door latch behind them.

Shit! Watson's washing his hands. He's abandoning us.

Peter felt a growing sense of deep fatigue. *It's not just today. It's day after day. How long does it go on?*

He went to the chest and unlocked it. He pulled at the sample bags until he found the one he wanted, untied it, and pulled out the plastic bag with their passports and various identification and credit cards. Then he added the samples from his backpack to those in the chest and locked it again.

Peter stood up. *Well buddy, you've done what Watson wants, and you're on your own again. Saul better be good. Got to remind them. They don't have my report.*

Chapter 20

Irish was a tall but thin man. *I'd be better off shorter and thinner*, he thought as he lay in the heating duct. He had changed his clothes in the men's room. Then he had hoisted himself, a bag, and a briefcase into the duct above the stall before the Swiss International Bank closed for the day.

He checked his watch. Seven hours. He lowered himself to the floor, replaced the vent cover, and stood beside the door.

He was dressed in a skin-tight, black body suit, a black hood and black gloves. The body suit left no part of his anatomy to the viewer's imagination, but only his eyes were uncovered. Irish shivered slightly. He waited. He was good at waiting.

Just before midnight he heard steps in the hall. He transferred the weighted, rubber club to his right hand.

The door opened with a faint chattering noise. It hid Irish. As it closed, the guard turned and saw him.

Irish brought the club down on the guard's head with a sharp crack. The guard grunted and collapsed onto the tile floor.

Irish leaned down and checked the man's pulse. It was strong. *Perfect. No need to kill him.*

He stepped up onto the toilet, reopened the duct, and pulled out his briefcase and a small bag. Opening the bag, he removed several short lengths of nylon rope and bound the guard's hands and feet. He covered the guard's eyes with a black blindfold and taped his mouth shut.

Irish put on a white shirt, black tie, and a black suit over his body suit. He removed his hood. He did a quick check. His clothing matched the guard's clothing almost exactly. Then he donned a pair of soft-soled shoes and picked up the guard's hat. The hat was slightly large for him.

It will work.

Irish looked down as the guard began to regain consciousness and struggled against the ropes. "Quiet, man. Struggling will do you no good." The guard was still. "You'll have a lush bump on your head, man, but you'll live."

Irish screwed the cover back onto the vent. He placed several small packages from the briefcase in his pockets. He took a larger, padded package from his bag, stuffed it under his shirt, and buckled his belt and pants over it. His shape was now similar to that of the guard. He put his gloves in his pocket.

Irish left his briefcase and bag, opened the door with a paper towel, and stepped into the hall. He kept his gaze lowered to hide most of his face from the security camera located in the hall closer to the guard's desk. He had darkened his skin and died his light blond hair a dark brown.

Your guard is returning to his station.

Irish walked slowly to the guard's desk. He put his gloves on again and checked the motion detectors. Off. He clicked off the cameras aimed at the main floor and the vaults. There were no other indoor video cameras except for one that showed part of the hallway between the guard station and the men's room. He left that camera on, but he turned off the outside camera that covered the seldom-used side entry.

Terrible security.

He almost laughed at the bank's misplaced confidence in stone and mortar.

He crossed the main floor of the bank to the stairwell and glided softly down the stairs to the level of the cash and client vaults. The cash vault, with its massive door and timed locking mechanism, tempted him.

Complicated, but I could do it.

He turned to the heavy steel entrance door to the client vaults. It had a simple combination lock. He removed the package from under his shirt and adjusted his belt. He took a few tools out of the package and changed his gloves to a set of surgical gloves. He held a stethoscope to the door, next to the dial. He turned the dial slowly, listening. He remembered the lock from before, but he would take no shortcuts. After thirty minutes he replaced his tools and opened the door.

In the dim light he could see a hallway in front of him, and he reached with his gloved left hand for the light switch on the inside wall. Six lights illuminated the hallway, which was painted light gray. A series of dark gray steel doors punctuated the left side of the hallway. On the right there was only one, large steel door.

Easy.

It was as he remembered. The locks were simple double-key locks, like those found in most safe deposit vaults. The doors to the left, for storage of valuables and papers for important clients, had one set of two locks. The large door on the right had three sets of double-keyed locks.

Annoying.

He set to work with his picks on the three sets of locks on the large door. Each lock, when he finally turned it, made a soft squeal of protest. After thirty-five minutes he opened the last set of locks and pulled the door open. He faced a Chinese folding screen that discretely hid the contents of the vault. A small, antique Persian rug covered the floor immediately in front of the screen.

He found the light switch and turned on the lights. He pulled the heavy door closed, but left it unlocked. When he stepped around the screen, he stopped, puzzled. Heavy, dusty, tan canvas tarps formed a seven-foot wall within the vault. They were anchored to the floor.

Irish pressed his gloved hand against the tarp. He shook his head. He couldn't be sure. He walked down the side of the vault, occasionally rubbing against the white, smooth plaster wall. He stopped where two tarps overlapped and were laced together with a rope.

He looked back and saw that he had left faint footprints in the dust on the floor. *I must remember to destroy these shoes.*

He bent down and untied the rope at the floor and pulled the tarps apart. He smiled.

The gold bars in front of him glistened in the low light of the bare bulbs in the vault. He continued to unlace the tarps until he got to the top of the pile. He pulled down six of the bars, examined each one, and laid them on the floor.

Each bar carried the mark of the refiner, in this case SIR. Each was stamped .9999, indicating an international standard purity of 99.99 percent pure gold.

Irish returned to the door and retrieved a small scale and a tape measure from the package he had carried under his belt. Seven inches long, a little over three and one-half inches wide, and one and three-quarters inches thick. Each one weighed very close to 400 troy ounces, a little over 27 pounds. *International standard.*

He measured the height of the stack, and he paced off the length and width. He did a quick calculation. He whistled, and he did the calculation again. *More gold here than in most central banks.*

He spent a little less than an hour in the vault. He examined and weighed selected gold bars at several other points along the pile, carefully replacing the bars and lacing up the tarps.

He opened a small filing cabinet in one corner.

That's curious.

He pulled out the only thing in the cabinet, an old folder with two sheets of yellowing and brittle paper. He photographed the sheets of paper. He did not read them.

He took a few minutes to examine a large steel plate, bolted to the wall at the far end of the vault. Beside it, on the wall, was a black button in a brass plate, like a call button for an old elevator.

An elevator? In a bank vault? Irish nodded. *Of course.*

Irish made one last circuit around the vault to make sure he had collected all his tools and had left everything as he had found it. Then he exited. He picked up the padded package, returned the scale and tape measure, and put it back under his shirt.

He relocked the door to the vault, shut and locked the main door at the end of the hallway, and returned the picks to his pocket.

Just over two hours after he had left the men's room, Irish returned to check on the guard. He kneeled down beside him and placed the man's hat back on the floor. Irish unbuckled the guard's belt and unzipped his pants. The man grunted and moved, as much as he could, in protest.

"Stop moving, or I'll hit you again. I'm giving you an injection. You'll be fine, but you'll sleep."

And you won't remember anything.

Irish pulled a syringe out of his bag. He rubbed a small alcohol swab over the guard's inner thigh and jabbed him with the needle. He zipped up the man's pants and rebuckled his belt.

Irish stood watching the guard until the man's breathing slowed and he was no longer moving or groaning. Then Irish untied the man's legs and hands, removed the tape over his mouth, and removed the blindfold. The guard lay still, eyes closed, breathing in a slow, steady rhythm.

"Sleep well, chum."

Irish collected his bag and briefcase. He picked up all the debris and checked that he had properly replaced the cover over the ventilation duct.

At the side door, Irish put on a hat he retrieved from his bag. He exited into an alley on the other side of the bank from the vaults. There was no video record of his exit.

Jan Kwak, Chairman and majority owner of the Swiss International Bank, sat in his office. He was a large man, not obese, but years of good living had added some extra pounds to his six-foot frame. Jan had what some call a "presence." He could intimidate most people without saying a word.

The office was meant to impress. Heavy red drapes framed the tall windows, and two small Rembrandts hung on the walnut-paneled wall to Jan's left. A painting of his father hung beside the door.

Jan sat in his black chair, behind his desk, an antique, carved Italian monster. Karl Westra, his aging chief teller, sat across from him.

"You found nothing missing?" Jan asked.

"Absolutely nothing, and everything was locked tight, just as it should be."

"But three video cameras were turned off."

"The guard must have done it for some reason," Karl said, "but he doesn't remember a damn thing. The fall, when he hit his head, must have given him amnesia. It sure put him to sleep for the night."

Jan breathed deeply. "I don't think he fell. Stand beside me. I want to show you something."

Jan pulled up the night's video record from the hallway on his laptop. "Watch this closely. This is the guard going to the bathroom. Look at his wrists. His shirt does not show." Jan skipped forward in the recording to where the guard returned from the bathroom. "You see? The cuff of his shirt is certainly visible now."

"I didn't notice that, but it's not much to go on."

"His shirt cuffs didn't show below his suit jacket when we found him this morning. Besides, this man does not walk like our guard," Jan continued.

"Well, if it isn't the guard, who is it? And if he didn't take anything, why was he here?"

"There are footprints in the great vault."

Karl raised his eyebrows. "You're joking."

"I am absolutely serious. We know what he stole, don't we? He stole something that could destroy this bank and all of us with it."

"Who is he?"

"Does it matter?" Jan asked.

"No. Probably not."

Karl returned to his seat. "What do we do?"

"We sure as hell don't call the police." Jan rubbed his chin. "Uehara has to start moving the gold now."

"It'll take a year. It's over three thousand metric tonnes. We have to fix the freight elevator. He has to find reliable people. Nobody can know what we're doing, and the damn thing is it's just one truck-load at a time."

"He has to start right now, and the ten years he proposes is too long." Jan paused. "For the cut he's getting, he can find a way."

They sat in silence for half a minute. "You'll call him?" Karl asked.

"I'll call him tomorrow morning." Jan managed a somewhat rueful smile. "If we pull this off, when I sell the bank you'll be a very wealthy man."

"And if we don't pull it off, we'll both be paupers in prison."

"Most likely."

"I'll get back to work, then." With a shrug, Karl stood, turned and left the office.

Jan looked at the painting of his father. His father was in his fifties when he commissioned the portrait. *Damn you. You dealt with the Devil. Now I have to pay his bill.*

Chapter 21

Peter joined Watson and Maria in the dining room. He handed their original passports to Watson. "We'll get these back tonight?"

"No. I'll meet you here at the hotel at five in the morning. I'm checking in for the same flight to Singapore on my way to Washington. I'll have tickets tomorrow for David and Nancy Madeaux, and I've changed the hotel reservations."

"And what do we do about our buddy, who's sitting at a table at the other end of the dining room?"

Watson glanced at Bandage and turned back to Peter. "Yes. Well, I'm beginning to agree with you. Let's see what I can do tomorrow."

"Okay," Peter said, and he picked up the menu. "Have you ordered?"

"Not yet. I should tell you. The embassy is sending a car to pick up the samples. Are they ready to go?"

"Yes, and to be honest I'll be happy to get rid of them. They make us more of a target. When will they be here?"

"Should be any time now."

"They have to go to a specific lab in Canada, and I have very specific instructions on how to handle them. I'll send all the instructions to you in an email."

"That should work," Watson said. "First we get them to Washington unharmed. There's a US military plane in Jakarta at the moment. They'll go directly to Alden Sage at the White House."

"It seems strange to send a pile of rocks to the White House," Maria said.

"A lot of strange things end up at the White House. The driver from the embassy will find us. One of you can lend him the key to your room or go up with him."

Peter put the menu down. "I can't provide any report until I have the assay results."

"Understood. Just get the report to Saul and me as soon as you can."

The embassy driver arrived a few minutes later. Peter took him to the room, checked to make sure there was nothing they needed in the chest, and gave the keys and combinations to the driver.

Peter made it back to the dining room just as the salad course arrived. The conversation was not particularly lively during the meal.

"Look, Watson, I know you didn't like me insisting you be here in Jakarta," Peter said, "but I'm not sure how we would have fared without your help."

"Thanks," Watson said. His phone beeped, and he picked it up and looked at it.

Shit! Peter took a deep breath. He waited. *I won't compete with his damn telephone.*

Watson looked up. "You were saying?"

"It's obvious you're pissed off about our exit from the camp. We had to make some really tough choices, fast, with almost no information. We're here. We're alive. Considering your background, I think you should appreciate that more than most."

Watson stared at Peter. "I won't second guess you, but I don't have to like all your decisions."

"Well, thanks for being here, and thanks for helping us get to Singapore."

Watson put his phone away. "I have to admit your reasons for having me here were valid."

"Thanks."

"Be ready to go at five tomorrow morning." Watson paused. "I have to leave you. I have to make a phone call from the embassy, which is a pain, considering the traffic this time of night. Actually, the traffic's awful most anytime in Jakarta."

"I think we're done anyway," Peter said. "If we have to be ready to go at five, I want to get to bed."

Watson pushed his chair back and got up. "All right. I'll see you tomorrow morning."

Peter watched him leave. "I don't know about you, Maria, but I'm a little annoyed with that man. I didn't figure him for a thin skin."

"I think I understand better now I've had some time to think about it," Maria said. "We took control out of his hands. He knows we did the right thing, but losing control is hard. You should understand that. Who knows, maybe we should have used his passports from the beginning."

"You're right, but it still annoys the hell out of me." Peter turned to Maria and smiled. "I'd still like to spend a couple of days in Japan. What do you think?"

"Watson thinks it's a bad idea."

"Hell, we're just Watson's tools. He doesn't care about us. He only cares about the results. If he really cared about us, we would have had serious security at the camp."

"People in his business have to accept collateral damage," Maria said flatly.

"I guess I'm tired of being disposable."

They sat in silence before Maria said, "Let's pay the bill and go to bed. It's been a long day."

"That's an understatement."

Peter watched Bandage look up and across the room at him.

Peter stared back at him.

Bandage looked down again and tapped a message into his telephone as he and Maria left the dining room.

Who the hell is he contacting, and what is he saying? Peter felt too tired to care.

As soon as Peter and Maria lay down in the bed, they each reached for the other. "How are you doing?" Maria asked.

"I'm good. I'm tired, but I'm good, as long as you're here."

"What are we going to do?"

"We've got one or two days in Singapore," Peter said. "No one should be able to find us. We've changed identities twice. We'll spend a couple of days in Japan, and then head back to Toronto."

"Canada won't be happy to see us back again, and I'm not sure I want to be there either."

"I've been thinking about that. I have a few ideas of how we can disappear for a while. Move back to Toronto later, different apartment, different identity."

"Sounds crazy," she said.

"True. Might work though. I do want Peter and Maria to reappear when the time is right."

Maria caressed him, and then she kissed him. "I wouldn't mind Peter remaining visible, right here, for a little while. I'd miss him if he disappeared completely."

Peter smiled in the darkness. "Suddenly I don't feel quite so tired."

"Peter?"

"Yes."

"Can you be really rough tonight?"

"That's a bit out of character for me."

"I know, but I want you to be an animal. I want to know you're really here."

"You're sure about that?"

"I'm sure. Don't stop, no matter what I say, or how much I struggle."

"Okay. But your safe word is 'Ontario', in case you need it."

God help us. I don't understand it, but I think we both need this tonight, Peter thought. *And I hope nobody's trying to sleep in the next room.*

Watson found his way back to the embassy. As the text message had told him, one of the agents from the Selective Service had flown to Jakarta with an envelope from Alden Sage, with instructions to hand deliver it, personally, to Watson. They met in the secure conference room.

"Hi," Watson said. "You have a package for me?"

"Sorry. I have to see identification."

Watson showed him his passport. "You do realize that in the business I'm in, identification is not particularly reliable?"

The man shrugged. "I know who you are, but it's all by the book, or my job is toast."

"You headed back on the military flight tonight?"

"Yes."

"I have a package for Alden Sage. It's the metal chest in that corner. I have to label it as a diplomatic pouch and give you the keys. Get it to Alden's office."

"How heavy is it?"

"It's about eighty pounds."

"Not a problem. I'll be heading out to the airport in about an hour."

"It'll be ready."

After he attached diplomatic seals to ensure the chest could not be opened without detection, and after he added a larger seal marking the chest as diplomatic baggage, he handed it over to the agent.

Watson returned to the conference room, unlocked his briefcase, and pulled out his computer. He checked that he was not hooked up to the internet, opened the envelope and pulled out the small memory card. He put on his headphones and prepared to listen.

"Good news and bad news about IG," Harold started.

"Let's start with the bad news," Brayden Davenport said.

"For once I agree with you," Gerhardt said. "What's the bad news?"

"Watson got access to Endang and got Peter Binder, and Maria Davidoff, to the property. I assume Binder's supposed to examine the property and report back to Watson. That's Binder's business, and he's very good at it."

"Christ, Harold. I told you to get rid of that damn geologist," Gerhardt said. "Couldn't you get it done? IndoGold should want to keep their little game afloat a while longer. That's all we need. They should be able to kill off a geologist in the middle of the jungle."

"Well… That brings up the good news. IndoGold plans to do just that when they head out from the camp to the airport in Manado. Shoot them. Drop them in the jungle. Let the animals dispose of the bodies."

"A bit risky, don't you think?" Brayden asked.

"Actually, the jungle's a big place. I suspect it'll work just fine," Harold said.

"You know that my Japanese buddy, tried to take them out in Jakarta, right?" Gerhardt Weber said.

"Another one of your genius plans that worked so well," Brayden said.

"Yeah, well I don't see you with many good ideas for how to make this work."

"It's pretty hard with the dumbest plot I've ever seen, and the cast of total idiots we seem to be working with," Brayden shot back.

"Look," Harold James said, "there's no sense fighting over this. None of this can be linked back to us. We just need a little more time."

"Eventually, someone has to move it," Brayden said. "That's when we have to make our move."

"Unless somebody else, with more guts, gets there first," Gerhardt replied.

"Let's see if IndoGold can keep things going for a little while longer," Harold said. "I should mention that Watson contacted our embassy in Switzerland. He wanted the contacts for Irish."

"Shit," Gerhardt said. "Is he that crazy lock and key guy you told me about?"

"That's him, which means Watson wants to get into something really secure. I don't know what, at least not yet."

"He's vulnerable," Gerhardt said.

"Yes. I know," Harold said, and that was the final word on the very short recording.

Watson removed the headphones and sat very still. *I wonder how long Peter and Maria can remain invisible?* Watson thought the answer was rather obvious.

Watson picked up his briefcase and let himself out of the room. He would sleep in one of the rooms in the embassy tonight. He thought about Bandage.

Who is he? And he works for... whom?

Watson didn't know the answer, and he didn't have time to find out.

I have to shut him down.

Watson nodded.

Tomorrow. At the airport. I've got everything I need.

Chapter 22

Watson arrived promptly the next morning at five. He wore a rather rumpled, dark gray suit. Peter and Maria were ready at the front door and joined him in the embassy car.

"A little early this morning," Peter said.

I'm not going to tell you how little sleep we got last night.

"Not too bad," Watson said. "When we get to the airport, keep your distance. I've got something I have to do by myself. I shouldn't interact with either of you."

As they pulled away from the curb, Peter looked behind them. "Bandage is in the taxi behind us."

"Not surprised," Watson said.

"You have our passports and our tickets?" Peter asked. "And our hotel?"

Watson reached into his jacket pocket and pulled out two envelopes. "Everything's in there. Tickets and hotel for David and Nancy Madeaux. You should sort everything out and put the extra passports in your checked bags. Well-hidden if you can. They don't look at checked baggage that carefully, but theft can be a major problem here."

They rode the rest of the short distance to the airport in silence.

The Jakarta airport was crowded and chaotic as always, but Singapore Airlines performed its usual magic act of creating order out of chaos. Check-in was slow, but as efficient as could be expected.

There were two lines for business class. Peter and Maria checked in with one agent, while Bandage checked in with the adjacent line.

Watson cleared immigration and security as a diplomat. Peter and Maria were a bit slower.

After Watson stopped to buy several news magazines, Peter and Maria followed him down the hallway to the gate, lagging behind by fifty to seventy feet. Watson carried his briefcase, marked as diplomatic baggage. As he approached the departure lounge, he stepped into the men's room.

At the gate, Peter stood in a corner with Maria. They could easily view the entire gate area. "Let's watch Watson when he gets back," he said to Maria.

When Watson returned, he maneuvered through the crowd. He settled down about fifteen feet away from Peter and Maria, and only a few feet from Bandage. He did not sit down. *What's he doing?* Peter wondered.

Bandage focused on his phone. Periodically he looked up at Peter and Maria. Peter did not look away, and the man seemed to get more and more nervous as time passed.

Bandage stood up. He started to move away from his seat, and Watson moved as if to sit down in the now empty space.

Watson's briefcase struck the man in the thigh.

"I'm sorry," Watson said.

Bandage looked at Watson. He didn't say anything. He moved a few feet away and rubbed his thigh. Watson sat down.

Peter looked at Watson and then Bandage. *What just happened?*

Peter glanced at his watch.

Gate staff announced that Preferred boarding and First-Class boarding would begin shortly. Peter watched Bandage.

Peter noticed a change and looked at his watch again. *Seven minutes. That's quick.*

Bandage suddenly had a wide-eyed look. He began to tremble. Then he started to drool. He held his phone loosely in his left hand, and the trembling became more pronounced, almost violent.

Watson got up and went to the man. "Are you all right?" Watson asked with a note of real concern in his voice.

Bandage did not collapse. He wilted. It appeared that his muscles simply refused to support him.

Watson reached out, as if to catch him, but he did not. Bandage hit the floor. Peter noticed that the man's phone had disappeared. *Smooth!*

"Someone get a doctor!" Watson shouted.

Bandage was now suffering violent convulsions. He vomited. His breathing was rapid and shallow. He made incoherent noises. His fingers suddenly turned blue.

In the commotion, as several of the Singapore Airlines staff rushed to help the man, Watson discreetly backed away. After one or two minutes passed, Peter watched Watson return to the men's room.

"That was interesting," Peter said to Maria.

"Yes. Well done… I think."

A lot happened all at once. Paramedics arrived and tended to Bandage. Men came with mops to clean the floor. Singapore staff began boarding the aircraft.

Watson calmly returned to the gate area, and Singapore Airlines announced Business Class boarding.

Watson was near the head of the line. Peter and Maria let the line form and waited.

Bandage turned a bluish gray. His convulsions were less dramatic, but he was barely breathing. His eyes were wide open. He tried to speak. He could only make nonsense noises.

The paramedics became frantic.

The last of the Business Class passengers were boarding.

"Let's go," Peter said.

Maria nodded.

They scanned their boarding passes and walked down the jetway.

After they sat down, they looked at each other.

"What do you suppose it was?" Maria asked.

"It looked to me like he ate a badly prepared pufferfish."

"What?"

"Yeah. What's the name of that poison? Tetrodotoxin, I think. It's a neurotoxin. It paralyzes the nervous system. You die because you can't breathe, or your heart stops, or both."

"Nice," she said.

"Well, it's quick, but from what we just watched, if that was tetrodotoxin, I don't think it's quick enough."

While they were still at the gate, Watson pulled Bandage's phone out of his pocket. He checked the text messages.

An unfinished test read, *On 7:55 Singapore Air flt. Names are…*

Watson checked the addressee. Akihiko Uehara.

Isn't that interesting?

He checked the earlier text messages. There was a long string to Uehara. They stated the itinerary as 1-2 days in Singapore, 2-3 days in Tokyo with a side trip to Kyoto.

A busy boy, this guy. Well... no longer.

Watson pulled the battery out of the cell phone. He dropped the phone into his briefcase. He spun the combination lock.

Watson sat back in his seat, closed his eyes, and tried to think.

He opened his eyes and sat up. They had not left the gate yet. Watson pulled his own phone from his pocket and tapped out a message to Saul.

Uehara knows they're coming. Doesn't know the name. They're your problem now.

He thought about it. Then he sent a message to Peter. *They don't know your name, but they're expecting you and know about Kyoto.*

Watson smiled. *Maybe I can get a little sleep on this damned flight.*

The flight departed only a few minutes late. Peter and Maria dozed for most of the short flight. Watson exited in Singapore ahead of them, and they didn't see him again.

They passed through customs as David and Nancy Madeaux without incident, collected their baggage, and arrived at the Village Hotel Changi a little before noon.

"I'm sorry," the desk clerk said, "but your room will not be ready for two or three hours. You are free to use the gym or spa. You can shower and change there if you wish. And you can leave your baggage with the bellman."

"You must be close to Changi Beach Park," Peter said.

"Yes, sir. It's quite close."

"As I recall, there are some good jogging trails in the park."

"I can give you a map with some jogging routes marked on it if you'd like."

"What do you think?" Peter asked Maria.

"I'm still a little tired.... A short run wouldn't hurt."

A few minutes later they were jogging toward the Changi Beach Park. After they entered the park, Peter stopped at a monument to the Changi Beach Massacre.

"It's a small monument," he said.

Maria read the brief inscription. "Sixty-six. It's a rather small number of victims for massacres in the Second World War."

"The Japanese pushed them into the water and shot them. Those who survived were bayonetted, or forcibly drowned. Singapore says the Japanese murdered over 70,000 ethnic Chinese after the surrender in a killing spree called Sook Ching. They did it all in fifteen days."

They resumed jogging along the pathway by the beach.

"Makes you wonder if we should be going to Japan," Maria said.

"Nobody should know our name. Besides, these days the Japanese are a very peaceful people, and there are almost no firearms in Japan. We should be fine." He did not mention the text from Watson.

Chapter 23

Akihiko Uehara looked up from the small stack of papers on his otherwise empty desk as Isamu Uno slipped into his rather stark office. Akihiko considered himself a traditionalist and an extreme Japanese nationalist.

The spare, black lacquer furniture and elegant black Japanese calligraphy was set against the brilliant white walls of the office. A short ceremonial sword lay in its dark, wooden cradle on a small table near the window.

"What is it?" Akihiko asked.

"Susilo should be in Singapore," Isamu said with a small bow. "I can't reach him. His cell phone no longer answers."

"And what of Binder, and his wife?"

Isamu shook his head. "There is no record that they were even on that flight. Susilo said they checked in, under a different name, but he did not send the name."

"He said they will stop in Tokyo?"

"Yes. And visit Kyoto."

"Kyoto is good."

"But I cannot find them."

Akihiko frowned. "I have no one I can trust in Singapore." He folded his hands on the desk. "Gather our most loyal men. Give them the photographs. Monitor arrivals of every flight from Singapore into Narita."

"How long?"

"Start tomorrow. Continue for three days. Find out where they are staying, and their plans."

"Yes, sir," Isamu said with a bow.

"Prepare the two shinobi to deal with them in Kyoto." Akihiko paused. "I know the people at Ryōan-ji. They owe me a favor. If not there, perhaps Tetsugaku no michi."

"As you wish." Isamu bowed more deeply.

"It is your assignment, Isamu. Do it well." Uehara looked down at his papers.

With one more bow, Isamu turned and silently left the office.

Akihiko looked up again as he heard the door close with a click. *Kyoto, the ancient city of intrigue and murder. Perfect.* He smiled. *Too bad I was not born a Samurai, when bushido was still the way of Japan.*

His phone rang.

"Yes?"

"You have a call. From Jan Kwak."

"He should not be calling."

"Do you wish to talk with him?"

"Did he say what it's about?"

"No, sir."

Akihiko drummed his fingers on his desk. "I will speak with him."

Akihiko waited until his assistant told him that Jan Kwak was on the line.

"This is highly irregular," Akihiko said.

"It is critical."

"What is it?"

"Someone broke security. They inspected the package," Jan said.

"Who was it?"

"I don't know. Does it matter?"

"Perhaps. What do you want me to do?" Akihiko asked.

"We may have little time. You must begin the move sooner than we planned."

"Impossible. We won't be ready for at least six months."

"I am not an unreasonable man, but if you expect your payment, you should start now. Unfortunately, we are not ready either. We will be ready in four months. You must start removal then. You must also speed up the process and finish in no more than a year."

After a short pause, Akihiko said, "That's not possible. It's over 3,000 metric tonnes. Removal will take time."

"That is your problem, not mine. If you cannot do the job I must find someone else."

"Do not threaten me, Mr. Kwak."

"This is no threat, Mr. Uehara. It is reality. The danger is real. Time is running out, and you have made certain promises to me."

Akihiko let the silence stretch out. He expected Jan to break it and speak, but he did not.

"If you double-cross me," Akihiko said softly, "you and your family will regret it most painfully."

"If you cannot perform, I will make sure your failure is well known. You will receive none of your payment. You will lose face and be humiliated." Jan Kwak paused. "Do your job. Am I clear enough?"

Akihiko waited. After fifteen seconds, he said, "It is clear."

"Good. I expect you to be here and ready to begin the removal in four months. Good day, sir." The call was over.

Akihiko held the phone in his hand, waiting, but there was nothing. He felt the raw anger rising, but, as was his practice, he closed his eyes and breathed slowly and deeply. He carefully constructed a mental box to hold the anger. Then he gently pushed the box to the side.

Anger is my weakness. I will not let it hold me.

He repeated the mantra twenty times until the sense of calm returned.

Kwak is panicking. Panic brings opportunity. He just needs to keep believing. His panic will let us gain control very soon.

Akihiko smiled.

Ivan Dinisovich exited the creaking elevator in the basement of the old building. This was once his domain.

It used to be darker, he thought, *but my memories are still as black as ever.*

He walked slowly down a stuffy corridor and passed three heavy metal security gates.

They would have been closed.

He frowned as he passed several rooms.

I can still hear them.

Long ago he had lost count of the men he had destroyed.

Halfway down the hallway, Ivan opened a heavy oak door on his left. He stepped into a reading room, rather typical of some old libraries. A throw-back to another age. At the end of the room, a woman, well past middle age, sat behind an oak counter reading a book. A chain-link barrier extended from the counter to the ceiling, with a small opening in front of her.

A large oak table with six chairs dominated the room. A card catalogue was housed in a modest filing cabinet at one end of the table.

"How are you Olesya?" Ivan asked.

She looked up from her book and smiled. "Ivan Dinisovich! It has been so long. How can I help you?"

"I have to find some old reports."

"Old reports we have, but few are interested in them these days," she said. She smiled again. "Nothing has changed from the last time you were here. It's still the old card catalogue."

"The digital age has passed us by?"

"Thank goodness! I'd be out of a job."

Ivan turned to the table. "I think I remember, but I'll let you know if I need help."

The detailed cross-referencing in the card catalogue always impressed him. He started with the name, Friedrich Glock.

There he is. There were many files under his name. Ivan ignored all the later listings and focused on 1940 and 1941. After fifteen minutes he shook his head. He couldn't find any specific reference to a contract with the Swiss International Bank in either year.

He considered one final category labeled *Other Miscellaneous Files.*

He wrote down the reference number for each file, got up, and handed the slip of paper to Olesya.

"These two files, please."

Olesya looked at the references. "This shouldn't take more than a few minutes, but I don't walk quite as quickly as I once did."

"I'm sure you're fast enough."

Ivan returned to the table and waited.

Perhaps I'll be lucky. I was lucky with some of the men, some of the women, too, particularly the Germans. They were weak.

Olesya returned. Ivan collected the files and sat with them at the table.

Most of the papers were handwritten notes of no importance. Some appeared to be grocery lists. In the 1941 file, he found it. Two brittle and yellowing sheets of foolscap paper. The odd size of the paper amused him.

Ivan began to read. Unlike his Italian, French and English, his German was not perfect, but it was sufficient.

The first page defined the simple terms. *Receive jewelry, precious stones, gold and silver, stocks, bonds, works of art… sell them… turn the proceeds into gold bars… store the gold bars for the benefit of the listed beneficiaries. Heirs have no claim. A commission of 3.0% for Johan Kwak…*

The signatories were Friedrich Glock and Johan Kwak. There was no mention of the bank other than Johan's vault.

Amazing that this still exists.

Ivan turned to the second page and inhaled sharply. The listed beneficiaries were all from Hitler's inner circle of advisors and sycophants. Himmler, Goering, Hess, Doenitz, along with numerous SS generals and, curiously, Eva Braun, the lone woman.

Ivan sat back in his chair.

What is this? He shook his head. *It's grand theft. That's what it is. Skimming a share of the war booty, from right under Hitler's nose.*

How much?

It would depend on the skill of the thieves, of course.

He looked at the list of beneficiaries again.

They would have been very good thieves.

Olesya was snoring softly.

Ivan carefully folded the two sheets of paper and dropped them into his jacket pocket. He stood up, picked up his briefcase and the two folders, and dropped the folders on the counter.

At the sound, Olesya jerked awake. "You're finished? Did you find what you wanted?"

"These files may be of interest to historians, but there's nothing here for me. Do you need to look at my briefcase?"

"Yes. Even you. You made the rules." She completed a cursory examination of his briefcase and handed it back. "Doesn't look like you stole any of the precious files."

"Have a quiet day, Olesya."

"Yes. Not like the old days in France."

"Neither of us have the body for that kind of work anymore."

Olesya laughed. "True."

As he shut the door behind him, Ivan smiled at the memories of Olesya in Paris.

What a woman she was in those days.

He walked through the open doors in the hallway.

It's too easy now.

Back at his office, Ivan closed the door and removed the papers from his pocket. He spread them out on his desk and read them one more time. He looked at the list of beneficiaries.

There's no one left. They're all dead.

Ivan tapped his fingers on the papers.

How much? If Watson's interested it's got to be a hell of a pile. At least ten to twenty million ounces. Maybe more?

Who knows about this contract? I know about it, and so does the banker. If I'm careful....

Perhaps there's enough to take control.

Ivan got up, made a copy of the contract, and placed the original and the copy in his personal safe. He returned to his desk, opened his laptop, typed in his password and another to open a list of contacts. He found the Zürich number. He called on his secure line.

"Hello." The voice was deep and carried the rasp of a life-long smoker.

"Yuri?"

"Yes."

"Ivan Dinisovich in Moscow."

"Yes sir. How can I help you?"

Ivan paused to phrase his question properly. "Tell me, Yuri, who runs the Swiss International Bank these days? Is it still a family owned bank?"

"It's a public company now, but the Kwak family holds a majority position. Jan Kwak is the Chairman and CEO. He's still active, but he's over seventy now."

"His father was Johan Kwak?"

"I think so."

Ivan contemplated his next move. "I want you to arrange a meeting for me with Jan Kwak. Try for two days from now."

"That won't be easy," Yuri said. "He's a very prominent banker in Zürich."

"Tell him our central bank wants me to meet with him to discuss using his bank to handle a major portion of our foreign transactions."

"That should get you a meeting, but he'll be petrified that you're involved in money laundering."

"See what you can do, Yuri. I'll call you tomorrow."

Chapter 24

Peter's eyes snapped open. For a moment, in the darkness of the room, he was still in his dream, hands dripping with blood, and surrounded by the confusion and stench of the battlefield. Then reality rose into his awareness, and the blood was only sweat, and the stench was just his own fear. The visions of his destroyed SEAL team lying on the desert mountainside, were slower to fade.

He got out of bed, sat naked in the desk chair, and stared out the window. He was not in the mood for meditation, but he forced himself to breath slowly, deeply. He waited patiently for his heart rate to slow.

I have to face my fears, but what was Bandage? Was he an ending, or a beginning?

After half an hour, Peter crept back into the bed. He lay with his eyes wide open.

I was never afraid before. I'm afraid of everything now.

Peter grew tired of lying in the bed, wide awake. He gave up trying to sleep, returned to the desk and opened his computer.

I have to get David and Nancy Madeaux to Tokyo, with a place to stay, and home, if home will have us.

Once he completed his travel plans, he sent an email to Saul with the itinerary attached.

Saul:

We're in Singapore, thanks to your contacts and Watson's help. The exit was rough. We need to talk. Please meet us in Tokyo. You know where you can find us.

Peter and Maria

Maria did not rise until after eight. Once they were both dressed, Peter said, "It's a little late for breakfast. Would you prefer to go to Raffles for an early lunch?"

"Sure. Raffles sounds good."

"It's not the best restaurant in Singapore, not even the best hotel in Singapore, but it's definitely worth a visit," Peter said. "You can almost imagine being in colonial Singapore in the late nineteenth century."

"Hopefully they've added air conditioning," Maria said. "Are we dressed for it?"

"Business casual. I checked. I think we're fine. I know you like curries, which is good. That's what the Tiffin Room is all about."

As they walked through their hotel lobby, Peter noticed one man sitting alone near the main entrance. He was reading a newspaper, but he folded his newspaper and stood up as they walked by.

Short hair, slightly gray, modest height, thin, looks Malay, Peter thought.

Peter and Maria took the first taxi in line. The man with the newspaper took the second.

Their taxi dropped Peter and Maria at the front of the brilliant white façade of the main building at Raffles.

"This does feel like stepping into colonial Singapore," she said.

"This part of the hotel opened in 1899," Peter said. "Sometimes I try to imagine what the world was like then, being an officer, or a clerk, in the British Colonial Service. I can't do it."

"You'd be a minor lord in one of the most racist exercises the world has ever seen," Maria said.

"I bet they didn't think they had a racist thought in their heads. They just knew they were superior."

"Probably true," Maria said as they approached the front door. "Colonial masters always think their subjects are somehow sub-human."

Peter glanced back. Newspaper was paying for his cab.

Who the hell do you work for?

Peter followed Maria into the lobby. "When you see the Tiffin Room and the waiters," he said, "I think you'll have the uncomfortable feeling that you're a colonial overlord. White linens, white uniforms, dark skin. I suspect it doesn't look all that different from 1899."

From their table Peter gestured toward the buffet. "It's all buffet, except for the drinks. I think you can order some a la carte items, but I recommend the buffet and a cold Tiger beer."

"Seems like we should be drinking whiskey in a place like this."

"Suit yourself," Peter said with a smile. "Shall we look at the buffet?"

Over the next hour and a half, they tested most of the available curries. The waiters were attentive but not overbearing. The chef checked on their happiness twice.

"I am beginning to feel like a colonial overlord," Maria said. "A very well-fed overlord."

Peter looked at Newspaper across the room. *We're being watched, and I don't know why, or who's doing the watching.* He looked back at Maria across the table.

"If you're interested, I'd like to show you the Chinese garden," Peter said. "It's huge, and it has a wonderful collection of miniature landscapes."

And it's open and usually empty. Let's see what our buddy does.

"You mean bonsai trees?"

"Not exactly." Peter signaled the waiter. "Let's pay the bill and grab another taxi. I'll show you."

When they entered the large Chinese garden, it was nearly deserted, as Peter had hoped. He lingered near the entrance long enough that he could see the watcher, Newspaper, show up.

"Singapore is so busy and noisy, but this garden is usually relatively empty," Peter said. "Let's just walk a while, then I'll show you the little trees."

Peter looked back. Newspaper had settled onto a bench near the entrance. *Why should he bother to follow us? There's only one entrance.*

After their walk, Peter guided Maria into an enclosed area with the collection of small trees and miniature landscapes. Newspaper hadn't moved.

"I love these," Maria said.

"None of these would survive a month in my hands."

"Aren't these the same as the Japanese *bonsai*?"

"The Japanese call the little trees *bonsai*," he said, "which translates roughly as tree in a pan. These are probably called *penjing*, which is the art of creating miniature landscapes. The Chinese think the Japanese are too impatient and maybe too simplistic."

They spent nearly an hour in the display. When they left, Newspaper was still sitting by the main entrance. They stopped on the path. *What do I do next*, Peter wondered.

"I do know what you're doing," Maria said.

"Okay. What do you think?"

"He's persistent, and very patient. A bit obvious, but it's hard not to be obvious in a place like this."

"Who do you think he works for?" Peter asked.

"I have no idea."

Peter reached out and took Maria's hand in his. "I suggest we ask him," Peter said.

"I'm not sure that's a great idea."

"I'm not either, but he seems pretty tame, and I'd like to know, wouldn't you?"

"Yes."

"Let's go then."

Peter took Maria's hand and they started toward the entrance. Newspaper looked up at them briefly, and then looked back at his paper. They stopped abruptly in front of him.

"Good afternoon," Peter said.

Newspaper looked up, expressionless, and said, "Good afternoon."

"Do you work for the Singapore Police?"

The man hesitated before answering. "Yes."

"Why are you following us?"

"I am not following you."

"It sure feels like you're following us. Would you mind showing me your identification?"

After a moment, the man pulled an official identification card out of his pocket, showed it to Peter, and started to return it.

"Just a moment, sir," Peter said. "If you don't mind, I'd like to take a closer look at that."

He held it out for Peter without comment.

"That looks official enough." Peter smiled. "Just to make life easier for you, we're headed back to our hotel. We'll go out to dinner tonight, and we'll be leaving for Tokyo tomorrow afternoon."

"Have a nice afternoon," Maria said.

Peter and Maria walked out the entrance and took the first available cab.

"He thinks we're drug couriers," Maria said.

"Probably. You don't have any drugs with you, do you?"

"Nope."

"Good, because I'm sure our luggage has been, and will be, searched more than once."

The next day found David and Nancy Madeaux exiting the jetway at the Narita airport in Tokyo. It was early afternoon, and the airport was busy. At any airport there are a lot of people moving, and a lot of people standing still. What is uncommon in this age of heightened airport security is to see someone who is not traveling and is obviously waiting for someone to enter the terminal from a jetway.

It was only a second or two. The man looked at a piece of paper in his hand, then directly at Peter and back at the piece of paper. He looked at Peter again, pulled his phone out of his pocket and appeared to send a text.

Peter turned his head toward Maria. "I think someone was waiting for us, and he just told someone else we've arrived."

"I think there's not much we can do about it," she said.

"Why don't we just walk over and ask him where we can find Akihiko Uehara?"

"Forget it. Let's get our baggage instead."

Peter looked at the man one more time. He was busy texting. "A missed opportunity." He began to walk with Maria. "I agree, though. Too many people."

They took the bus into the city and sat in the back. Peter watched the other passengers, mostly Japanese.

The bus made slow progress in the dense traffic. *How do we check for watchers and followers with this mob of people?*

When they arrived at the train station, Peter said, "Let's do a little walkabout to confuse any followers, if there are any."

They walked into the train station, out another entrance, back into a third. They sat on a bench for a while.

"If someone's following us, I can't spot them," Peter said.

"What's the matter? They all look alike to you?"

"Ouch! You're nasty."

"Well, I'm convinced there was no one on the bus."

"That's no surprise, but what about the guy in the gray shirt that's been standing by the news shop since we sat down?" Peter asked. "I think I may have seen him when we exited customs."

"You sure?"

"Nope."

"I think we're starting to see ghosts," Maria said. "Let's get a taxi to our hotel."

Before they took the first available taxi, Peter watched the man in gray get into a black Toyota SUV with dark tinted windows.

Easy to remember that plate, 21-48.

"Our gray ghost just got into a black sedan, and I bet he pulls out behind our taxi," Peter said.

Peter asked the driver to go to the American Embassy. When they got there, he watched the black sedan drive past. Then he asked the driver to go to their hotel.

Their room was ready, and they got on the elevator for the twelfth floor. When the elevator door opened, Peter said, "I'm going back down. Just to see if the gray man found the hotel. You coming?"

"I'm coming."

When the elevator door opened, they looked across the lobby. The gray man was at the registration desk.

As they watched, the man appeared to be in an animated conversation with the clerk. The clerk pointed in their direction and the man turned around. He looked at them, spun around, and walked out of the hotel.

"Maybe we should have asked him who he is," Maria said.

"Actually, I don't think that would have been a good idea."

They turned with their baggage and took the elevator back to the twelfth floor. Peter pressed the key card against the lock and pushed the door open. As he walked down the short hallway, past the bathroom, and entered the room, he stopped abruptly. Maria almost ran into his back.

"Jesus!" Peter said.

"What the hell?" Maria asked as she recovered, and the door shut behind her.

"What the hell are you doing here? You could get yourself killed surprising us like this."

Saul put his cup down on the coffee table and stood up from the sofa at the end of the room. "Sorry. We need to talk, sooner rather than later. It seemed like a good idea at the time. Besides, what are you going to do? Throw a chair at me?"

"You might be surprised what I could throw at you. How the hell did you get into the room anyway?"

"We have some excellent contacts in the *kōanchōsa-chō.*

"What the hell is that?" Maria asked.

"The Public Security Intelligence Agency for Japan. They're kind of like the FBI and the CIA rolled into one."

"You're a man of many talents," Peter said.

"Not as many as you, apparently." Saul gestured at the sofa. "Let's sit down. You can bring me up to date on what happened in Indonesia."

Peter pulled a chair over. Saul and Maria sat on the sofa.

"Thanks for your help in Indonesia," Peter said. "That woman, Atin in Manado, was perfect."

"I don't actually know her." Saul paused for a moment. "You are both officially missing at the moment, along with the IndoGold geologist, the pilot, and the helicopter. You think it'll stay that way?"

"They'll never find the bodies. They certainly won't find the two of us, but I would like Peter and Maria to reappear in a few months. We'll have to work on that."

"Any family members I need to talk to?"

"Not for me," Maria said.

"Me neither," Peter said, "but if some distant cousin, and I'm sure we both have a bunch of them, finds out how much we're worth, they might push to declare us legally dead and come after the money."

"I can help with that, but what do you want to do? Right now?"

"Short term is easy. Kyoto tomorrow. A couple of days in Tokyo, and head back to Canada. But we can't be Peter and Maria in Canada, can we? And it wasn't exactly safe when we left."

"I gather you had an Indonesian follower?" Saul asked.

"Yes. Watson took care of him. Seems to have injected him with some fast-acting poison."

They lapsed into silence.

"Actually," Peter said, "we had a follower in Singapore, but he was with the Singapore Police."

"How do you know that?"

"We asked him," Maria said. "He showed us his ID."

"Somebody met us at Narita, too," Peter said. "And somebody followed us to the hotel."

"You sure about that?"

"It was pretty obvious," Maria answered.

Peter got up and went to the small fridge in the room, took out three beers, and opened them. He brought them back to the table, handed one to Maria and Saul, and took one for himself.

"I don't know what we should do next," Peter said. "We've done what you wanted us to do, and you'll have your report as soon as the lab gives me the gold assays." Peter drank some of his beer. "We're in deep shit right now, and we could use a little help."

"I've been thinking about that." Saul set his beer on the table. "I've got a proposition for you. It involves an extension of your contract."

"Doing what?" Maria asked.

Saul hesitated. "Before I answer that question, let me lay out a little of the background." He turned to Peter. "What's your preliminary conclusion about Endang?"

"I've got no hard evidence yet. My guess? I don't believe it's a gold mine, not even a small one." He paused. "There's always a chance it's something entirely new, but I don't believe it."

"You think it's a fraud?" Saul asked.

"Yes, but if I'm right, I don't know how a fraud of this scale could continue as long as this has. It's way too complicated. Too many people involved. Too many opportunities for leaks. It can't work long term."

"I don't think it has to work long term," Saul said. "The worst thing for IndoGold insiders would be to have to develop a mine. They're all selling out as fast as they dare, and they're making huge profits."

Peter shrugged. "It can't hold together much longer. They've got to know that."

"I think they're hoping for another year, maybe two. You did them a favor getting rid of Teunis. And Peter and Maria for that matter."

"How's that?" Maria asked.

"Well, no negative report, and an excuse to stop drilling. Less chance of discovery, and no real ongoing work to maintain the fraud."

"They have to keep a lot of people happy and quiet," Maria said.

"They're keeping quiet because the longer it goes on the more money they make," Saul said.

"There's got to be more to this than simple greed," Peter took another drink of his beer. "Watson told us that he believes there's a huge pile of dirty gold out there and that Endang may be a giant gold laundering scheme. That sounds impossible."

"Impossible as it may seem, I think Watson's right." Saul smiled. "There is a huge pile of dirty gold out there. Endang is the story that has convinced someone to move the gold, to yield control."

"Who could possibly believe this would work?" Maria asked.

"Desperate men grasp at straws," Saul said. "They'll even believe in shadows."

"So how do we fit into this scheme, other than me proving Endang doesn't exist?" Peter asked.

"I think I know the location of the dirty gold." Saul drained the last of his beer. "The myth of Endang suggests it's a very large pile. After all, it's all the gold that's supposed to be at Endang. All I want from the two of you is to help me get my hands on that gold and return it to its rightful owners."

"What do you want us to do?" Maria asked. "Rob a bank?"

Saul smiled. "Let's just call it a little mining operation."

"And what's your timing?" Peter asked.

"You want to have the extension?"

"I didn't say that. I asked about your timing."

"Look, I want your report on Endang as soon as possible. You can stay here a couple of days, but then I want you to fly to Zürich and do this job for me."

"And you're not going to tell us anything more?" Maria asked.

"You already know that I take care of the people who work for me. I got you out of Indonesia. Watson couldn't do it. This is a simple project management job, and it's in Switzerland. What more do you need?"

"We both appreciate what you did for us in Indonesia," Peter said, "but you didn't do it alone. Watson did take care of our tail. And your simple job in Indonesia nearly killed us."

"And you're still alive because of me."

"We're still alive because of us," Peter said.

"Without my help you'd be in an Indonesian prison."

Peter glared at Saul. "Don't push it. We'll take our time deciding on this proposed extension to our contract, and you'll have to tell us a lot more."

They sat in silence for a minute.

"You're heading to Kyoto tomorrow?"

"That's the plan," Maria said.

"Be careful," Saul said.

"Why?" Maria asked.

"I don't fully understand the Japanese connection," Saul said with a shrug. "And you say you've already picked up somebody watching you here."

"So how the hell are we supposed to 'be careful'?" Peter asked.

"Just be alert. We'll talk when you get back to Tokyo. I'll need an answer by the next day."

After Saul left, Peter and Maria talked with the hotel concierge about Kyoto. Then they walked the short distance to the grounds of the Imperial Palace. They stood at the top of one of the outer walls of the grounds and looked out over the manicured grass and trees to the densely packed city beyond.

Peter was still on edge. He had watched everyone around him all day. It was almost automatic. *I don't like the follower in Tokyo, or the warnings from Watson and Saul.*

"I know you pretty well, Peter Binder. You're going to accept this extension, but I don't really know why."

Peter liked the emptiness that surrounded them on the grounds. Emptiness was good. He could see any threats, and for the moment he could almost relax.

He took a deep breath. "I'm not sure how to explain this to you. I thought I had returned to being just another consulting geologist. It turns out I've become some sort of hit man and troubleshooter for the CIA. Maybe the Mossad, too."

"It doesn't have to be like that," she said.

"I'm tired, but I don't know how to escape, and I can't seem to give it up. It's like I'm a SEAL again, except my enemies tend to be invisible."

Peter continued to stare out at the city. "I'm scared to go home," he said, "but I'm more scared by the fact that I seem to need this. I think I'm addicted."

Maria reached out and grasped Peter's hand. She said nothing.

"You don't have to come with me," he said.

"You say you're addicted? Well, with my background it makes no sense for me to say this, but I think I'm addicted to you."

Peter felt her grip tighten.

"I'm not walking away," she said.

"You won't have much of a chance of a long and peaceful life with me."

"I know. I've lived in your crazy world before. I'll take my chances, as long as they're with you."

Chapter 25

As they stood on the train platform in the early morning, Peter said, "I love the Japanese trains."

They settled into their assigned seats, and the fast train raced by the coastal scenery, a mix of industrial centers and short intervals of more open, agricultural land.

"Look at the green patches next to the factory buildings," Peter said. "I assume they're little rice patches, stuck in anywhere there's room."

The blue sky gave way to clouds as they sped south. Peter watched small ribbons of water slant down the windows by the time they approached Kyoto.

The temple grounds will be deserted.

They stepped onto the platform in Kyoto, along with almost everyone else on the train.

The crowds and shops are the same as I remember.

He tried to ignore his growing anxiety.

Something bad is going to happen today. I know it.

They stopped at one of the shops, bought two umbrellas and a bilingual map of Kyoto. When they stepped back into the crowd, it carried them along, almost involuntarily, to the exit onto the street.

"I think there's a taxi stand across the street," Peter said.

"Can't we walk to the temples?"

"We could, but I'd rather spend more time at the Ryoan-ji and Ginkaku-ji temples. We can walk down the Philosopher's Path and back to the station. The temple gardens are wonderful and peaceful places. They should be deserted in the rain."

Good places to watch people.

They found the taxi stand and stood patiently in the queue. When their turn came, they climbed into the spotless back seat of the taxi. Peter reached forward with his bilingual map and showed the driver the symbol for the Ryoan-ji temple. The taxi surged into the narrow streets and traffic of the old city.

In spite of the light rain, as they entered the temple at Ryoan-ji, the long, neat rows of shoes and umbrellas told them they would not be alone. Peter took off his shoes and laid them and his umbrella with the rest.

He sensed Maria's hesitation. "Don't worry about it. No one would think of stealing anything here. I think it's beyond their imagination."

Even before they entered the viewing area for the famous Zen garden, Peter felt the enduring age and peace of the building enfold him. His feet moved smoothly over the dark wood flooring, polished by thousands of shoeless visitors.

They walked down a short corridor, turned a corner, and with soft suddenness the Zen garden became the whole world. Twenty or thirty people sat quietly on the dark brown planks, under a simple overhanging roof, along the edge of the garden. Peter and Maria took their place at one end of the group, where all of the garden was within their view.

After a few minutes of silence, Peter whispered, "Can you see my Ontario garden here?"

"I think I can. Tell me about it."

Peter put his arm around Maria. "This, to me, is the epitome of the art of the Zen garden. It dates back to about 1680. The patterns of the raked stones suggest waves. The major rock groupings are set in interlocking triangles, islands in a calm sea. If you can let go, the garden can capture you." Peter smiled and pulled Maria closer to him. "It releases you only when it desires to do so."

Without consciously deciding to do so, Peter's mind explored the garden. He closed his eyes. His anxiety and tension slipped away. In quiet silence his mind wandered down his normal path of meditation. Into the white sea he knew so well. Into the darkness. Into the endless stars and the empty universe. His mind rested and floated in solitude.

Peter opened his eyes with a shudder. He was terrified. He looked frantically at the small crowd around them. Instead of the slow heartbeat of meditation, his heart was racing.

Idiot! You can't do that. Not now. Not today.

"Where were you?" Maria whispered.

"Sorry. It's a long way from here."

They sat silently. Peter tried to enjoy the peace of the walled garden, but he was afraid. Finally, Peter stood and said, "There's a pathway around the temple pond. It's quite beautiful."

They retrieved their shoes and umbrellas. Rain still fell in a light drizzle as they walked slowly and visited the shrines dotted along the path. Halfway around the pond they stopped and looked at the hazy pattern of trees hanging over the edge of the water.

Peter suddenly tensed.

"What's wrong?" Maria asked.

"I don't know."

Peter looked around. He saw an old man sitting on a bench, several hundred feet along the pathway. There was nothing else.

He doesn't look like a threat.

"Someone's watching us. Maybe following us," he said.

"Where?"

"I don't know. I just feel it. Let's get out of here."

As they began to walk, two men materialized in what had been an emptiness. They were dressed in black, and they both held small, double-edged swords.

"Good God," Maria said. "We're being mugged by two men from a bad Japanese movie."

"This is no mugging, and it's no movie either."

The four of them stood motionless for several seconds. "Come and get us boys," Peter said softly. "It's showtime."

Peter and Maria dropped their umbrellas and moved toward the two men.

Their move made the two men hesitate briefly, but with rapid and fluid movements they closed on Peter and Maria. The bright flash of the two swords was unexpected in the gray light.

Peter heard no sounds except the sudden, sharp breathing and soft grunts of exertion. The short swords slipped toward Peter and Maria, but their targets seemed to vanish.

Maria connected with a well-placed kick to the ribs, accompanied by a sharp thud and the sound of breaking bones. The man stumbled forward, and Maria slipped behind him.

Peter aimed a little higher. His kick connected with the second man's jaw. He could hear the distinct snap. The man staggered backward and spit out two teeth.

Neither man had time to recover fully. Peter followed-up with a kick to the man's temple. As the man in front of her turned toward her, Maria closed on him with an upward blow to his nose and a punch with all her strength to his solar plexus. Both men dropped their swords and crumpled to the ground, unconscious.

The old man watched intently from his bench. He didn't move or speak.

Peter and Maria, panting, looked down at the two men on the packed earth of the pathway.

"You okay?" Peter asked.

"I'm fine. How about you?"

"They cut a hole in my jacket, but I think I'm fine."

"What the hell do we do now?"

"Well, I don't want these two following us," Peter said as he looked down at the two men. One of them began to stir, and Peter kicked him savagely in the head. He lay still again.

Peter reached down and pulled a black glove off one man's hand. He picked up the small sword with the glove. A quick slash severed the Achilles tendon on the right leg of each man. A surprisingly small amount of dark red blood fell into the soil. He dropped the sword on the pathway and put the glove in his pocket.

Peter looked up. "Let's get out of here... while we still can."

Maria picked up the umbrellas and handed one to Peter. A few beads of sweat showed on her forehead. "No sense getting any wetter than we already are," she said with a smile.

They walked briskly down the path. As they approached the old man, he rose from his seat and faced them.

"Oh, God. Not again. And an old man, too," Maria said.

"I don't think he's very old."

The man smiled.

"Shit!" Peter said. "I am in no mood for this."

As they continued walking, Peter said, "You take the right side. I'll take the left."

They walked out of the temple grounds with no further challenge and got into a waiting taxi. Peter showed the driver the symbol for Ginkaku-ji.

"Why are we doing this?" Maria asked as they wove through the traffic. "We should get on the next train back to Tokyo."

"I think you're wrong. None of those three men can follow us, and I'll bet they won't say anything to the police."

The taxi dropped them off at the end of the small street that led to the Ginkaku-ji grounds. As Maria paid the driver, Peter looked around. More crowds of tourists.

The temple garden will be a good place to watch. The Philosopher's Path, too.

Peter and Maria sat in the garden for a long time, contemplating the field of white sand, the roughly incised patterns, and the perfect, flat-topped cone. Peter could feel that Maria could not relax.

I can't either.

He talked softly, trying to regain a sense of calm. "I feel very different in this garden," Peter said. "To me it's less about peace and more about confronting myself, and my life's contradictions."

"We've got plenty to confront at the moment," Maria said.

"True."

They sat quietly for a while longer. The light rain had stopped, and they folded their umbrellas. Peter said, "The grounds away from the sand garden are very different. More of an ancient water garden. Shall we take a walk?"

They silently toured the water garden, full of sluggish koi and luxurious moss. Most visitors focused on the sand garden. Peter and Maria had the water garden almost to themselves. They sat and watched the crowd at the pavilion on the other side of sand garden.

"Do you see those two men standing together by the pavilion?" Maria asked.

"You mean the ones that haven't moved for at least fifteen minutes? They were at Ryoan-ji, too." Peter paused. "Dark complexioned. Black, curly hair. The older has a bit of gray. He's heavier and more powerfully built than his younger comrade, but the taller one's no slouch. Fancy dark glasses. Middle Eastern maybe?"

"I guess you did notice them."

They sat a little longer until Peter said, "Let's see how quickly they move when we leave. They should be easy to spot. They're the only pair of Caucasian men visiting the temples today."

"We might as well get on with it."

Peter pulled his map out of his pocket. He pointed to the Tetsugaku-no-Michi. "That's the Philosopher's Path. It's full of little teahouses, obscure temples, and little Shinto shrines. We can watch for our friends and have lunch at one of the teahouses."

As they left the temple grounds, Peter looked back. He couldn't see the two men. He was sure Maria had noticed.

"So... What's next?" she asked.

"We play tourist, and watch the watchers."

They walked slowly down the narrow lane, crowded with souvenir shops and small restaurants. They turned left onto the Philosopher's Path which ran along the edge of a small canal. Two narrow lines of paving stones sat in loose gravel.

With the turn, they left the crowds behind. Dense, green foliage seemed to silence the city. Cherry trees hung over the sides of the canal and walkway, and layers of green moss covered the rocks.

"I love the quiet and the sense of age," Peter said. "I can almost feel the poets and sages of six hundred years ago walking with us."

"Your imagination is better than mine. I'm too busy watching."

"Actually, I think it got its name from a local philosophy professor who took his morning walk along this pathway around the year 1900 or so."

"So the sense of age you feel is an illusion?" Maria asked.

"You're mean."

Peter looked back. "They're behind us. They seem to be keeping their distance."

"I know."

The light rain returned, and they opened their umbrellas. They stopped at several of the small shrines. Strips of cloth wrapped around the smooth, oval, upright stones.

After they had walked for fifteen minutes, they crossed a small arched, stone bridge and slipped into a quiet teahouse. They ordered lunch, mostly by pointing at the pictures on the menu.

"It's just as well the cherry trees are not blooming," Peter said. "It would not be quiet and peaceful if they were."

They ate at a dark brown, polished wooden table under the overhanging roof. They were alone at the teahouse, and they watched in silence as the two men from the temple walked by.

Maria looked past Peter and said, "They're sitting on a bench, less than a hundred feet from us."

Peter turned briefly to look at them and then returned to his lunch. "I vote we enjoy our meal. They're not going anywhere."

Maria nodded. "I have to admit that these encounters are... stimulating." She picked up her chopsticks. "They always have been."

"First sign of addiction," Peter said with a small smile.

After they finished their meal and the sharp, green tea that came with it, Peter paid the bill.

He stood up. "There has to be a back entrance. This is as good a place as any to confront those two."

When they approached the door to the kitchen, the staff met them with an effusion of bowing and gestures. Peter and Maria simply bowed in return and kept saying "Thank you!"

Shortly, they found their way out the back entrance, into a narrow alley lined with neat rubbish bins and smelling only slightly of old fish. The alley pavement, clean and recently washed, extended several hundred feet in both directions, before it curved out of sight.

"Let's come at them from both directions," Peter said. "You double back to that bridge we saw before the restaurant. I'll go forward and come back. Whoever sees them first, wait. We need to confront them together."

Maria nodded. "I'll let you take the lead."

"Nice holiday, eh?"

"My choice, I think. See you in a few minutes."

Peter watched her walk away. Then he turned and walked rapidly down the alley. The small teahouses and foliage hid him from the Philosopher's Path until he came to a narrow, cobbled street and a bridge over the canal.

As Peter came to the pathway the foliage provided some concealment, but he could see the two men, about one hundred and fifty feet from him. They were standing and looking back at the restaurant. He couldn't see Maria.

Patience. Patience.

Peter watched the two men. They were conversing in short bursts. Peter couldn't make out the words or even the language.

Who are you? You don't look like anyone a Japanese mobster would hire.

Maria came into view, and Peter stepped out into the pathway. One of the men turned and saw Peter, spoke to his companion, and he turned as well.

I hope you saw what happened at Ryoan-ji. Can we make this quiet and peaceful?

Peter began to walk slowly toward the men, and Maria did the same. Peter felt the building tension in his body. He and Maria stopped about fifteen feet from the two men, and Peter said, "We noticed that you were sitting here for a long time. Can we help you?"

The older man hesitated. "No. No. We're fine."

Peter couldn't place the accent. "That's good," he said. "Did we see you earlier at Ryoan-ji?"

"You might have."

"Did you see two men in black attack a couple on the path around the temple pond?" Peter asked.

"No."

"A pity."

Peter moved slightly closer to the two men, and Maria did the same. He held his hands to his side, fingers close together. He could see the two men tense in response. The younger one was already standing on the balls of his feet.

This will not be fun.

"Perhaps you could tell us why you are following us," Peter said.

After a moment's hesitation, the older man asked, "Does the name Saul Bernstein mean anything to you?"

Peter and Maria both stopped.

"What's your relationship with Saul?" Peter asked.

"We work for him. My name is Alon, and this is Gershon. We're supposed to make sure no one bothers you today." He looked from Peter to Maria. "We haven't done a very good job, and Saul is not happy."

Peter looked intently at Alon and said, "I seek the golden star of David."

"It will be found on an island nation," Alon responded with a small smile.

Peter contemplated the two men and finally said, "And just what the hell does Saul want us to do next, Alon, after that mess at Ryoan-ji?"

"Saul wants both of you to go back to your hotel in Tokyo on the next available train. The police will not interfere."

"Just like that?" Maria asked. "Like nothing happened?"

"Yes," Alon said.

"You know, you could get yourselves killed pulling shit like this," Peter said.

"True."

They stood silently, staring at each other.

Finally, Maria said, "Tell Mr. Bernstein trust is a two-way street."

Peter and Maria walked away. They did not look back.

Chapter 26

In the basement of the White House, Watson MacDonough read the document Irish had sent him one more time. He looked at the signatures. Johan Kwak and Friedrich Glock. And the list of beneficiaries.

Christ almighty! If Ivan Dinisovich finds a copy of this… Watson frowned. *He still won't know how much gold is in that vault.*

Watson looked at his watch. Twenty minutes.

The phone rang.

"Watson.",

"Secure line?"

"Yes."

"Your old company doesn't want me to work for you. They're hunting me."

"I'm sorry to hear that."

Watson thought about the old castle where Irish lived, which was complete with moat, drawbridge, and portcullis. Watson assumed there was more than one priest hole, secret passageway, and escape tunnel.

"No need to be sorry," Irish replied. "I accepted the risk, but I have only a few minutes."

"What does the vault look like?"

"Plaster walls, painted white."

"What's in it?"

"A series of tarps, stretched tight, hide one hundred million ounces of gold, plus or minus, in standard 400 ounce, .9999 gold bars."

"Yes!"

"Another thing," Irish said, "no one goes into that vault."

"How do you know that?"

"The floor's dusty, and, except for mine, there are no footprints in the dust."

"Interesting." Watson paused. "Can you disappear?"

"I have before. How long?"

"Three to four months. You'll know when to resurface."

"Send the money as usual."

"A double payment is on its way. Find me if I can help."

"It was a beautiful."

Watson heard a pounding sound.

"Ah! They're here," Irish said. "Sorry. Got to go."

Irish left the phone on, and Watson heard a creaking and scraping sound, followed by the sound of heavy gunfire, then silence, and finally what sounded like pounding to smash a heavy wooden door.

Someone said, "Be careful in here. This place could be wired."

Shit! That's Terry Whincup!

"We've got to take the chance. We can't…"

As Watson reached to cut off the call, he heard an explosion, and the line went dead.

Watson sat back in his chair.

Irish cut that a bit close. Somehow, I've got a feeling he'll survive.

Watson closed his eyes.

Terry. You were a good man, but you dropped into their world, didn't you?

Watson didn't know how long he sat there before he finally got up, packed up his computer, and left the secure room. His phone buzzed immediately as he exited. A message to call Alden Sage. He tapped in the number.

"Alden Sage."

"Watson."

"Where the hell were you?"

"In the black room."

"I wondered. I couldn't reach you. Come up to my office. I've got something for you."

When Watson got to Alden's office, he rapped on the door jam. "What have you got?"

"Come in and sit down. The Secret Service guys just sent me a note from Zürich. I was about to call off that stakeout, but they saw one of your targets. Your old buddy, Ivan Dinisovich. Turns out he had a one-on-one with the top man at the bank, Jan Kwak."

Watson sat down heavily. "When did that happen?"

"Yesterday. Early in the morning."

"They're sure about the meeting with Jan Kwak?"

"One of them was in the bank. He saw Ivan come out of Kwak's office."

"I think I've made a very bad move."

"What?"

"It's a long story, but let me tell you about a call I just received. You remember I told you that I asked this guy Irish to find out what's in the owner's vault at the bank?"

"Yeah."

"Well, he got in and did a little inventory. We just talked. He calculates a hundred million ounces of gold, in standard four nines gold bars."

"Jesus!" Alden said.

"And he sent me a copy of the original contract between Johan Kwak, the father of the current head of the bank, and the Nazis. A bunch of Hitler's inner circle were skimming the take from the Jews, and even from the eastern European treasuries, converting it all into gold."

"Greedy little bastards, weren't they?"

"I'd say so. But this gets even more interesting. While we were talking, Irish told me the CIA is after him. They showed up when we were still talking."

"Did Irish escape?"

"Don't know. There was a hell of an explosion. Knowing him he's already on his way to a tropical island retreat. I'm pretty sure I recognized Terry Whincup's voice just before the explosion. I assume he died, along with several other agents."

"We should take them down," Alden said.

"Can't."

"Why not? Isn't this enough?"

"There's no clearly illegal intent," Watson replied. "They can justify an action against Irish for any number of reasons. They've said they want to eliminate Binder, but those efforts have all failed. Anyway, so far Harold can easily and plausibly deny any involvement in any attempt on Binder's life. Too many layers of removal."

"So… just keep Binder and Davidoff out there as bait? That's your plan?"

"More or less."

"Binder knows what you're doing?"

"Yes, but he's stuck. He's threatened to quit, but where can he go? We're the only security he's got."

"You're pinning a lot on him and giving him nothing. What about Davidoff?"

Watson shrugged. "She's well trained. She knows."

"You're playing a nasty game."

"I know. How's their security clearance going?"

"It's done. It wasn't easy."

"Good. They're going to need it."

"They have it, but POTUS needed some cover on this, particularly with Davidoff."

Watson stood up. "Thanks. I really do appreciate your help on this."

As Watson turned to leave, Alden asked, "What did you mean that you made a bad move?"

Watson stopped at the door. "I didn't expect Irish to find the contract. I asked Ivan to look for one in their World War II archives."

"You did what?"

"I asked him to look for a contract. He owes me… big time."

"Did he find it?" Alden asked.

"I assume so. Why else is he talking to the Swiss International Bank?"

"So now the Russians are in the middle of this?"

"I'm not sure. Unless Jan Kwak told him, Ivan has no idea of how much gold is in that vault. I think he's in this for himself."

"He's gone rogue? Is that good or bad?"

"Hard to tell. No official constraints, but the Russians rarely have many anyway."

"If he's on his own, maybe we can scare him a little," Alden said.

"You don't scare Ivan. The best you can do is make him angry. When he's angry he sometimes takes stupid and deadly risks." Watson paused. "If he learns how much gold is there, and if Bernstein steals it, he'll be really pissed. He'll do something monumentally stupid."

"I couldn't live in your world, Watson."

"It's a living, I think," Watson said with a smile. "Right now, I think I'll go and poke at a Russian bear."

Watson turned and walked down the hall, picked up a fresh cup of coffee, and returned to the secure room in the basement.

He opened his computer and found the number.

Only two months old. It might still work. He punched it into the telephone on the table. It rang twice.

"*Da?*"

"Watson."

"Ah! Watson! Good to hear your voice. How are you?"

"I am well, Ivan, and you?"

"Quite well, thank you."

"Did you have any success finding that contract?"

"No. Sorry. I found no trace of it. If it existed, it must have disappeared in the last days of the war."

"Those were crazy days."

"Yes."

"It was worth a try," Watson said.

"Sorry I couldn't help."

"Well, no matter." Watson paused. "When do you head home?"

Ivan hesitated, just a tiny moment. The moment was not lost on Watson.

"I should be home tomorrow," Ivan said. "Why?"

"No reason. I trust the weather has been good for your visit to Zürich." Watson smiled.

"It's been beautiful. I actually walked by the Swiss International Bank."

"Did you go in?"

"Yes. It's quite impressive. I think you could hide almost anything in that pile of rocks."

"I suspect you're right. Well, thanks for trying, Ivan. It would have been nice to see that contract, but it was a long time ago."

"Yes. It was a long time ago. Sorry I couldn't help. *Do svidaniya.*"

"*Do svidaniya.*"

Watson terminated the call and laughed out loud.

"Chew on that, you old bastard," he said.

He was still chuckling as he left the room.

Chapter 27

The light mist of Kyoto evolved to a more substantial rain as the train raced north to Tokyo. Peter and Maria sat across from each other, alone at the back of the rail car.

Maria stared out the window. "I don't trust Tokyo."

"I agree. After today Japan doesn't feel very safe."

"I thought we came here to get away from Rostov and his thugs," she said

"Oh, we managed that all right," Peter said, "but Endang seems to have its own constellation of evil."

They fell into silence for the rest of the trip, took a cab from the station directly to their hotel, and went straight to their room.

Maria lay down on the bed and covered her eyes with her forearm. Peter lay down beside her.

"We're fighting a two-front war," Maria said.

"Yes."

"Where do we go to live in peace?" she asked.

"It's not where. It's what we have to do to get there. I think there's a lot of blood and violence on the road ahead of us."

Maria propped herself up on one arm and looked at Peter. "Are we on our own?"

Peter didn't answer immediately. "We're not alone. Watson and Saul will help us, on their terms, and if we fit with their plans and objectives." He paused. "They have to tell us what they want, and how we fit in."

"They'll never tell the truth," she said.

"Maybe. I'm not sure we have any choice. If we want their help with personal security, imperfect as that may be, we have to help them."

"Lovely."

Peter's cell phone rang. He pulled it out of his pocket. Saul Bernstein. He answered it on speaker.

"Hello, Saul."

"Hello. You're both okay?"

"What the hell is going on?"

"Not quite what I intended," Saul answered.

"Good, because I'm tired of being blindsided. You're playing a dangerous game, and you're not telling us a damn thing."

"Alon told you that the police are under control?"

"Yes," Peter said.

There was a long pause before Peter asked, "Is there anything else you want to talk about?"

"Neither of you is safe in Tokyo."

Peter took a deep breath. "It's a little late to tell us that. We'll head home tomorrow."

"What about working with me in Switzerland?"

"I don't think either of us is super excited about it," Peter said. "You had to know what we were walking into in Kyoto. After today it's hard for us to trust you."

"Look, I knew you were followed in Indonesia, but you knew that, too. I've suspected a Japanese connection since the first attack in Jakarta. Kyoto just confirmed that. That's why I think you should get out of Tokyo as soon as you can."

"Saul, we don't like being hunks of bait," Maria said, "just so you can identify the sharks."

"I warned you and gave you some protection."

"Some bloody protection," Peter said.

"Fair enough." Saul paused. "We can't talk on the phone. If you're willing, Alon will pick you up at ten in the morning. Be packed, checked out, and ready to go with your baggage. We'll have lunch and talk. You can make a final decision on Switzerland tomorrow afternoon."

After a pause, Peter said, "You have to tell us the whole story, Saul. Otherwise, forget it."

"I'll do the best I can," Saul said. "I'll see you tomorrow morning."

Peter disconnected and looked at Maria.

Maria was lying back on the bed with her eyes closed. "I'm exhausted. I'm taking a nap. Wake me in an hour, and we can get something for dinner."

Peter watched her as she rolled over and settled her head into the pillow. In less than a minute she was snoring lightly.

I wish I could do that.

Peter went to the desk and opened his computer. He worked a while on the outline for the Endang report. He didn't have the results, but he was pretty sure he knew what they would be. He drafted a short email.

Watson:

Saul wants us to work with him in Zürich. He says he'll give us the details tomorrow. I assume it has something to do with the dirty gold you mentioned.

How's our security clearance? You need to start telling us everything you know. We're having too many surprises. We'll go to Zürich, but only if we think Saul is telling us the whole story. Otherwise we go home.

Rostov's another matter. We want him as much as you do, but we won't operate half blind.

Peter & Maria

Peter leaned back in his chair and closed his eyes. After a minute he heard the computer ping. He looked up. It was Watson.

Go to Zürich. I need you there. I'll meet you in Zürich and explain everything. You both have full security clearance now, almost as good as mine.

"Shit," Peter muttered.

In his room, Saul pressed his fingers against his temples.

It's coming. It's going to be bad this time.

He exhaled sharply and turned to Alon. "Make sure the house is ready. Lunch. Tell Gershon to make it special. Some good single malt scotch. Pick them up promptly at ten in the morning. I need time to bring them on board."

"It's back?"

Saul nodded. He got up from the chair, shaking slightly, and he lay down on the bed. He shut his eyes. He heard Alon shut the door softly as he left the room.

The pain crashed down on Saul like a tsunami.

"*Scheisse!*"

The pain and his body were the same thing. The hallucinations would come later. Always the same. His parents would scream his name in the agony of their tortured death.

His tears began to flow, and he cried out again, like a child, "*Mutti! Mutti!*"

The morning dawned slowly. Thick clouds obscured the sun. Peter woke at six and quietly got out of bed. He checked the latest releases from IndoGold.

"Interesting," he muttered.

IndoGold had announced the loss of the helicopter, without further comment.

He heard the bed squeak. He waited. He heard the soft sound of her coming to him. She massaged his shoulders. He turned his head.

"Good morning. You slept very soundly last night," he said.

"I'm awake now."

"So am I." He stood and embraced her. "You are absolutely beautiful this morning."

"Thank you." She kissed him. "You're not bad yourself."

"What do you think? Should I carry you back to bed?"

"I'd love that, if you feel up to it," she said with a smile.

"I'm up to it."

At ten, Peter and Maria stepped out of the hotel with their baggage.

Alon and Gershon were waiting with the car. Gershon swept their bags into the trunk. Peter and Maria settled into the back seat.

"So, what's the plan?" Peter asked.

"We have an apartment near the airport," Alon said. "We'll meet Saul there."

Does Gershon ever speak? Peter wondered.

The car slogged through the heavy traffic. Just short of the airport, when Peter began to wonder when they would stop, Alon turned off the main road into a working-class neighborhood.

When they approached one of the newer and larger buildings, Alon turned, stopped to press a card to the sensor, and opened the overhead door to the basement parking.

They rode the small elevator to the top floor, where the door opened directly into the entryway of a penthouse apartment. Though it was on the top floor, it was modest in size and sparsely furnished. An outdoor terrace and garden occupied a portion of the rooftop.

"Come in! Come in," Saul said, and he gestured to the sofa and chairs in the small living room. Alon and Gershon disappeared.

Peter sat in one of the chairs, and Maria and Saul sat on the sofa.

"We can talk quite freely here," Saul said. "This is maintained by the Mossad. I've borrowed it for the day." He pointed to a side table. "Help yourself to some Sulawesi coffee."

Peter got up. "You want a coffee, Maria?"

"Sure."

Peter returned with two cups of coffee and handed one to Maria. After he sat down he tried the coffee and said, "Not bad. I rather like it."

For a short while, perhaps thirty seconds, they sat in silence.

Saul's not eager to get down to business, Peter thought. *I think I can wait.*

"You look a little rough around the edges, Saul," Peter said.

"It was not a great night."

Maria put down her coffee and turned to Saul. "I'm going to be blunt. You and Watson both have the bad habit of putting us out as bait, and not bothering to tell us what's going on. I have no intention of having anything more to do with you unless you're more open and honest with us."

That should start something, Peter thought.

Saul smiled slightly. "I understand. I'd like to talk about Kyoto first."

Maria picked up her coffee. "When you're done with Kyoto, I'd also like to know if the police will arrest us when we try to leave Japan."

Saul nodded. "The police will not arrest you. You tangled with Isamu Uno and two shinobi, modern-day ninjas who work for him. Uno is the enforcer for a rather nasty representative of the Japanese mob."

"Akihiko Uehara?"

"Yes, though I'm surprised you know the name. We're pretty sure that Uehara was behind the attack on you in Jakarta. He's an ultranationalist whacko."

"We left his nasty boys pretty badly damaged," Maria said. "This didn't happen in a back alley in some dark and failed country. This is Japan. The police know what happened? And they're still not going to bother us, not even question us?"

"The Japanese police know exactly what happened. They will not bother you."

"That's a little hard to believe," Maria said.

Gershon entered with three bowls of soup, placed them on the table by the window at the end of the small room. He spoke briefly to Saul in a language Peter did not understand. *Must be Hebrew.*

Saul smiled. "Lunch is served. We start with Gershon's ton-jiro soup."

They moved to the table, sat down and started to eat.

"This is good," Maria said.

They ate in silence until Peter put his spoon down.

"You've asked us to decide this afternoon whether we continue to work for you," Peter said. "Before we decide, you have to open up about Zürich. You have to tell us exactly what you have in mind."

Saul pushed his empty bowl away. "You believe Endang is a fraud?"

"Yes, but I have no proof yet."

"I told you earlier that I'm part of an Israeli effort to recover the missing Holocaust gold. I'm supported by the Mossad, but the effort is essentially unofficial."

"Yes," Peter said. "I remember."

"What the banks have identified and paid out is a pittance," Saul said. "I believe there is a significant amount of missing gold from the Holocaust, and the treasuries of the countries overrun by Hitler's armies. It's still sitting there, somewhere, hidden and unaccounted for."

Gershon returned. He brought plates of dark-green seaweed salad and removed the soup bowls.

Peter picked up his chopsticks. "That's all fine," he said, "but what does any of this, other than Endang, have to do with us?"

"Patience," Saul answered with a small smile. "Endang is a myth, created deliberately to convince someone to release a large amount of dirty, well-hidden, Holocaust gold. The myth says the gold will be ground up, mined at Endang a second time, and made into new, clean, and legitimate gold."

"Watson suggested something like this," Peter said. "It's crazy. It won't work. You can't keep something that big and that complex a secret, particularly not for a mine life of ten or twenty years."

"You're correct. But people who are afraid, who possess a toxic and evil secret, they can convince themselves to do some strange and illogical things."

"If that's all true," Maria said, "how much gold are you talking about?"

"How much gold," Saul asked, "is supposed to be in Endang's mythical ore reserve?"

"About a hundred million ounces," Peter answered, "though IndoGold keeps saying it's still expanding."

"There's your answer, Maria."

"Jesus Christ!" she said.

"You do realize," Peter said, "that, with no hard evidence, you're talking about roughly $130 billion US dollars?"

Saul nodded. "Yes. A few years ago, with higher gold prices, it was nearly $200 billion. It's about 3,000 metric tonnes of pure gold. It's a very large pile."

"All in one place?" Peter asked.

"We think so."

"Has anyone actually seen it?"

"Nobody we know and trust, and is willing to tell us, has seen it."

Peter put down his chopsticks. "Suppose I believe this insane story, what the hell is Uehara doing in the middle of this?"

Saul shrugged. "I think he's the facilitator, maybe the creator of the Endang myth. He hopes to gain control of the gold and take a portion, maybe all of it, for himself."

"So, if my report is released, Endang collapses. He loses his myth before he's ready, and he loses his opportunity to take control of the gold. He needs the myth to survive a while longer."

"Therefore, he orders the attacks on the two of you in Indonesia and Japan."

Gershon arrived at the table again, this time with a large bowl of gyoza dumplings, clean plates, and assorted sauces.

"Thank you, Gershon," Peter said. "This is a lunch of my dreams." He picked up ten of the dumplings and put them on his plate.

Gershon smiled and retreated to the kitchen.

"If the gold is all in one place," Maria asked, "where is it?"

"The evidence we gathered over the years, along with several other intelligence services, points to a bank in Zürich. I own the building next door. My building shares a foundation with a very large vault in the basement of the bank."

"I think I've seen this movie before," Peter said.

"You're asking us to help you rob a bank?" Maria asked.

"I'm not robbing the bank," Saul responded. "Officially the gold does not exist. The discovery of this gold could destroy the bank. If we take the gold, we actually do the bank a favor."

"I suspect most people would still say you're robbing a bank," Maria said.

"It's the biggest bank robbery in history," Peter said. "But if this is German gold, from the Second World War, how could it just sit there? After all, Germany was desperate for hard currency and gold to pay for essential raw materials during the war."

Saul nodded. "We think this was an effort by some Nazi insiders to steal from the German war effort to ensure a comfortable life after the war, win or lose. The war ended. Most of them died. The few survivors were in no position to collect their share of the gold."

"If you can steal the gold, what do you do with it?" Maria asked.

"I'll take it to Israel as compensation for the Holocaust. Incomplete? Yes. How do you compensate for mass murder? But it will be far better than anything else that has been done to date."

"That's a bit simplistic," Peter said. "A significant portion of this gold must be from looted national treasuries, like Lithuania and Ukraine."

"You could argue that point, but many in those countries were fully complicit in the Holocaust. The Germans could not round up and murder the Jews without local help. The gold has a value approximately equivalent to what Germany stole and looted from the Jews. The payment is long overdue."

Peter nodded slowly. "I guess I can accept that, but I'm still uneasy."

"Uneasy? You say that in response to mass murder?"

"That's unfair, Saul, and you know it," Peter said.

Saul remained silent, and Peter could not read his expression.

Peter finally continued. "If you do this, unlike the movie I remember, this isn't a job for a long weekend," Peter said.

"No. It's complicated and prone to discovery," Saul said. "It's a big job. You represent fresh eyes and fresh thinking. You both tend to see the whole picture. I want your help in planning and execution. I want to extend your contract, with a bonus for success."

"You do know that I'll have to tell Watson and get his approval?"

"Yes, Peter. Watson knows most of this, and he supports our efforts. I cannot tell you, at least not precisely, why he has been so supportive."

The three of them sat in silence for several minutes. Peter reached out and took four more gyoza. "These are really superb," he said.

After Peter ate the gyoza, he looked at Saul. "I think I'll choose to believe what you've told us, as long as Watson confirms most of it. Maria has to speak for herself, but there are several reasons I would like to help you. Some are deeply personal, and some are simply practical, considering our current situation."

"Thank you."

"Don't thank me quite yet," Peter said. "I need you to promise that you will hide nothing about this project. You will tell us everything. If you hide anything, and I discover it, I will walk away, regardless of the consequences."

Peter paused and turned to Maria. "You have anything you would like to add?"

"Only that I expect to work with Peter. I will not work for you if you hide critical information. Already, your secrets have almost killed us."

"With your backgrounds," Saul said, "you know that complete transparency is not always possible."

"There are no excuses on this one, Saul," Maria said. "I will accept nothing less than complete transparency."

"You may find that my 'truth' and Watson's 'truth' are somewhat different."

Peter shrugged. "Yes, there may be differences, but we must be able to believe in Watson's truth as much as we do in yours. We'll see him in Zürich. We'll commit to go to Zürich, but we cannot commit to the project until we talk to Watson."

Saul looked from Peter to Maria and back again. "All right. You have my word that I will be completely transparent with regard to the project in Switzerland."

Peter looked at Maria. "Are we ready to go to Zürich?"

Maria hesitated only a moment before she said, firmly, "Yes."

"Not that it really matters, but you mentioned a success bonus earlier," Peter said.

"Oh, yes. A quarter of a percent of the gold that reaches Israel."

"That's impressive," Peter said. "At least it's potentially impressive."

Saul smiled. "I thought you'd find the math easy."

Chapter 28

At the Air Canada gate at Narita Airport, Peter watched the noise and confusion prior to boarding. He scanned the crowd.

I can't tell. Peter saw Alon and Gershon. *I wonder what they see.*

"You ready?" Peter asked.

"Yes," Maria said.

The gate attendant announced First-Class boarding.

Peter and Maria stood up, picked up their carry-on bags, and walked briskly away from the gate. Peter looked back. Gershon and Alon had each accosted a Japanese man in a very animated fashion. *Were they really coming after us? Here?*

Peter and Maria disappeared into the crowd in the main hallway, passed two gates, and turned into the gate for the Swissair flight to Zürich.

Peter looked back again. *Nothing.*

They stepped into the empty First-Class line, boarded, and found the two First Class seats assigned to Cynthia and Richard Paine.

After she stowed her carry-on bag, Maria turned to Peter. "I'm starting to feel somewhat schizophrenic."

"Just be yourself."

The flight to Zürich was completely uneventful, but at more than twelve hours it was far too long for comfort, even in First-Class.

Swiss customs waived them through, and they arrived at their Zürich hotel in the early evening of the same day that they had departed Tokyo.

At check-in the hotel clerk handed Peter two envelopes. Peter ripped them open. One was a note from Saul.

I'll meet you at 8:00 AM for breakfast in the hotel's main restaurant.

The second note was from Watson.

Call me when you get in. We should talk before you meet with Saul tomorrow.

Peter showed the notes to Maria.

"Not much rest," Maria said.

"Nope."

Once they got to their room, Peter called Watson.

"When do you meet with Saul?" Watson asked.

"Breakfast. Eight. Tomorrow morning."

"Listen to his spiel. We want you to work with him, and I'll explain later. Tell him you're meeting with me at noon. I'm borrowing a house on the east shore of the Zürich Zee." He gave the address. "It's one of the grand old houses built after the First World War. It's about twenty minutes by cab from your hotel."

"We're not committing to Saul until we talk with you."

"That's not a problem." Watson paused for a moment. "Be a little careful. You're probably fine for a couple of days. With the switch of names and flights in Tokyo, nobody should know you're here, but the world will catch up to you. Saul and I will discuss security tomorrow. It's important. Particularly if you plan to run every day."

"We usually run in the morning or evening."

"I know. We'll talk about it. See you tomorrow."

"He wants us to work with Saul," Peter said as he disconnected, "and he'll talk to us tomorrow. He's also saying that we should be careful."

"Probably closer to Rostov now than we've ever been."

"I hadn't thought about him, but you're right." Peter frowned. "You want to clean up and get something light to eat?"

"Sounds good. Then I'll try to sleep."

Peter woke only once in the night. His dreams were quiet, but he was wide awake at a little after five. He got out of bed quietly and brushed his teeth. He pulled out his razor, thought about it, and put it back. He put on his running shorts and a shirt, and left Maria sleeping in the room.

The hotel catered to old money. All conversations, particularly those between the members of the staff, were carried on in muted tones. Large bronze doors framed the revolving door at the main entrance. An understated doorman, dressed in a dark gray business suit, stood in front of the door to assist and welcome guests.

Peter ran down to the strip of parkland along the north shore of the lake.

A nice city. Human scale. Comfortable. Maybe too comfortable. Definitely too rich.

He had the trail to himself, and he quickly increased his speed until he reached a pace of five-minutes per mile. He felt his body shift into a higher gear. Breathing deeply, his heart rate climbed to a comfortable plateau of 130 beats per minute. After twenty minutes he stopped and walked slowly for five minutes. Then he turned back.

This empty path makes for a great run. And maybe a dangerous one.

Maria looked up from the bed as he came into the room. "You're ambitious. What time is it?"

"About half past six," he said as he stripped out of his shorts and shirt. "I've been thinking that we need some better clothes for this hotel."

"Perhaps." Maria sat up, and the sheets fell away to reveal her naked body. "Actually, I rather like what you're wearing right now."

Peter smiled and sat on the bed beside her. He embraced her and they kissed.

"Sorry. I'm a little sweaty."

"If you recall, I rather like sweaty sex."

"I do recall." Peter lay back on the bed and pulled Maria down with him.

She pushed him on his back and began to kiss him and lick him. "I like your salty taste," she said with a smile.

"My little Russian spy. I think you've captured me."

"We've captured each other."

Peter rolled her over and began to explore her with his tongue. He tasted his sweat, and he tasted her. When she pushed back and lay on top of him again, the warmth of her body seemed to consume him.

She is devouring me. There will be nothing left.

He surrendered.

As they lay quietly in bed, Peter said in a whisper, "Do you remember a breakfast meeting?"

"Vaguely."

"Maybe we could be a little late?"

Maria raised her eyebrows. "Really?"

"Really," Peter said with a smile.

Maria laughed. "Sorry, my eager lover. I'm hungry. I want to take a shower and get downstairs for breakfast."

"You're being very sensible," Peter said, still smiling, "but I wouldn't mind being a little late and a little hungrier." He embraced her again.

Laughing, she pushed him away.

"Okay. You win," he said. "We'll plan on a rerun later. You get the first shower."

A few minutes late, Peter and Maria exited the elevator and strode across the lobby. Peter smiled at the concierge. He was already busy answering questions from guests in at least two or three languages. They paused for a moment in front of the jewelry store, and Peter pointed at the display of high-karat gold chains, bracelets, and necklaces set with large sapphires and emeralds.

"Before we head home, you should see if there's something here or in some other store in town that you'd like." Peter smiled.

"Actually, I prefer the white gold settings for sapphires and emeralds, but I'd be happy to look around."

They continued down the hallway and entered the dining room, which was set with white linen, in stark contrast to the dark wood paneling.

"You're right about our clothes," Maria said. "I feel like a country cousin visiting the big city."

"In Zürich we are country cousins. This city positively drips money."

Saul waved to them from a table in the far corner.

"Sorry we're a few minutes late," Peter said as they sat down. "Too many time zones for us, I'm afraid."

"No problem at all. I hope you don't mind the hotel. It's a bit stuffy and pretty quiet, but it's convenient to our work." Saul smiled.

He might be over eighty, Peter thought, *but he doesn't act it.*

"I always assume young couples can create their own entertainment," Saul said, still smiling.

Peter glanced at Maria.

My God, he thought, *you're actually blushing.*

Peter stifled a laugh and picked up the menu. "Right now, I'm starving. The light dinner I had last night has evaporated."

Once they had ordered, Peter watched Saul as he launched into a brief history of Zürich, how it prospered in the Second World War.

He's more relaxed and animated than I've seen him before.

"I've spent a lot of time here," Saul said. "It almost feels like home."

"Have you ever visited where you were born?" Peter asked.

"Once. The house was still standing. The owner wouldn't let me in. I found out later that he became convinced I had come for the family gold. He tore the old house apart, board by board, until there was nothing left but a pile of lumber." Saul closed his eyes.

"Did he find anything?"

"There wasn't anything to find. We were never wealthy. The final destruction of that house is crazy, but somehow it seems fitting... I guess."

Breakfast arrived, and they ate in silence for several minutes.

"You know, Saul," Maria said, "we don't really have the clothes for this sort of place, or for this city for that matter."

"I wouldn't worry too much. This hotel's pretty tolerant." Saul nodded. "Just the same, we could probably go out tomorrow and do a little shopping. There are worse places than Zürich to buy clothes, but not if you're looking for bargains."

"What's on the schedule for today?" Peter asked.

"I gather you're meeting Watson for lunch?"

"You're well informed," Peter said.

"We have to work together," Saul said. "First, I'll take you to the site. We can talk freely there. You can look around, and I'll arrange for someone to drive you out to your meeting with Watson. We'll play it by ear from there."

Peter picked up his coffee cup. "As soon as I finish my coffee, I'm ready to go."

"Just as a side note, Watson told me that he'll have your assay results today or tomorrow."

"That's quick," Peter said. "He must have paid a premium for that."

After breakfast, they exited the hotel to a waiting car. After driving away from the hotel for a few blocks, the car doubled back. They passed an undistinguished office building across the street and half a block from the hotel. The building was empty and obviously undergoing a major renovation. The sidewalk was closed off, and a tall, wooden fence made it impossible to see the first floor.

They turned a corner and entered an alley behind the building. They got out of the car next to three loading platforms at the end of the alley.

"This is the building I told you about," Saul said. "We're gutting the interior and making major changes to the front entrance area and access to the parking garage." He climbed a set of stairs to the level of the loading platforms, punched a code in a keypad and opened a small door.

"It doesn't look like much," Saul said as they entered, "but it will be the best office space in Zürich when we're done."

A group of construction trailers gathered in a little white flock to one side of the gutted first floor.

"Follow me," Saul said. "I'll introduce you to Levi. He's the project manager, in more ways than one. He's an engineer by training. He's also an Israeli commando."

"Interesting combination," Peter said.

"He's an interesting personality. He's never happy standing still."

Saul walked up the four steps to the nearest trailer and opened the door. "Is Levi around?"

"I'm here," was the booming response. "You have our visitors with you?"

"Yes. We need the tour."

Peter studied the man who appeared at the door to the trailer with three hard hats in one hand.

He may be short, but good Lord he has massive arms and legs. And his shoulders? He looks like he could explode.

Levi jumped down the four stairs two at a time and stuck out his hand to Peter. Peter smiled at the strength of his handshake.

"I'm Levi Singer. I'm happy to meet you." He turned to Maria and shook her hand as well.

"I've heard a little about your recent work in Japan and Indonesia. Welcome aboard." He handed a hard hat to each of them. He asked Saul, "You want to start with the garage?"

"That's the best place."

"Follow me, then," Levi said and started off. He led them down a flight of stairs to the first level of the parking garage and across the floor to the cement wall.

He doesn't walk, Peter thought. *He marches.*

Saul walked up to the wall, where blue paint outlined a rectangle about five feet high and three feet wide, starting at two feet above the floor. He patted the concrete that still showed the wood grain of the original forms. He turned around to face Peter and Maria.

"This foundation abuts the foundation of the Swiss International Bank. Six feet away, the other side of the two foundations, there's a large vault. It contains a hundred million troy ounces of gold, or about three thousand metric tonnes."

Saul turned back to the wall to pat the cement again. "I want you to help us remove the gold. It does not belong to the bank. It does not belong to the Swiss government. In many respects it does not exist at all."

They stood in silence for a full minute.

"I'm a geologist. I'm not a construction engineer," Peter said.

Saul turned to Peter and nodded. "True, but you and Maria both think in a holistic manner, and, in my opinion, you underestimate your abilities. You, Peter, have a lot of experience around mines, their tunnels, logistics, security, and shipping issues. That's what this is, a very high-grade gold mine. What I want from you is a complete proposal for taking the gold from this vault and getting it to Israel."

"This is a dangerous project, as Maria and I have already discovered," Peter said. "Large amounts of gold always attract bad actors."

"Yes. We have to think about security, and I think you may have some good ideas in that area as well. Nothing can go wrong. There is no second chance. We have to do it right the first time."

"What's your time frame?" Peter asked.

"I want your plan in two days. We've got two months to move the gold, maybe a bit more."

"Jesus," Peter said, stepping up to the wall. "That's tight." He put his hand on the cold concrete. *Why am I doing this?*

Peter turned back to Levi. "Tell me about the foundations."

"We're between the main supporting pillars for this foundation It's about two feet thick, concrete, with minor amounts of rebar. There's some packed fill between this foundation and the foundation for the bank. Maybe an additional foot thick."

"What about the bank's foundation?"

"We don't know. It's an older masonry building. We suspect the foundation is two to three feet thick, concrete, probably with a considerable amount of stone. Putting a major opening in the bank's foundation could cause localized structural failure in the building itself."

"The bank has all the normal alarms," Saul said, "including some very sensitive motion and vibration sensors. However, they're doing a major remodel themselves, possibly taking advantage of the disruption we are creating. They've told the private vault owners that they'll be repainting the vaults in three months. The whole upgrade will go on for at least four or five months."

Peter closed his eyes for a moment and listened. *All I can hear is the jackhammers working on the floor above us. Lots of vibration.* He opened his eyes and looked at Saul. "You're taking the gold to Israel by ship?"

"Yes."

"Departing which port?"

"Genoa."

Peter stared at Saul. "So… All we need to do is figure out how to break into the bank, silently and unnoticed. Remove 3,000 metric tonnes of gold, if it really exists, in less than two months. Move the gold out of Zürich, across the Alps and down to Genoa. Load the gold on a ship and get the ship and the gold to Israel. We've got two months, and we have to make sure no one hijacks the gold shipments."

"Exactly."

"A piece of cake," Peter said. He laughed. No one else laughed.

"Levi can provide all the manpower you need," Saul said, "plus plans and photographs. For your own safety, and the security of the project, please do not show up at the front of this building. Do not linger in front of the bank, or enter it. You will be delivered and picked up each day the same way as this morning."

"We can handle that," Peter said.

Saul looked at Peter. "You're growing a beard?"

"I've been thinking that a small change of appearance might be a good idea."

"I agree." Saul paused. "Do you have any more questions?"

Peter looked at Maria. She shook her head.

"I don't think so. We need to spend some time with Levi and learn a lot about this building." Peter turned and put his hand on the wall again. "Fascinating. Is it really a crime to steal something that doesn't exist?"

Watson sat in the two-story library, full of oak and musty books. MI6 maintained the grand old house on the east side of the lake. Watson knew the CIA had a house nearby, but that was the last place where he wanted to be.

He inserted the memory card into the computer and listened to the latest recording.

"There's a sizeable gathering of the faithful in Zürich," Harold James said. "In spite of Irish escaping, I think we can start to connect the dots."

"The failure with Irish was expensive," Braden said.

"The man disappeared like a puff of smoke, and, yes, we lost four good men. Ivan Dinisovich is sniffing around the edges. I don't think he knows much. Hard to tell whether he's official or not. We can be certain that Watson knows what's in the vault, and by definition so does Saul Bernstein. We can assume that by now they know the source of the gold."

"What's next?" Braden asked.

"They have to move the gold," Gerhardt said. "Too much to fly out. They'll truck it to one of the ports in Italy. That's a bunch of truckloads. Then they'll have to store it and get it on a ship. Lots of opportunities to relieve them of their precious cargo."

"The key is the ship," Harold said.

"Yes. We arrange for a hijacking," Gerhardt said.

"And what if, like most of your ingenious plans, it fails miserably?" Braden asked.

"Parts of the Mediterranean are very deep."

Harold laughed. "True enough."

"The gold doesn't do us any good if it's sitting on the bottom of the Mediterranean," Braden protested.

"At least it keeps it out of the hands of the Jews," Gerhardt said.

"Sick!"

Watson clicked off the recording and removed his headphones.

Might have a little spell of peace, until the ship sails.

Watson shut his eyes and frowned.

Just the same, you'd better stay on your toes, Peter my boy, and you, too, Maria. And what about you, Rostov? I think you're nearby. I can almost smell your stink.

Chapter 29

Gershon delivered Peter and Maria to the front door of a large and somewhat forbidding old house on the east side of the lake. It was one of many built by the wealthy bankers of Zürich in the first decades of the twentieth century.

Just as Peter touched the heavy brass knocker, a young woman opened the door. "Please come in," she said softly.

She directed them through the open doors into the library. "Mr. MacDonough? Your guests have arrived."

"Thank you, Jane," Watson said. "If you could bring us a fresh pot of coffee and then see that we are not disturbed."

"Certainly. I'll bring in the coffee trolley with lunch. It will be a few minutes."

Jane disappeared, pulling the pocket doors shut behind her.

Peter looked around at the two-story library. The narrow leaded glass windows offered glimpses of the lake. Oak paneling filled the spaces between the narrow windows and the bookcases.

"This is quite the house," Peter said. "We can talk freely here?"

"Oh, yes. This is maintained by the British. MI6. We won't say anything that our hosts don't already know. They're happy to provide support for this project, while we take the lead."

Peter and Maria sat on a brown leather sofa by the oak coffee table, and Watson sat on a matching leather chair across from them.

"What did Saul say?" Watson asked.

"Oh, it was a pretty uneventful morning," Maria said. "He just asked us to plan the biggest bank robbery in history, secretly move 3,000 metric tonnes of gold out of Zürich, across an international border to Genoa, load it on a ship, and get it to Israel. As Peter said to Saul, no Biblical allusion intended, it's a piece of cake."

Watson smiled. "You going to do it?"

"You want us to do it?" Peter asked.

"Yes, I very much want you to do it. The President of the United States wants you to do it."

"You believe the gold is really in that vault?" Peter asked.

"Yes."

"Saul uses the Endang resource estimate to come up with the number of one hundred million ounces," Peter said. "He thinks Endang is a gold laundering scheme. I think it's much more likely it's a gigantic stock fraud."

"Saul's right. Endang was created as a tool to launder a huge pile of dirty gold."

"That's very hard for me to believe. What do you have to support that?"

Watson smiled. "Let's start with the vault. Someone I trust has been in the vault. The vault has lovely, white plaster walls. A series of tarps, pulled tight, cover a huge pile of gold bars. He did a rough inventory. He estimated one hundred million ounces."

"How the hell did he manage to do all that?"

Watson made a small gesture with his hands. "I don't know. He doesn't talk about his methods, and I don't ask."

"Does the bank know he was in the vault?" Maria asked.

Watson hesitated. "I'm not sure. Probably. He left footprints in the dust on the floor of the vault."

"No action by the police?" Peter asked.

"Not so far," Watson said. "He also copied an original contract that explains where the gold came from." Watson picked up two pieces of paper from the table. "Do you read German?"

"Not well enough to read a legal contract. You, Maria?"

"Sorry," she said. "Not German."

"Well, then I'll summarize for you," Watson said. "This document is a contract between a Nazi named Glock and the owner of the Swiss International Bank. It was signed back in 1941. A group of Hitler's inner circle of Nazi leaders skimmed about ten percent of the take from the Jews and from the treasuries of eastern Europe. The owner of the Swiss

International Bank agreed to turn it all into new, clean gold bars. The Nazis would pick up the gold after the war. That's the story of the gold."

"That's nuts," Peter said. "They stole the equivalent of one hundred million ounces of gold, and nobody noticed?"

"It was easy. Most of the upper level Nazi officials were in on it."

"And it's still there?" Maria asked.

"Sure. Most of the beneficiaries died at the end of the war, either by suicide, or in battle, or by execution. The survivors were too deeply in hiding to show up for their share. So there it sits."

"It doesn't make any sense," Peter said. "Too many people. Somebody would have told Hitler, or maybe told the victors after the war."

"I think the Nazi leaders mostly came to think Hitler was completely crazy," Watson said. "And they weren't just stealing gold, it was diamonds, other precious stones, art, stocks, bonds, all kinds of stuff. The banker turned it all into gold."

"It still sounds totally crazy," Peter said.

"Maybe crazy," Watson said with a small smile, "but it's what happened. Hitler probably knew about it. They must have sold it to him as some sort of hidden emergency account."

"Okay," Maria said. "I get it. You know the gold's there. You know where it came from. Why not just tell the Swiss government and let them take care of it?"

"Knowing the Swiss record so far on Holocaust gold, we don't trust them to do what's right. We're afraid the gold could end up in the hands of some really bad actors."

"You obviously don't think much of the Swiss government," Maria said.

"After all their denials, this would be a huge embarrassment." Watson said. "And this amount of gold, in the wrong hands, could have some extremely unfortunate consequences. Revolutions. Civil wars. Maybe elect a dictator in the United States. The president wants to make sure it goes where he thinks it belongs."

"So you just steal it and give it to Israel?" Maria asked.

"Why not? There's a certain amount of elegance to that. President Pelton likes elegant solutions."

With a knock, Jane entered with the coffee trolley. A second woman brought a serving table holding an assortment of plates, beverages, sandwiches, salads, cookies and cakes.

Once the two women left, Watson gestured to the coffee and food. "Help yourselves. It's not a five-star lunch, but they do make rather nice sandwiches. The desserts are actually quite good. We also have beer and whiskey over in the corner, but I suggest we save that for later."

Peter poured two cups of coffee.

"I'd rather we sort out some of the issues in front of us before we start to eat," Peter said.

As he sat down he handed one cup to Maria.

"I have some real conflicts with this," Peter said. "My Ukrainian grandfather comes to me in my dreams sometimes. Usually he shouts at me and tells me about his youth and the Ukraine he knew. Sometimes he tells me what happened to his Jewish family. I know it's strange, but lately he's been telling me to do this. He says the gold belongs in Israel." Peter paused. "He can actually get quite loud about it."

Watson smiled. "I think you should listen to him."

"I'm sure my grandfather appreciates your support," Peter said, "but I suspect the majority of this gold came from the treasuries of eastern Europe, not from the Jews. It seems to me that part of the gold ought to go back to the Ukraine, or Latvia, or wherever it came from."

"Okay," Watson said. "In an ideal world we'd try to divide it all up according to where it came from. Trouble is, we don't know where it came from, not in detail. And I think time is running out."

"Time's running out?" Maria asked. "Why is time running out?"

"You do realize you have top security clearance, right?"

"Yes," Peter answered.

"Everything I tell you is top secret. Discuss it with no one, including Saul, without my approval. For example, I haven't told him I know how much gold is in that vault."

"Why not?" Maria asked. "It seems like he ought to know."

Watson shut his eyes. "The CIA is hunting the man who got into the vault for me, and I don't want to make his life any more dangerous. Saul's educated guess on the amount of gold is right." He opened his eyes again. "And now you know he's right."

"You haven't answered Maria's question about time," Peter said.

Watson sighed. "It's clear that the current owner of the Swiss International Bank is eager to get rid of the gold. There's no other possible reason for inventing the Endang fraud."

"I don't necessarily agree with that," Peter said, "but go on."

"Okay. Akihiko Uehara wants the gold. A Russian, Ivan Dinisovich, number two at the SVR, wants the gold. That's partly my fault. Finally, there's a cabal of traitors in the United States who want the gold. Sorry, high as your security clearance is, it's not high enough for details on those guys."

Watson paused. Peter and Maria both drank some of their coffee

"If we don't move that gold to a safe location, very soon," Watson said, "it will end up creating major problems. It could threaten the existence of the US government. Israel's a good destination, for a bunch of reasons. We help the Israelis. We pay reparations for the Holocaust. And we have plausible deniability."

"If Maria and I get caught, we will not have plausible deniability."

"Who's going to catch you?" Watson asked. "The gold doesn't exist as far as the Swiss are concerned. The banker wants to get rid of it. How does he report a theft of something that he doesn't want, that doesn't exist on his ledgers, and that could destroy the bank if the government knew about it?"

"And if it all goes wrong?" Peter asked.

"We might have a lot of explaining to do."

Peter stood up. "That sounds like an understatement to me, but I think I'll see about lunch."

He stepped over to the second cart. Watson and Maria followed him.

"Ah," Peter said. "That looks like curried egg salad on wheat bread, one of my all-time favorites."

They collected what they wanted and sat at an oak reading table. They ate in silence for a few minutes.

"The sandwich is as good as I hoped," Peter said. He looked at Watson. "It's a good story, but it wouldn't sell as a novel. Too unbelievable."

"It's not a novel, it's reality."

"I'm not sure how much of this I actually believe, but you know we're kind of stuck working for you. We're being attacked by at least two different groups, and until at least some of that is resolved we need some security help. I don't think my camp on the lake works anymore."

"I think you're right," Watson said.

Peter looked at Maria and raised his eyebrows. She nodded.

"We're ready to commit to continuing with this project," Peter said. "But… we need assurances of security backup. You have to pull us out if things get too dicey. You also have to promise to tell us everything you know. We've been blindsided too many times already."

"I'm being as transparent as I can be. I told you that I can't give you details about the cabal in the United States. As for security, Saul and I have some young men following you on your runs, and quite a bit of security around the hotel. If you have an unscheduled run, or you want to go out to dinner some night, let me or Saul know. We can adjust, within reason."

"Just a side question," Peter said. "Has our hotel room been swept for bugs? Is it safe to talk there?"

Watson smiled as he nodded. "As a matter of fact, yes. The room is safe, but I wouldn't talk when you're looking out the window."

Watson's phone made a small sound, and he pulled it out of his pocket to look at it.

"Ah," he said, "it's reminding me that I have the preliminary assay results for your samples."

"Can you give them to me?"

"Sure." Watson got up. "Come with me to what I use for an office here. I'll print them out for you."

"I'll wait here," Maria said, "and have another sandwich."

Peter followed Watson to an interior room with no windows. Watson closed the door. He turned and faced Peter.

"This is a secure room with no recording devices. I'll give you your sample results in a moment, but I want you to do something for me."

I don't think I'm going to like this, Peter thought.

Watson reached into his pocket and took out two small, plug-in memory cards.

"I want you to take these memory cards and protect them. You should treat them as if they're unstable explosives."

I don't like this.

"What the hell is on them?"

"As you know, I'm working directly for President Pelton. My main job is investigating a dangerous plot, deep within the US government, the cabal I mentioned. They are powerful people. I am beginning to worry about my personal safety. This contains all I know about the plot. If I die before I tell you to return or destroy these memory cards, call Alden Sage in the White House." Watson handed Peter a small slip of paper. "Here's his direct number."

"Christ!"

"I need someone I trust completely to safeguard this information. It has to be someone not completely obvious and someone not in the government. Don't tell anyone you have it, not even Maria."

"Does anyone know you're doing this?"

"No. Of course not. The President and Alden Sage know some of this information, but they don't know all the details, or that you have them."

"Should I look at the files?"

"Only if you must. I advise against it. The access code is also on that paper I gave you. Enter it backwards. Lower case and upper case are reversed."

"I don't have to do anything? Just hold these?"

"Correct, unless I die prematurely." Watson paused. "Please."

"Jesus! Now I know I'm completely nuts."

Peter took the memory cards and dropped them into his pocket.

"Thank you."

"I don't think I'll say that you're welcome," Peter said.

"Probably wise. Now let's get your copy of the assay results."

Watson picked up several sheets of paper and handed them to Peter.

"You had it printed and ready?"

"Of course."

"You know, sometimes you are a devious son of a bitch."

"In my business, that's how you stay alive. When you aren't devious enough, you're dead."

"Is that a warning?"

"Perhaps."

Chapter 30

After dessert and a final cup of coffee, Watson arranged for a driver to return Peter and Maria to their hotel.

Once in their room, Peter sat at the small desk. "I'm going to try to complete my Endang report in the next couple of hours," he said.

"Won't it take a while to evaluate the results?"

"Hell, the report's complete except for the results. I just have to fill in the numbers on the tables, plot the graphs, and finalize my conclusions. From a quick glance at the assays, it won't take long."

"Writing the report before the sample results are in? That's real confidence." She waved her hands. "Don't tell me. I'll wait for the formal conclusions."

She went to the closet and began to undress. "While you're finishing that, I'll go the gym and do something useful."

"I might be done when you get back."

Once Maria left, Peter entered the assay results in the tables in the report. He compared the gold values. *Just as I thought. No surprises here.*

He completed six graphs to go with the tables.

That should make it clear enough.

He went on to the conclusions. By the time Maria returned after two hours in the gym, he was reviewing the just-completed first draft of his report.

"So, what's the official conclusion?" Maria asked.

"I'll show you six graphs of the assay results. You tell me." He pulled up the first one. "These are the results from the sampled from the surface of the high-grade outcrops. Okay?"

"Yeah."

"The gold values are all over the place, but all are in the range of quarter to half an ounce of gold per ton. Really high grade. Average gold grades for an open pit gold mine are usually less than a tenth of these grades, in the range of hundredths of an ounce per ton."

"It's just like what they report for the deposit."

"Right. Look at this next graph. These are the gold values for the second set of samples we took, just below the surface of the outcrops."

"Wow!"

"Yep. Except for a few traces, no gold at all. Gold was added to the surface of the outcrop, but it's only skin deep. It doesn't matter how they did it. It's a fraud."

Maria shook her head.

"Of course, the assays for the resource come from the drilling. You remember I had the workers cut the samples in half?"

"Yes. I wondered about that."

"The workers at Endang washed the samples and labeled them. It's easy during that process for someone to dip the samples into a gold chloride solution, or rub a bit of a wedding ring on the surface of the samples. No easy way for me to stop either of those actions without a major confrontation, and either technique would result in some great gold grades."

Peter pulled up the third graph.

"Here are the results when the lab just ground up one half of the sample, with no special cleaning or washing. Gold values all over the place, but they still range from a tenth of an ounce to almost a whole ounce of gold per ton."

"That fits with what they reported from their drilling, right?"

"Yes, but I asked the lab to treat the other half of each sample differently. They did some cleaning and washing to try to get rid of contamination, but it wouldn't affect any gold naturally in the samples."

Peter showed her the fourth graph.

"Here are the results from those samples."

"Nothing?"

"Exactly. No gold at all, except for a tiny trace of gold in a couple of samples, which might be contamination at the lab for all I know."

"The whole thing really is a fraud," Maria said.

"Let me show you the two final graphs." He brought them up on the screen, side by side. "The one on the left shows the two sets of results from the surface samples. The one on the right does the same thing with the two sets of samples from the drilling. Pretty dramatic."

"Rather obvious," Maria said. "So... You know it's a fraud. What's IndoGold worth on the market?"

"It's down a bit after they reported that Teunis is missing, but it's still worth about $5 billion Canadian, maybe a little more."

"And it's actually worthless?" She paused. "So what do you say in your conclusions?"

"I say I'm 98 percent sure it's a fraud. To get to 100 percent, someone should drill two or three holes through the highest-grade portion of the reserve and carefully supervise the sampling and assaying." Peter took a deep breath. "In my opinion, the property has absolutely no value."

"Ouch."

"Yeah. If this story Saul and Watson tell about the reason for Endang is true, the conspirators know we survived. At least that crazy Japanese guy knows, and that's probably enough. They should know there's a good chance I discovered the fraud."

Maria said, "There are lots of people hovering around this pile of gold. Canadians, Russians, Indonesians, Japanese, Swiss, and some unknown Americans. They'll be really angry about your report, just because it screws up their plans. They'll be royally pissed if we succeed in stealing the gold."

"To put it mildly."

"I'm beginning to think I should be afraid of shadows," Maria said.

"I'd guess any of them would kill us over losing a hundred billion dollars. And then there's Rostov. He's still out there, somewhere, still trying to kill us."

"I lumped him in with the other Russians."

Peter sat back in his chair, and Maria sat down on the sofa.

"Okay," Peter said. "I'm going to finalize this report and print out two copies downstairs at the business center. I'll tell Watson and Saul that it's ready." He looked at Maria. "Then I think we need to start planning a bank robbery."

"You said it'd be a piece of cake."

"I do remember that."

That night, they began to work on their plan to move the gold.

After a long night, they headed out in the morning for their scheduled six-thirty run along the lake.

"Full speed today?" Peter asked.

Maria stretched. "I'm game if you are."

"Well, my brain's been in high gear. It's time to give the heart some exercise." He looked down the path. "Looks like Alon and Gershon are waiting to escort us today. Let's see if they keep up."

In the cool, clear air of the morning, the run along the lake was pure joy. The mountains in the distance were sharp and clear.

In the beginning of the run, Peter pushed to a little faster than six minutes per mile. He looked back. Alon and Gershon were following at a discreet distance. "Doing okay?" he asked Maria.

"I'm feeling great. Let's go."

Both of them sped up to five minutes per mile.

Peter smiled. *We're almost breathing in unison.*

In the second half of their out-bound run, as they came around a curve in the trail, they passed a group of six other runners. At the same time, Peter saw the man sitting in his usual place.

The man sat on a bench facing the lake. He wore a light-weight jacket, crisp dress pants, and held a furled umbrella. A broad-brimmed hat hid most of his heavily bearded face as he looked down at his feet.

Peter looked up at the sky. *Not a cloud in sight.*

After they passed him, Peter looked back. The man was watching them, but he quickly looked away. In that brief moment, Peter saw his face. *He looks familiar.*

Peter and Maria kept running. At twenty minutes Peter said, "Let's take a short break and head back." He looked back along the path. "I think we outran Alon and Gershon."

"They'll catch up," Maria said.

They were both breathing deeply, but not particularly quickly. They walked slowly and Peter checked his heart rate. *Good.*

"Did you notice our friend back there?" Peter asked.

"The man on the bench?"

"Yeah."

"Looks the same. Looking down at his feet."

"I looked back. He was watching us. He looks familiar somehow."

"Who do you think he is?" Maria asked.

"I don't know, and I don't know why he has an umbrella on a day like this."

Maria shrugged. "Maybe he knows something we don't?"

"I have an uncomfortable feeling about him."

"Did you really have to say that?"

"Sorry. I can't help it," Peter said. "When we get to him, let me run ahead about twenty or thirty feet."

"Fine."

"I'm probably crazy."

"I hope so."

"I still don't see Alon or Gershon," Peter said.

"Probably decided to wait for us."

They started back, quickly picking up speed.

When the man on the bench came into view, Peter ran a little faster and pulled in front of Maria. The man stared directly at them. There was no one else in sight.

He's waiting for us.

The man stood up.

Shit. He's not as old as I thought.

The man was tall. His broad shoulders were not hidden by his jacket. Peter moved to the right side of the path.

Just as Peter reached him, the man raised his unopened umbrella and lurched forward. He appeared to be falling, but the tip of the umbrella was clearly aimed at Peter's chest.

What the hell?

Peter quickly twisted counterclockwise. The umbrella missed him, and the man struggled to keep his balance. Peter swept his right leg across the man's lower legs, just above his ankles. The man fell heavily to the ground, and his umbrella skittered down the path toward Maria.

Maria scooped up the umbrella. She was shouting. She charged the man.

She's yelling at him in Russian.

The man tried to get up, and Maria slammed the tip of the umbrella into the man's abdomen, then into his chest and into one of his thighs. All the time she was shouting at him.

The man made a grab at the umbrella.

Peter kicked him in the ribs.

The man exhaled loudly but managed to stagger to his feet. With a horrified look on his face, he turned and ran through the bushes to the roadway. He climbed into a waiting car and disappeared.

"You fucking bastard," Maria said as she watched him disappear.

"What the hell just happened?" Peter asked.

"That man… He's Russian, and I think I just sent him to hell."

"How do you know that? What did you do to him?"

Maria backed away. "Don't touch this umbrella." She laid it carefully on the ground.

Peter raised his hands.

"I don't know what I did," she continued. "This is a classic Russian assassination attempt. The end of the umbrella probably holds several small tablets of something that's fired into your body when the tip hits you."

"Jesus!"

"Probably polonium. I hope so. It's a very painful and disgusting death."

"You know," Peter said slowly, "if that man's really Russian, I think I know who it is."

"Who?"

"His beard changes his appearance a lot, but I'm pretty sure it's Zakhar Rostov."

"Damn! You may be right. Now I really want that to be polonium. He deserves it."

Alon and Gershon ran up to Peter and Maria.

"Glad to see you guys… finally," Peter said.

"You were a little too fast for us today. What just happened?"

"Be careful of that umbrella," Maria said. "That man tried to assassinate us. It's a classic Russian operation. Probably fires poison pellets of some sort."

"I'm pretty sure he's Zakhar Rostov," Peter said.

"Really?" Alon asked.

"Yeah. I've never met him, but I've seen lots of pictures. Looked like him, but he's grown a beard."

"I struck him three times with the umbrella," Maria said. "If I just injected three polonium pellets into him, he's already dying."

"Where'd he go?" Alon asked.

"He had a really shocked look on his face," Peter said, "and he ran through the bushes to the road. A car was waiting and they took off."

"Anything special about the car? Did you see the license plate?"

Peter shook his head. "The bushes screen most of the road. The car was black, a Mercedes maybe, like about a hundred thousand others in this town."

Alon stooped and picked up the umbrella. He looked at it very carefully.

"Okay," Alon said. "Let's run back to the hotel together, and a little slower than your top speed, please."

Once they were back in their room, Peter started to strip off his clothes.

"Shit," he said. "That never should have happened. Alon and Gershon are supposed to be with us, not relaxing on a damn park bench."

"Well, we were running pretty fast today."

"Having security isn't much help if they're too far away to do anything. Rostov wouldn't have tried that if they'd been with us."

"We survived, and Rostov will die."

"True, but it happened only because you recognized a Russian operation going down."

Maria sighed. "Just shows you that there are advantages to falling in love with a Russian spy."

Peter turned to look at Maria. He shook his head. "It's not usually at the top of my list of favorite benefits, but it might be today."

Chapter 31

Peter and Maria focused on their planning, perhaps to rid their minds of the image of Rostov. They skipped lunch.

At three, Watson called. "I hear you ran into our old friend."

"Yes," Peter said. "Rather nasty."

"You sure it was Rostov?"

"Maria's sure. I'm almost sure."

"You outran your security detail?"

"If they'd been there, Watson, this wouldn't have happened."

"You were moving fast."

"Not a valid excuse," Peter said.

"Agreed, but you're alive."

"Watson, I like Alon and Gershon, but I'm tired of security showing up just to congratulate us for being alive."

"Talk to Saul. It was his day."

"Yeah. Why don't you talk to him?"

Watson hesitated. "Maria was right about the umbrella. We suspect it fired pellets of polonium, designed to dissolve in the blood. We'll know for sure sometime tomorrow, after the FBI lab gets a crack at it."

"Have you found Rostov?" Peter asked.

"Not yet, but you've stirred up a real hornet's nest. Everyone wants a piece of that man, the CIA, the Swiss, Interpol, the works. Even Russia. He'll turn up. If it's polonium, he's already losing control of his bowels, vomiting, generally having a really lousy day."

"Glad to hear that."

"To change the subject, I read your report, Peter. I noticed you didn't sign it."

"I agreed to make a report to you and Saul. I've done that. I don't want my name on it, and I don't want it released."

"We might start a rumor when it makes sense, but we won't release the report."

"To absolutely nail down the fraud, someone has to do some careful drilling and sampling."

"What you've done is sufficient for us." Watson hesitated. "How are the bank plans coming? You making any headway?"

"I'm planning to give Saul a review, at his building, at three tomorrow afternoon."

"If you don't mind, I think I'll attend."

"You're the boss, Watson, not me."

"True."

"Before you hang up," Peter said, "I'd like to take a break and just head down to the lake with Maria."

"I'll make arrangements."

"Tell them to keep a discrete distance."

"But close enough to respond."

"Not so close they're listening to our conversation."

After Peter disconnected, Maria stood up and stretched. "What did he say about Rostov?"

"Everybody's looking for him, and you were right about the umbrella."

"Do they know what was in it?" she asked.

"Not yet."

Peter stood up. "Let's head down to the lake. I need some fresh air."

"I'm not excited by the lake, not after this morning," Maria said.

"There are lots of people this time of day. Besides, with Rostov out of the picture we're probably safer than we've been in a long time."

"There's always someone else," Maria said softly.

"I have to admit, it's a beautiful day," Maria said as they walked.

Peter held her hand. "The mountains are so sharp. I feel like I could touch them."

"Maybe we can come back someday and climb some of them."

"Maybe."

They sat on a bench beside the path they had run along earlier in the day. After a while Peter broke the silence.

"Do you know why I want to work on this project?"

"I think your grandfather is a persuasive ghost."

"He is," Peter said with a small smile. "I still have some misgivings, but the more I think about it, the more I tend to agree with Saul. Morally, it just seems right to send it to Israel."

"I can accept that, I guess."

"Rostov's out of the picture, Maria. At least I hope so. But this project is dangerous as hell."

"Yes."

Peter looked at Maria. "You ready for this?"

Maria hesitated. Peter watched as she stared out over the lake toward the mountains. *What are you thinking about? Do you still owe somebody?*

Without looking at him, she said, "Yes. I'm ready."

Peter and Maria stood with their backs to the wall in the first level of the garage in Saul's building. They faced Saul, Watson, Levi and Alon.

"We have nothing written," Peter said. "Our approach is simple. Nothing fancy."

"I like simple," Saul said.

"We seem to have a couple of strange advantages," Peter began. "Essentially, the gold does not exist legally. It's been kept secret for a long time. Probably only one or two people in the bank know anything about it, and it's most likely quite rare for anyone to enter the vault."

"We assume the time limitation is because of the planned painting of the vaults," Maria said, "but you've said there's only two or three months to complete this job. Presumably that frequency of visits to the vault will not change for at least two months."

"That's reasonable," Saul said, "but you can't rule out an unexpected visit."

"It's not foolproof," Peter said. "Nothing about this project is foolproof. We should keep the tarps in place, some sort of frame to hold them up, so a quick peek into the vault might not discover we're removing the gold."

"Unlikely," Watson said.

"You're probably right," Peter said. "The chance of discovery is significant, and we can't do much about that. The first major problem is the vibration and the noise we'll make getting through the two foundations. We have to have some sort of symphony of jackhammers working on something very visible and legal while we work on the foundations. Perhaps a new entrance to the parking garage, and hopefully right next to the bank. They have to turn off the alarms and get used to noise and vibration."

"It's already in the plans," Levi said. "We'll just move up the timing."

"We'll need steel bracing for the opening in the bank's foundation," Peter said. "It'll take three days or so to complete the opening into the vault."

"Getting the gold out of the vault is straightforward," Maria said. "Get a silent conveyor system into the vault, out the opening, up through a hole in the floor above us, and out to the loading docks."

"It's brutal, physical work," Peter said. "To be safe, plan on forty days to get the job done. We're talking about a quarter of a million gold bars, each weighing a little over twenty-seven pounds. We need to move 6,250 gold bars every day. That's nearly eighty-six tons, every single day, and most of it hand work."

"Most of the time, it'll be nearly impossible to get more than twenty workers in the vault at any one time," Maria said. "Each day, assuming twenty workers, every worker will have to lift and move over four tons. That's a long, hard day."

Peter and Maria waited for a response. An uncomfortable silence continued for almost a full minute.

"We can get the men from the Mossad and the Israeli military," Levi finally said. "We'll have to put extreme security measures in place, but we're good at that."

"So, you get it up to the loading docks," Watson said. "How do you get it over the Alps and on the ship to Israel?"

"It's really a simple trucking issue," Peter said. "You've got three loading bays. Each can handle a twenty-foot container on a truck trailer. Each container has the capacity of about twenty-four tons. Load two layers of gold bars into the container, protected by layers of felt. That's about 1,600 gold bars per container, just under twenty-two tons of gold."

"What about customs?" Watson asked.

"Our understanding is that the truck x-ray is not available on the Swiss-Italian border crossing for trucks headed to Genoa," Maria said. "Cover the gold with piles of construction debris, which some entrepreneur in a coastal African country will accept for a relatively small charge. It's more economical to ship the debris, rather than pay the fees to dispose of it in Switzerland."

Levi laughed. "That's probably true."

"We have to fill and haul away at least four containers every working day. You have enough rubbish to cover the camouflage effort, Levi?"

"That's one thing we have in abundance," he answered.

"They'll be very heavy containers," Saul said.

"They're legal on the highway," Peter said. "Who will question their weight since they're supposed to be full of construction debris? Pack heavy debris, like gypsum board, up against the access to the container. It will look like the whole container is full of heavy waste."

"Okay," Levi said. "We need a quiet conveyor. That's fairly easy, except for some sharp corners. It's going to take a lot of people. You plan on twenty-four hours a day?"

"We've planned on eight-hour days, at least to start, with construction noise covering any noise in the vault," Maria said. "If the operation is very quiet, we might be able to extend that a bit. But hauling away more than six or eight containers in a day, particularly when you're not working on the building, except maybe Saturday, might bring unwelcome attention."

"With a little luck," Peter said, "if things are quiet enough, we might be able to speed up the process and get it done in as few as thirty to thirty-five days. I wouldn't hope for anything less than that."

"We should push it as much as we can," Saul said.

"What about security?" Peter asked. "It'll have to be tight as hell. We're stealing over three billion dollars in gold every day."

"As Levi said, we know security," Saul said.

"What about unexpected inspections of the building, Levi?" Maria asked.

"I don't expect any, but there are ways of covering this activity. I can use dust control on the debris as an excuse."

No one spoke for a moment, until Saul said; "I want to hide all our activity when we're done. Even if everything goes perfectly, when we finish removing the gold, how the hell do we do that?"

"Ah," Peter said, "That's a bit of a problem, but I think we can do it, with a little help from Watson."

"Really? What kind of help?" Watson asked.

"First of all," Peter said, "you seem to know how to get someone into the vault. Let's call him the Magician. It's complicated, but we may need the Magician to get someone else either in, or out of, the vault, or both."

Saul raised his eyebrows. Watson remained silent.

"We need someone to remove the forms from the inside of the vault that are used when we fill in the access with cement," Peter continued. "We can probably pass them through a small hole into the adjacent building. We repair that hole at the last minute."

Peter took a deep breath. "Then someone has to re-plaster the patched wall and paint it. The Magician almost surely needs to be on the painting crew for the bank, and particularly for the crew that paints the vaults. One thing for sure, the Magician has to get the plasterer and painter out of the vault. If the man working in the vault is dressed like a painter, he can leave unnoticed with the other painters."

"That's a rather amazing ask," Watson said.

"Depending on how we finally organize the repair job, the finishing of the plaster on the vault wall may require someone to stay in the vault for several days."

"Jesus Christ," Watson muttered.

"With a big enough bribe to the painting company, and a man who can get in and out of the vault, when he needs to do so, we should be able to pull this off."

Saul glared at Watson.

Watson said nothing for almost a minute. Finally he said, "It won't work."

"Who the hell is this guy, this Magician who walks in and out of the vault?" Saul asked.

Watson ignored the question.

"If he's good," Peter said, "this should all be doable."

Saul was getting agitated. "Who the hell is he?"

Watson shut his eyes. "I can't answer that question."

"You bastard!" Saul said.

Peter waited.

"I'm not sure I can make the Magician appear," Watson said softly.

Peter waited.

Watson opened his eyes. "Okay. If we're really lucky, and if I can raise the Magician, possibly from the dead, this can work. We've got a little time to find him, to work out some of the details… and to work on the painting company." Watson paused. "You've got one huge problem, though."

"What's that?" Peter asked.

"The tiniest slip-up, the smallest unexplained noise, maybe just a passing whim, will bring the owner into the vault. If it's more than a casual glance in the door? Empty tarps won't help us much if he goes around the back and finds twenty Israelis and a conveyor belt full of gold bars heading out a hole in the vault."

"Yes," Peter said. "That's the one major risk we cannot control. If it happens, we're in deep shit."

In the silence that followed, Peter could almost feel the thoughts bouncing around in their brains.

Saul finally spoke. "I think it'll work. The banker may not be as much of a threat as you think."

"What do you mean?" Watson asked.

Saul smiled. "I don't think I'll answer that."

"Fuck you," Watson said.

Saul laughed.

"I sure as hell hope you're right," Watson said with a note of exasperation, "because I'll bet anyone standing here today that the banker will walk into that vault before we're done."

Watson's offer met with nothing but silence. He looked pointedly at Saul and smiled.

Over the next five days, Peter and Maria tried to stay out of the way, while activity in Saul's building reached a level of frantic intensity.

"I've never seen anything quite like this," Peter said to Maria.

The new conveyor system reached from the top floor of the garage, through a brand-new hole in the ceiling, to the loading docks at the back of the building.

"How do they get this stuff so fast?" Maria asked.

"I don't know," Peter answered. "It could take a year at a normal mining operation."

A new chute for the construction waste, to camouflage the gold, entered the first floor, near the loading bays.

The workers chipped away at the bank's foundation, the sounds lost in the cacophony of jackhammers assaulting the new entrance to the parking garage. When they were about a third of the way through the foundation, Peter insisted they place the first of three planned steel supports.

"We want at least three," he said, "and we need some space between the last one and the inside of the vault."

Peter and Maria joined Watson, Saul, Levi and Alon in the garage early on the fifth morning. Each of them held a flashlight.

Peter watched as the workers, amid waves of noise from the other jackhammers, chipped away at the last of the rock and concrete. They started at the top of the opening. They worked slowly and carefully. When the opening was complete, Peter helped set the last of the steel supports.

Along with the other workers, Peter stepped back. He smiled slightly at everyone's hesitation. *No one wants to be first.*

Watson final spoke. "This is your baby, Saul. You first."

Saul stepped into the opening. He carefully walked over the irregular surface, through the six-foot tunnel, and stepped down into the vault. He turned on his flashlight. The others followed.

Peter watched Saul put his hand on the tarp, and he did the same. Peter felt the hardness behind it. *I think so.*

"I can't be sure," Saul said.

They all followed Saul as he walked down the side of the vault. He came to where one tarp overlapped with another. Just as Irish had done before them, Peter and Saul untied the tarps and untied their connections with the recessed hooks in the cement floor.

They all watched in silence as Saul pulled back one of the tarps.

Peter heard a gasp from someone, when the light from the flashlights reflected off the shiny and dust-free gold bars.

"I'll be damned," Peter said.

"It really is here," Saul said.

He actually sounds surprised, Peter thought.

Chapter 32

They moved the first gold on the eighth day. Two loaded containers departed for Genoa the next morning. After some practice, the work became completely silent, but silence required great care, and the work was exhausting and mind numbing.

Security was intense. All of the work – removing the gold from the vault, the conveyor system, and loading it into the containers – was walled off from the construction activities in Saul's building. Every shipment to a heavily guarded warehouse in Genoa was accompanied by security provided by the Mossad and the Israeli military.

On the fifth day of moving gold, Peter and Saul watched the men pack the containers.

"It's hard to increase productivity and maintain silence," Peter said.

"How many days do you need?"

"Seventy days, with Sundays off to rest the men and make repairs."

Saul frowned. "It's too long."

"Silence takes extra care, and it's inefficient. We could do two shifts if you can get the men, but moving them back and forth to the building could raise suspicions."

"It has to be forty days or less."

"You can't fit more men in the vault and still have room to work."

Peter watched the flow of gold bars. The containers came to the docks with rolls of felt. The workers laid down felt, then a layer of gold. Another layer of felt, and another layer of gold. A final layer of felt covered the top layer of gold. The process was very quiet.

"Maria did suggest a way around the problem," Peter said.

"And?"

"Keep the men here. Set up a bunkhouse in the second level of the garage, behind a wall, with a hidden door. Bring the food in every day with the containers. Do two shifts five days a week. One or maybe two shifts on Saturday. It would be like living in a dungeon for the men, but they'd be done in about thirty days. Maybe a little longer."

"How do we handle toilets and showers… laundry?"

"There's still plumbing on the second level," Peter answered. "The men would need to be very quiet, though, even during their time off."

"Sound-proof the off-duty area."

"Possibly."

Saul looked at Peter. "Why not work twenty-four hours, seven days a week?"

"You might be able to do two ten-hour shifts, but you've got only three loading docks. You take out three full containers early in the morning and replace them with empties. Maybe move and replace two or three during the day and make one final exchange for three more at about six at night. You can't be moving them at midnight."

"Why not?"

"Somebody will complain, and that will bring unwelcome attention. Anyway, we can't camouflage the gold without construction debris, and we can't be making a lot of noise with the construction debris when there's not supposed to be anyone working here." Peter paused.

"Go on," Saul said.

"I figure during the week we can fill the chute with debris late in the day to handle any night work, and maybe a bit extra on Friday, to provide the needed debris for Saturday's containers. We'll have to be careful to not jam the damn thing."

"What about the noise of using the debris at night or on Saturday? We won't have any construction workers here then. How do you explain that?"

"You don't. You fill the three containers with gold on Saturday and stop when they're full. You cover the gold with debris first thing on Monday, before the containers are replaced. Same thing at night during the week. Load the gold, cover with debris first thing in the morning."

"If you do all this, how long?" Saul asked.

"Thirty to thirty-five days total, if we ramp up five days from now."

They watched the loading a little longer. *Those guys are tough*, Peter thought.

Saul took a deep breath. "Let's go talk to Levi. He has some work to do."

Once the gold was moving out of the vault at the higher rate, the gold bars flowed steadily into the containers, and the days settled into a routine. Levi had nearly eighty full time workers, and nearly the same number of guards for the building, and for the trucks going to Genoa.

Peter and Maria had little to do, but they assisted where and when they could. This day the security team was short several workers due to a stomach flu. Peter and Maria stood on either side of the main, heavy steel door from the bank into the vault. As long as the door remained closed, their job was perhaps one of the most boring jobs ever created.

Peter looked at his watch. *Five o-clock. The bank will close soon, and we'll be able to leave, too.* Twenty-five days elapsed, and they were down to just over 60,000 bars remaining. *Right on schedule.* He stretched and yawned.

He turned to look at Maria. She smiled.

The only problem is the Magician is still missing, Peter thought.

A barely whispering fan moved air through the vault.

Peter heard a faint squeal from the door, then a second.

He jerked his head around. The sound came from his side of the door.

Shit! Someone's at the door. They're unlocking it!

Peter signaled for Maria to flatten against the wall. He reached and switched off the light in the vault.

The workers halted their work.

Peter heard another faint squeal. A slightly different tone. Then another.

That's the second set of locks.

Peter heard the soft sound of movements in the vault

Must be the armed Israelis.

He listened. Silence. Then he heard the third set of faint squeals.

That's it. That's the third set of locks.

He tried to become part of the wall as someone began to slowly heave the door open into the hallway.

At first only a small sliver of light entered the vault and fell on the Chinese screen. As the door opened fully, Peter could see the shadow of a large man.

The man stood there, in the center of the now open entrance to the vault, just out of sight. He didn't move.

Peter barely breathed.

He's not coming in.

A minute passed. Though the ventilation system was off, Peter felt a faint flow of air passing him as it flowed out of the vault.

He'll feel that. It will force him to enter.

The man stood still. Then he turned to grip the door.

He's not coming in!

Another moment passed, and the shadow turned again. The silence was almost overwhelming. Slowly, the man stepped forward. He reached around the entrance and flicked on the lights in the vault.

Peter recognized him immediately from pictures he had seen. In one quick motion, Peter gripped Jan's right arm and pulled him roughly into the vault. Jan squawked in surprise before Peter clapped his left hand over the banker's mouth.

Peter tightened his grip and shoved Jan's right arm high up along his back.

He'll feel that.

"Be still," Peter hissed in Jan's ear. "Don't make me break your fucking neck."

Jan tensed at the words, but he stopped struggling. Peter continued to hold him. Jan moaned softly.

Maria turned toward him. She had pulled a black balaclava over her face. Two armed Israelis, the men Peter had heard moving in the darkness, stood behind her. They carried Glock pistols with silencers. One holstered his pistol, moved behind Peter, and pulled a balaclava over his head.

"Shut the damn door," Peter whispered.

Once the door was shut, Peter spoke to Jan. "If I let go, will you be quiet?"

Jan nodded his head.

"You will not make a sound. You will not move. If you do either, one of these men will kill you, and your body will disappear. You understand?"

Jan nodded again.

Peter loosened his grip and slowly released Jan's arm.

Jan massaged his right arm. He took several deep breaths. He said softly, "You are stealing the gold. You must work for the Russians."

Peter ignored Jan's comment. He jerked his head at one of the armed men. "Go get S from the hotel. He has to make a decision."

The man hesitated.

"Shit! Get going, and be quick. Who knows when the guard will come looking for this guy."

The Israeli offered his pistol to Peter, but Peter shook his head and nodded toward Maria. The Israeli shrugged and handed his pistol to Maria, turned, and jogged out of sight.

"Can I move?" Jan asked.

"No," Peter said. "And keep your mouth shut."

"How much…?"

Before Jan could finish his question, Peter's left hand was over his mouth again, and Peter forced Jan's right wrist almost to his neck. Jan made muffled sounds through Peter's grip on his mouth.

"I told you to shut your damn mouth. You will be quiet. Understand?"

Peter forced Jan's wrist a little higher. Jan made more urgent, but still muffled sounds. Peter slowly lowered Jan's wrist again. He loosened the pressure of his left hand on Jan's mouth. Other than rapid breathing and soft moaning, Jan was quiet. Peter released him.

Six more minutes passed in tense silence before Saul came into view. A scarf covered his face and most of his head, except for his eyes. He studied Jan in silence.

"May I speak?" Jan asked.

"Yes." Saul said, "but softly. If you shout for help, you will die."

"You are stealing the gold. For whom?"

Saul shook his head. "Stealing? I don't think so. This gold does not exist. It does not belong to you, or the bank. It is already stolen gold. We are claiming it for those who truly own it."

Jan stared at Saul. "I know you. I know your eyes, and I know your voice, Saul Bernstein." He paused. "You're taking the gold to Israel?"

Saul looked past Jan to Peter, but Peter simply shrugged.

"Yes," Saul said. "We are taking the gold to Israel. You have a choice. You can help us… or you can disappear."

Jan began to giggle. It sounded strange coming from such a large man, particularly under the circumstances.

This is weird, Peter thought.

"I'm sorry," Jan said. He wiped his eyes. "This is unbelievable. I've been trying to do this for years, and now you're doing it for me? You think I won't help you?" He took out a handkerchief and softly blew his nose. "Unbelievable!"

Saul said nothing.

"You will have to let me go. The guard will begin to wonder where I am."

"Why should I trust you?" Saul asked.

"You don't know what a gift this is? Really?" He blew his nose again. "You're right about the gold. I can't call the police. I don't want to." Jan paused. "You're operating from the office building next door?"

Saul nodded.

"Good. Let me go. I'll come there directly."

Saul looked at Jan. Saul did not speak for a full minute. The silence grew thick and heavy. Finally he said simply, "Go."

Jan put his handkerchief away. "I'll meet you at the front door to your building in about ten minutes." He turned, pushed open the vault door and stepped out.

In the vault they all waited in silence, until the door was closed, and they heard Jan turn the keys in all three sets of double locks.

They pulled off their balaclavas and Saul undid his scarf.

Maria shook her hair free. "Christ! You're taking a hell of a risk."

Saul shook his head. "I don't think so." He turned his attention to the Israelis. "Get everybody back to work."

Then to Peter and Maria, "You two come with me. We have a meeting with our personal, Swiss banker."

Chapter 33

Once they stepped into the garage, Saul turned to Peter and Maria. "Give Jan a tour. Show him everything. I have to get Watson."

"Everything?" Maria asked.

"What difference does it make? He knows we're taking the gold. The details are not important. Meet him at the door, give him the tour, answer his questions, and bring him to Levi's office when you're done. Once he's inside, make sure he doesn't leave. I'll alert our security."

Peter and Maria met Jan at the door to the office building.

"We've been asked to give you a tour," Peter said. "We'll answer any of your questions, if we can."

They started at the loading docks and worked their way along the conveyor system to the vault itself. Peter provided a brief commentary on the different aspects of the project.

"Sorry for my rough treatment earlier," Peter said.

"You didn't have much choice," Jan answered.

Jan touched some of the gold bars as they traveled along the conveyor system. He stepped into the vault.

"How much is gone?" he asked.

"We've shipped almost 190,000 bars.

"Three quarters."

"That's about right."

"Amazing. When will you finish?"

"Five or six days."

Jan nodded.

"I think we should see Saul now," Peter said.

"Yes."

As they walked up to the first floor, they passed two armed guards. They climbed the steps into Levi's trailer, and Saul, Watson and Levi were waiting for them. Jan looked out of place in his banker's suit.

Jan sat down heavily in a folding chair. "What do you need from me?"

"You do realize," Saul said, "that you know too much. You have no choice but to cooperate."

"Yes, that's painfully obvious. Will I be allowed to go home tonight? My wife is expecting me for dinner."

"I don't know. Perhaps you should call her and tell her you will be a little late."

"How late?" Jan asked.

"That depends on you and your story." Saul looked at his watch.

Jan called his wife on his cell phone and spoke to her in German. Then he called his driver and told him to wait.

When he disconnected from the second call, he asked, "What do you want to know?"

Saul leaned forward like an eager student. "Just tell us about the gold."

"I will have to summarize. I can give more details later."

"Just start."

"You probably won't believe me, but I didn't know about the gold until just before my father died. I will start with a gift." He pulled two sheets of paper out of his pocket and handed them to Saul.

"My father signed this contract in 1941 with a group of Nazis. Hitler was robbing the Jews and all the treasuries and museums of eastern Europe to finance the war effort. This group of Nazi insiders was skimming a share of that treasure, gold, jewelry, art works, stocks, bonds, all sorts of things."

Saul handed the contract to Watson, but Watson just shook his head.

"My father," Jan went on, "was supposed to turn it all into gold, and that's the gold you are stealing now."

"We are not stealing the gold. We are returning it," Saul said.

Jan raised his hands. "Call it what you will. We are all thieves. My father and I possessed the gold, but we never owned it. It owned us. By the time you deliver the gold to Israel, it will have been stolen at least four times."

Jan paused. "My father believed he was guilty of helping the Germans murder his own half-Jewish family, millions of other Jews, and many other unfortunate people, all while profiting from that murder. I think the guilt killed him. He made me promise I would return the gold to the Jews."

"How did you plan to do that?" Saul asked.

"Ah! Your approach is so much simpler. I planned to ship the gold to a mine with no gold, pretend to mine it again, and produce clean gold. I planned to send most of the profits to Israel as dividends."

"Endang," Peter said.

Jan turned to Peter. "How did you know?"

"Lucky guess?"

Jan sighed. "It seemed all very neat, if complicated. I think it would have worked, but then the Russian showed up."

Watson spoke for the first time. "Ivan Dinisovich."

"*Mein Gott!* You really do know everything," Jan said.

Saul glared at Watson. "Not everything," Saul said. "What was your discussion with Mr. Dinisovich?"

"He has a copy of the contract. He assumes there is a lot of gold in the vault, but he has no idea that there is, or was, so much. He gave me sixty days to agree to give him the gold, in exchange for Russian bonds. I have thirty days left before he makes enough noise that the regulators will visit the bank and demand I open the owner's vault."

"What about Akihiko Uehara? How's he involved?" Saul asked.

Jan sighed. "That's one frightening man. He's the brains behind Endang. He created the illusion of the great mine. The Canadians think they're running a stock fraud."

Jan rubbed his right arm and frowned. "I have come to believe Uehara wants all the gold. He plans to legally transfer the ownership of the gold to his company within thirty days, with an extensive paper trail to explain its existence. He also knows about the Russian and his demands."

"The timing will work," Saul said. "With your help we can quickly cover our tracks. We will show them an intact vault without a speck of gold."

"The Russian will be angry," Saul said, "but the Japanese will try to kill me. I expect he will succeed."

"Don't underestimate Ivan," Watson said softly. "If he discovers how much gold was there, and what we've done with it, he'll do something monumentally stupid, and almost surely deadly."

Jan looked from Watson to Saul. "I've told you essentially everything I know. Granted, it's a summary, but my father burned the detailed records after the war. All I have is the contract. It's damning enough."

"As I understand it," Watson said, "every listed beneficiary is dead."

"There is no record of exactly where the gold came from, and no one alive to claim it," Jan said.

"Fascinating," Watson said. "It's almost as though the gold does not exist."

"It's much worse than that. It does exist. It sits in my vault, or did. It's covered in blood, and the only way to change that is to get it to Israel."

"That's the plan," Saul said softly.

"And I owe you a debt of gratitude." Jan paused. "I've told you what I can. I can fill in details tomorrow. Is it possible for me to go now?"

Saul did not answer immediately. Finally, he said, "You can go, but we need to talk tomorrow, and we will need to talk often. Can you to come to this office through the back door by the loading docks? I can give you the combination for the keypad."

"That will work... at least temporarily."

Watson smiled at Saul after Jan left. "I have to hand it to you. You were right about the banker. I'm glad, because my Magician has managed a rather convincing disappearing act."

The removal of the last of the gold came quickly. Peter, Maria and Saul watched as the last container was sealed, locked, and pulled away from the loading dock.

"Congratulations to both of you," Saul said. "This went much more smoothly than I expected."

"Actually," Peter said, "I think you deserve the real congratulations."

"When do you load the gold on the ship?" Maria asked.

"The ship should be there in two weeks at the latest. I've told them we want our containers loaded first, deep in the hold. The firm date for sailing is..." Saul looked at the calendar on his phone. "It's eighteen days from now. I want to be on the ship and out to sea the day after the bank regulators make their inspection."

"Why wait?" Peter asked. "We should get out of Zürich as soon as we can."

Saul nodded. "You're probably right. However, the ship is not loaded or ready to sail. We have a lot of work to do to repair the vault, hide the entrance from my building with a new cement wall, and finish it all with a nice fresh paint job in the vault. I want to be absolutely sure the job's done right. Then we have to fill it with something, old files, antiques, art."

"Why not leave it empty?"

Saul smiled. "What an interesting idea. It would make the inspection much more amusing."

"Ivan Dinisovich called today," Jan said as he pushed a large, sealed envelope across his desk to Karl Westra, the senior teller. "He wanted to know if I had made my decision on his Russian bonds."

"What did you tell him?"

"I told him I wasn't interested in Russian bonds."

Karl smiled. "How'd he take it?"

"Not very well. To put it mildly, he became quite agitated. When I could get a word in, I told him about the inspection and invited him to attend. I warned him that he would probably be disappointed."

"And?"

"I think he's confused."

Karl laughed. "I dare say. What about that bastard Japanese?"

"Ah! I told him that we could have a major problem with the inspection. He plans to attend."

"A major problem indeed. What do you suppose he'll do when he finds out the gold has vanished?"

"I expect him to kill me, probably in some particularly gruesome fashion. You should stay clear of this." Jan gestured toward the envelope on his desk. "You have a copy of my will now. If I die, you have the authority to sell the bank and settle with the shareholders, including my wife."

Karl frowned. "You need more security, at the bank and at home."

"Saul is providing some already, and I'm working on a more permanent solution. I'll retire to my mountain home when this is over. It can be made quite secure."

"The vault is ready?"

"The painter finishes today." Jan smiled. "It looks wonderful. Intact. Fresh paint. Completely empty. It's beautiful."

"I'm really sorry I won't get to see their faces when they see the vault," Karl said. "I will see them when they leave the bank, though. That should still be interesting."

"Yes. 'Interesting' is perhaps an understatement."

On the day of the inspection, Saul, Watson, Peter and Maria showed up early at the bank. The guard let them in, and Jan took them down to the vault.

"The paint still smells, but we're painting everything in the bank, including the vaults." He gestured at the hallway. "They're still working on these walls, so the smell of fresh paint should be expected."

Jan opened the vault door. The Chinese screen was still in place. Peter and the others stepped inside.

"Wow! This looks a little different," Peter said.

The empty vault seemed even larger than before. The hooks for the tarps were still there, but they were painted the same dark gray as the rest of the floor. The walls and the ceiling were all bright white.

"Uehara knows what was in this vault," Jan said. "He will be extremely angry."

"You are prepared to take on your own security?" Saul asked.

"Yes."

"Uehara has few assets in this part of the world," Watson said. "Dinisovich is another story. He wants the gold, and he's dangerous. Kidnapping, torture, and a hijacking, are all very real possibilities."

Interesting, Peter thought. *He's not mentioning the US group at all.*

"Should we change our plans?" Saul asked.

Watson shook his head. "I don't think so. Our best defense is to move fast after the inspection is over."

"The ship will complete loading tonight," Saul said. "The gold is on board, buried in the hold. We'll sail early tomorrow morning."

Jan looked at his watch. "We should lock up and go upstairs. We'll be opening soon, and I expect everyone to show up promptly."

Watson pointed to Peter and Maria. "These two should be introduced as Richard and Cynthia Paine."

Jan raised his eyebrows. "Actually, I thought I wouldn't introduce anyone, unless I'm forced to do so, but I will if you wish."

"I think you should introduce us," Watson said.

Peter helped Jan close the vault door.

While they waited on the main floor of the bank, Watson said to Peter, "You know that Dinisovich and Uehara are staying at your hotel?"

"That's interesting. They must have seen us already."

"Almost surely, and I'll bet they know exactly who you are."

"Why play with names then?"

"Who knows? It might spread some tiny bit of confusion."

They watched Jan greet four men at the door.

"With Dinisovich in play, we're going to need all the confusion we can muster," Watson said as Jan and the four men headed toward him.

Jan made the introductions. Peter almost laughed at the regulators' names, Win Wright and Ami Lange. Peter looked closely at the reaction of Uehara and Dinisovich when Jan introduced them as Mr. and Mrs. Paine.

Maybe a flicker of surprise from Dinisovich. Absolutely nothing from Uehara.

"Shall we head down to the vault?" Jan said.

"Sounds good," Watson said.

Peter and Maria followed the group as they descended the steps to the vaults. An attendant opened the barred door that was kept closed during business hours. With a few more steps they all stood in front of the steel door to the owner's vault.

Jan pulled the three sets of keys out of his pocket. "This is a large vault. Many clients used it during the war to store art works and valuable antiques. There's not much call for that service these days."

He turned to the door, inserted the first set of keys, and turned them.

"There have been rumors that this bank holds a huge hoard of gold bars."

He inserted and turned the second set of keys.

"I, and my father before me, have maintained that such rumors are libelous lies."

He inserted and turned the final set of keys.

"There is no huge hoard of gold in this bank."

Peter thought he could hear Uehara breathing a little faster and deeper.

"Mister Paine," Jan said. "Perhaps you could pull the door open. It's a little heavy for an old man." Jan smiled.

Peter stepped forward and pulled on the door. It opened without a sound.

"Please pardon the smell of paint. We are planning on leasing this space, or dividing it into five or six smaller vaults. We needed to make it presentable. Please follow me."

Peter watched Dinisovich and Uehara as they entered and walked around the Chinese screen.

Uehara glanced at Jan but quickly looked away.

Can't see his expression, Peter thought.

Peter smiled as he watched Dinisovich.

His anger is rather obvious.

Dinisovich glared at Jan. "You moved it," he said with venom.

Jan pulled himself to his full height and said, "Moved what?"

"You had a large pile of gold bars in this vault," Ivan said.

"Where? I don't see any."

"You moved it," Ivan repeated.

"And how exactly would we have done that?" Jan asked.

Jan turned to the regulators. "Has anyone complained of a long line of armored vehicles leaving the bank at all hours over the last several months?"

Win Wright shook his head.

Jan turned back to Ivan. "The only way to move a large pile of gold bars would be to carry them up the stairs and out the front door. The elevator we used during the war has been sealed off and out of service for years."

"What about the other vaults?" Dinisovich asked.

Jan raised his hands. "Those are client vaults…"

Dinisovich interrupted. "You must open them."

"That's really quite unreasonable," Ami Lange said flatly.

"I have been granted the authority to open the client vaults this one day," Jan said. "However, some contain highly sensitive files, and you are not allowed to enter the vaults."

Jan opened each small vault in turn. There was no sign of a pile of gold bars. When they returned to the main floor of the bank, Jan turned to the regulators. "I assume that this inspection puts to rest any of the libelous rumors that this bank holds a hoard of Holocaust gold?"

"I think you can safely assume that," Win Wright said. "Ami and I have spent more than enough time on this, and we should return to work."

Once the regulators had left the bank, Jan said to Ivan Dinisovich, "I trust you're satisfied. I have told you all along that the gold did not exist."

"You have played me for the fool," Ivan said. He looked at the others. "And I think you had a little help. Do not rest lightly. Good-bye." He bowed slightly and turned to go.

Akihiko Uehara spoke for the first time. "Wait for a moment, won't you Mr. Dinisovich? I'll walk with you to the hotel."

Ivan stopped and turned back.

Akihiko turned to Jan. "You do not need the papers I prepared?"

"No."

"Very well. I will be in touch," Akihiko said. He turned to Ivan. "Shall we go?"

Once they had left, Watson said, "Ivan will soon know how much gold was there. They're not stupid. They know what happened, and neither one enjoys losing. Jan, you should double your security."

"Yes."

"And the rest of us had better go over our security arrangements for tonight's trip to Genoa."

As Saul and Watson drove back to the hotel with Peter and Maria, Watson said, "The Swiss authorities found Zakhar Rostov today."

"Oh," Maria said. "What's his condition?"

"Quite dead. Gunshot to the head. Apparently self-inflicted, which is no surprise. He was in very bad shape, in a huge amount of pain."

"One down," Peter said. "How many to go?"

"That's the way it always is," Watson said.

In the hotel, Watson put his hand on Peter's arm, and they lagged behind Saul and Maria. He handed Peter two memory cards. Each was labeled with a neat "2".

Peter raised his eyebrows.

"Just an update, Peter," Watson said. "The same keys apply."

"Just what I need."

"It's not long now. I head to Washington after Genoa, but this is a very high-risk time. You remember what I told you to do with these if I die?"

"Yes," Peter said.

"I'll let you know when you can destroy them."

"Thanks, I guess."

Chapter 34

Alon drove the heavily armored Mercedes sedan aggressively. Saul sat beside him in the front seat, and Peter and Maria, with their waterproof Gore-Tex jackets and gloves beside them, occupied the back seat.

"You sure you want Splügen Pass?" Alon asked. "The tunnel would be faster."

"We'll have the pass to ourselves on a night like this."

"It'll be a bitch. It's raining heavily near the summit, with a lot of fog. Those hairpin turns will be a hell of a challenge."

"You like driving challenges," Saul said.

Alon did not respond.

Peter thought about their security. *Not much more we can do. The cars can handle small arms fire, and we're well armed. AK101's for me and Maria, two Uzis for Alon and Saul. Gershon's driving the lead car, with Levi and two others, all of them well armed. Same for the vehicle behind us.*

Saul broke into Peter's thoughts. "I don't know why we're so paranoid."

"I bet Ivan Dinisovich knows and is in a car behind us… somewhere," Peter said, "and Uehara's with him. It doesn't take a genius to figure out we'd leave tonight, and Splügen Pass is the only bet for them."

"What do you mean, 'only bet'?"

"Genoa's the closest port, and the tunnel road is too busy for an ambush."

"This is hardly Afghanistan," Saul said.

"Suit yourself," Peter said.

They rode in silence for several miles.

Peter turned to Maria. "Make sure you can find your rifle, and put the extra clip in your pocket. If something goes wrong, we may not have much time."

As they gained altitude, the fog closed in around them, and the rain increased in intensity. Sudden gusts of wind shook the car.

Peter and Maria put on their jackets and gloves.

Peter's nervousness increased with each mile. The windshield wipers fought to clear the rain. They were near the summit, alone, with an invisible world around them.

With the suddenness that a foggy night carries with it, the lights of the border crossing broke through the fog. As expected, the gate was raised.

A few miles past the border, around a corner, Gershon's lead vehicle flashed its brake lights.

Peter leaned forward. He could barely make out a van parked sideways, blocking the road, about three hundred feet in front of them.

"Stop here!" Peter shouted. "Shut off your lights and tell the car behind to keep back."

Alon reacted as Peter spoke. In a moment they were in darkness.

"Grab your rifle, Maria. I don't like the looks of this."

Peter looked out the window. They were too close to the summit for trees. There was a slight hill above the road on the passenger side. He saw a few rounded boulders and rocky outcrops.

It'll have to do.

"Head up the hill on your side, Maria. I'll be right behind you. Duck down between the boulders and outcrops. Grab as much cover as you can."

Maria opened her door and started up the low hill.

Peter slid across the seat to follow her. He softly closed the door behind him. As agreed, Saul and Alon stayed in the car.

The grassy hillside was slippery and muddy. Even with their heavy boots, they both fell several times, and Peter felt the cold rain running down his face and neck.

He cursed softly as he caught up with Maria.

Peter looked back at the rear car in their convoy. Another car blocked the road behind it. At least one of the Israelis was outside of their car.

Peter and Maria could hear the muffled sound of automatic gunfire.

"Jesus Christ," Maria said.

"Nice ambush."

Peter looked back and forth along the road.

"We've got our hands full, Maria. I'll try to get closer to the lead vehicle."

Maria squinted, trying to see through the rain. "I'll head the other way. It looks like they already need help."

"Stay out of sight. They're either in the road, above it, or both."

Maria nodded and started to walk away. With her hooded camouflage jacket and dark pants, she was almost invisible.

Peter turned and headed toward the van, slipping and sliding in the mud, just above the road, as he made his way between outcrops and boulders.

Invisibility and surprise are our only allies.

Peter saw a bright light from up the hill. He ducked behind a boulder. In an instant the lead car exploded in a flash and a sudden blaze of flame.

Christ! An antitank weapon.

Another explosion. Behind him.

Peter glanced back to see the flames.

"Shit!"

Peter shuddered as he heard one of the men in the lead car scream.

He had a good view of the road and the lead car. He waited for the attackers to expose themselves. He didn't wait long. Three men clambered down the slippery bank toward the still-burning lead car. One of them shot a survivor in the head. Another spoke into a handheld radio.

"Shit," Peter said.

The wind brought the sound of laughter as the three men walked toward the car holding Saul and Alon.

Peter waited.

When they were within fifty feet, Peter fired half the magazine at the small group. They fell awkwardly onto the wet pavement.

Peter waited. *Okay, buddy. If you're out there, come to the rescue.*

After a minute or so, Peter grew impatient. He could hear small arms fire behind him, in the direction of the rear car in their small convoy.

Maybe nobody's left here. I've got to take the chance. Maria may need some help.

Peter turned and struggled through the mud and slippery grass back toward Maria. As he slipped around another boulder, he saw some movement in the limits of his peripheral vision. He dropped into the mud and heard the ricochets as the bullets hit the boulder.

He peered around the boulder.

There he is! Be patient. Wait.

There was one man. Peter watched as the man hesitated, reconsidered, and exposed himself in some open ground about forty feet away.

Peter aimed. By now he had no emotion left. He fired the remainder of the magazine. He watched the man crumple to the ground as he replaced the magazine.

Peter moved as fast as he could on the slippery ground above the road. About a hundred feet behind Saul and Alon's car, Peter settled down where he had some large rocks for cover and a good line of fire.

He watched as three men, silhouetted against the lights of the blocking car, approached the back of the burning Israeli car.

"Not too bright, guys," Peter muttered.

They prodded each Israeli.

A fourth man slid down the bank above the road, threw an empty launch tube into the blocking car, and joined the others. The four began a slow walk toward Saul and Alon. They moved in a ragged line, almost touching each other.

A dozen shots, thirty feet in front of him.

Maria!

Three of the men on the road were down.

The fourth started a clumsy run toward Peter. When he was twenty-five feet away, Peter fired five shots. Maria fired ten.

The man spun around as the bullets hit him and fell backward onto the rain-soaked pavement.

Peter listened to the sudden silence.

That's it. There's nobody else. Four to a car.

"Maria?"

"Yeah."

"Come on back. I think it's over. Let's get back to the car."

Peter stood up and watched Maria as she struggled in the mud. When she got to him, he asked, "You okay?"

"Not really. Who's left?"

"Alon, Saul, you and me."

"Damn."

Peter put his arm around her. "We have to get going."

Time enough to scream in the night later, Peter thought.

As they slid down to the road, Peter heard a cell phone ring. It was coming from the last attacker they shot.

Peter jogged back to the man and fished the phone out of his pocket.

Peter hesitated, but he answered the phone. "*Si?*"

"This is Ivan. You have them?"

"*Si*. We have them."

"Excellent. A black Mercedes is coming. Kill them."

"*Si*," Peter said. He disconnected and dropped the cell phone into his pocket.

He jogged back to Maria, and together they ran up to Saul's car.

"Alon," Peter shouted. "It's Peter and Maria. Let us in."

Peter watched Alon get out of the car cautiously, holding his Uzi in both hands.

"You alone?"

"We're alone, Alon. Let us in. We're getting soaked."

Alon looked around. "What about the others?"

"Dead."

"*S'Emek*," Alon said through clenched teeth. He unlocked the doors as he got into the car.

Peter and Maria tumbled into the back seat and set their rifles on the floor.

Saul turned to them. "What happened?"

Peter looked at him. "Sixteen dead. Eight attackers and everyone in the front and rear cars."

"Everyone?"

"We've got to get out of here," Peter said. "I intercepted a phone call to one of the attackers. From Ivan Dinisovich. He asked, 'Do you have them?'. I said, 'Yes', and he told me to kill everyone in the black Mercedes that's coming." Peter paused. "That's one cold son of a bitch."

"Watson's got to be the target. He's supposed to be following us." Saul turned to Alon. "Get going, Alon."

Alon hit the steering wheel. "What about the others?"

"We'll deal with the dead later. Deal with the living now."

Peter picked up his rifle again. "Let me move some bodies out of the way and move the van."

"I should push the van over the edge," Alon said.

"Safer to move it, if I can."

Peter ran toward the van. He pulled two bodies off the road. When he passed their lead car, he grimaced when he confirmed that Levi had been the one shot at close range.

He came up to the driver's door on the van and looked in. Nobody. He climbed in and drove the van to the side of the road.

Alon pulled up beside the van, and Peter climbed back into his seat.

"Let's get the hell out of here," Saul said.

Alon began the down hill run to Genoa, driving as fast as he dared.

Peter stripped off his jacket, and his gloves, and turned up the heat. He leaned over and put his head in his hands.

"Shit," he said.

Saul turned to look at him. "Thank you. Both of you."

"They were quick," Peter said, looking up. "We were slow."

"It all rests with me," Saul said. "I was too confident."

Saul's phone rang. Leaning forward, Peter could hear the conversation.

"This is Watson. How are you guys doing?"

"We were ambushed on the Italian side. We lost the front and rear cars."

"You okay?"

"Yes," Saul answered.

"Get moving. I think Ivan and Akihiko are right behind us. I'll try to slow them down."

"Ivan called one of the dead attackers, Watson. Peter took the call. Ivan wants to kill you, too."

"Get out. I'll take care of Ivan."

"You're crazy," Saul said.

"Probably."

At the top of the pass, Watson's driver picked his way past the vehicles and bodies. Watson took in the results of the ambush in silence.

"Stop by the burned-out car. Block the road but leave enough space that Ivan can pull up beside us on my side."

Watson called his contact in the US embassy in Rome. He used every source of authority he had, including Alden Sage and President Pelton.

"I don't give a damn how you do it. Just get it done. Make it a Mafia assassination."

Watson disconnected.

"What a fucking mess," Watson said.

"You're crazy," his driver said.

"No. I know Ivan. This'll work."

His driver remained silent.

Five minutes later, Watson saw headlights approach the rear of the ambush. The black Audi wove its way toward them.

"Get ready," Watson said.

His driver clicked off the safety on his AR15.

When the Audi slowly pulled up next to them, Watson rolled down his window. He waited. Nothing.

Maybe this is a mistake.

Watson shouted over the rain and the slapping wipers. "Your choice, Ivan. We can talk or not."

Watson waited.

Forget it. Time to move on.

The driver in the Audi began to lower his window. Ivan. Akihiko sat beside him, staring ahead.

"What the hell are you doing here?" Ivan said with a snarl.

"We need to talk."

"You're a son of a bitch."

"Me? You're the one who called in the ambush. You're responsible for the dead, not me."

Ivan said nothing.

"I wouldn't plan on hanging around. The authorities will arrive, even on a night like this."

Watson looked at Ivan, trying to read his mind. *He's close to losing it.*

"I'll take care of it." Watson paused. "If you're staying in Genoa, I'll buy you lunch at the Marina Hotel. One o'clock." Watson looked at his watch. "Today."

When there was no response, Watson rolled up his window and signaled the driver to go.

"Take it slow," Watson said. "I don't want to catch up with Saul."

Watson looked at his watch again. *We'll see the sunrise before we get to Genoa.*

"I wonder what Akihiko Uehara is thinking right now?" Watson answered his own question. "He's wishing he never met Ivan Dinisovich. That's what he's thinking."

Chapter 35

Peter woke up as Alon pulled up beside the Greek-registered container ship in the darkness before the dawn. All the cargo on this ship was destined for Israel. Saul had paid for a fast passage, and the ship would make no stops before Haifa.

After Saul, Peter and Maria exited the car, Alon drove it into a waiting container. He removed the weapons and ammunition, adding them to the baggage that went to Saul's cabin. The dock workers lifted the last container into place.

Once the four of them were on board, the crew cast off the lines, and with the help of harbor tugs sailed into the Mediterranean as the morning sun broke the eastern horizon.

In their small stateroom, Peter and Maria stripped off their wet clothes and fell into bed. With the gentle swell of the Mediterranean, sleep came quickly, but Peter woke with a start several times in the night.

I'm amazed I can sleep at all.

Just before noon, Peter rolled over and massaged Maria's back.

"Hmm…"

"I wondered when you'd wake up," Peter whispered.

"I was dreaming that a tall, handsome man was rubbing my back." She rolled over. "Oh! It wasn't a dream."

"Nope."

She wrapped her arms around him and kissed him.

"You do know how much I love you, don't you?" Peter asked.

She kissed him again. "Not a clue. Not a clue."

"I think we'd better get dressed and find some food."

Maria smiled. "That's a bit out of character for you, when we're both naked in bed."

"I suppose, but I'm really hungry," Peter said.

"Well then, lover, let's get dressed and find where the food is on this boat."

When they stepped out on the deck, the immense size of the ship was obvious to them for the first time. Over a thousand feet long, containers were stacked eight high above the main deck, with more below in the hold.

Small, puffy clouds sailed across a deep blue sky. They inhaled the fresh air and looked out over a placid Mediterranean.

"This is peaceful," Maria said.

"You see those two ships in the distance? They're both destroyers, I think. I wonder why they're sailing along with us."

"Peter! Relax already."

"Okay. It's beautiful, destroyers included. Let's find lunch."

It wasn't hard. The ship was large, but it had a small crew. Accommodations for the crew occupied a small area, though there was a lounge, and each crew member had their own private cabin.

"This looks like food," Peter said.

They stepped into a narrow room. Most of the crew were finishing lunch at two tables. Saul and Alon sat in the far corner and waved them over.

"Welcome to lunch," Saul commented. "I missed breakfast, too. Too long a night for an old man."

"Too long for anyone," Maria said.

The food was laid out on the table family style. It was plentiful and nourishing, if somewhat uninspired.

"What's with the two destroyers? Are they shadowing us?"

"No one seems to know for sure. I'm told the Russian came along shortly after we sailed. The American followed shortly after."

Peter looked out the window at the two ships. "Well, with both of them accompanying us, it seems like we ought to be covered."

"Exactly."

Maria looked up from her food. "So, Saul, how long is this cruise anyway?"

"About three days. We paid the Detros II to sail at higher speed, just over twenty-three miles per hour."

"A fairly tranquil pace," Peter said.

"All a matter of economics. Full speed is just over thirty-one miles per hour. Speed costs money," Saul said.

Watson sat by the window of the Il Gozzo restaurant. He dressed like an American tourist, slightly baggy jeans, not quite so baggy on his frame, and an open-neck, knit shirt. Besides its excellent selection of Ligurian specialties, Watson liked the restaurant for its view of the harbor.

Perhaps a bit too elegant for my taste.

He sipped at the strong coffee. Most spies fought tension in the field. Watson experienced a slow-down, and his awareness became excruciating acute.

He looked at his watch. Quarter after one. He had no doubt Ivan would appear.

He'll enjoy making me wait. Watson smiled.

When he finished his coffee and put his empty cup down, Ivan slid into the seat across from him.

"The view is good," Ivan said in Russian, "but the ship I really wanted to see has already left the harbor."

Also in Russian, Watson said, "It was in a hurry."

"I can believe that."

Watson's rumpled shirt and jeans set a strong contrast to Ivan's sharply tailored Italian suit. Watson's face, too, round and full, with an out-of-control bushy, gray moustache, and his balding head, seemed almost comical compared with Ivan's narrow, angular features, tightly trimmed beard, and full, well-brushed head of hair.

Watson leaned forward and said softly, "Last night I was afraid for you."

"An interesting statement."

"There is no reason for us to tell lies, Ivan. We have known each other too long."

"Old habits die slowly."

The waiter arrived. They ordered, and the waiter returned quickly with their bottle of Italian wine.

"Let the gold go where it belongs," Watson said.

"I can't do that."

"Stalin came close to destroying you and your family. You should understand more than most."

Ivan shook his head. "I'm sorry."

Watson swirled the well-aged Barolo in his glass. "Nice choice of wine, Ivan." He paused. "You do know that your Russian escort has a US companion?"

"Yes." Ivan smiled. "We both play a waiting game. We wait… for a mistake… or a lie."

When their meal arrived, they broke away to English, and they spoke of their countries and the political rot they both despised.

As they finished, Ivan put down his glass of wine. He reverted to Russian. "There is a matter I would like to discuss with you, but I cannot do so here." He contemplated the wine again and drank a small amount. "Can you come to the Consulate at four?"

"If I must. You sure you can't talk here?"

"I cannot." Ivan paused. "I will tell you this. It has nothing to do with the gold, but everything to do with the larger issues of your current assignment."

The taxi stopped in front of the ten-foot stone wall with a spiked steel fence along the top. A flock of security cameras covered every approach to the wall.

"Wait here until they let me in," Watson said.

He pressed the intercom beside the green door. "Watson MacDonough. I have an appointment with Ivan Dinisovich."

When he was buzzed in, he waved to the driver, passed through a security screening, and met a pleasant young woman.

"I hope you don't mind me practicing my English," she said with a smile. "We don't get too many Americans visiting this Consulate."

She opened a door. "*Signore MacDonough è qui.*"

"*Grazie!* Come in, Watson." Ivan gestured toward a small table with two chairs. "Have a seat. Would you like coffee?"

"No. I'm fine, thank you."

"Sorry to drag you out here, but I need a little security for this conversation."

"You're afraid of the hotel?"

Ivan said nothing for a moment, got up and retrieved his coffee from the desk, and sat down again.

Watson waited.

"With regard to the ship, I can tell you nothing more than quite a few people are determined to see that it does not reach Israel."

"That includes you?"

"Forget it."

Watson tapped his fingers on the table. "That's not why you dragged me out here."

"You saw the news? About the pass?"

"Mafia turf war, apparently," Watson said.

"Sometimes you do good work, Watson."

"Not my work, but thank you." Watson smiled. "And you're stalling."

Ivan was silent for more than a minute.

Watson waited. *I won't rush him.*

"Uehara told me about the gold, Watson. I didn't know it was quite so much. I was very angry. I apologize, but sometimes there is a price that must be paid."

"I understand."

Ivan paused again. "We know you're working for President Pelton. We know what you're working on. Your problem affects the whole world." He drank the last of his coffee. "Harold James."

Watson raised his eyebrows. "What about him?"

"He regularly meets with Brayden Davenport, Gerhardt Weber, and Derek Bunting."

"And?"

Ivan frowned. "They are rogue. They are undermining the authority of your President. We believe that many in your military follow their orders. We have hard evidence that they were helping Rostov. They wanted Rostov to succeed in destroying modern Russia."

"It didn't work," Watson said.

"It was a close thing. And they betrayed Peter Binder and Maria Davidoff to Rostov."

"And that didn't work either. Rostov's dead."

"There are plenty more like him."

"Most of this is our problem, not yours, Ivan."

"These men Harold James meets with are far worse than Rostov. They have manipulated more than one of your presidents. What they want to do could destroy us all."

Interesting, Watson thought.

"Can you give me any supporting evidence? Documents? Communications?"

"I cannot."

"Anything more you want to tell me?" Watson asked.

"They are determined to kill you. Watch your ass and get some help." Ivan paused. "I owe a great debt to Peter Binder and Maria Davidoff. Get them off that ship."

They sat in silence. Watson realized Ivan would say no more.

"I should head back to my hotel," Watson said.

"We'll call a cab for you."

Watson stood outside the green door of the Russian Consulate.

Ivan tells me to watch my ass? Jesus!

He was so lost in thought that he didn't notice the taxi until the driver honked his horn.

Shit! Wake up, you idiot.

He directed the driver to the American Consulate, and he called a number in Rome.

"Yes?"

"This is Watson MacDonough. I'm in Genoa. I need a secure telephone. Can you arrange for someone to let me into the Consulate?"

"It won't wait?"

"No."

"When will you get there?"

Watson consulted with the driver. "About five-thirty."

"No problem."

"One more thing. I need some help. Send Jimmy Louderbough up here. Today. You'll have him back tomorrow."

"It has to be him?"

"I need somebody good."

"Be careful of what you ask for. I'll get him up there, probably about eleven."

"Thanks."

He's the best watcher… and the best assassin we have in Italy. I have to take the risk. Besides, I like him. I think.

Watson watched everything, all the cars and scooters that pulled up beside them. He hated the scooters. When they got to the Consulate, he waited in the cab, watching. He saw nothing. He paid the driver, walked quickly under the arches and into the building. The Consulate was one of many tenants.

The Consulate offices were dark, but an obviously annoyed young woman opened the door and let him in. She was attractive and dressed for a night out.

That's one spoiled evening, Watson thought.

She showed him to the telephone, gave him instructions on locking up, and disappeared as quickly as possible.

Watson punched in a number.

"Alden Sage."

"Watson here." He rattled off a series of letters and numbers.

"I'm alone in the Consulate in Genoa," Watson said. "I just met with Ivan Dinisovich. He nearly killed me last night, but today he invited me for coffee. He confirmed everything we know about the cabal."

"What?"

"He had all the names. He knew they supported Rostov. He's scared."

"Jesus."

"Where are we on your end?"

"We're ready," Alden said.

"Is the President ready?"

"You should know better than I do."

"He'll support it, unless Harold gets to him."

"He hates that man, Watson."

"Harold can be persuasive."

"Not that persuasive."

"It's time," Watson said. "Set it up the way we planned, but make sure you have enough force to control Weber. And coordinate with Toronto."

"POTUS won't sign the order unless you bring the silver bullet in person."

"I'm on my way tomorrow morning," Watson said. "I've asked for Jimmy Louderbough to watch my ass."

"You really think you need that guy?"

"They're close. Even Ivan warned me."

"And you really want Jimmy around?"

"We're old friends, Alden. If things get too hot, get Peter and Maria off that ship."

"I have the ship covered. Just remember Jimmy's line of work. He doesn't have any friends."

Too close to the truth, Watson thought.

"I'll see you tomorrow, Alden. Probably late. You know the drill if anything goes south. Peter Binder has the updates"

"Will he look at them?"

"Probably."

"Well… for God's sake be careful, Watson, and I really mean that."

"Thanks. I appreciate it."

Watson sat at the telephone for a long time. He got up, turned off the lights, and locked up. He waited in the recessed doorway and watched. Then he moved in the shadows under the arches, walked around the corner and watched the Piazza De Ferrari. Three taxis waited in line along the curb, beside the large fountain.

Watson watched two of the small clutch of tourists enter the first taxi. He quickly crossed the street, got into the next taxi, and directed the driver to his hotel.

He relaxed when he saw the entrance to his hotel, and a bit more when he entered the crowded lobby.

He went to the bar and ordered a drink.

Chapter 36

Watson was on his second drink, after a light dinner. His phone rang. An Italian number.

"Yes?"

"I'll be there about eleven." A pause. "Get lost."

"Really?"

"Really." The caller disconnected.

Shit! Was that Jimmy Louderbough? Watson wasn't sure.

He looked at his watch. A few minutes past eight. He paid his tab and went to his room.

The room's safe? For now? Holy shit!

He pulled the extra currency and passports out of the room safe. He called and reserved a room for Irving Barrymore at the Hotel Continental Genova, and he made a reservation for him to depart for Paris on Air France at 7:25 in the morning, connecting to a flight to Dulles in Washington, arriving at 4:15 in the afternoon. He paid for everything with Irving's credit card.

Slow down. Don't make any mistakes.

He left the reservations intact for Watson MacDonough. *Damn waste of money.*

His phone rang. *Saul.*

"Hello."

"Saul. Any news?"

"Expect an attack."

"Unlikely with a Russian and an American destroyer shadowing us."

"Things can change. Is Peter Binder there?"

"I'll get him."

After a pause, "This is Peter."

"Things are getting hot. I told Saul to expect an attack. Stay on your toes. You know what to do if something happens to me."

"I don't want to hear this," Peter said.

"Yeah. It's getting real."

When he ended the call, Watson pulled the battery out of his phone. He pulled a sports bag out of his suitcase. He dropped the extra passports onto a cut-out portion of the bottom lining. He added the basics for two days, his Italian currency, $3,000 in hundred-dollar bills, and looked at his watch.

Nine. Two hours to go.

Watson left the room and took the elevator to the lobby. He walked out of the hotel and took the first taxi in the line. In the half-mile ride, Watson MacDonough disappeared.

Irving Barrymore's passport comes from the oval office. As secure as I can make it.

Watson settled into his new hotel room, looked out the window and smiled. "Thank you, Jimmy," he said softly. "You're a friend after all."

Maybe I should move one more time. I could.

"Screw it," he muttered. He looked at his watch. A little after ten.

Plenty of time.

He went to the bar.

He returned to his room a few minutes before eleven.

As he walked past the bathroom, into the bedroom, he caught a flicker of movement at the edge of his vision.

He heard the shot. With the silencer, it was no more than a sharp pop.

For a split second, before the bullet hit him in the head, halfway between his eye and his right ear, Watson knew, for the first time in his career, that he had been a fool.

The tall man stepped out from beside the bed. His black clothes and hood covered him, except for his eyes.

He fired two more shots in quick succession as Watson lay face up on the floor.

The first shot entered Watson's skull just at the top of his nose. The other hit his chest just to the side of the breast bone and tore a ragged hole in his heart.

The man bent down and picked up the shell casings. He had to hunt for one of them. He would leave nothing of himself in the room, other than the bullets themselves.

I've got what I need.

The DNA of hundreds of guests would cause enough confusion that what little he might have left would never be identified.

The tall man looked down at Watson and shook his head. *"Durak,"* he whispered in Russian.

A few minutes later, at a back entrance, the man pulled off his hood and put on a floppy hat. It covered his face from any security cameras. He walked out into the dark, onto Via Arsenaledi Terria, and disappeared.

The maid discovered the body at nine in the morning, with the usual screams, followed by shouts and the arrival of several earnest detectives.

The US consul in Genoa did not know of anyone by the name of Irving Barrymore, though the face looked familiar. A search of the database for the passport came up with a blocked entry and a request to call Mr. Alden Sage of the White House in case of injury or death.

It was almost eleven in the morning when the consul made the call, catching Alden just as he swung his feet out of bed.

Alden swore. "How did he die?"

"Three gunshots, close range," the Consul said, "two to the head and one to the heart. It was an execution."

"I'm not surprised. You have a photograph?"

"No, but he matches the passport photo for Barrymore."

"Do you have his laptop?" Alden asked.

"The police didn't find one."

"Shit. Well, if they do find one, send it to me."

Alden disconnected and consulted his calendar.

Good. POTUS is in today.

He called the President's chief of staff.

"This is Alden. Sorry to bother you so early. Get me fifteen minutes with him, alone, this morning."

"He's up. You could catch a breakfast meeting at seven."

Alden looked at his watch. "Thanks. That'll work."

Alden Sage looked out the window, thinking, for several minutes.

Time to move.

He ran at full speed through his morning rituals, dressed and headed for the White House. In the early morning traffic, he made good time and was at his office well before six. He unlocked his safe file, pulled out a folder labeled WM in bold, red letters, slapped it on his desk, and called the Detros II.

Peter, Maria, and Alon sat with Saul in his cabin just before noon on the second day of the voyage.

"What happened to our destroyer escorts?" Peter asked.

"According to the captain, the US destroyer pulled out just after three this morning, and the Russian followed shortly after," Saul answered.

"I'm feeling naked," Peter said.

Saul shrugged. "We're a fantastic target for a hijacking. A hundred billion dollars in gold, and no ransom notes required." He paused. "And too many people know about us."

"Not a happy thought," Peter said.

"Thanks to Alon, we've got four guns under the bed and about 120 rounds of ammunition for each one."

"What the hell are we supposed to do with them?" Maria asked.

Saul looked at her. "Repel boarders, just like the movies."

Peter shook his head. "This is no movie. They'll come at us with RPGs and hand-held missiles."

"Let's be honest," Saul said. "If we're boarded none of us will survive. The crew might, but we'll be executed. If we fight like hell, we might be able to discourage them."

They heard the knock on the cabin door.

Saul nodded to Alon, who pulled one of the Uzis out from under the bed.

"Who is it?" Saul asked.

"I have a message for Peter Binder."

Peter and Maria stood on both sides of the door as Saul opened it.

"What is it?" Saul asked.

"He's supposed to call Alden Sage."

"That's all?"

"Yeah. Uh, no. He's supposed to use your satellite telephone."

Saul thanked the man and closed the door. He stepped over to a small bureau and pulled out his satellite telephone.

Saul handed it to Peter. "You familiar with this?"

"Yeah… I think I'd better find a private place for this call."

"You want me to come with you?" Maria asked.

"I don't think so," Peter said as he exited the cabin.

He ran up three flights of stairs to the left bridge wing and out to the end. He was alone. The emptiness below him was a bit unnerving. He faced the stern of the ship and pulled a slip of paper out of his wallet. He dialed the number Watson had given him.

"Alden."

"Peter Binder, sir. What's up?"

"Watson's dead."

It took a moment for Peter to absorb the news.

"Damn! How did it happen?"

"Don't know the details, but it looks like a professional assassination."

"Bloody lovely."

"I need you back here as soon as possible. I'm going to ask the US destroyer to take you off the ship.

"That'll be a little difficult, sir."

"What do you mean?"

"The Russian and the US destroyers both left early this morning. Right now we're quite alone out here."

"You're joking."

"I'm serious. They're gone."

"Those bastards!" Alden fell silent. "Hang on for a moment. I have to make call."

"Sure."

Peter could hear Alden shouting and swearing. *Admiral Ben Riggins… The USS Jason Lawrence… Flank speed… Helicopters…* Then a lot more swearing.

"The destroyer is headed back to you at highest possible speed," Alden said. "You'll have a helicopter on site in about an hour. You prepared to defend against a hijacking?"

"Not really," Peter said.

Peter stared at the horizon behind the ship. *What is that?* He squinted. *It's a small boat, and it's moving fast.*

"I hate to tell you, sir, but we're not alone anymore. There's a small boat… actually several small boats. Coming on from behind. Moving fast. I don't think they're a welcoming committee."

"Shit! I'll call the captain and tell him to go to full speed. Hold on as long as you can."

"I gotta run," Peter said.

"Before you go. You still have Watson's little gifts?"

"Yes."

"Don't lose them. You have to get them to Washington."

"I really have to go. Now." Peter shut off the phone.

He looked back at the little flotilla. It was definitely getting closer. *Jesus Christ.*

He ran down the stairs two at a time. He could feel the ship increasing speed.

It might help.

He swung open the door to Saul's cabin. Alon and Maria were still there with Saul.

"Small boats are coming up from behind us," Peter said. "Looks like we're being hijacked."

He got down on the floor and began to pull the weapons out from under the bed.

"We have to find the captain. Maria and I will cover the stern with the heavier AK-101's."

Peter looked at them. No one was moving.

"Come on! Let's go, damn it."

As they barged out of the cabin, they nearly collided with Captain Stavros, who was armed with a 12-guage pump shotgun.

"We've been through this before," the captain said. "We've dogged down all outside entry points, and we're breaking out high-pressure water hoses along the sides and at the stern." He was sweating heavily.

"Maria and I will head to the stern. Maybe we can break this up before it gets started. Saul and Alon can help along the sides of the ship. The Uzis are best suited for that." Peter looked around. "Everybody good?"

"It's good," Captain Stavros said.

"Okay. Good luck. Let's go."

Peter and Maria ran down the stairs to the deck level and jogged toward the stern.

Peter stopped just short of the stairs down to the lower level of the stern. He looked out. The small flotilla was about a mile away.

"Looks like three inflatables and the one larger boat," Peter said, "something like a fast patrol boat. They'll try to board at the stern. It's the lowest point on the ship."

Maria said, "You know, I was beginning to enjoy this cruise." She made sure her rifle was ready to fire.

"Can't complain about being bored," Peter said.

He pointed down.

"There's good cover behind the steel lip at the lower level, and the openings for the mooring lines will give us good firing positions."

Two crew members were readying the fire hoses, one on each side.

"You focus on the small boats," Peter said. "Wait until they get really close. We have to make every shot count. We don't have much ammunition. I'll try to take out the larger boat if it gets close enough."

Peter settled down behind one of the openings for the mooring lines, on the far side of the stern.

You should have been waiting for us. That's your first mistake.

He waited. He wanted to be sure.

Each small boat carried four men. One of them opened fire with an assault rifle. Peter could hear the bullets hitting the steel of the ship.

"That's good enough for me," Peter muttered.

He could see one man in front of the wheelhouse of the larger boat. He held an RPG with the tell-tale bulbous warhead on his shoulder.

Peter fired two shots. Too low.

He fired five more. One of them hit the man holding the RPG.

As the man fell backwards, he fired the RPG. He disappeared into the blue-grey exhaust cloud as he fell overboard.

The warhead exploded in the wheelhouse of the small boat. Two men immediately dove overboard. In a bright orange explosion most of the top of the boat disappeared. It turned sharply, nearly capsized, and stopped, dead in the water.

"Yes!" Peter shouted.

Two of the three inflatables sped up and made a run at the stern of the Detros II.

There were three armed men in each boat, and all six began to fire at Peter's position. The bullets ricocheted off the steel around him.

As the two boats got closer, the crewmen opened up with the high-pressure water hoses. The force of the deluge came close to capsizing the small boats.

Peter and Maria took the interruption of the gunfire from the boats as an opportunity. They both sited on the nearest boat and fired fifteen or twenty shots. Peter slapped a second clip into the rifle.

With a dead man at the helm, one of the boats took a hard turn and flipped over. The other turned away and quickly slowed to a halt. Peter saw no signs of life.

The third, and last, inflatable ramped up to top speed and made a run at Maria's side of the ship. Maria's gunfire and the water hoses did little to impede its progress.

Peter watched it disappear up the side of the Detros II.

What the hell are they doing?

He ran over to Maria's side and looked along the side of the ship. One man in the boat held a second man. As the small boat moved down the side of the ship, he attached small black objects to the hull of the ship, right at water level. He prepared to place a fifth.

A third man in the boat fired his assault rifle at Saul, Alon, and the crewmembers. The fourth man was steering.

The small boat struggled to stay close to the ship.

"Mines!" Peter yelled.

He yelled back at Maria. "Stay put! One of those boats might come at us again."

Peter ran up the stairs to the main deck level and leaned over the side. Saul and Alon were firing at the boat. He could hear the occasional bark of a shotgun.

Peter took aim. The first person hit in the crossfire was the holder for the man placing the mines. They both disappeared into the small space between the boat and the ship.

Peter fired another five rounds at the boat. One round must have hit a mine. The boat disappeared in a flash, an explosion, and flaming bits of debris.

A moment later, Peter looked behind the ship. He could still see smoke from the burning boat, but it was too far away to see either of the inflatables.

No threat for the moment.

Peter heard shouts and began to run. Several men tended someone on the deck. Peter stopped. Saul lay, quite still, in his own blood.

Peter spoke to Captain Stavros. "If there's anyone below decks, get them out. They laid five mines on the side of the ship."

The captain seemed to shrink. He turned and spoke to one of the crew in Greek, and the crewman headed to the bridge.

Peter knelt down beside Saul. Alon had stopped first aid and was simply holding Saul's hand.

"Peter," Saul said.

"How are you doing?"

"Not good," Saul said and coughed. "I heard you. We're going to sink?"

Peter nodded. "Looks like it. Sorry."

"Don't be sorry. Thank you… for everything."

"Didn't get to Israel."

"No, but the gold is safe." He grasped Peter's arm. "It almost worked….. I will sleep with the gold."

Saul grimaced with pain when the first mine exploded and shook the ship. His eyes opened wide. "Goodbye, Peter… my miracle man." Saul smiled, took a sharp, sudden breath, and his hand slipped away.

The second mine exploded, a bit closer, and the ship shuddered a second time.

"He asked me to put him on his bed," Alon said.

"It's a lot of stairs. You want some help?"

"No. I'll carry him, but come along, just in case."

On the way to Saul's cabin, two more mines exploded. Alon nearly fell with the second.

"You okay?" Peter asked.

"I'll make it."

By the time they got to Saul's cabin, the ship had a distinct list.

As Alon laid Saul on the bed, the fifth mine exploded, followed this time by several secondary explosions.

"I'm sorry, Saul," Alon said. "I have no minyan. I will return with your friends, and we will pray over your grave."

Alon wiped tears from his face, and he and Peter stepped out onto the deck. Maria was waiting. The list was increasing.

"The captain wants us in the lifeboat right now," Maria said.

As they ran down the stairs and along the deck to the lifeboat at the stern, they collected all the weapons they could find. The lifeboat was bright orange and attached to a steeply inclined launch ramp. They climbed in at the back and clambered down the slope, found two seats, and buckled into their safety harness. The boat was a little over half full.

A crew member dogged the entry closed. He shouted to the captain. "All secure. Sixteen on board."

"How do they launch this thing?" Maria asked.

"We fly," Peter said. "It dives into the water."

"Oh, my God!"

They made sure their weapons were safe and wedged between their feet and the seat in front of them.

Peter heard someone working the hydraulic pump that would release the boat.

"How high are we?" Maria asked.

"Oh, I don't know. Probably sixty feet or so," Peter said, just as the lifeboat plunged free.

In a matter of seconds, they went from nearly weightless to hitting the water and straining at their safety harnesses.

The boat dove under the water for a moment before it popped to the surface like a cork. In spite of the drama of the moment, everyone laughed.

Chapter 37

The captain pulled away from the sinking ship. Peter unbuckled his harness and joined Alon at the back of the lifeboat. They watched the ship in its death agony.

"I'm sorry Alon."

"No. Saul found his gold. It's covered with the blood of my people. The sea will wash it clean."

The wave of his own emotions over Saul's death surprised Peter.

Gradually, most of the crew joined them. The great ship's list increased, and the leaning towers of containers finally broke away and cascaded into the sea with great crashes of metal on metal. The containers churned the sea near the ship into froth and waves.

The ship screamed in protest. Everything loose crashed loudly into the metallic skin and skeleton of the ship. Some of the containers sank immediately. Others continued to float and jostled noisily with the others.

"I wonder how deep the Mediterranean is here," Peter said.

One of the crew answered. "It is very deep, almost fifteen thousand feet."

"Saul will rest quietly," Alon said softly.

As more of the deck cargo slid into the sea, the ship seemed to right itself, but the stern was already slipping under the water. As the bow rose, in a great scream of tearing metal, the ship tore itself in half. The stern sank quickly with a rush of water and air.

The front half of the ship settled back into the water, almost level, before it slid, slowly and gracefully, into the water. After the eruption of air and water and debris subsided, the only sound remaining was the softer metallic clanking of the containers hitting each other in the waves.

Some of the crewmembers wept.

"It was not a bad ship," Captain Stavros said.

Peter heard another sound. He looked up and spotted two helicopters.

"Well, captain, I was told that the US destroyer would come back to rescue us."

"Too bad they left in the first place," the captain said.

"Why did they leave?" Maria asked.

Peter watched the helicopters. "I have no idea."

The lead helicopter dropped two swimmers. One approached the lifeboat and climbed on board.

He shouted above the noise. "We're from the USS Jason Lawrence. We can take five in each helicopter, so we'll be making two trips. They'll drop a sling. I'll help you into it, and you're off."

He turned to Maria.

"You're first, ma'am. It's two at a time. Who do you want with you?"

She pointed to Peter.

Once the first five were hoisted aboard, the pilot immediately turned for the forty-five-minute flight back to the destroyer.

As they approached, Maria said, "That's an impressive wake."

"Yeah," Peter said. "I think it's got over a hundred thousand horsepower. Probably doing forty miles an hour, which is damn fast for a ship that size. They'll slow down for the helicopter to land."

Several members of the destroyer crew guided the new arrivals to the crew mess. Coffee, sandwiches, cake.

Maria shut her eyes as she sat down. "What a day."

"Not over yet," Peter said.

A young man sat down across from them. Two armed seamen, a man and a woman, stood directly behind him. Peter raised his eyebrows.

"I'm Captain John Hodges. I assume you are Peter Binder and Maria Davidoff?"

"You're correct," Maria said.

"Welcome to the USS Jason Lawrence. I'm sure you need some time to relax. However, I've been instructed to ask you, Peter, if you still have a package from Watson MacDonough."

"I do."

"All right, then. As per orders, the armed guards behind me will accompany both of you, anywhere you go, while you are on this ship."

"Are we under arrest?" Maria asked.

Captain Hodges smiled. "No. This guard is for your personal safety only, and the safety of the package."

"I'm not sure I like that any better than an arrest," Maria said.

"There are a few details I must attend to. I'll be back shortly. We need to talk in my quarters."

"We're not going anywhere," Peter said.

Captain Hodges smiled again. "True."

After the captain left, the two seamen retreated to the entrance to the mess.

"What the hell was that all about?" Maria asked.

"I can't talk about it. Not here."

"It better be good."

Peter shook his head. "It's not good at all."

"Jesus."

They each had some coffee and a sandwich. They sat in silence.

Captain Hodges returned. "Ready?"

"Good a time as any," Peter said.

As they headed to his quarters, the captain said, "You may have noticed that we slowed down for a while."

"Yeah," Maria said, "but it feels like you're back up to full speed again."

The captain stepped into his quarters and pointed to a small table with four chairs, all anchored to the floor. "Have a seat. We slowed down to search for survivors from the attack. We found one and hauled him aboard."

"Find out anything?" Peter asked.

"Not yet." Captain Hodges paused for a moment.

"I don't know what you're involved in, but I'm not used to receiving orders directly from the President of the United States."

Peter and Maria remained silent.

After another pause, the captain continued. "We'll deliver you at best possible speed to Souda Bay. Once we're close enough, we'll fly you to the airstrip. I understand the White House is sending a plane. I'm giving you my quarters until we fly you to Souda Bay. I'll be on the bridge, and this is as private as it gets on a destroyer."

He pointed to a telephone on a small desk. "That phone connects directly to the bridge if you need me. Feel free to use my bed. Clean sheets, just for you." The captain smiled. "At this speed, it won't be a quiet night."

"I would like to connect to the internet, and I'd like to look at some classified files on a memory card," Peter said. "My computer's at the bottom of the Mediterranean. Can you loan me one? I might need to take it to Washington."

"I'll have someone to bring one for you."

"Thank you," Peter said.

The captain stood up. "Keep the door closed. It's not completely soundproof, but if you speak softly you will not be overheard, particularly when we're running at high speed." As he exited his quarters, he said, "Even I will knock before entering." The door closed.

"Peter? What the hell is going on?"

Peter closed his eyes. "You remember that Watson told us he was investigating a cabal in Washington, a group that was working to destroy the US government?"

"Yeah."

"Well, he gave me a couple of memory cards. He told me to get them to the President if something happened to him. I think they contain his report and all the information he's collected on the cabal."

"And you still have them?" Maria asked.

"Oh yes."

"Good God."

"Yeah. I'm not sure I want to, but I have to look at them. I'd rather be petrified than ignorant."

"I do not like this," Maria said.

Someone knocked on the cabin door.

"Who is it?" Peter asked.

"Lieutenant Marjorie Pierson, sir. I have a laptop for you."

"Come on in."

A young woman entered the room. She placed a duffel bag on the floor and a laptop on the table.

"This uses Windows," she said. "You're comfortable with that platform?"

"Yes," Peter answered.

"Good. This will automatically connect to the general internet on the ship. Do not send or receive any classified information on that connection. If you are looking at classified information, do not download it to the hard drive, and disconnect from the internet."

"Thank you," Peter said.

"I brought a change of clothes for you in the duffel bag. A couple of sizes, so just try them on. Standard Navy stuff. No insignias. Some toilet articles. The captain suggests you use his shower, short please, and join him in the Officer's Mess when you're ready."

"You've thought of everything," Maria said.

"I'm sure that's not true," Lieutenant Pierson said.

"Please tell the captain," Peter said, "that we should be in the Officer's Mess in thirty minutes."

When the lieutenant left, Maria said, "So who's first in the shower?"

"You can go first, but when she says short, she means it. A minute to get wet. Soap up. Another minute to rinse off." He unzipped the duffel bag. "Let's see what fits in this gift bag."

A little ahead of schedule, they were clean, dressed, and ready for the captain. They opened the door, and Peter said to the older guard with the sidearm, "We're ready to go to the Officer's Mess."

"Yes, sir. Just follow me."

Peter fell in behind the first guard, Maria behind him, and the younger, female guard with the M16 took up the rear. *We're a little parade*, Peter thought.

They stopped by an open door. "Officer's Mess, sir. We'll be waiting outside."

"Thanks," Peter said.

A steward pointed them to a table. "The captain will join you in a few minutes."

A minute later, Captain John Hodges slid into the seat across from them. "I've taken the liberty of ordering up a full steak dinner for both of you. Medium-rare, unless you object."

"I think we can handle that," Maria said.

"I don't know what you two are involved in, but you sure have some well-placed supporters in Washington."

"And they're responsible for our guard detail?" Peter asked.

"As a matter of fact, yes."

The steward arrived with soup.

"You know, captain," Peter said, "when I was a SEAL, I was not used to this sort of fare on ship."

"Well, today you are the guest of the captain, and you're getting the best we have to offer."

As they ate, Maria said, "We'd like to thank the captain of the Detros II and his crew for taking care of us."

"I would also like to talk to Alon," Peter said.

"Actually, your guards are not preventing you from moving around. The people you wish to speak with will still be in the Crew's Mess when we're done."

"Could you ask the guards to be a little discreet?"

"Sure." Captain Hodges looked at Peter and Maria as the steward delivered the steak and a salad. "Perhaps in return, you could tell me what happened on the Detros II."

"You must have talked with the other survivors. What do you need from us?" Peter asked.

"You were associated with some of the cargo, some of the containers, weren't you?"

Peter looked directly at the captain. "Yes."

"Can you tell me what was in those containers?"

Peter frowned and spoke slowly. "Captain Hodges, you'll have to talk to the White House."

"And how did you end up with a couple of Russian assault rifles and two Uzis?"

Peter looked at Maria and back to Captain Hodges. He looked around the room. They were alone. "You already know my answer." Peter hesitated. "Why are you asking these questions? If you have direct orders from the President regarding the two of us, isn't that enough?"

Captain Hodges nodded with a trace of a smile. "You're right. However, you might like to know that those orders directly contradicted earlier orders, which came from a level not much lower than the President himself."

"And?" Peter asked.

"It suggests to me that you are personally threatened by some very powerful forces."

"That's really not news," Peter said.

"This is different. This is really high-level stuff."

Peter and Maria remained silent.

"Okay," the captain said, "let's talk about other things."

After they enjoyed their dessert, a large piece of chocolate cake, the captain stood. "Perhaps this is a good time to do your duty in the crew's mess. Israel is sending an aircraft to Souda Bay to pick up Alon."

"Interesting," Peter said. He looked at Maria. "You ready to go?"

"I'm ready."

The captain left them at the door to the crew's mess. Alon sat in a corner, nursing a cup of coffee, and looking down at the table. The captain and crew of the Detros II sat together at a large table. They were a boisterous group, noisy with relief.

Peter and Maria thanked the crew from the Detros II, expressed regret about the sinking, and shook hands all around. As soon as it was polite to do so, they went to Alon's table and sat down.

"I'm sorry about Saul," Peter said. "I had grown to have a lot of respect for him."

"He knew he would die, but he did think he'd get the gold to Israel. Who knows? It might still get there. Someday." Alon looked away for a moment. "I will miss him."

"We all will," Peter said.

Alon nodded. "You seem to be well guarded. Are you in some sort of confinement?"

"I think we're being protected," Peter said.

Alon smiled. "Sometimes protection and prison can be the same thing."

Peter nodded. "True. Keep in touch, Alon."

"I will do that, Peter. Please travel well, and find only protectors and not prison guards."

Peter and Maria left with their guards.

Peter sat at the small desk in the captain's quarters. He disconnected from the internet. He inserted one of the two memory cards labeled *2*. He pulled up the list of files. At the top of the list was *Summary and Conclusions T-1*. The remaining files were labeled *Support-1* through *Support-53*.

Peter clicked on *T-1*. The computer asked for a password. Peter searched his wallet for the small piece of paper Watson gave him in Zürich and opened the file. The words, *TOP SECRET*, appeared in bright red across each page.

These conclusions are based on a nearly year-long review of information from wiretaps, from clandestine searches of personal and governmental computers, from listening devices placed in homes, offices, conference rooms, and vehicles, and from clandestine video observations of meetings, coupled with information from the Canadian, Russian, British, and German intelligence services. This review has confirmed that the following individuals form a cabal that is guilty of conspiracy to commit murder, conspiracy to undermine and destroy the US government, and numerous other acts of treason and sedition.

1. *Harold James – current director of the CIA*
2. *Brayden Davenport – current assistant to the US Secretary of State*
3. *Gerhardt Weber – former Vice President of the United States*
4. *Derek Bunting – Major General, military intelligence*

Peter frowned and began to skim the remainder of the file. In several places it mentioned him and Maria as instrumental in foiling or destroying key aspects of the group's plans. He mostly skipped over those sections.

These men have conspired to assist Russian terrorists to steal and install a fully operable nuclear-tipped intercontinental ballistic missile … to return Russia to full Communist rule… attempted to fund extremist "patriot" groups in the United States with up to $100 billion to destabilize the government and allow for the introduction of fascist, strongman rule… planned to fund terrorist groups to destabilize the Middle East and use the violence that followed to put their extreme right-wing candidate in the White House.

The four individuals listed above have operated illegally, undermining the authority of the President, the elected government of the United States, and the chain of command of the US military. They have assisted our enemies.… Many people supported them.… They could not operate without many supporters who knew exactly what was planned…. A list of supporters can be found in file Support 53.

These four individuals and their network form a clear and present danger to the welfare and very existence of the United States…. They must be taken into custody immediately…. Inaction, or even a short delay in taking action… presents an extreme danger to the fundamental foundations and stability of the United States government.

He stopped reading and looked up at Maria.

"What did you just read? You look terrified."

"I am." He turned the computer to Maria. "Here. You read it. This is just the summary and conclusions."

Peter paced around the small room as she read. He looked in several cabinets. *God! What I'd do for a drink right now.*

Maria looked up when she finished.

"This is crazy. The only thing missing is a former President."

Peter removed the memory card and shut down the computer.

"I wouldn't be surprised if a former President isn't in there somewhere," he said. "The fallout from this could be monstrous."

"And we're named… as critical to their failure."

"It was nice we could help, but now we're major targets." Peter held up the memory card. "And this is the reason."

"We've been targets for a long time."

"This is different. I can't wait to see what happens when we get to Washington."

He put the memory card in its plastic bag and dropped it back into his pocket.

He looked at her and smiled. "Right now, I'd like to try out the captain's bed. I think there's room for two. Barely."

"I think we can make it work."

"We'll have to be quiet."

Maria smiled. "We can make it work."

The bed was narrow, and the sense of privacy incomplete, but they both felt a desperate need for each other.

"Just hold me and love me," Maria said. "Maybe, for the first time, I need you more than you need me."

Before he surrendered himself to his love for her, he did ask himself the obvious question. *Why?*

They fell asleep cradled against each other.

Chapter 38

Peter woke with a start to a firm knock on the door. He looked at his watch. 5:30 AM.

He raised himself up on one elbow. "What is it?"

The door opened a crack. A male voice said, "The helicopter will be ready to take you to your plane at Souda Bay in forty minutes." The man closed the door again.

Peter got out of bed.

"Maybe you can get our clothes packed up," he said to Maria, "and put the computer in the duffel bag."

"Just take your shower before I get tired of dealing with the laundry."

The eastern sky held a faint tint of pink when they stood on the deck, waiting to board the helicopter. The ship slowed in anticipation of the takeoff, and the cool morning breeze ruffled Maria's hair.

"Beautiful," Maria said.

Peter nodded. "Yes."

Captain Hodges came over to them and shook their hands. "I've talked with Alden Sage. He gave me some background. I wanted to shake your hands before you left."

"Thanks for your help," Maria said.

"Sorry we weren't there when you really needed us."

"Fog of war," Peter said. "Did the survivor give you anything?"

"Not yet. We'll turn him over to intelligence at Souda Bay."

A member of the flight crew signaled to them.

"That's your invitation to board. By the way, you'll fly in style from Souda Bay. The White House sent the Vice President's plane."

The sun was shining brightly as they approached Crete. The helicopter flew over the two peninsulas that reach out into the sea along the northwest coast of the island.

Maria looked out the window. "Looks like a desert."

They dropped in altitude, crossed the runway, banked to the left, and settled down on a taxiway at the eastern end of the airbase.

Peter pointed out the window at the blue-and-white Boeing 757. "There's our ride."

"A little bit of security," Maria said.

"Yeah. Four personnel carriers, .50 caliber machine guns, and armed guards all over the place."

A man and a woman boarded the helicopter. They were dressed exactly the same as Peter and Maria, standard Navy uniforms, no insignias.

"We're your escorts to the airplane," the man said. "Mr. Binder, you have a package for Aldon Sage?"

"Yes."

"On your person?"

"Yes."

"You go first with my associate. Please jog to the airplane and up the stairs. Once you are safely inside the aircraft, I will follow with Maria."

This is about as extreme as it gets, Peter thought.

Aloud, he said, "Understood."

A tall man in Airforce blue met them inside the plane. "Welcome aboard. I'm Captain Lyman, and I'll be your pilot for your trip to Washington. I need to prepare for takeoff, but Master Sergeant Mark Reynolds will take care of you. You're the only passengers today, so we are completely at your service."

"Mr. Binder, Ms. Davidoff," Reynolds said, "welcome aboard. Please call me Mark."

"And you can call us Peter and Maria," Peter said.

"That's against protocol, but I'll do my best. We have a few minutes before we start to taxi. Let me show you around."

Mark walked toward the back of the plane. "I suggest you ignore the first section. It's normally for staff and press. You can seat yourselves in the third, or conference section. You can eat and work at the tables there. Later, I'll set up a video call with Alden Sage."

As they passed a doorway in the second section he said, "This is the stateroom. It's at your disposal once we're airborne. I've made up the two sofas as beds for you, whenever you want them."

In the conference section, Mark pointed to the forward-facing seats. "It's probably more comfortable sitting in these seats for takeoff and landing. We'll have breakfast for you shortly after takeoff, cheese and bacon omelet with sausage, fruit, and yogurt."

"Sounds good to me," Maria said. "I'm starving."

"The flight will be about eleven hours. We should arrive a little before noon, local time. A car from the White House will meet you. Since you lost most of your belongings in the sinking, we have some clothes in the stateroom. I think we have your size, and they should make you feel more comfortable in Washington."

Peter heard the engines wind up and felt the airplane begin to move.

"I have to return to my station," Mark said. "Please take a seat and buckle in. I'll be back with breakfast shortly after takeoff."

Peter sat and looked out the window. "Interesting," he said. "The security is moving with us. I bet we do a war-time take off, too, steep and fast."

"It can't be any scarier than the flight of a lifeboat."

Peter laughed.

Peter was right about the takeoff. He looked out the window. *Impressive. And the pilot must have a full fuel load for this trip.*

As soon as Captain Lyman slowed the rate of climb, their breakfast appeared.

"Better china than mine," Maria said, "and a better omelet, too."

"No comment," Peter said.

When Mark cleared away the breakfast dishes, he turned on the large, flat-screen monitor on the wall for the video call with Alden Sage.

"It will be a few minutes, but Mr. Sage's call will come through automatically. Just speak normally."

After Mark left, Peter said, "This should be interesting."

"That's an understatement."

At that moment, Alden Sage appeared on the screen.

"Good to see the two of you."

"Good to be here," Maria said.

"Did you look at Watson's files?"

"We looked at the summary," Peter answered. "That's it. We were using a borrowed computer from the USS Jason Lawrence."

"Do you still have the computer?"

"Yes. I'm supposed to give it back to the Navy."

"Give it to Sergeant Reynolds. He'll set you up with secure computing capability. Read, or at least skim, as much of Watson's report as you can, but get some sleep. You have two copies of the memory cards from Watson?"

"Yes," Peter said.

"Please give one set to Sergeant Reynolds. He'll transmit it to me."

"Watson fingered Harold James, Gerhardt Weber, Brayden Davenport, and Derek Bunting as the four key conspirators," Peter said. "I'm sorry, but I have to ask if that's really true."

"You've seen more of Watson's report than I have, though I do know about some of his information. I believe what you just said is true, though there are at least another fifteen to twenty high-level people in the government and the military who are part of the supporting cast. Perhaps five or six additional people in Canada, Germany, Russia and Japan."

"How many people know about this?" Maria asked.

"Besides the conspirators," Alden said, "now Watson is dead, I think the number is four, the two of you plus the President and myself."

"How could this conspiracy survive?" Peter asked.

"It hasn't, largely because of the two of you and all of Watson's efforts."

"You put a lot of security on for us," Maria said.

"To be blunt, a lot of powerful people want you dead, and until we arrest the key people in this mess that's likely to remain the case. You're the only people alive who have actually witnessed, on site, most of the efforts of this cabal. They nearly swept us into a nuclear disaster. They were trying to use the gold to finance a revolution in the United States."

"And what happens to us now?" Maria asked.

"Hang in there a little longer. When this job's done, once this gang's in prison, you're done if you want to be. You'll be able to go back to living your life as you wish."

"That sounds a bit optimistic," Maria said.

"We're landing at Andrews?" Peter asked.

"Yes. The Secret Service will pick you up with one of our limos and a fully armed escort."

"I want a good, semiautomatic handgun for each of us."

"That's really not necessary, Peter."

"Perhaps, but you're not the target. We've survived by being over-prepared."

"I'll see what I can do. You can't have them at the White House."

"No problem," Peter said. "It's the drive to the White House that has me concerned."

Shortly after the call ended, Mark returned. Peter gave him the computer from the USS Jason Lawrence and one set of Watson's memory cards. Mark set up a computer attached to the large monitor.

"We'll leave you alone," Mark said. "If you want something, please remove any high-security or top-secret information from the screen before we serve you."

"Perhaps a pot of coffee?" Peter asked.

"I'll have that for you in a couple of minutes."

Peter and Maria began to examine Watson's full report. There was a lot of detailed information. They skimmed most of it.

About two hours later they turned off the computer, sat back, and contemplated what they had just read.

"What's amazing," Peter said, "is the number of recordings, some from meetings inside CIA headquarters. The emails, telephone calls. And what the former Vice President has been up to."

"I'm not surprised that my old buddy, Dick Durban, is in this up to his eyeballs," Maria said.

"At least now we can understand some of what we were facing."

"But now the President has all of this information. Why do they need anything from us? This is a no-brainer," Maria said.

"They want us as the human witnesses. They want us to testify."

"That's a scary thought."

"Yeah."

"Once they round these guys up and throw them into some federal penitentiary, aren't we home free?" Maria asked.

"Maybe, but Rostov was a surprise in Zürich, and what about that crazy Japanese guy who's already tried to kill us at least once, and Ivan the Russian? They have lots of resources."

"You're making me feel so secure, babe."

"Sorry," Peter said. "It's just reality, I think."

Peter sat back and exhaled. He looked at Maria. "Let's try out the stateroom, and get some rest... or something."

"Sounds good to me," Maria said with a small smile.

They stood up and made their way to the stateroom. Peter shut the door behind them, put his arms around her, and they kissed.

"Crazy," he said.

"Yeah." She kissed him again.

Chapter 39

Peter woke to the insistent ringing of the telephone on the table next to the sofa-bed. It pulled him from his vivid dream, and he found himself sweating and breathing hard as the images refused to fade. He fumbled around the table until he found the phone.

"Yes?"

"Hello, Mr. Binder. This is Mark. We'll be landing in about two hours. You might get dressed and have something to eat before we land. You prefer breakfast or lunch?"

"Let's make it lunch."

"I'll have lunch ready in the conference area in forty-five minutes."

"Thanks. We'll be ready."

He turned to Maria, who was sitting up. "We've got forty-five minutes before lunch is served. You first for the shower?"

"I'm on my way."

Peter sorted out clothes for himself and looked at what someone had selected for Maria and laughed. *A trifle conservative.*

Thirty minutes later Peter had shaved off his beard, and they were dressed and ready to go.

"I feel almost human again," Peter said with a smile.

Maria shook her head. "In these clothes I feel like a prim librarian."

"Better than fish bait in the Mediterranean."

Maria laughed. "Put that way, the clothes are exquisite."

Once settled into the seats in the conference area, they enjoyed a light lunch of sandwiches, soup, and a salad. Almost as soon as they finished, Peter heard the sound of the engines change, indicating the beginning of their descent to Andrews.

After a seamless landing on a clear and cloudless day, they taxied to the hanger for Air Force One.

Mark appeared. "You can disembark now. Your baggage and extra clothing are already in the limo. Please move quickly to the limo, once you exit the plane."

They stepped down the stairs in bright sunlight to the pavement, where a black, heavily armored White House limousine waited for them. A Secret Service agent held the passenger door open for them. As soon as they were seated and the door was closed, the limousine started off, led by a black SUV.

Probably four armed men in that SUV, Peter thought.

The agent riding in the front passenger seat carried a Heckler & Koch MP5 submachine gun on his lap. He turned around to face Peter and Maria, and he handed back two SIG Sauer P229 pistols, each in a small leather holster.

"They're standard issue, .357's," he said. "One round in the chamber. Safety on. First shot requires a long, double-action pull. After that they're semiautomatic. From what I know about you, I think you can handle them. Shouldn't need them anyway."

"I'll relax when we get to the White House," Peter said.

As they exited the base, the lead SUV popped on its lights and siren and cleared a path in the moderate midday traffic. They headed west on I-95 south at a relatively sedate pace of sixty-five miles per hour.

They exited onto northbound I-295 and headed into the far-left lane. The two vehicles began to increase speed again and passed several cars.

When the front wheels of the SUV were adjacent to the rear wheels of a garbage truck, the truck veered sharply into the left lane, striking the SUV.

"What the hell?" the limo driver shouted, as the SUV was flipped into the median, rolled several times, and came to rest on its left side against the cement barrier.

"Jesus Christ!" Peter said.

"Get down," the agent in the passenger seat shouted.

The garbage truck, now out of control, swerved across several lanes of traffic, hitting one Prius, and slammed into the barrier on the right side of the highway.

The limo driver braked hard, and a black van hit it from behind.

Their driver jerked one lane to the right, which was blocked by a semi, and then jerked one more lane to the right. Peter felt the driver accelerate to get around the truck on the right, but the heavy limo was slow to respond.

The black van that hit them pulled up on their left side.

"Get down! Get down!" the agent in the front seat kept shouting.

Peter and Maria didn't move.

I have to know what the hell is happening, Peter thought. He pulled his pistol out of the holster. He glanced at Maria. She had done the same.

As the limo moved along the right side of the semi, the truck moved sharply to the right. The limo driver cursed again, blew his horn, and hit the brakes.

The truck grazed the front bumper of the limo, crashed into the right cement barrier and mounted it.

"Holy shit!" Maria said.

The truck scraped along the cement barrier, shedding parts and pieces until, quite gracefully, it tipped over the side of the road and dropped, upside down, into the swamp and trees below the road.

As the limo pulled back into the center lane, the black van pulled in front of them. The rear doors opened. Three men appeared with heavy-caliber assault rifles.

Peter shouted, "Get down!"

Peter and Maria flattened themselves on the rear seat just as rapid fire began to impact the windshield.

The thick laminated glass absorbed the initial shots, but as the glass fractured the driver had to lean to the edge of the windshield to see enough to drive.

After eighty to a hundred rounds, the windshield began to break down. Rounds began to strike the rear window.

Before he could trigger much defensive fire from the vehicle, the agent in the front passenger seat was struck by several rounds.

Peter popped up long enough to see that the agent was hit in the head and was out of action.

The limo driver swerved to the left and accelerated again. Peter looked over the seat as the front of the limo came level with the left rear wheels of the van. Bullets were striking the thick windows on the passenger side of the limo.

The limo driver turned hard and struck the rear of the van. The collision sent the van into a sharp skid and ejected two of the gunmen. They were promptly run over by a semi that was smoking its brakes trying to avoid the developing chaos.

The van turned sideways and rolled four times down the highway and into the center barrier, spewing van parts, rifles, ammunition, and several passengers in the process.

The limo driver braked hard again, bumped over one of the ejected van passengers, and managed to stop on the extreme left side of the highway, thirty feet short of the mangled van.

Wrecked cars and trucks completely blocked the highway behind them. Peter could hear the squeal of tires as cars and trucks continued to crash into each other.

Peter unbuckled his seatbelt. "Jesus H. Christ!"

He put on the safety and dropped the pistol into his pocket. He stretched over the front seat, and grabbed the MP5 from the dead agent. Piles of shattered glass littered the front seat. The engine was still running. Peter opened his door.

"What the hell are you doing?" Maria asked.

"I don't want to hang around. There may be more out there."

As he stepped out, he looked back and said, "You're a better driver than I am. The agent's dead and the driver's dying. Cover me while I drag them out. Then get into the driver's seat."

He yanked the passenger door open and dragged the agent out.

Maria exited on the left, holding her pistol in both hands.

Peter set down the MP5 and pulled the dead agent to the divider.

"Get down!" Maria screamed.

Peter dropped to the ground and looked toward the van, just as Maria fired four shots at a man raising an assault rifle. Her shots stitched a neat dotted line from his chest to his left eye.

Peter looked back at Maria. She had lowered her pistol. He jumped up.

"Bastards!" he said.

He ran around the limo, picked up the MP5, and ran to the van. A quick look told him no one was left alive.

He ran back to the limo. The driver had died, and Peter pulled him out, ran around to the passenger side, and jumped in.

Peter looked to his left. Maria was trying to brush glass off the seat.

"Get in!" he shouted. "Better glass in your ass than a bullet in your head!"

Maria sat down with a grimace and shifted into drive. They heard the first sirens. She stepped on the gas and lumbered back onto the highway.

"This feels like a tank," she said. "Do you know where you're going?"

"Sort of, but take it easy. I want to call Alden Sage."

Peter scrolled down his contacts list on his cell phone and called Alden's direct number.

"Alden Sage."

"This is Peter Binder. We were ambushed on I-295. Everybody's out of action or dead."

"What the hell?"

"We're coming in with the limo, but it's all shot up. Can you get an escort for us?"

"Where the hell are you?"

"We just crossed into DC on I-295."

"Stay on the line."

Traffic was blocked behind them, but they were picking up cars from the entrances of the highway as they passed them. Peter found the switches for the police flashers in the front grill, the strobes for the headlights, and a siren. He plugged one ear with his finger, and pressed the cell phone to the other.

He could barely hear Alden Sage. "The police helicopter has spotted you… You should have an escort on the ground right about… now."

Peter looked around. Four police cars closed on the limo with lights and sirens running. Two positioned in front. Two in back.

"We're set, Alden. See you soon."

Peter flipped off the siren. "Follow them. Don't stop for anything."

As they approached the White House, Maria said, "Look at that."

"Impressive," Peter said.

Besides the DC police, members of the Secret Service's counterassault team, or CAT, seemed to cover the White House. Black body armor, black helmets, and most with SR-16 CQB assault rifles.

"You sure these are our friends?" Maria asked.

"Hope so."

Armed officers stopped them at a barrier and asked Maria to roll down her window. To Peter's surprise, it still worked.

"Put any weapons on the floor and exit the vehicle. Walk around the barrier and get into the black SUV on the other side."

As they got out of the limo, Maria took a moment to brush some broken glass off her pants. Peter did the same.

"I must look like a total wreak," she said.

"You look fine," Peter said.

An armed officer opened the SUV's door for them, and they slipped into the back seat. The driver turned to them, "We'll run you over to the entrance to the West Wing. Alden Sage will meet you there."

Peter's heart rate was still not back to normal. He looked at Maria. "You okay?"

"Are you kidding?"

In less than a minute, the SUV stopped by an entrance to the West Wing. An armed man opened the door to the SUV and ushered them into the White House, where Alden Sage was waiting.

Alden put out his hand to shake theirs, and said, "Welcome to the White House. I am really glad to see the two of you."

"I think the feeling is mutual," Peter said.

"I can imagine."

"How are the agents who were in the SUV in front of us?" Maria asked.

"From what I've heard so far, pretty badly injured, but they'll survive."

"Do you know who's behind this?" Maria asked.

Alden took a deep breath. "Too early to tell. You've read Watson's report?"

"Yes," Peter said.

"Then your guess is probably as good as mine." He shrugged. "If you'll follow me, I'll give you a few minutes to yourselves. Then, after I update you, the President wants to talk with both of you."

"Really?" Peter said.

"Yes, really," Alden said as he opened a door and gestured for them to step inside. "Have a seat at the table. I'll be back in a few minutes." He closed the door behind him.

Maria sat down. "Christ. There's no way I'm ready to talk to the President."

"I don't think we'll have much choice," Peter said.

Maria stood up and picked at her pants. "I'm still picking pieces of glass out of my pants."

Peter laughed. "I'm having the same problem," he said, "but fortunately they're not chopping me up much."

Alden opened the door and sat down at the end of the table. "I know I'm not giving you much time to get yourselves together, but President Pelton wants to talk with you as soon as possible. How are you doing?"

"I think we're starting to calm down," Peter said. "Maria?"

"I'll be okay," she said. "It sounds like a command performance."

"President Pelton likes face to face discussions on the most serious matters." Alden paused. "You have both read Watson's report?"

"We have," Peter said.

"And?"

"I was a little shocked," Peter said, "but not totally amazed. I always thought that Gerhardt Weber would be happy to destroy most of the world if he thought it would benefit his family business."

Alden smiled. "Interesting."

"I don't understand why we're so important, or why people want to kill us," Maria said. "You have Watson's report. We can't add much to that."

"The fact is," Alden replied, "no one knows that Watson completed his report, or that you forwarded the report to us. You're the only people left who have been involved in this mess from the beginning, and we're about to create a governmental crisis not seen since the Civil War. We need witnesses, and you're all we've got."

"What Watson has presented isn't enough?" Maria asked.

"We need living speakers of truth," Alden said. "We need witnesses, and President Pelton wants to talk to you about the need for you to testify. Please understand that you are now privy to the most sensitive and top-secret information in this government."

Peter and Maria remained silent.

Alden stood up. "Shall we see the President now?"

Peter looked at Maria. "You ready?"

Maria frowned. "No, but let's go."

The Oval Office was steps away. Alden Sage stopped, made a minute adjustment to his tie and jacket, and tapped lightly before he entered.

President Pelton stood up behind his desk and said in his rich voice, "Come in. Come in."

Peter and Maria followed Alden sage into the room. There were two other people, a woman on one side of the President's desk, and a man on the other side.

"Mr. President," Alden Sage said, "Mr. Peter Binder and Ms. Maria Davidoff."

The President shook hands with Peter and Maria. Patricia Pennell, the Attorney General, and Richard Bentley, Director of the FBI, both introduced themselves.

"I am truly glad to meet the two of you," the President said. "From all the reports I've read, you're an amazing couple, and you look remarkably good, considering your entrance into Washington."

The President gestured to a sofa and several chairs.

"Let's sit over there."

"I'm sorry our visit has already cost the lives of at least two Secret Service agents," Peter said.

"Yes. A terrible loss. I will have to meet with their families tomorrow morning."

There was a moment of silence. It seemed to Peter that no one in the room really wanted to speak after the President spoke of the families.

Finally the President said, "I am curious. In the last year and a half, how many times has someone, or some group, tried to kill one or both of you?"

"I've lost track," Maria said.

"I actually thought about that, on the flight from Souda Bay," Peter said. "Counting today, seventeen."

The President inhaled deeply. "Well, the Attorney General has a few questions for you."

"What did you think of Watson's report?" Ms. Pennell asked.

"Frightening… on many levels," Peter said.

"It confirmed a few suspicions, like Dick Durban," Maria said.

"You had a personal relationship with him at one time?"

"Yes," Maria said, "and I assume you know how and why that ended."

"And you had a professional relationship with him and the RCMP?"

"Yes. I severed that relationship, with the help of the Prime Minister."

"Just so you know," Ms. Pennell said, "when we take the group of four and their supporters into custody, the Canadians will collect Mr. Durban."

"That will not upset me," Maria said.

"And you, Mr. Binder. Somehow you seem to simply drop into major trouble."

"I'm a geologist," Peter answered. "I end up in strange places. I've also worked with Watson MacDonough for a long time. The business with the mine with no gold, and the Holocaust gold in Zürich, all came to me via direct requests from Watson."

Peter noticed Maria give him a strange look. *She didn't know about Watson and me. That's a surprise.*

"The two of you have left an astonishing trail of mayhem behind you," Ms. Pennell said. "The State Department has been very busy cleaning up after you."

"I'm sorry," Peter said.

"I think you're being a bit hard, Patricia," President Pelton said. "After all, to put it bluntly, these two have saved this country from potential disaster more than once. They may have kept a fascist dictator out of this office."

The Attorney General nodded and said nothing.

"It seems to me," Peter said, "that your opponent in the upcoming election, Axel Wisser, might fit that role quite well."

"He is only the leading edge of the problem. We live in an era of politics by fear and anger, supported by lies and propaganda. The economy is good. People should be happy, but they are not."

The President looked at Peter.

It feels as though he can read my mind, Peter thought.

"I have to know something," the President said. "Considering what you have been through, are the two of you willing to take the risk of testifying in open court when we try these people? We need someone with courage to testify to the truth of their charges, but I will not force either of you to do so."

"I think we both want to lead normal lives," Peter said. "I doubt either of us wants to testify, but if you need my testimony I will certainly provide it."

"I agree with Peter," Maria said. "I don't want to, but I will."

Richard Bentley spoke up. "We will have a heavy security blanket on you while you are here. You will stay at Blair House. Please do not venture outside without security. Once we round up the conspirators, you should be able to begin to relax, at least a little."

"We plan to collect three of the gang of four at CIA headquarters tomorrow," Patricia Pennell said. "Gerhardt Weber will be arrested at his ranch in Wyoming. Considering your involvement, if you would like, Alden Sage could arrange to accompany you to the entrance hall of the CIA in Langley to see three of the ringleaders removed from the building."

"I think… that would be good," Peter said.

The President stood up. "Now, thank you all for your time." He shook hands with Peter and Maria. "Enjoy your stay at Blair House, if you can."

Before they left the room, Richard Bentley said, "You say you want to lead normal lives. You can't. Even after we shut down and put this whole group in prison, you will still be targets. You will be able to begin to relax, but you can never let your guard down completely. Do not forget that."

Peter looked at the FBI Director. Then he looked at Maria. Without a word they turned and exited the Oval Office with Alden Sage. They walked toward the exit from the West Wing.

Alden said dryly, "The President has decided. I will make sure you witness a little history you helped create." He gestured to two Secret Service agents. "These gentlemen will walk you to Blair House. I'll see you tomorrow morning."

Alden Sage shook their hands at the door.

"I don't want to exaggerate," Alden said, "but what we will be able to do tomorrow will save this government… and this country."

Chapter 40

When they walked into their room at Blair House, Peter looked at his watch. In spite of the ambush on the highway, and the meeting at the White House, it was still only half past three in the afternoon, Washington time. His body didn't know what day it was.

They stood for a moment in the room, like stunned animals, not quite in touch with reality.

"I feel like," Peter said. "Actually, I don't know what I feel like. Maybe like I've been in a boxing match for two days."

"Yeah," she said.

He found her hand. "Thanks."

"For what?"

"For saving my life... again."

She looked at him. "You're welcome."

She's completely exhausted, he thought.

He put his arm across her shoulders. "You okay?"

"No."

Peter turned and held her with both arms. "I'm sorry you had to learn about me and Watson that way."

"You still don't know all my secrets."

"That's okay."

"Just hold me."

They stood, holding on, as if each of them would drown without the other.

Peter guided her to the bed. They lay down and embraced.

He could feel the tightness and tension everywhere he touched her.

"What about you?" she asked.

"I'm afraid to sleep."

"Oh, God, Peter. Where are we?"

"I think we're home."

They took their supper at Blair House. The meal was excellent. They were alone. They didn't talk much.

At the end of the meal, while they finished off the wine, Maria said, "I didn't like Mr. Bentley's comments as we left the Oval Office."

"You mean, when he said we'd never lead a normal life again?"

Maria nodded.

Peter took several deep breaths. "He's right, but I think, with some reasonable precautions, we'll be able to relax."

"He doesn't think so."

"No, he doesn't."

They got up from the table and returned to their room.

In their room, Peter stood by the window, looking at the White House. Maria joined him and reached for his hand.

"Amazing, isn't it?" Peter said. "It's beautiful, peaceful, orderly, and it all hangs by a thread."

"It all depends on people of good will," Maria said. She tugged at Peter's hand. "Let's go to bed. We're both exhausted."

Peter turned and they embraced. They kissed, stepped apart and began to undress. When they climbed into the large bed, they rolled together and embraced again. They held each other tightly.

"Go to sleep, Peter."

"I'll try."

"Peter?"

"Yes?"

"If you have one of your dreams, and if you wake up in the night, don't be alone. Wake me."

"You don't have to do that."

"I know, but I want to."

"Thank you."

Peter heard Maria's soft snoring a few minutes later. It took him almost a half hour, but he finally fell into a restless sleep.

He dreamed of his grandfather. His grandfather spoke angrily.

"Live a life of truth!" he shouted. "Be a righteous man!"

But Peter stood naked on the top of a small hill in Afghanistan. All his friends lay dead and dying around him. Their blood flowed over his bare feet. He was defenseless. He was alone, except for the powerful man, wrapped in black wool, who had visited him in his dreams so many times.

The man in black stood close, in front of him, and he laughed.

"You are but one defenseless man," the man shouted. "Give it up!"

For the first time, Peter saw the man's eyes, and he saw his reflection in them.

"I know you!" Peter screamed at him.

Peter lunged. He stretched out his arms.

The tall man laughed and raised his rifle.

Peter jerked upright in bed, wide awake. He was panting, sweating. He got out of bed and stumbled to the bathroom. He knelt in front of the toilet and heaved. Then his stomach was empty. He couldn't stop. There was only the bitter taste and bile.

He stood up and flushed the toilet. The nausea was retreating. He washed his mouth out and walked back to the bedroom. He stood for a long time at the window.

He heard Maria get out of bed and walk to him. She took his hand in hers.

"You okay?" she asked.

"No."

"I heard you. You shouted in your sleep. Who was it?"

"No."

"Peter."

He shuddered. "I can't."

Maria put her arm around him.

"I saw... I saw... myself."

After a while she said, "Come back to bed."

The sound of the telephone woke Peter from a deep sleep. He looked at his watch. Six. He answered the phone.

"Hello?"

"Peter, this is Alden Sage. We'll drive to the CIA headquarters at nine. Be ready, but stay inside Blair House."

"We'll be ready."

Peter, Maria and Alden stood to one side of the entrance hall of the CIA headquarters. It seemed as though all the CIA staff had flocked there as soon as the armed agents and the head of the FBI had entered the building. They all wanted to see for themselves.

When the three men entered the hall in handcuffs, a low murmur passed through the otherwise silent crowd. Few loved Harold James, but the shock was still real.

Harold's head moved, as he scanned the crowd.

He's looking for us, Peter thought.

Harold found them at the edge of the crowd. He looked first at Peter, then Maria, then Alden Sage. He stopped and nodded. The FBI agents pushed him forward, and he was gone.

"He will not forget us, and neither will his supporters," Maria said.

"You're right about that, Maria," Alden said.

On their way back to Blair House, Alden answered his phone.

"Yes?" he said. "No. I'm not surprised. Thanks for letting me know."

Alden disconnected and turned to Peter and Maria. "A modest armed force landed at Gerhardt Weber's ranch in Wyoming to arrest him. He shot himself in the head with a shotgun."

"Thorough, if rather messy," Peter said.

"That's a description of his life," Alden said with a grimace.

The arrests of the gang of four and their supporters extended across the Pentagon, the CIA, the State Department, the President's own staff, and several members of Congress.

Watching the news, Peter said, "I'm surprised there hasn't been a complete riot in the House of Representatives. This has to guarantee a Pelton win."

After depositions, promises of testimony, visits to the wounded Secret Service agents, and visits to the families of the dead, Peter and Maria escaped to the cabin on the lake. They didn't feel safe in Toronto, in spite of assurances from Bill Branch.

A few weeks later, along with millions across the globe, they watched in horror as the voters in the United States calmly and deliberately elected Axel Wisser for President of the United States.

Two months passed. It was another cold and snowy night in January.

"I'm off for my cross-country ski run," Peter said at the door. "Don't forget to lock up."

"Don't worry. I'll remember. Keep warm."

Outside, Peter shrugged on a small pack with some water and a few energy bars, and he stepped into his skis. The snow squeaked. He looked at the thermometer.

Minus ten. This will be a cold one.

He skied onto the edge of the lake and headed south. A light snow fell, and a soft westerly wind blew the snow across his trail. He shivered. The clouds hid the moon, and only a faint touch of light showed him the way.

Have to make it a fast one tonight.

Three miles down the lake, he skied off the lake and onto the road that accessed the fishing lodge in the summer. He headed back to the main road.

The trees sheltered him from the wind. *I'm getting too warm.*

He stopped and unzipped his jacket part way.

He came out onto the main road and turned north. He stopped to listen and take a short break. With a light snow falling, the silence was heavy. He heard a wolf howl, and Peter smiled. *He's close.* He saw no one on the road.

Almost unconsciously he patted his jacket pocket for the P229 pistol. He shook his head. *What am I thinking?*

He started up the side of the road. He pushed himself to go faster.

That poor young cop at the end of the road. He'll be bored tonight. It's such a waste.

He was making good time. He came around a corner and saw the patrol car. He smiled. *I'll sit with him for a while.*

He skied closer, but he stopped, puzzled. *It's too dark. I can't tell, but I don't think the engine's running.*

He skied cautiously forward, stopped again, and skied down to the road. He took off his skis and left them and his poles behind. He took off his right glove, reached into his pocket, gripped the pistol, and flipped off the safety.

His boots squeaked in the snow. The noise startled him.

He approached the car from behind. He paused and looked around. Nothing. With the pistol in his right hand, he opened the driver's door with his left.

The dome light switched on.

Peter flinched as he saw the body of the young officer lying across the seat. The small bullet wound was clear, just in front of his left ear.

"Shit!"

Peter shut the door and listened. *Nothing.*

He looked down the road toward the cabin but could see very little in the snow and darkness. There was nothing but a nearly snow-covered set of tire tracks. They were not his.

He put his hand on the hood of the cruiser. *Cold. It's been a while.*

Peter opened the door again. *This is stupid, but I have to do it.* He checked for a pulse. Nothing. The body was already cool.

He quickly walked around the car, opened the passenger door and pulled the body onto the passenger side and closed the door. Back on the driver's side, he slid behind the wheel, started the engine, and pulled the radio mike from its holder.

"This is Peter Binder. Anybody hear me?"

"What's going on?"

"I've got a problem. You have an officer at the end of my road. Somebody shot him, and they drove down my road. I need some help out here, and I need it now."

"Who's talking?"

"This is Peter Binder, damn it. When can you have someone here?"

"Someone shot officer Barnes?"

"Christ! Yes! He's dead."

After a pause, "It'll be twenty minutes at least before we can get someone there."

Peter hesitated. "I'm on my way down to the cabin. Tell your guys to be careful. I don't know what the hell is going on."

"Stay put. We'll get there as quick as we can."

Peter didn't respond. He replaced the mike, shut off the car's engine, and took the keys out of the ignition. It took a moment to find the key to unlock the shotgun from the dash. With the shotgun in hand, he sprinted back to his skis.

"Shit! Shit! Shit!"

He shoved the shotgun, butt first, into his pack, slung it on his back, and adjusted it so the barrel wouldn't hit his head. He stepped into his skis, grabbed his poles, and raced for the road to the cabin.

He glided down the small incline and made good time down the road. The first gate was open. Someone had used a cutting torch to take out the lock.

"Maria."

The trail that ran parallel to the road was well packed from his regular trips. The wind blew snow into his face. He was moving fast. He barely noticed the snow.

He stopped at the sound of high-caliber rifle fire.

"Maria!"

He raced down the trail again, moving even faster.

Breathing hard when he came to the end of the groomed trail, Peter took off his skis and maneuvered through the small trees to where he could see the cabin. He saw flames flickering on the outside walls.

Two armed men stood in front of the cabin, watching the door, which was illuminated by the headlights of their car.

You bastards.

Peter looked at the cabin's windows. *The shutters are closed.*

He carefully maneuvered back to his skis. He shrugged off his pack, pulled out the shotgun, pumped a round into the chamber, and leaned it against the pack.

I have to find Maria.

Heart racing, he searched for the opening to the escape tunnel from the cabin, but as he bent down to dig through the snow, the snow began to move.

Christ!

Peter stepped back and grabbed the shotgun.

He waited.

THE END

Printed in the United States
By Bookmasters